WELCOME TO PLUCKLEY GREEN
A MURDER MYSTERY GAME BOOK

Text copyright © Charlie Revelle Smith

All Rights Reserved

Proudly made without the assistance of A.I.

*For Graham.
Here's to the many days we have spent
solving mysteries together!*

INTRODUCTION

Pluckley Green is an ancient, idyllic and beautiful rural village, nestled in the Somerset countryside.

To the west there are woodlands, to the east there is heathland. A tranquil canal runs along the south of the village and to the north, the bright lights of the bustling city of Brigstowe illuminate the night sky.

When the villagers are not scrumping for apples in the local orchard or playing cricket on the green, they are frolicking in the many lush and colourful parks or enjoying a warm pint of beer in the village pub.

Pluckley Green may seem like the quintessential English village, the kind you will find sprinkled across the countryside. However, something is very strange about this bucolic paradise.

For reasons unknown, the residents of Pluckley Green will brutally murder each other over the slightest disagreement or rivalry. The cake you win in the church raffle may well be laced with poison, tea with the vicar could easily end in a bloodbath and the village's prize winning flower beds hide the countless corpses buried beneath.

Strangest of all is that none of the residents seem to be aware that the murder rate of their sleepy little village is staggeringly high and they seem almost bewitched into believing that this state of affairs is normal.

For centuries, the villagers have entrusted their safety to "The Pluckley Green Sleuths" - an organisation of volunteers who are primed to visit any crime scene at any hour of the day or night. Over their many, many years of operation, The Pluckley Green Sleuths have nurtured a peerless reputation for solving crimes and apprehending killers. Not only do they reach the murder scene long before the police, but they are far more reliable and successful in their investigations than they are.

Our story begins on the 1st of January, 1956. It may be a new year for Pluckley Green but the same old murders seem likely to plague the village. Throughout this game book you will assume the role of a Pluckley Green Sleuth. It will be up to you to visit the crime scenes, talk to suspects and above all else, catch the killers…

HOW TO PLAY

The Basics:

There are three different ways to play "Welcome to Pluckley Green." You can choose to investigate as a solo sleuth, cooperate with friends as a team or you can play with friends competitively - where the winner is whoever successfully solves each mystery.

For all three forms of play, the basics remain largely the same.

"Welcome to Pluckley Green" features an ongoing story which runs throughout the course of a year and as a result, you must play the mysteries in the CASE FILE in order.

The book is divided into three main sections, THE CASE FILE, THE EVIDENCE FILE and SOLUTIONS.

The story begins with Case 1 "Bloodshed at the Bloodied Axe", which is set on New Year's Day, 1956. You can find this mystery at the start of the CASE FILE.

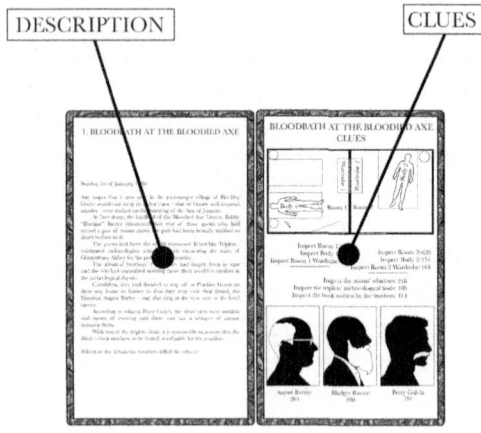

Begin by reading the description. This will always be the page on the left. If you are playing with other people (competitively or cooperatively) one member of the group should read the description aloud to the other players.

On the opposite page, you will see where to find the clues in the EVIDENCE FILE. This page (always on the right) may be a map, diagram or a sketch of the crime scene.

Once the description has been read, it is time to start looking for clues. In the first case, "Bloodshed at the Bloodied Axe" you may want to check the windows of the bedrooms. To do so, you would turn to the corresponding entry (in this instance, entry 218) in the EVIDENCE FILE. Once you have read this clue (or read it aloud if playing with friends) return to the "Bloodshed at the Bloodied Axe" page in the CASE FILE and continue searching for clues.

After that, it is simply a matter of repeating that process until you think you may have solved the mystery.

Now for some specifics regarding how you play solo or with friends…

Playing Solo:

The most straightforward way of playing "Welcome to Pluckley Green" is to do so solo.

As a lone sleuth, you will be tasked with solving 50 perplexing crimes and will rely on your own wits and skills of deduction.

Begin at Case 1 in the CASE FILE - "Bloodshed at the Bloodied Axe."

Read through the description on the left page and study the clues on the right page. Then, you must decide where you would like to investigate first.

As a solo sleuth, you can search the EVIDENCE FILE no more than 9 times before making your deduction.

For instance, in Case 1 - "Bloodshed at the Bloodied Axe", you may want to investigate the windows of the bedrooms. The page of clues will tell you to go to entry 218 in the EVIDENCE FILE.

When you find this entry in the EVIDENCE FILE, read the clue and return to the CASE FILE for "Bloodshed at the Bloodied Axe"

This counts as one turn and you can do this eight more times until you make your deduction.

Occasionally, when you go to an entry in the EVIDENCE FILE, you will be given the option to go to an additional entry in the EVIDENCE FILE to uncover further information. If you decide to visit this additional entry, it also counts as a turn, so choose wisely if you think the additional information will be of use. (If you choose not to visit this additional entry, you cannot return to it later in the investigation.)

Once you have visited the EVIDENCE FILE 9 times, you must decide what you think the solution to the mystery is. When you think you have an answer, turn to the SOLUTIONS section of the book to discover if your deductions were accurate.

This solution will also tell you of a place to go in the EVIDENCE FILE to collect an additional clue about the larger mystery of the village - but you are only permitted to read this entry if your deduction on this case was correct!

Good luck and happy sleuthing!

Playing Cooperatively With Friends:

Playing "Welcome to Pluckley Green" cooperatively with friends is a great way to sleuth as it allows you to swap theories and work towards a solution together.

The rules are very similar to playing solo as you have 9 opportunities to search the EVIDENCE FILE before you can make your deduction.

To begin, decide upon the order in which your team will play (for instance, your team members could play alphabetically).

The first mystery you will be investigating is Case 1 - "Bloodshed at the Bloodied Axe." A member of your group should turn to this page in the CASE FILE and read the description (on the left hand side) to the rest of the group.

The first player must then use the clues (on the right hand side) to decide where they would like to search for evidence.

For example, in the first case "Bloodshed at the Bloodied Axe", the first player may decide that they would like to check the windows of the bedrooms, in which case the clues page will tell them to go to entry 218 in the EVIDENCE FILE. They should then read this entry to the rest of the group.

The player will then return to the CASE FILE entry for "Bloodshed at the Bloodied Axe" and pass the book to the next player.

This counts as one turn. After 9 turns, the group will have to make a deduction and decide what they think is the solution to the mystery.

During a player's turn, they may stumble upon an entry in the EVIDENCE FILE which gives them the option to gain further information by visiting another entry. The group must decide if they want to go to this secondary location in the EVIDENCE FILE. If they choose to do so, this will count as an additional turn and the player must read this secondary piece of information to the group.

Choose wisely, because if you do not take this opportunity to visit this secondary information in the EVIDENCE FILE you will not be able to access it later on in the investigation.

Once all 9 turns have been used, the group must make a deduction (in most cases, this will mean accusing someone of being a killer but some cases will ask for a different answer). A player from the team must then turn to the SOLUTIONS section of the book and read the entry for the case to the rest of the group.

If the group has been correct in their sleuthing, they can access an additional piece of evidence from the EVIDENCE FILE. The solution will tell you where to find this additional clue.

This clue will help you solve the bigger mystery of the village - the mystery you will be tasked with unravelling at the end of the game.

Good luck and happy sleuthing!

Playing Competitively With Friends

Playing "Welcome to Pluckley Green" competitively with friends allows you each to work against one another to see who will be the first to crack the case!

When playing competitively, there is no limit to the number of turns you take - but some evidence will be uncovered solely by individual players and not the rest of the group.

To begin the game, choose which order your team of sleuths will play (for instance, you could go alphabetically).

The first player reads the left page of the case in the CASE FILE to the rest of the group (begin with Case 1 and then proceed through the other cases in order.)

Once the player has read the description of the case to the rest of the group, all of the sleuths should have a few minutes to study the page of clues (this is the page on the right.)

The players will then take it in turns to investigate the evidence in the EVIDENCE FILE.

For instance, if the group are playing their first game, they will be investigating Case 1 - "Bloodshed at the Bloodied Axe." The first player may want to investigate the windows in the bedrooms. The player should turn to the corresponding entry in the EVIDENCE FILE (in this instance, entry 218). They should then read this piece of evidence aloud to the rest of the group.

Once they have finished reading the evidence, the player should return to the "Bloodshed at the Bloodied Axe" page in the CASE FILE and pass the book to the next player.

Occasionally a sleuth may stumble over a piece of evidence in the EVIDENCE FILE for which there is additional information. The entry will tell the player where to go in the EVIDENCE FILE to find this additional information. The player whose turn it is can go to this entry and read the entry (in silence and to themselves) so that only they are privy to this information.*

The game ends when a player thinks they have solved the mystery - in which case, they must declare what they think the solution is (they can do this at any point of the game, regardless of it being their turn). The game can also end if all the evidence has been uncovered but nobody has managed to solve the mystery (in which case, the investigation has failed and players should go to the case's page in the SOLUTIONS section to find out what happened).

Turn to the case's corresponding page in the SOLUTIONS section of the book and one of the players must read the solution aloud to the rest of the group.

If the player successfully solved the mystery, that person is declared the "master sleuth" of the round and will be able to access a special piece of evidence in the EVIDENCE FILE regarding the village's grand mystery - the location of this evidence can be found at the end of the solution.

However, if the player has been wrong with their deduction, then that player has lost this round and all the other players can visit this special piece of evidence in the EVIDENCE FILE.

Good luck and happy sleuthing!

*An interesting, optional twist on competitive play is to allow players to exchange information. At any point during the case, two players can decide to swap evidence they have uncovered - either by whispering this information to each other or by passing each other notes.

A Few Additional Notes:

It is highly recommended that you keep notes in a notebook throughout the entirety of playing "Welcome to Pluckley Green." There is a large and complex mystery taking place in the village - one which you will be tasked with solving once you have played all 50 cases. Be sure to take notes regarding anything which seems strange, unusual or significant in the village.

Each character in the mystery cases is represented by a silhouette portrait on the page of clues. After a while, you may notice that some of these characters make appearances in other cases and seem key to a larger mystery in the village. Moreover, some character silhouettes have white features - such as white spectacles or beards - this denotes that this is a character who is significant to the main story of the book and is worth paying extra attention to.

Now, if you are ready to begin your sleuthing, get ready to go back in time to 1956. Turn to case 1 - "Bloodshed at the Bloodied Axe" in the CASE FILE and begin your adventure.

Welcome to Pluckley Green…

THE CASE FILE

1. BLOODBATH AT THE BLOODIED AXE

Sunday, 1st of January, 1956

Any hopes that a new year in the picturesque village of Pluckley Green would cast away its oldest curse - that of bloody and frequent murder - were dashed on the morning of the first of January.

At 7am sharp, the landlord of the Bloodied Axe Tavern, Bobby "Bludger" Baxter discovered that two of three guests who had rented a pair of rooms above the pub had been brutally stabbed to death in their beds.

The guests had been the world renowned Tchotchke Triplets - celebrated archaeologists who had been excavating the ruins of Glastonbury Abbey for the previous six months.

The identical brothers' endeavours had largely been in vain and the trio had unearthed nothing more than worthless trinkets at the archeological dig-site.

Crestfallen, they had decided to stop off at Pluckley Green on their way home to Exeter so that they may visit their friend, the historian August Barley - and also ring in the new year at the local tavern.

According to witness Perry Gulch, the three men were sociable and merry all evening and there was not a whisper of unease between them.

With two of the triplets dead, it is reasonable to assume that the third (who is nowhere to be found) is culpable for the murders.

Which of the Tchotchke brothers killed the others?

BLOODBATH AT THE BLOODIED AXE
CLUES

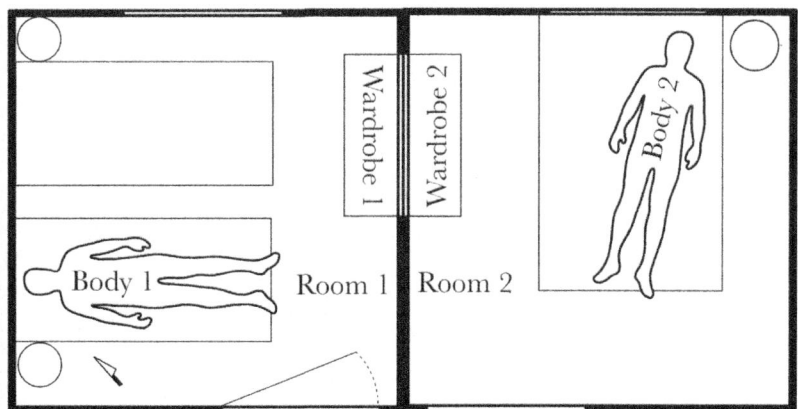

Inspect Room 1: 664
Inspect Body 1: 618
Inspect Room 1 Wardrobe: 31

Inspect Room 2: 620
Inspect Body 2: 154
Inspect Room 2 Wardrobe: 168

Inspect the rooms' windows: 218
Inspect the triplets' archaeological finds: 185
Inspect the book written by the brothers: 414

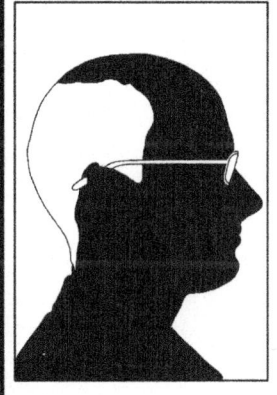

August Barley:
263

Bludger Baxter:
490

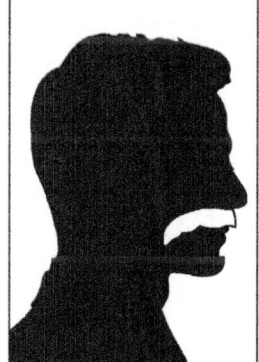

Perry Gulch:
191

2. FOR WHOM THE BELL KILLS

Thursday, 5th of January, 1956

One of the ways the residents of Pluckley Green fight the constant urge to commit murder is by developing hobbies.

Founded sometime in the 16th century, the Pluckley Green Ringers is one of the oldest campanology societies in England.

Until this evening, the bell ringing club consisted of four members; Gabe Ratchett - the head of the society; Frank Greenburg and his wife Joan and the newest member, Sebastian Turner. However, due to unforeseen circumstances, this quartet is now a trio.

As was their annual custom, the campanologists met at dusk on Twelfth Night in order to peel the four mighty bells which hang within the church tower of St Julian on the Edge church.

However, when Gabe Ratchett tugged upon the rope which swung from the fourth of the church bells, the entire half ton bell came crashing down from the rafters and flattened the man as if he were an overripe tomato.

In any ordinary village, this would be regarded as nothing more than a dreadful accident but in Pluckley Green, accidents are more often than not disguises for murder.

Aside from the ringers themselves, there were three other people in the church at the time of this incident; the Reverend Amos Harper; the church cleaner Daphne Robinson and her husband, organist Humphrey Robinson.

Who killed Gabe Ratchett?

3. 9.50 TO BRIGSTOWE

Friday, 6th of January, 1956

Nowhere in the picturesque village of Pluckley Green is safe from cold-blooded murder, not even the village's charming, Victorian train station.

A train to the nearby city of Brigstowe stops at the station twice a day, every weekday, and the Friday train was always the most popular - as that was market day in Brigstowe.

So it was quite a surprise that, as the Brigstowe train huffed and chuffed into the station that morning, a figure dressed all in white stepped out from the shadows and pushed a man in front of the train.

The man was killed instantly. His body lay in bits across the bloodied tracks as the figure in white fled into the morning fog.

Earlier that morning the victim had been seen coming from the pub by Roberta Agutter - a commuter at the station - who also witnessed the man's untimely demise. Furthermore, another witness to the murder was Albert Cribbins, the station's porter. But who was he?

What was the victim's first, middle and surname?

9.50 TO BRIGSTOWE CLUES

Inspect the victim's coat pockets: 477

Inspect the victim's wallet: 516

Check the shadowy corner where the killer was hiding: 92

Inspect the remains of the victim 425

Visit the pub: 400

Visit the waiting room: 694

Consult the train timetable: 347

Witness. Roberta Agutter 4

Porter. Albert Cribbins: 307

Train driver. Errol Frisk: 648

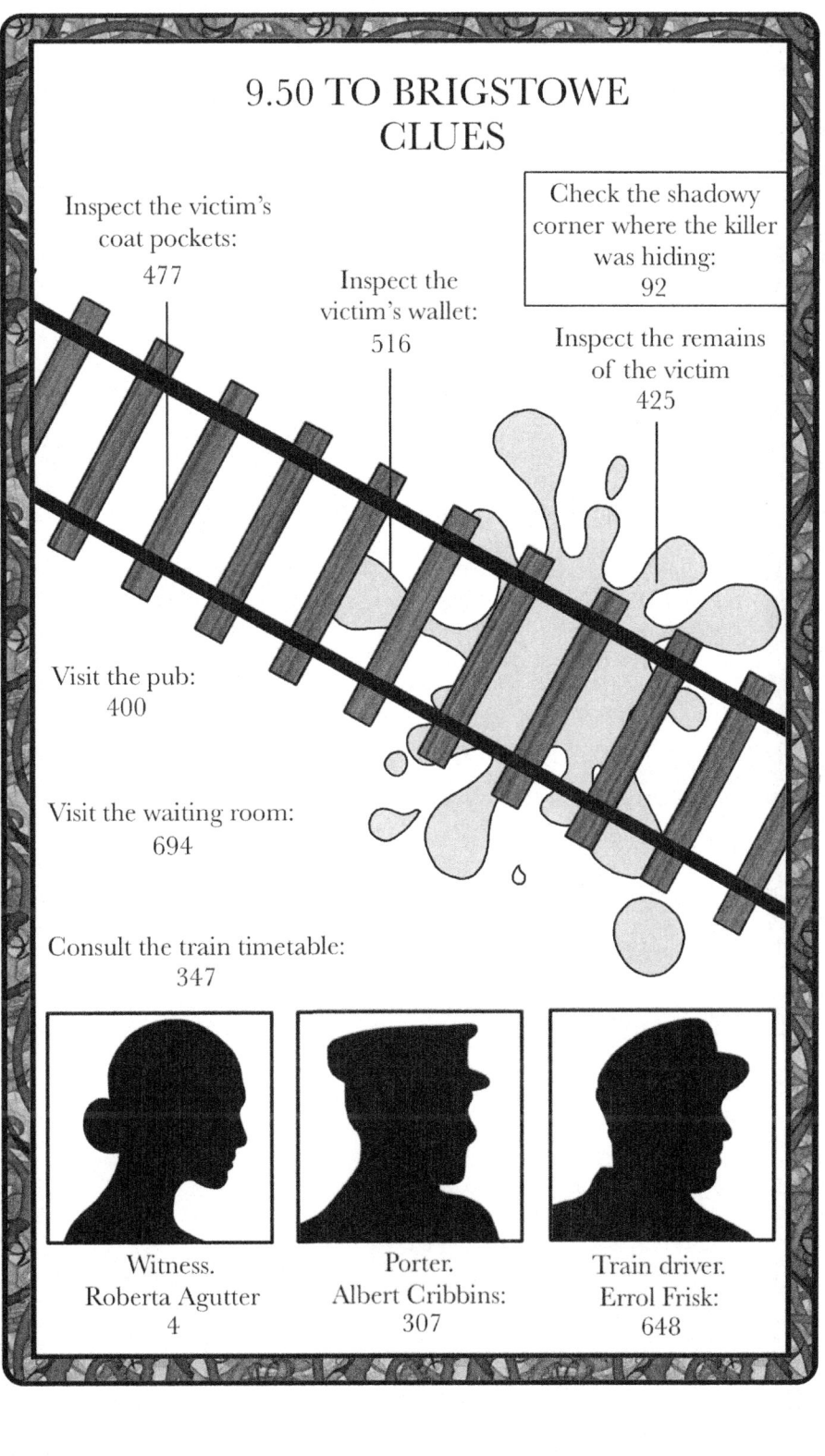

4. BLOOD ON THE STONES

Saturday, 15th of January, 1956

Whilst Pluckley Green remains a largely Christian and God-fearing village, there are still traces of the Old Ways, if you know where to look.

Nowhere is this more evident than with the Ancient Order of Pluckley Pagans - a secretive and centuries old society within the village.

Of the eight current members of this occult circle, seven keep their involvement with the nature-worshipping society a secret (and they attend all of the meetings draped in their ceremonial, hooded robes).

The eighth member, however - 92 year old Holly Merryfair - the "Grand High Wizard" of the organisation, has no such qualms and strolls about Pluckley Green in his white ceremonial garbs every day of the year without a care in the world.

Every morning Holly Merryfair would celebrate dawn at the mysterious Pluckley Stones - a prehistoric monolith on the heath at the edge of the village. The stones have stood for hundreds, maybe thousands, of years and are a place of worship for the Pluckley Pagans.

The morning of the 15th of January had been much like any other (save for the blanket of snow which had fallen overnight - the first snowfall of the winter) and Holly had traipsed to the standing stones as he did every morning. However, at 8am on the dot, a shot rang out across the heath - the Grand High Wizard of the Pluckley Pagans had been struck in the head by a bullet - somebody had shot him.

The only footprints which can be found in the fresh snow are those belonging to Holly Merryfair and the only homes within sight belong to local mechanic Gerald Ratchett, dog walker Helena Turner and retired English teacher Wilbur Charles - all three of whom happen to be members of the Order and moved so that they may live closer to their sacred stones.

Which one of them shot Holly Merryfair?

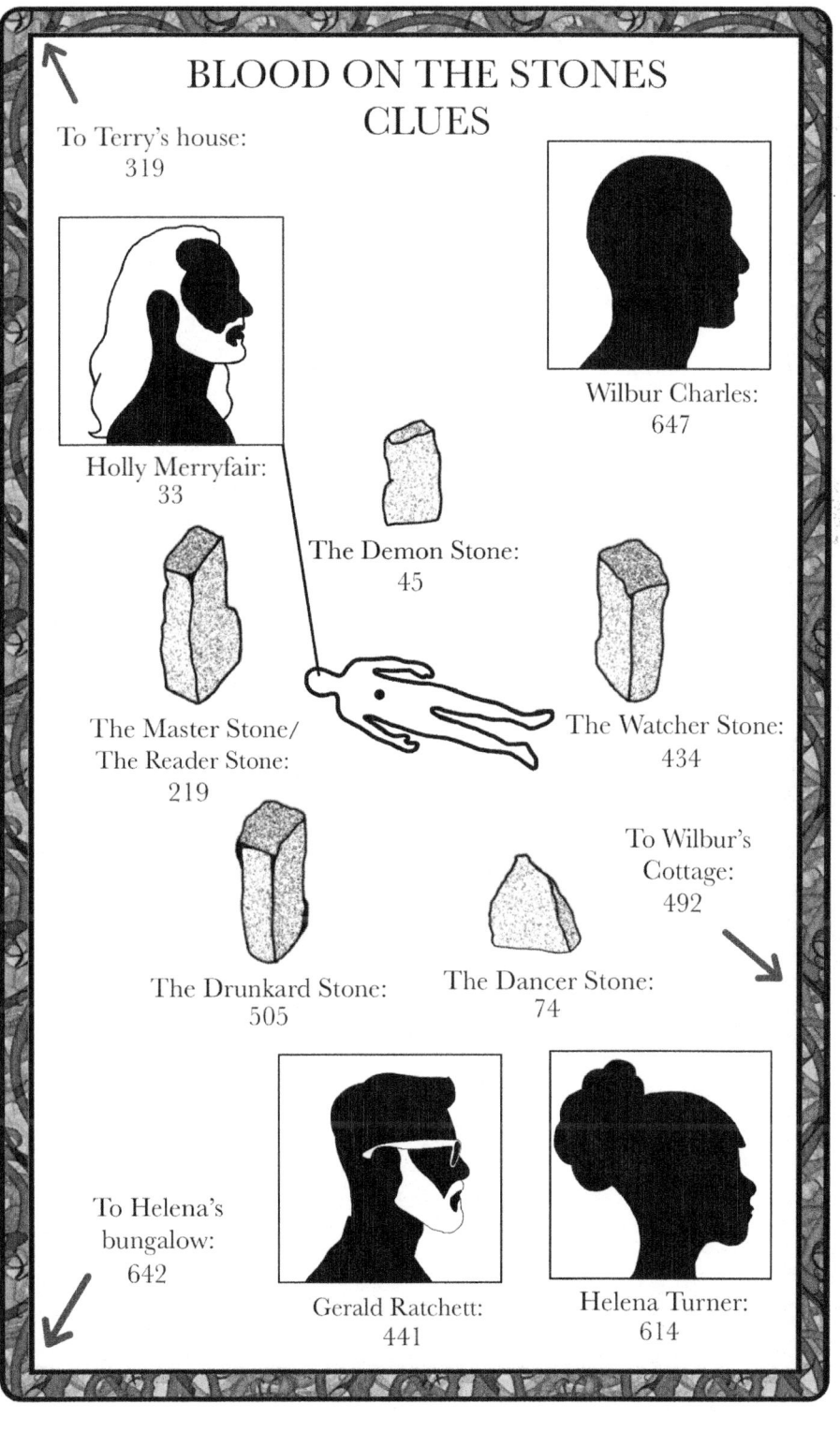

5. ATTEMPTED MURDER AT THE VICARAGE

Sunday, 5th of February, 1956

There has been an attempt on the life of one of Pluckley Green's most beloved residents.

Nagatha Christie, Reverend Amos Harper's adored horse has been poisoned!

As was customary for Sundays, the Reverend had invited a handful of the village residents to the vicarage for afternoon tea and cakes.

The invited guests were; Lord Lucien Pendergast and his wife, Lady Oxania Pendergast (also known as the Second Lady Pendergast); local conservationist and ornithologist Jeremy Trumble and two-time Somerset Junior Dressage Trials champion Judy Spiff - these four had also been guests of the Reverend on the prior Sunday.

Also present were the Reverend and his live-in cook of many years, Mabel Witherspoon.

It remains to be seen if Nagatha will survive this terrible ordeal but at the moment, only one question is on the lips of all the villagers.

Who poisoned Nagatha Christie?

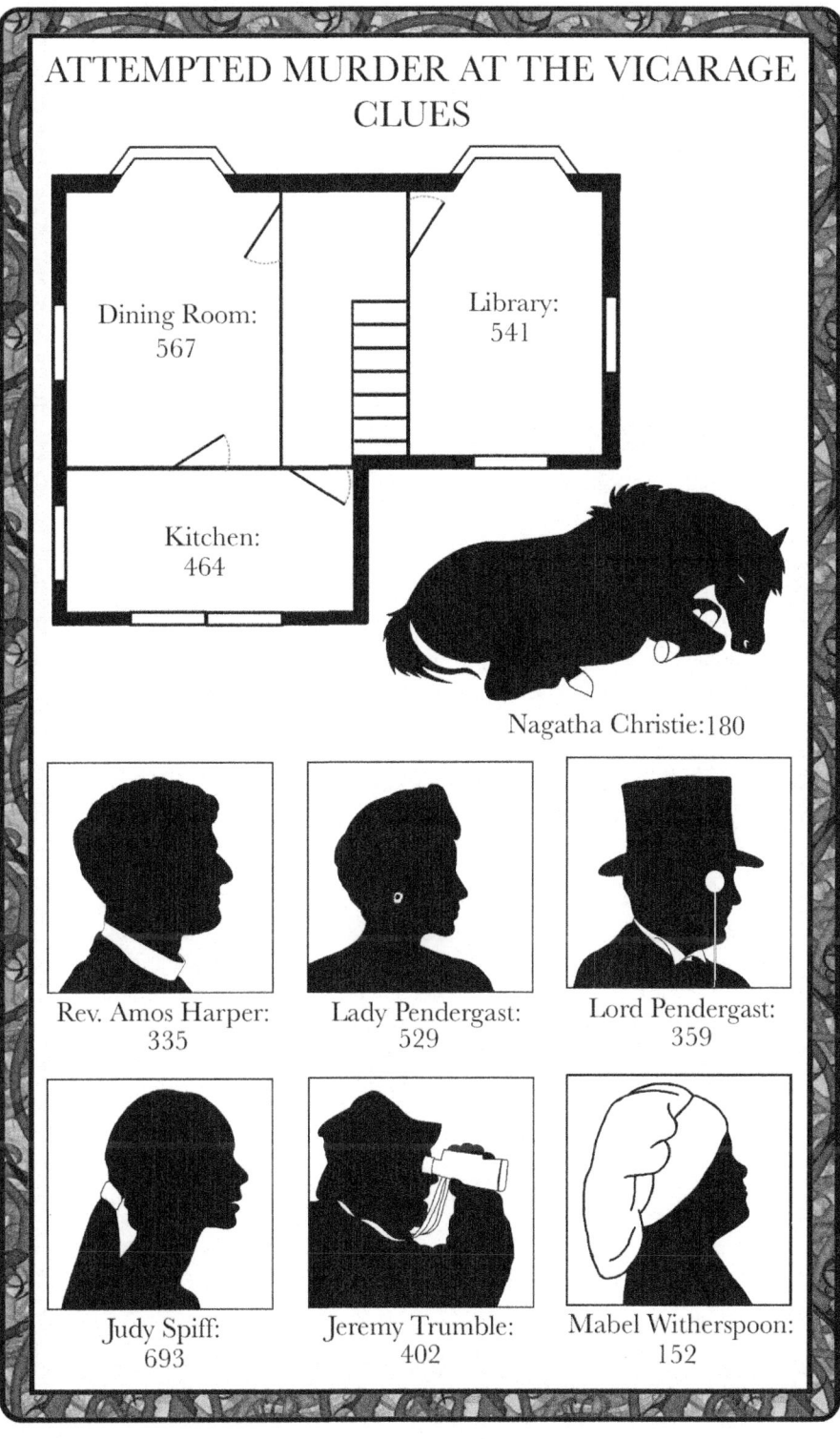

6. LOATHE THY NEIGHBOUR

Saturday, 11th of February, 1956

A years long dispute between neighbours came to a bloody end on Sunday, when the bodies of Harry Willis and Helen Dubois were discovered.

The corpses were in the adjacent gardens of 5 and 7 Henbury Street. Harry had been stabbed through the chest with a pitchfork and Helen had been strangled to death.

The two retirees had been engaged in a five year long boundary dispute. Mr. Willis had argued that official documents held at the library revealed that the edge of his garden was actually three feet beyond the existing garden wall.

Mrs. Dubois, however, was adamant that that the garden wall should stay precisely where it was and would not surrender even an inch of her land for the sake of an old document.

The widow and widower went from one-time friends to sworn enemies and soon there was a war between the two. Harry frequently dumped his rubbish over the garden wall and Helen took to feeding laxative laced meat to Harry's loyal beagle Darwin.

A call was made to the police at midday by Sophie Willis - the daughter of Harry (she would always visit her father at this time on Saturdays) who claimed to have discovered both bodies on the lawns of their own gardens.

Helen lived with her son Charles Dubois, who claims to have been at church that morning. She was due to be visited by her gardener Giles Greenham for his regular Saturday appointment at 2pm that afternoon (Giles had been witnessed working at Pluckley Green Park all morning).

Harry lived only with his dog Darwin.

Who murdered Harry and Helen?

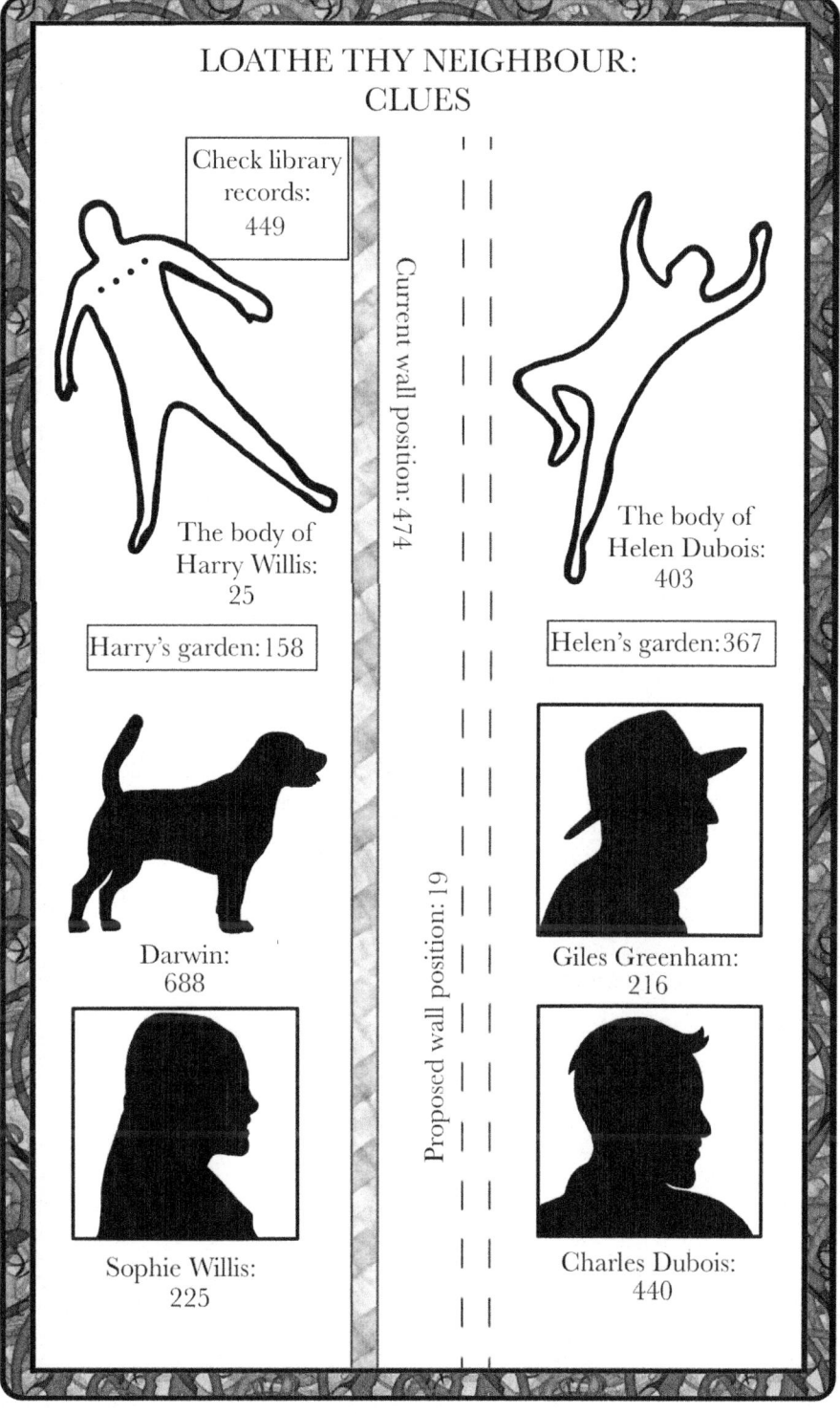

7. HATE EXPECTATIONS

Monday, 13th of February, 1956

Miss Faversham of Stasis House - the enormous mansion, which stands amidst the windswept loneliness of the heath - is a terrible, ruthless woman.

20 years ago, she was betrothed to a man who left her at the altar and eloped with a younger woman. Since that day she has retreated to her achingly huge mansion where she wanders the halls like a ghost - still wearing the tatters of her once beautiful wedding gown.

The house has fallen into a state of decay, as she has never cleaned even an inch of it since her wedding day and it now creaks beneath the weight of two decades worth of dust and cobwebs.

Quite surprisingly, Miss Faversham does not live alone in this tomb of a mansion, as thirteen years ago she took a baby into her home - a foundling named Esther, who she rarely allows to leave the house and who spends her days locked away in her bedroom.

Her live-in maid Genevieve Jensen is sighted by a handful of villagers every morning in the village buying groceries. It is often noted that this young woman will have scratches upon her face or be missing clumps of hair - as if fistfuls of it had been torn out.

The only other visitor to the house is Winston Lampeter, the handyman who takes care of the house and grounds and is the only one responsible for Stasis House not completely collapsing. He was present at the house early this morning.

At the same time, Holly Merryfair (who is recovering excellently from his brush with death) was greeting the dawn at the Pluckley Stones when he heard a bloodcurdling scream tear across the heath from the mansion. That was about two hours ago, at 8am.

Genevieve has not made her morning visit to the village greengrocers and the people of Pluckley Green are worried for her.

What happened to Genevieve Jensen?

HATE EXPECTATIONS CLUES

Miss Faversham: 202

Esther: 95

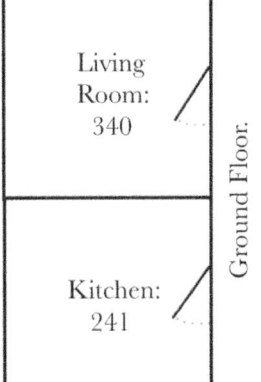

Ground Floor:
- Living Room: 340
- Kitchen: 241

First Floor:
- Miss Faversham's Bedroom: 522
- Genevieve's Bedroom: 352

Browse Miss Faversham's album of wedding photos: 408

Winston Lampeter: 448

Holly Merryfair: 233

Paddy Parson: 560

8. THE LONELY HEARTS MURDER

Tuesday, 14th of February, 1956

Marvin Makepeace has been murdered. The freshly divorced former surgeon was found on a bench in Pluckley Green Park with a knife stabbed through his heart. There were no witnesses to the attack, which is thought to have happened at around 3pm.

Mr. Makepeace had recently been exploring the world of dating, thanks to a lonely hearts ad he had placed in the local paper.

Over the course of a month he had met six women - all of whom he had deemed unworthy of his affections - and was due to meet a seventh that afternoon in the park. Whoever that woman was is assumed to have killed him.

All of the dates were arranged via letters sent to the offices of the Pluckley Green Press - the local paper which had originally printed Makepeace's lonely heart advertisement.

On all of these blind dates, it had been ensured by the newspaper that neither party had seen each other beforehand.

Marvin Makepeace had recently experienced a rather dramatic downturn in his life - having been fired from his job as a surgeon and then divorced from his wife of 10 years (after it was discovered that the man had been conducting an extramarital affair with a young woman.)

Who murdered Marvin Makepeace?

THE LONELY HEARTS MURDER CLUES

DIVORCED MALE, 45. WLTM petite, healthy and compliant woman aged 18-29 with intentions to marry. Tall or heavy ladies need not apply.

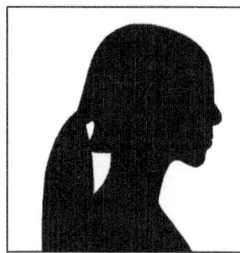

Ex-wife
Lola Dempsey: 163

The body of Marvin Makepeace: 697

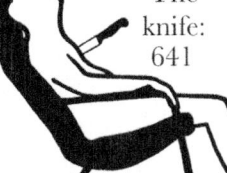

The knife: 641

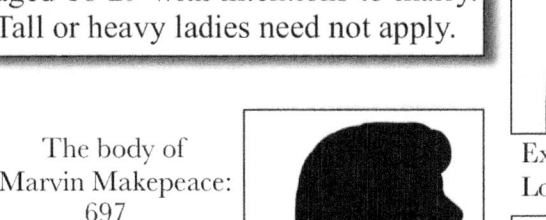

Newspaper editor
Sandy Tomlin: 479

Ex-mistress
Molly Mae: 184

Willow Carpenter: 470

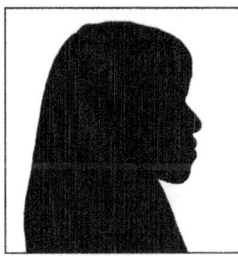

Rita Debbonaire: 611

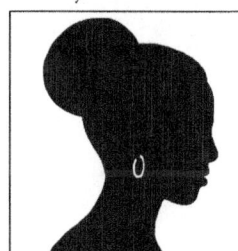

Daisy Doyle: 397

Debbie Salt: 6

Lucy Sparrow: 394

Rosemary Springs: 489

9. LOCK-IN AT THE BLOODIED AXE

Saturday, 18th of February, 1956

What began as a night of merriment ended in tragedy at the Bloodied Axe Tavern. The barmaid "Saucy" Sally Carter is dead.

Her body was found in the morning by Billy "Bludger" Baxter, following a raucous party at the pub. She had simply collapsed on the floor sometime during the night and the cause of her death is not currently apparent.

The party had been in honour of Bludger Baxter's 60th birthday. Beginning at 7pm, the party had continued past final orders and a few of his close friends had enjoyed an after hours lock-in, which went on until about 1am. Despite Bludger's ferocious reputation (he is infamous for keeping a loaded shotgun behind the bar) he is said to have been very fond of Sally, who was a kind and reliable worker.

Aside from Bludger and Sally, the guests at the lock-in were Jennifer Carter (the victim's sister), Norman Grebe (the victim's former boyfriend) and Donny Steadman (Sally's fiancée).

In addition, there was Walker Bradley (Bludger's friend), who was in attendance with his wife Lorraine, also present were Marcus Baxter (Bludger's brother) and pub regular Delia Steadman - mother of the victim's fiancée.

Also, the notorious village drunk - Perry Gulch - was in the nearby park late at night and claims to have overheard something he believes may have been a clue.

Nobody in attendance had a bad word to say against "Saucy" Sally but who killed her?

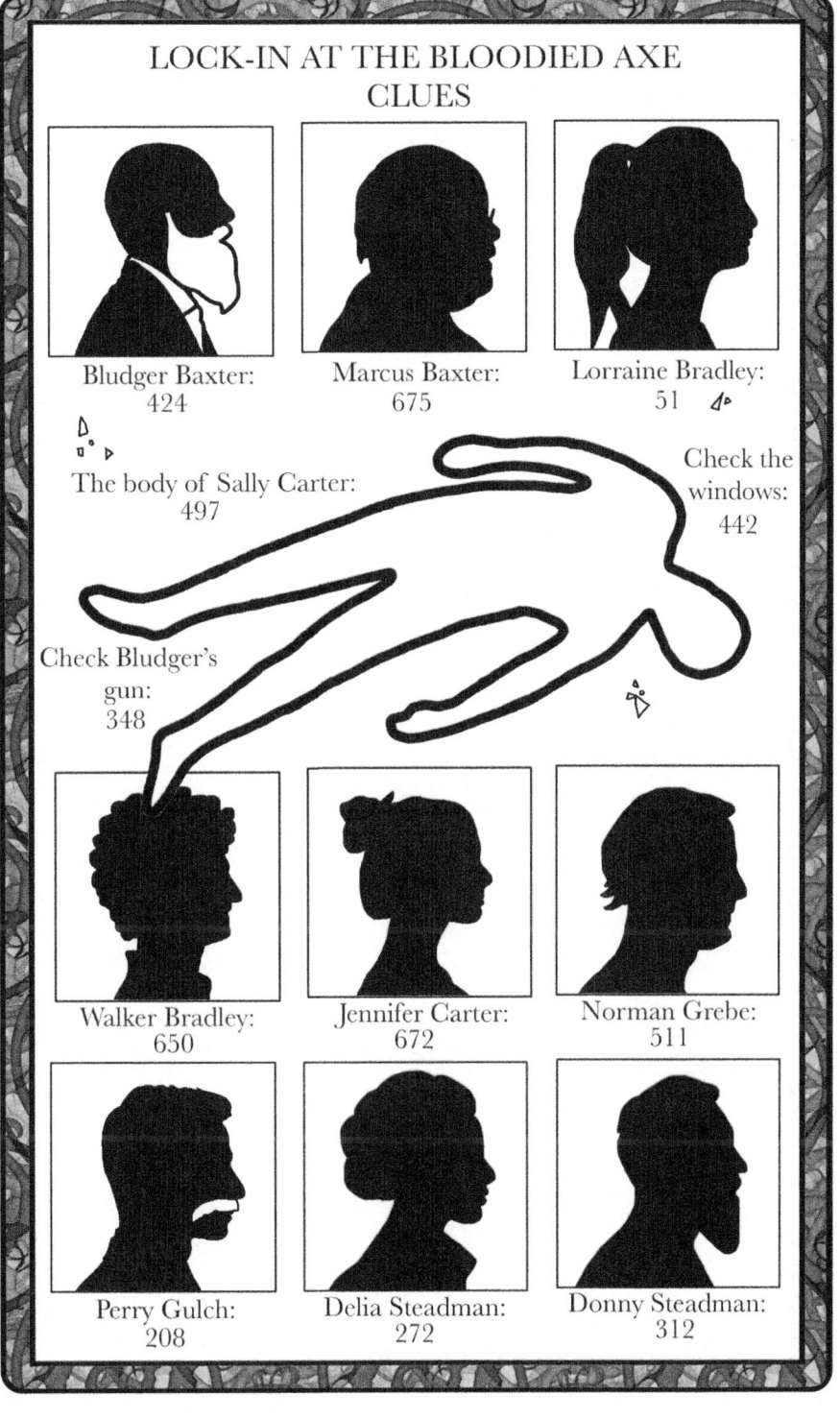

10. MURDER IS FOR THE BIRDS

Wednesday, 22nd of February, 1956

Pluckley Green has an abundance of hobby groups of all kinds and just like everything else in the village, once you peek behind the genteel facade of these groups, you'll find that they are a hotbed of jealousies, rivalries and personal vendettas.

One such hobby group are the Pluckley Green Birders - an ornithological group founded in the 1890s.

Until this morning, the group consisted of six avid birdwatchers, all of whom received an anonymous note through their letterboxes yesterday afternoon.

According to this note, the rare warbling snow dipper had been sighted in the river leading to the wetlands estuary. This enigmatic bird had been sighted precisely where the group had built their five hides (camouflaged, open-fronted huts from which the birdwatchers could discretely observe the local wildlife).

The following dawn - just as the winter snow was thawing - the group set out to the wetlands and each took to their regular hides.

At about 8am, any hopes of witnessing the rare bird were dashed by an enormous, ear-splitting bang - the unmistakable sound of a gunshot.

After a few minutes of confusion, five of the perplexed birdwatchers emerged from their hides. These were:

Conservationist and head of the Pluckley Green Birders, Jeremy Trumble; husband and wife ornithologists Barney and Tanya Flock; Tiffany Pearl and finally, Bill Barr.

The sixth member of the group, Pip Longfellow, was dead in his hide. He had been shot through the head.

Who killed Pip Longfellow?

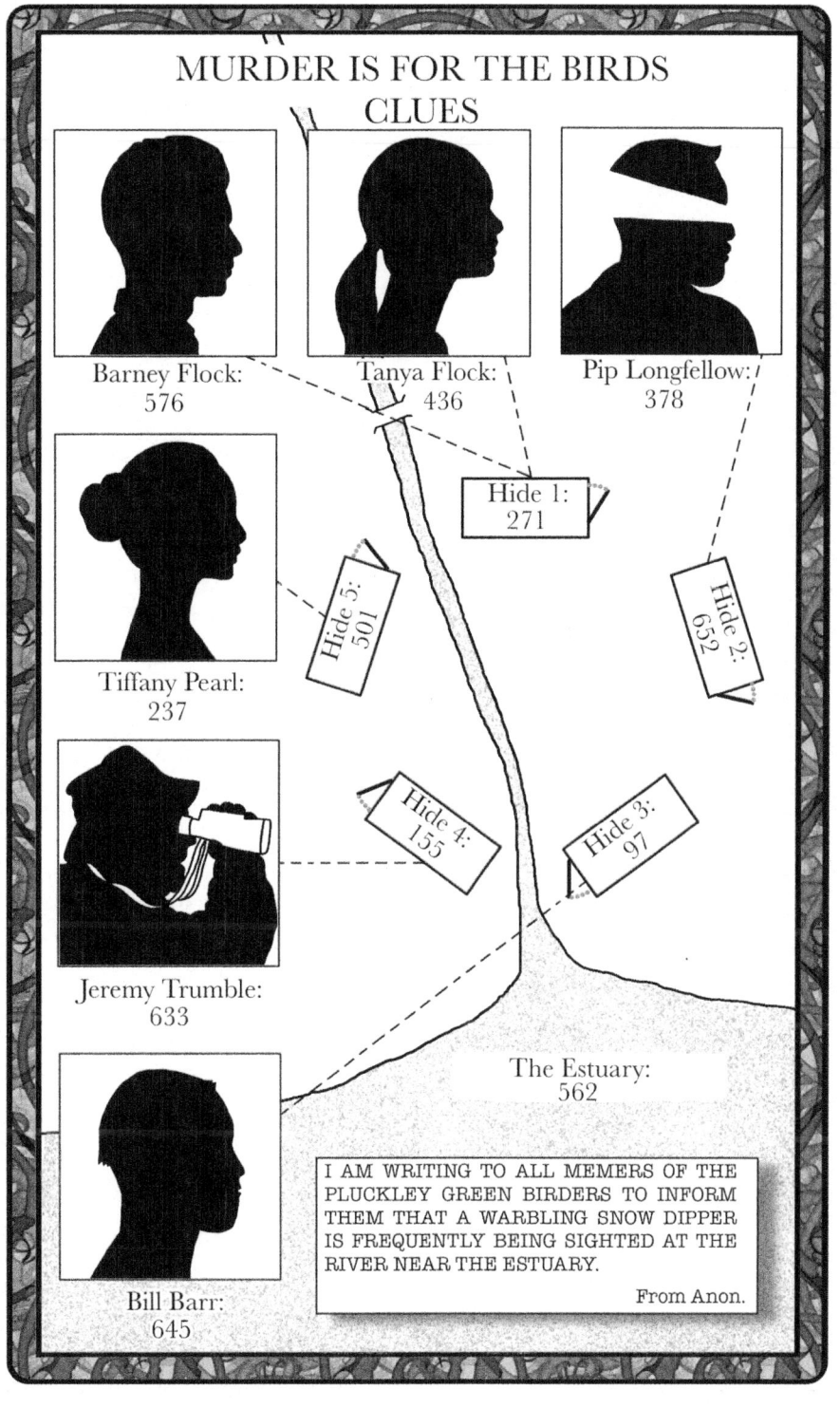

11. A LEAP OF LOVE

Wednesday, 29th of February, 1956

Traditions will always find a home in the unabashedly old-fashioned village of Pluckley Green.

One such tradition, which has survived for generations, is that Leap Day - that magical day that appears only once every four years - is the day that the tables are turned and a woman may ask her beau for his hand in marriage.

This year, one aspiring bride was Lana Finch, who had gathered a handful of friends and family in Pluckley Green Park to witness her proposal to her boyfriend Dickon Paisley.

Dickon had been informed that he and Lana were simply to go for a walk around the charming park, so that they may enjoy the blooming daffodils and other early spring flowers.

The witnesses invited to the secret proposal were; Lana's closest friend, Petra Blossom; Dickon's fishing pals Vernon Weathers and Colin Carnegie; Lana's father, postman Larry Finch and her mother, Rose Finch.

Halfway through the walk, when they were standing amid a carpet of crocuses and Dickon had his back to her, Lana got down on one knee. When he turned back around, she presented him with a ring in a jewellery box and said to her beloved:

"Now that we have truly moved on from all of that unpleasantness of last summer, I believe that it is time that you and I settled down and started a life together. Please Dickon Paisley, will you marry me?"

Dickon took no time to respond with an enthusiastic "YES!" And kissed Lana demurely upon the lips. His fiancee then proceeded to slip the engagement ring onto his finger.

A few moments later, as the onlookers cheered the happy occasion, Dickon Paisley dropped to the floor - dead.

Who killed Dickon Paisley?

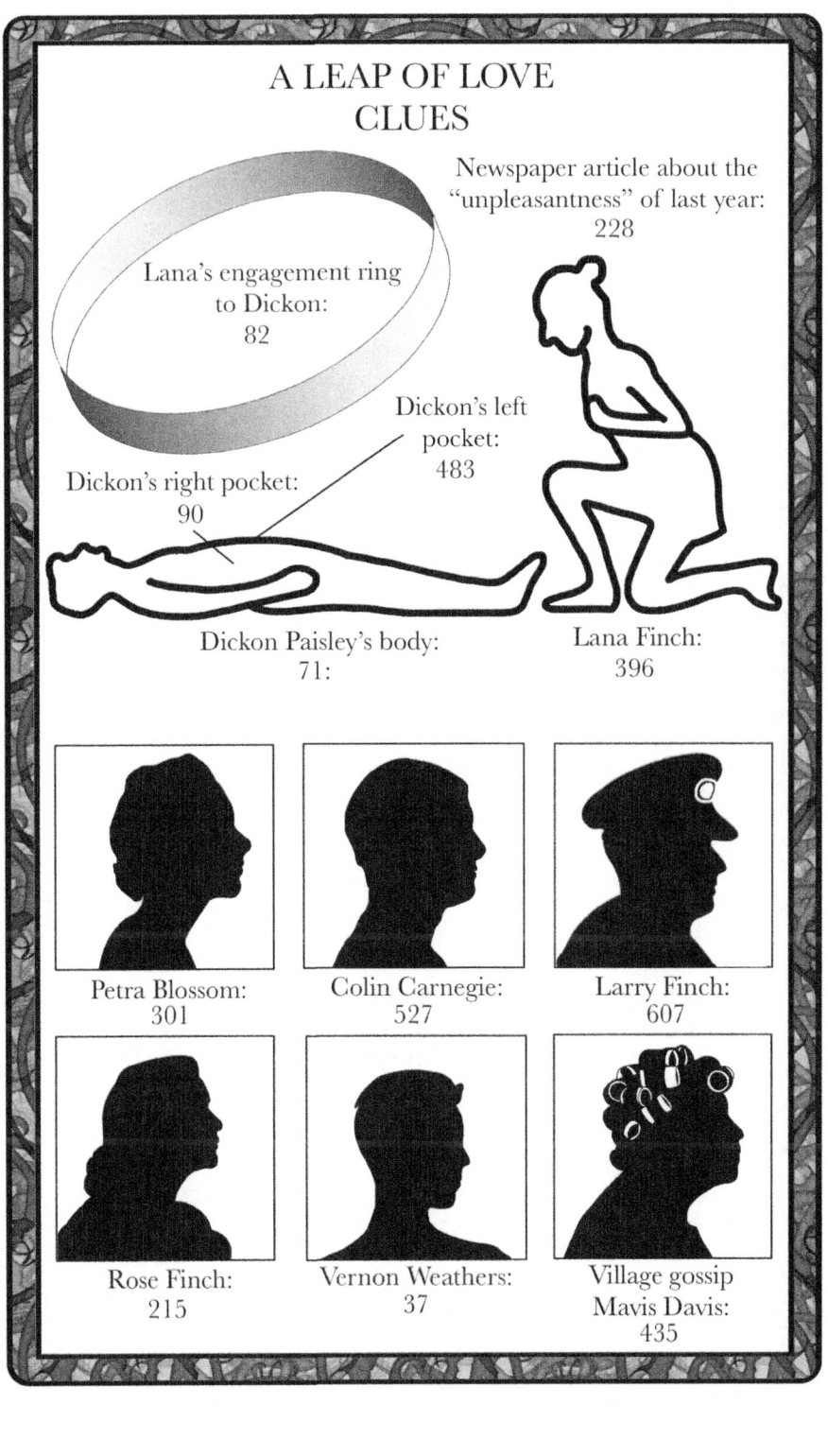

12. TOIL AND TROUBLE

Tuesday, 6th of March, 1956

The Pluckley Players are the village's merry band of actors who perform as an amateur dramatics troupe at the local village hall.

The Pluckey Players have been performing their definition of theatre since 1937 and are now a beloved institution in the village - for all the wrong reasons - as their performances are a parade of wooden acting, forgotten lines and collapsing scenery.

Rehearsals for the Pluckley Player's latest assault upon the arts was going as well as could have been expected. The production of Macbeth was due to open on Saturday and a handful of the cast were rehearsing a few scenes on Tuesday evening when murder struck.

Leon Cribbage, who was playing the part of Macbeth himself, was standing alone on the stage in a spotlight and reciting the character's famous "is this a dagger which I see before me" soliloquy when a figure dressed in black and wearing a white theatrical mask crept onto the stage from the wings, stabbed the actor with a dagger in the back, and fled from the village hall through the main doors.

As the hammy actor dropped to his knees, the man gasped his theatrical final words, which were intended to be "Sleep no more! Sleep no More! Macbeth shall sleep no more!" but as usual, he fumbled his lines and promptly died.

Following the shock and confusion of the moment, the cast and crew of the production rushed from backstage to the stage, these were;

Thalia Jones, the actress who was cast to play Lady Macbeth; her boyfriend, Melvin Pomene, who was the understudy to Leon Cribbage's Macbeth; Isobel Chance who was cast as Witch #3 and Eric Aria, who was playing the role of Macduff.

Also present were Colin Carnegie, the stagehand who was in the dark of backstage with the other actors when the murderer struck and director Stanley Slavsky, who was the only person watching the rehearsal from the front row of the seats.

Who murdered Leon Cribbage?

TOIL AND TROUBLE CLUES

Outside the village hall: 186

The stage: 59

Backstage: 57

Dressing room: 656

The body of Leon Cribbage: 267

Eric Aria/ Macduff: 692

Colin Carnegie/ Stagehand: 98

Isobel Chance/ Witch #3: 580

Thalia Jones/ Lady Macbeth: 282

Melvin Pomene/ Macbeth understudy: 566

Stanley Slavsky/ Director: 625

13. MURDER AT CROOKED COTTAGE

Wednesday, 13th of March. 1956

A storm is heading for Pluckley Green - figuratively and literally.

Meteorologists have been tracking this storm as it heads southeastwards, leaving a wake of destruction across Ireland and it is due to reach the quiet village on Friday.

Fears that the storm may be as huge and ruinous as "The Great Gale of '28" have led many of the villagers to board and barricade their windows in advance of its unwelcome arrival.

The village handyman, Winston Lampeter, has helpfully been assisting with preparations by offering to stormproof the villagers' homes - free of charge.

However, at about 2pm this afternoon, he attended Nightshade House - the oldest residence in Pluckley Green - a building so rickety and wonky with age it has come to be known as "Crooked Cottage" by the villagers.

The current occupant of the house is (or rather was) Lucy Sparrow, a 32 year old librarian whose family have owned Crooked Cottage for generations (however, owing to a curious superstition, Lucy was the first member of the Sparrow family to have lived in the house for over a century).

Once he had knocked upon the door and received no response, Winston Lampeter peered through the window and to his horror, saw Lucy Sparrow sat upright in a desk chair - with her severed head resting upon her own lap.

After battering the front door open and gaining entrance to the small home, Mr Lampeter (and later the police) discovered that not only had the door been locked from the inside, so had every other door and window in the cottage.

Beatrice Beauregard, who lives next door to Crooked Cottage, believes that she has information which may be of help.

How did Lucy Sparrow's killer escape from the locked cottage?

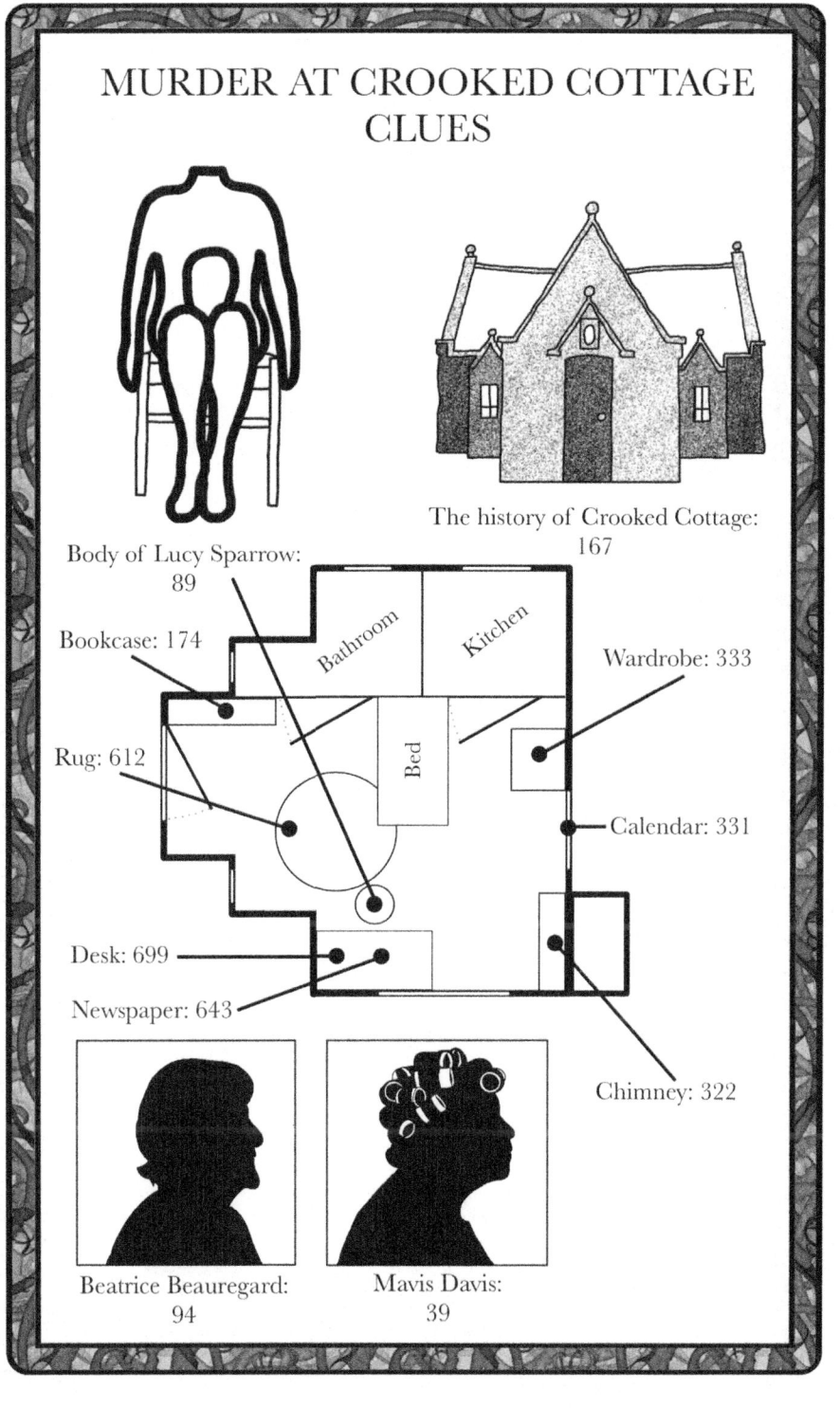

14. THE NIGHT OF THE STORM: PART ONE

Friday, 15th of March. 1956

For centuries, the church of St Julian on the Edge has provided sanctuary and refuge for the beleaguered residents of Pluckley Green.

Never was this service more needed than on the night of the 15th of March, 1956, when the ancient church threw open its doors so that the people of the village could find a place of safety in which to shelter from the storm.

The walls of the church were thick and far away from the threat of falling trees or the rising river and those in more perilous locations were drawn to the holy site as they had been for time immemorial.

Those arriving for a night at the church came laden with sleeping bags and pillows so as best to prepare for sleep upon the cold, stone floor of the church. They were (in order of arrival):

Local historian August Barley; Silas Marsten (another historian from an unfathomably wealthy background - who just happened to be writing a book on the history of the village); the village gossip, Mavis Davis and Holly Merryfair of the Ancient Order of Pluckley Pagans (who was an unlikely friend of Reverend Amos Harper). The last to arrive were botanist Wilma Rogers and Daisy Doyle, who worked part-time at the village greengrocers.

Reverend Amos Harper and his live-in cook Mabel Witherspoon were also present, with Mabel conjuring up a delicious vegetable soup for the guests.

Perhaps it was the storm which had set everyone on edge but there was a frosty, tense atmosphere in the church leading up to supper at 8pm.

The soup was served upon a folding table with all present seated along it. Each guest was given a bowl of soup from a large saucepan, along with two slices of buttered, crusty bread.

After saying Grace, the guests tucked into the soup and bread. All seemed to be going well until Silas Marsten slumped forward at the table, his face landing in his bowl of soup. He was dead - he had been poisoned.

Who murdered Silas Marsten?

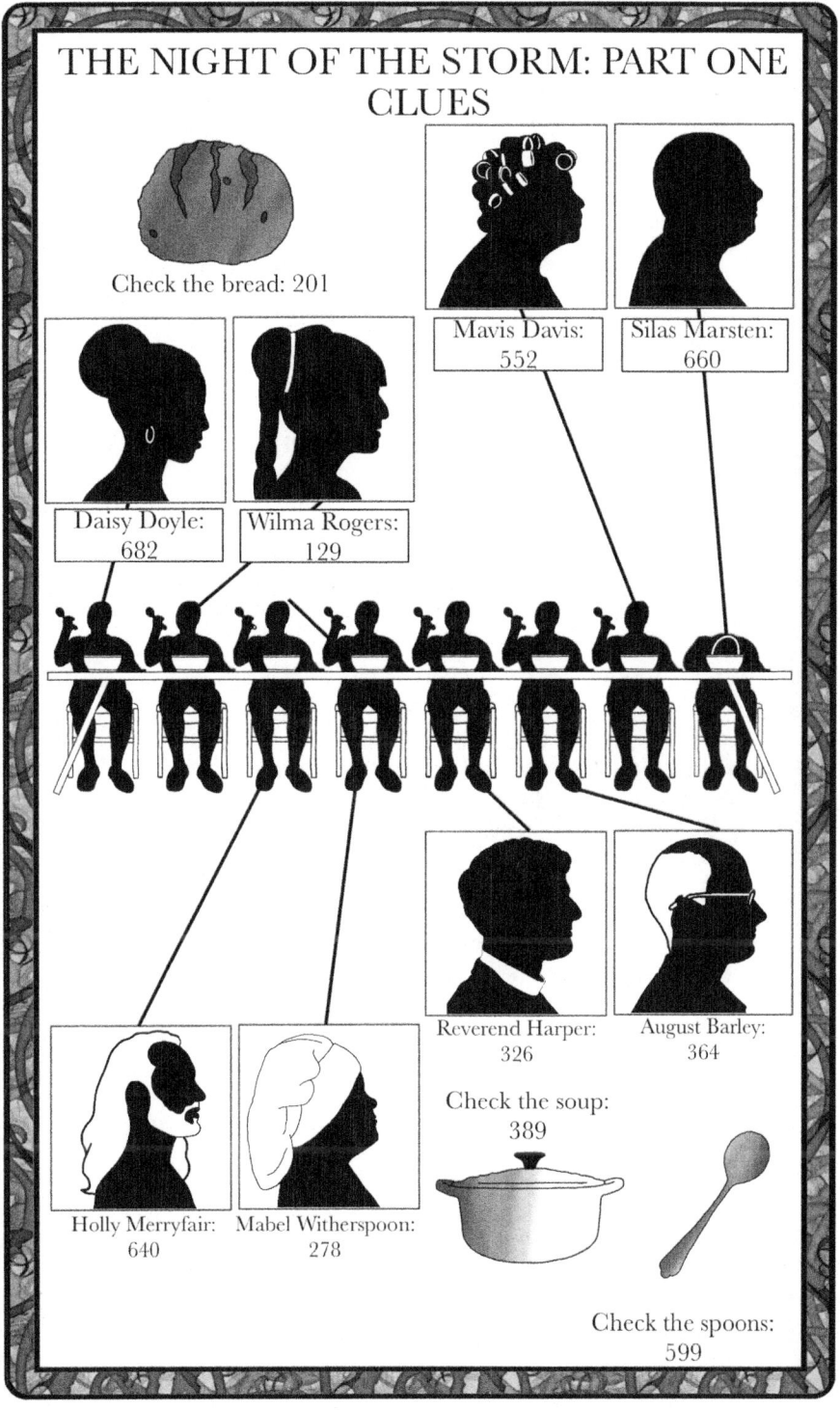

15. THE NIGHT OF THE STORM: PART TWO

Friday, 15th of March. 1956

The mighty storm lashed at the village with even more ferocity than had been forecast.

Whilst most of Pluckley Green's residents hunkered down for the night and sheltered from the weather, Lord and Lady Pendergast chose instead to host an impromptu "storm party" by inviting members of two of the village's most prominent families to spend the night with them at Pendergast Manor.

The guests - the Nolans and the Mertons - arrived at 7pm promptly, just as the storm began howling against the walls of the grand mansion and the rain battered at the windows.

The guests consisted of Gordon Nolan, a local businessman of note and his wife Matilda. They brought with them their fifteen year old daughter Nelly. Also present were accountant Damien Merton and his wife Charlotte (who happened to be Gordon Nolan's secretary).

Upon arrival, the Pendergast's maid, Mona Prim, invited the guests to explore the manor for half an hour before they all settled down for an elaborate feast.

At some point during the meal, Charlotte Merton discovered that a handwritten note had been tucked beneath her napkin. She discretely read it but did not disclose its contents.

As the guests knew all too well from previous Pendergast parties, after dinner, they were invited to partake in a game of hide-and-seek.

All of the guests, plus Lord Pendergast and Mona the maid, had until Lady Pendergast counted to one hundred in which to hide in the east wing of the mansion, after which Lady Pendergast searched the rooms in pursuit of the players.

She first found her husband, who had hidden beneath the dining room table. Next she found her maid Mona, who was in a wardrobe of the first guest bedroom. Both Mona and Lord Pendergast waited in the dining room for the game to end.

However, as Lady Pendergast searched for the third player, a gunshot rang out across the house.

The players emerged from their hiding places at once and after a frantic search of the east wing, the corpse of Charlotte Merton was discovered in the wardrobe of the second guest bedroom. She had been shot through the head.

Who murdered Charlotte Merton?

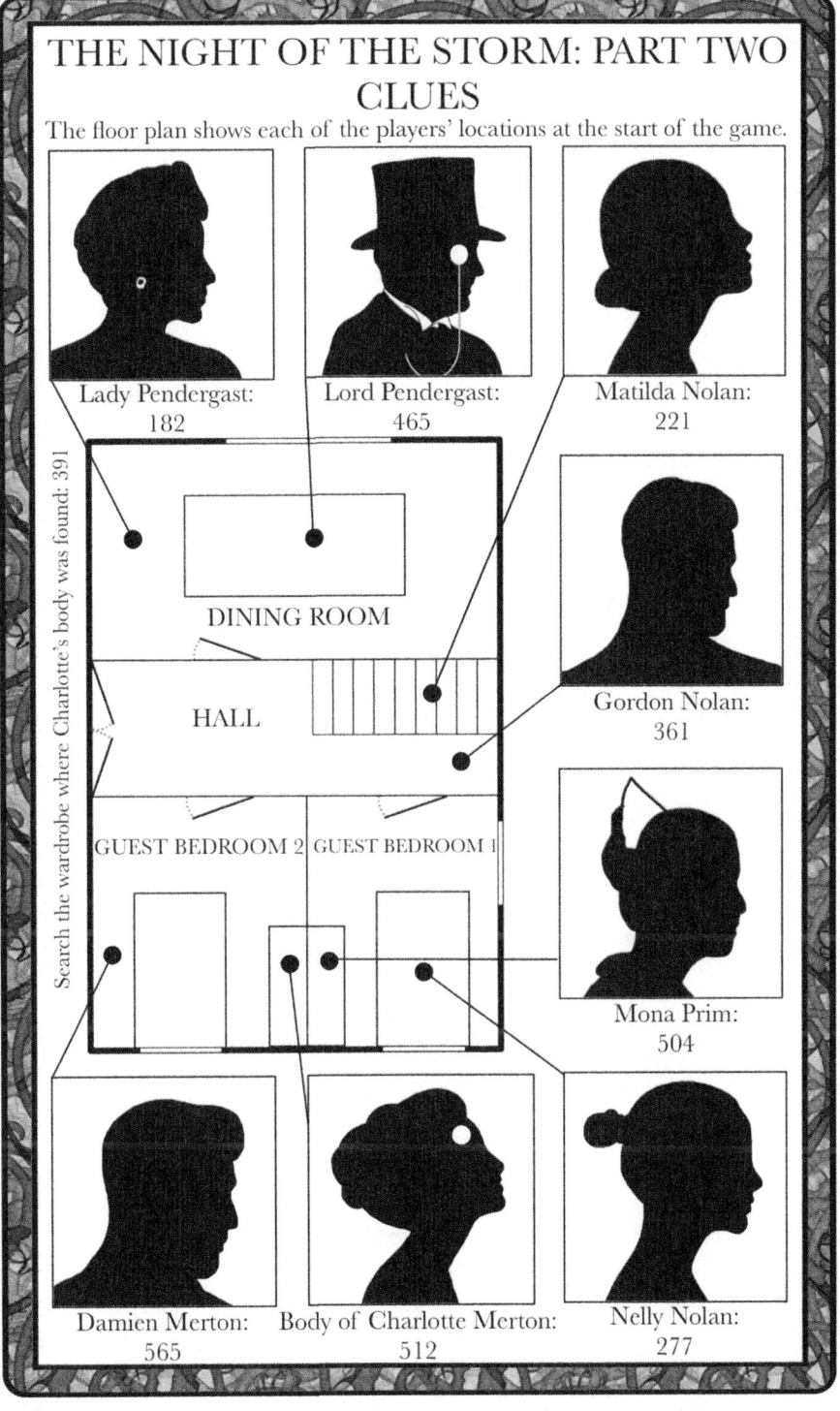

16. EASTER FOOL'S DAY

Sunday, April 1st, 1956

Pluckley Green's Easter parade is a beloved annual event whereupon almost the entire population of the village lines the high street - from the Bloodied Axe Tavern to the church - and cheers as a procession of local dignitaries and prominent members of the community promenade by. The women wear their finest bonnets and the men wear daffodils in the lapels of their jackets.

However, anxieties had been rising in the build up to the 1956 parade. Easter Sunday happened to fall on the very same day as April Fools' Day - and the opportunity for mischief was undoubtedly high.

Worse still, the Lord Mayor of Brigstowe, Lord Barclay Asquith-Hulme - a stern and humourless man - was this year attending the parade as guest of honour and would almost certainly be the target.

The culprit of such a stunt was likely to be Lester "The Jester" Pratt. Lester enjoyed a reputation as a prankster and mischief-maker and every April Fools' Day he revelled in staging a grand scale jape which would outdo all others.

The Lord Mayor arrived at the Reverend Harper's house on Friday evening and stayed at the vicarage with his assistant Carl Turpin throughout the weekend.

The plan suggested by the organiser of the parade, Frank Greenburg (who was now also the head of the Pluckley Green Ringers) was to have Lester's neighbour Sidney Snell (the village cobbler) visit the prankster in the morning and distract him until noon - after which time, April Fools' Day pranks were regarded as gauche.

However, upon arrival, Sidney witnessed postman Larry Finch fleeing from the front garden of Lester's home. Peering through the open front door of the house, Sidney discovered that Lester was laying dead upon the floor of the hall. It was not immediately apparent what had killed the man.

Doctor Henery White was first on the scene - just before the police.

Who murdered Lester "The Jester" Pratt?

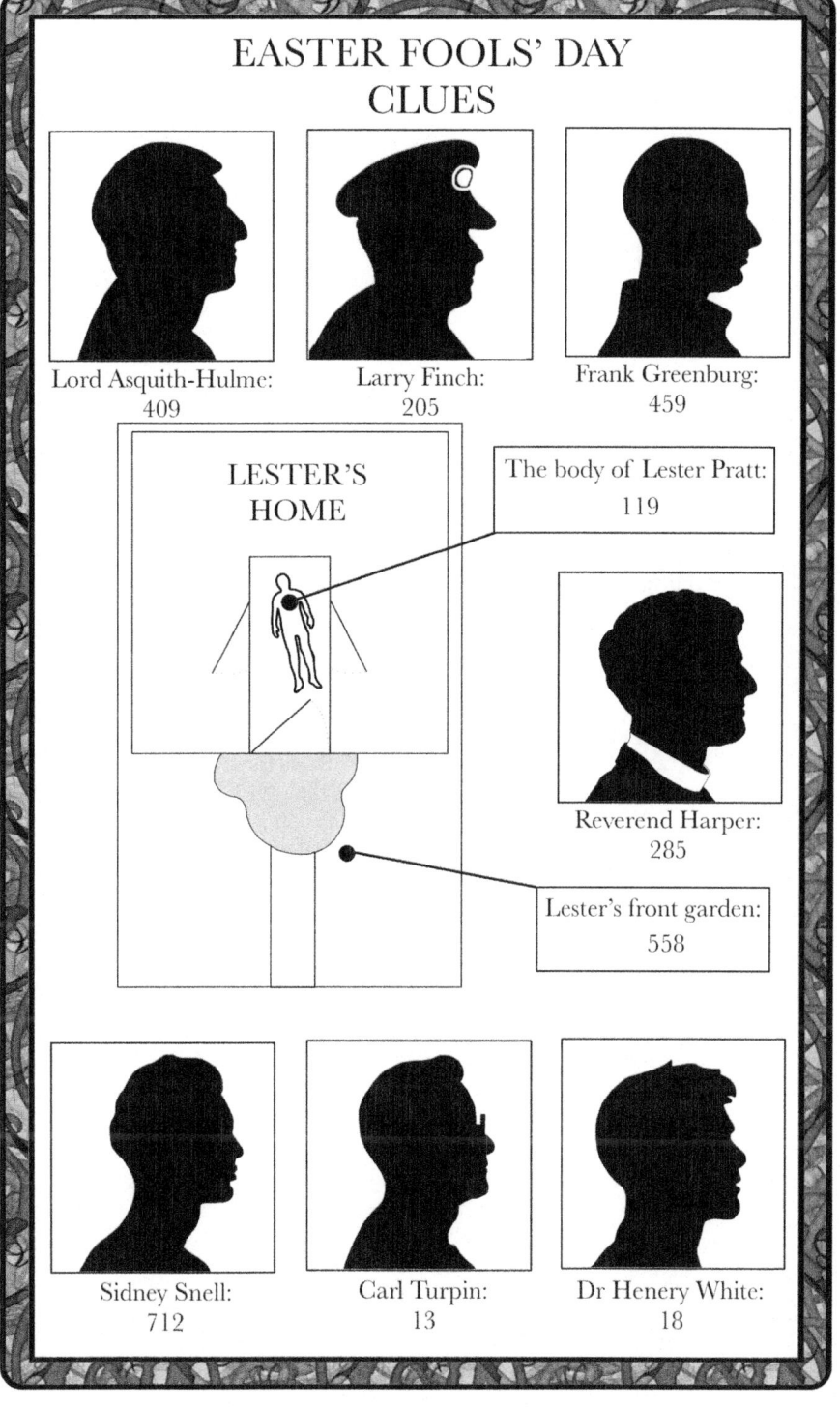

17. SEANCE ON A CURSED AFTERNOON

Friday, 13th of April. 1956

Whilst the storm had provided the residents of the village a much needed distraction, once the cleanup of Pluckley Green had been completed all talk returned to the grim subject of The Ghost.

Ever since the discovery of the headless body of Lucy Sparrow, the Pluckley Green Press had been filled with little else besides lurid details and fevered speculation on the unknown killer in the midst of the village. Who was the killer? When would he or she strike again?

Owing to the mysterious details of Lucy's murder (she had been killed in a supposedly haunted cottage which was locked and bolted from the inside) many of the villagers had concluded that these murders had a supernatural origin and called upon the services of the local clairvoyant, Adriana Arcana.

Adriana Arcana claimed to be in contact with the spirit realm and could foretell events which were yet to be. On the afternoon of the Friday the 13th of April - the cursed day - she summoned five curious visitors to her cottage so that she might conduct a seance which would draw out the identity of the killer.

The five guests were: local farmer Horace Scrub - who had recently inherited a large fortune from his departed father; his wife Helga - whose family had roots in the village for as long as records have existed; local historian August Barley; cider maker Ashton Egremont-Russet and Preston Gannet, a labourer at Horace's farm.

The guests were met at the door by Adriana Arcana's daughter Minerva, who led them to the drawing room but did not join them for the seance.

Once seated around a circular table in the small room, the guests and the medium first attempted a spirit board before joining their hands to form a ring around the table and closing their eyes for a seance.

Adriana Arcana informed her guests that once they opened their eyes, an ornamental dagger she had placed in the centre of the table would be floating in midair before them.

However, when they opened their eyes they discovered instead that Horace Scrub had been stabbed in the throat with the dagger.

Who murdered Horace Scrub?

18. RUN FOR YOUR LIFE

Saturday, 21st of April, 1956

The Pluckley Green Run began in 1936 as a fun race around the village, with any money raised going to the refurbishment of the church roof.

Over the following (non-war) years, the run has grown in size and reach, with spectators arriving from miles away to view the cross-country race.

Now in its twentieth year, the Pluckley Green Run is one of the most popular events in the village calendar.

The runners train all year for the big event, however, for the past five years the first place medal has gone to Milton West, who without fail crosses the finish line clear ahead of his competitors.

Second place has always been awarded to Bruno Brown, a gifted and determined runner who has nevertheless perpetually had to settle for silver.

Meanwhile, third place has always gone to Lyle Carmichael, who has simply been proud and pleased with this achievement.

The rest of the runners race to raise funds for local charities and none of them are regarded as true rivals to the three in the lead.

This morning at 10am, once all the competitors were lined up at the starting point outside the Bloodied Axe Tavern, the starting pistol was fired by Maximilian Prowse - a former long distance runner from Pluckley Green, whose Olympic dreams were never realised - and the runners were off.

At four points along the course, tables had been set up where runners could grab a beaker of orange squash. Race officials (known as spotters) were stationed at each of these tables to record the runners' times. These were situated (in order of the course) at the Pluckley Stones, outside the grounds of Stasis House, the edge of the Western Woods and finally, midway along the canal path. After that, the runners then had to make it back to the Bloodied Axe - the finish line.

As expected, Milton West was the first to finish. To some surprise it was Lyle Carmichael who came in second.

As more and more runners completed the race it became clear that Bruno Brown was missing.

That afternoon, a search of the course was conducted by many villagers and spectators. Among them was Bruno's girlfriend, Samantha Stein.

To the horror of everyone, Bruno's body was discovered in a ditch beside the canal.

Who murdered Bruno Brown?

19. MAYDAY MAYHEM

Tuesday, 1st of May, 1956

May Day in Pluckley Green is one of the most cheerful and spirited in the village calendar.

Pluckley Green Park is transformed into a celebration of spring and festooned with bunting. Games are played and food is enjoyed at the stalls dotted around the green. Morris dancers dance, folk singers sing and a spirit of gaiety and jubilance fills the air.

The May Day of 1956 was no different. As usual, Reverend Harper welcomed the festivities with a short speech to the assembled crowd. This year's theme was "It takes a village".

"How can a celebration on this scale be mounted?" he asked the crowds. "It takes a village. How did we build such a safe and peaceful community? It takes a village. And how will we catch The Ghost? It takes a village."

The centrepiece of the fete was the village's maypole, around which young women danced, their ribbons entwining into complex patterns before a delighted crowd. The choreographer of this dazzling spectacle was Judy Spiff (head girl of Unity Mitford Girls' School and two-time red rosette winning Somerset Trials dressage champion), who was dancing alongside the other Maypole Maidens.

In the afternoon, the biggest event was the crowning of the May King and Queen. Ballots were handed out and the winners were voted for. The winners were newlyweds Jessica and Kevin Waterstone, who sat upon thrones for the rest of the afternoon with crowns made of flowers upon their heads.

The evening party was held at the village hall and had been organised by Jack Quick and his girlfriend Aria Ford. A good portion of the village were in attendance for an almighty dance. Meanwhile, Perry Gulch - the village drunk - napped on a bench in the park.

At about 10pm, Virginia Day (Aria Ford's best friend) witnessed Jack Quick reading a note and at 10.30pm he discretely left the party.

As the party drew to a close at midnight, the partygoers filed from the village hall and one by one they witnessed to their horror that the corpse of Jack Quick was hanging by its neck from the maypole.

Who murdered Jack Quick?

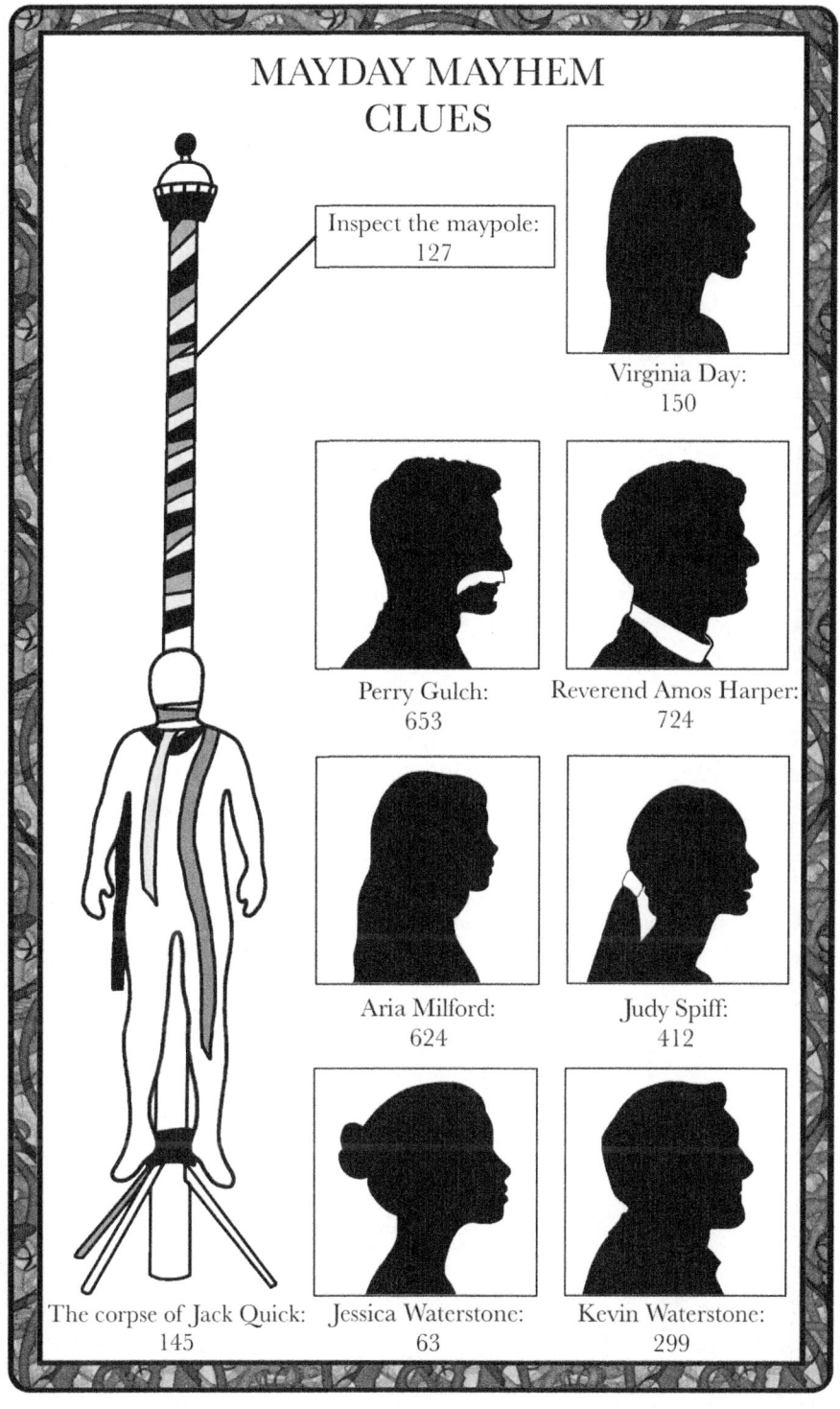

20. THE BODY IN PLUCKLEY GREEN LIBRARY

Saturday, 12th of May, 1956

The Pluckley Green Brights are a pub trivia team. Founded in 1946, the five-member group of self-described brain boxes travel around villages in Somerset and more often than not, win the local pub quiz.

What has proven most frustrating for the team has been the annual Bloodied Axe Tavern New Years Quiz - which has been won by the Pluckley Bird Brains five years in a row.

This year the team is more determined than ever to seize glory from their rivals and have vowed to spend every available Saturday brushing up on their trivia knowledge at the Pluckley Green library.

The Pluckley Green Brights are; Xander Meeks, the local butcher; Eustace Leadbetter, a history teacher; Wilma Rogers, a botanist; Cosmo Calder, a retired journalist and his wife Carrie Calder, a retired secretary.

In addition, for the past three Saturdays, Wilma Rogers has brought along her friend Calvin Copperhead to these study sessions. Calvin is an architect of fine repute.

As had been decided the previous Saturday, today the team were to each revise their weakest topic. For Cosmo and Carrie this was sport, meanwhile Eustace and Wilma studied geography and Xander went to the section on the arts. During this time, Calvin busied himself in the periodicals aisle.

At 12pm, all five members of the Pluckley Green Brights were in these sections of the library. At 12.05pm an almighty bang echoed across the room and Eustace Leadbetter dropped dead. He had been shot through the head. No trace of a gun could be found.

Also present in the library at this time were Esther of Stasis House, who was seated at a table in the centre of the room and the librarian Stacey Weedle who was seated at the library reception.

Who murdered Eustace Leadbetter?

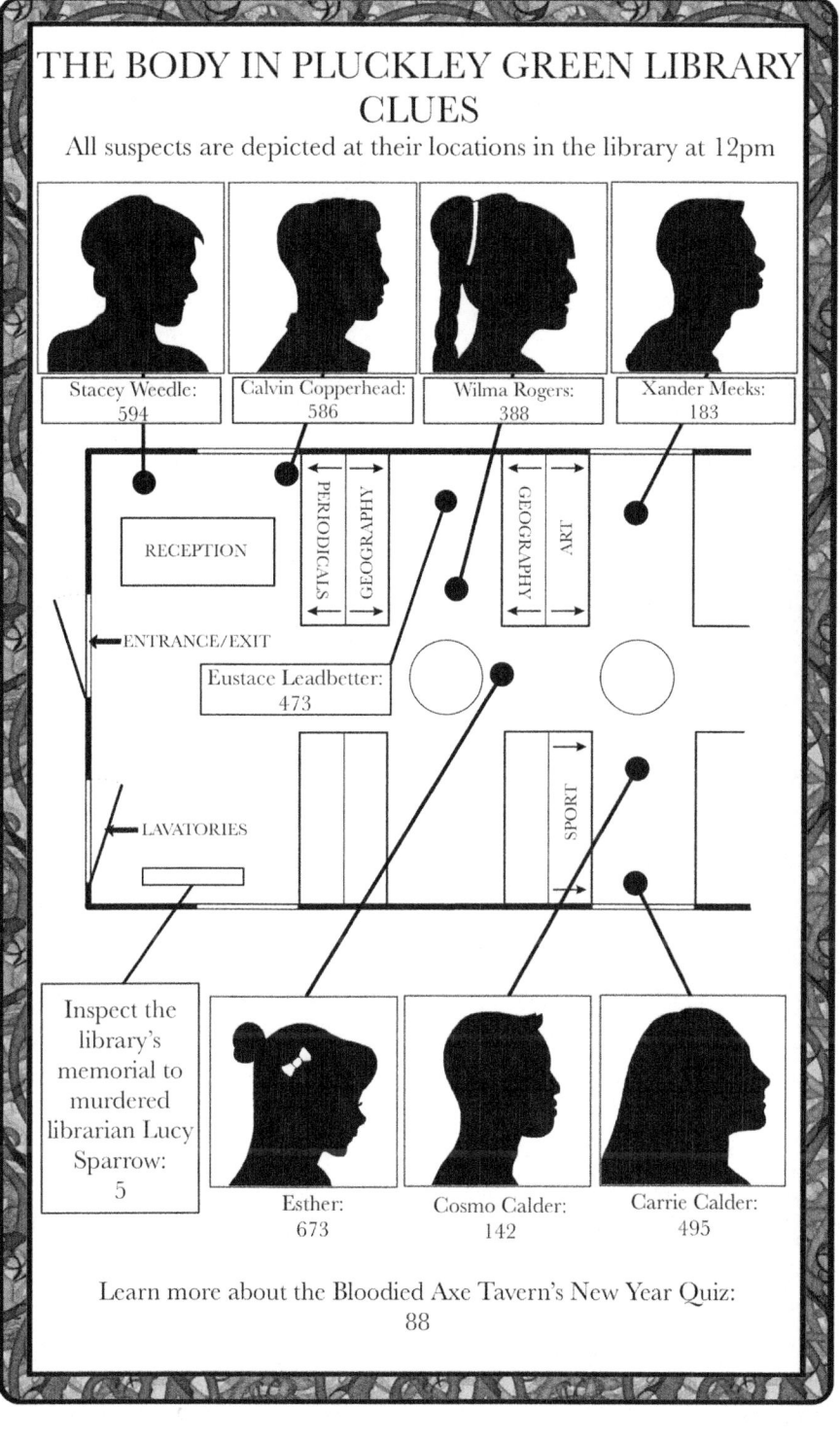

21. THE HOUND OF THE PENDERGASTS

Friday, 25th of May, 1956

For generations it has been said that the stark and lonely heath at the Northern fringe of Pluckley Green is haunted by a demonic black dog with glowing eyes.

Known to locals as the "gurt dog", seeing this huge and terrifying hound is said to be an omen of impending death.

For as long as anyone can remember, this phantom dog has been particularly associated with the Pendergast family - appearing to many of its members shortly before their deaths. The First Lady Pendergast (Lord Lucien Pendergast's first wife) is rumoured to have been the most recent victim.

This frightening legend has not however dissuaded campers from occasionally venturing to the heath. (Which borders onto the Pendergast Estate).

On Thursday, the 24th of May (the night of a full moon), five adventurous friends were spending the night in a tent on the heath. These intrepid campers were; Gary Grimpen and his girlfriend Tamara Stapleton - both of whom were from the city of Brigstowe; Donny Holmes, a resident of Pluckley Green and an enthusiastic rambler; Gustav Frankland, whose family had bred dogs in Pluckley Green for generations and aspiring poet Benjamin Selden, who has spent many years wandering the heath for artistic inspiration. The five friends all met at university and were camping to celebrate the end of their final academic year.

At midnight the five friends took a stroll to the middle of the heath, where they could get the greatest view of the breathtaking full moon. On their way they met Holly Merryfair who was heading to the Pluckley Stones. It was shortly afterwards that they witnessed the gurt dog.

The terrifying vision of the ferocious hound sent the friends running in different directions. When they finally regrouped at the tent they realised that one of their number, Gary Grimpen was missing.

It took until dawn to discover his body. He was trapped up to his waist in a quagmire on the heath - close to the home of plumber Gerald Ratchett. His body was in pieces as if savaged by a ferocious beast.

Who murdered Gary Grimpen?

22. BAILIFFS AND BULLETS

Saturday, 26th of May, 1956

Towards the end of each month, Lord Lucien Pendergast liked to indulge in one of his favourite hobbies - evicting his tenants who had not been able to pay rent.

As landowner of the majority of homes in the village, Lord Pendergast took particular delight in being present at the eviction of each and every one of his tenants and today - when the elderly widow Mrs Agnes Tipple was being evicted - was no exception.

At 7am on a Saturday morning, Lord Pendergast arrived outside of Agnes' cottage in his Rolls Royce and rolled down the window from his position in the backseat.

He produced a megaphone and loudly informed Mrs Tipple and her neighbours that the retired teacher had failed to pay her rent on time and was about to be evicted.

Lord Pendergast had with him two bailiffs; Alastair Lackey (who also served as his driver) and Lenny Goon.

To the lord's surprise, two young men appeared at the entrance to the elderly woman's home and linked arms to form a human barrier in front of the door. These were Colin Carnegie - Agnes Tipple's grandson - and his best friend Alvin Luft.

Agnes Tipple appeared at a downstairs window looking understandably distraught and to the horror of everyone present, began waving a pistol in the direction of Lord Pendergast.

Agnes had her friend Mabel Witherspoon with her. The cook was attempting to calm the panicked woman down.

Meanwhile, the retired army general Spencer McDonald appeared on the front lawn of his home across the street and began pleading with Agnes to put the pistol down.

It was then that a gunshot rang out. Inside the car, Lord Lucien Pendergast slumped down in the backseat. He had been shot in the shoulder.

Who shot Lord Pendergast?

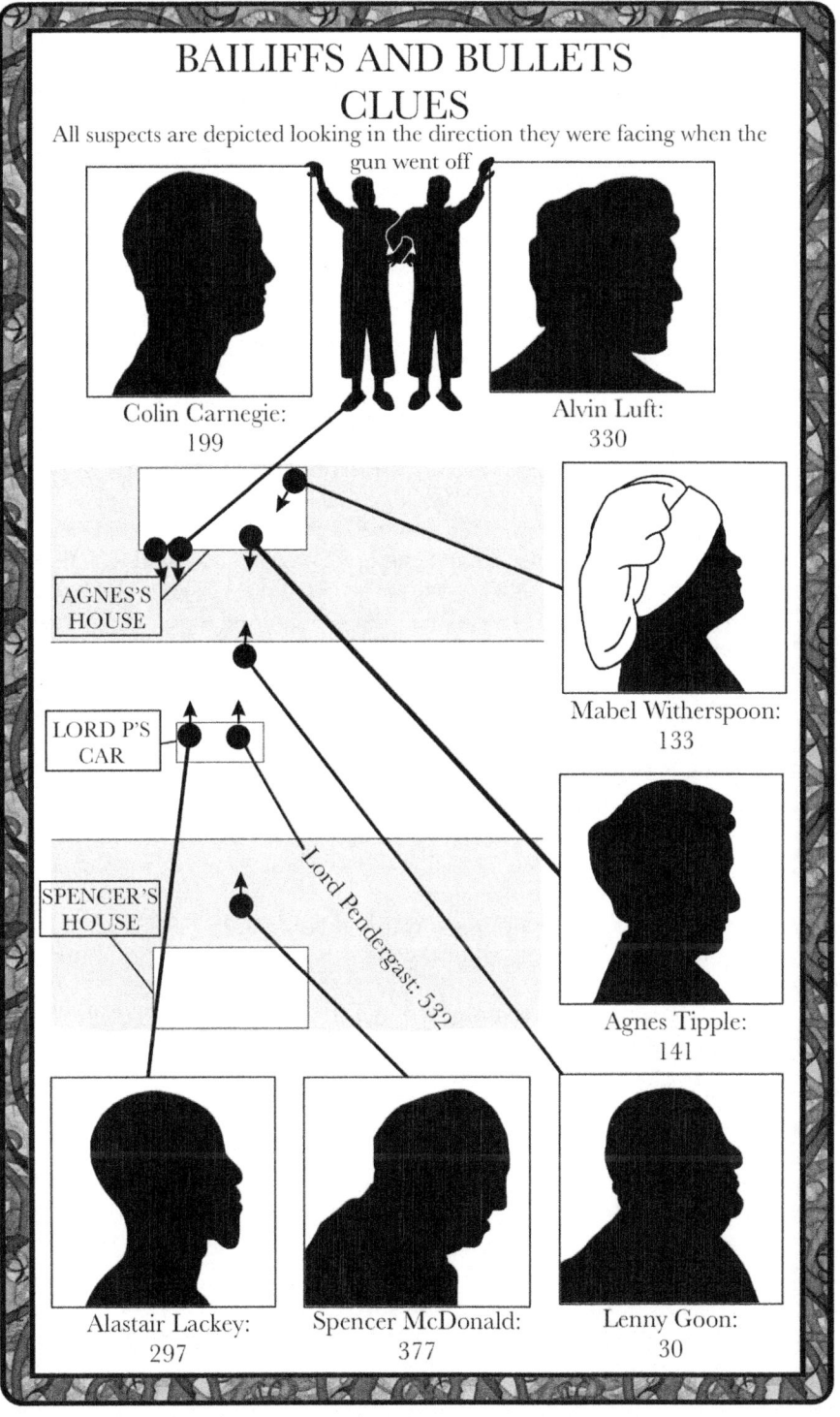

23. A STITCH IN CRIME

Wednesday, 3rd of June, 1956

The Pluckley Green Sewing Circle has been meeting at the home of Penelope Gannet every Wednesday evening for so long that nobody can quite remember when the group began.

Until the end of this evening's meeting, the group consisted of seven members. These were; Penelope Gannet, a housewife; Beverley Potter, a retired seamstress; Daphne Robinson, the church cleaner; Marcy Mathew, a nurse approaching retirement; Mavis Davis, the local gossip and Daisy Doyle, who worked at the village greengrocers. Much to the surprise of everyone, the seventh and newest member of the group was Miss Faversham of Stasis House. The reclusive woman had recently undergone a transformation in her personality and had become a rather outgoing, sociable person (although still always dressed in her tattered wedding dress and veil).

The seven women met at 7pm and spent the evening seated around the dining room table working on individual sewing projects whilst reminiscing, gossiping and talking about the upcoming Pluckley Green Fete - the two day, annual village celebration which was due to take place at the end of the month.

At around 9pm, once the ladies had finished their tea, a box of doughnuts was produced from the kitchen (as was customary at this time each week).

Beverley Potter was only one mouthful into her jam doughnut when she silently slumped back in her chair. She was dead.

Who murdered Beverley Potter?

24. A FETE WOSE THAN DEATH

Tuesday, 12th of June, 1956

The 12th of June began as a beautiful, sunny morning. The flowers were in full bloom, swallows and butterflies danced through the crisp air and Tommy Tomlinson came careening down the village high street in a car at a tremendous speed, blasting the horn all the way. He then crashed the vehicle into the ornamental fountain in the centre of Pluckley Green Park and was incinerated in a fiery explosion.

Tommy Tomlinson had been part of the village summer fete organising committee. His role had been as assistant to both Cuthbert Crookshank - chairman of the committee and his wife, deputy chair Eloise Crookshank.

Other members of the esteemed committee were; Lord Lucien Pendergast, who was fresh from his spell in hospital. The village fete's funfair was due to take place on part of his estate; Mona Prim, who was also the Pendergast's maid, who was generally called upon solely to make tea and coffee during committee meetings and Della Dempsey, who last year won the prestigious title of "Miss Pluckley Green" at the village fete's beauty contest.

Also on the committee were husband and wife Oswald and Diana Spiff, who each contributed a large sum each year to the village fete's fund and finally Dunstan Lavender, who recorded the minutes of each of the committee's meetings.

It would appear that the car Tommy Tomlinson was driving had been sabotaged.

Who murdered Tommy Tomlinson?

A FETE WORSE THAN DEATH
CLUES

The wreck of the car: 546

The corpse of Tommy Tomlinson: 686

Cuthbert Crookshank: 589

Eloise Crookshank: 514

Della Dempsey: 287

Dunstan Lavender: 523

Lord Pendergast: 42

Mona Prim: 350

Diana Spiff: 404

Oswald Spiff: 619

25. A MIDSUMMER NIGHT'S SCREAM

Tuesday, 21st of June, 1956

The Summer Solstice is a time of celebration and great joy for the members of the Ancient Order of Pluckley Pagans. Midsummer is the day when the sun sits higher than on any other and the daylight hours stretch long into the evening. It is when the Pluckley Pagans like to give thanks to the God and Goddess for the bountiful harvest the summer brings.

The number of Pluckley Pagans varies as new members join and others are either murdered or arrested for murder. The current membership of the Order stands at eight.

At 10pm on the day of the solstice, all members - dressed in their ceremonial cloaks - attended a ceremony of thanks at the Pluckley Stones.

The ceremony was led, as always, by Holly Merryfair, who stood in the centre of the stone circle as the seven other members formed a ring around him with their backs to the stones.

At the climax of the holy ritual, Holly asked that all members lower their hoods, raise their arms to the sky and gaze upwards at the beautiful, sun-filled evening.

"To the God and Goddess of the summer, may we give thanks for the season and for all the seasons you bring."

Unbeknownst to the Pagans, watching from afar was Esther, who was crouching behind a bush and watching the ceremony with much interest.

It was then that an ear piercing scream cut across the heath.

To the horror of all of those present, Wilbur Charles, a retired maths teacher lay dead at the foot of the Demon Stone.

Who murdered Wilbur Charles?

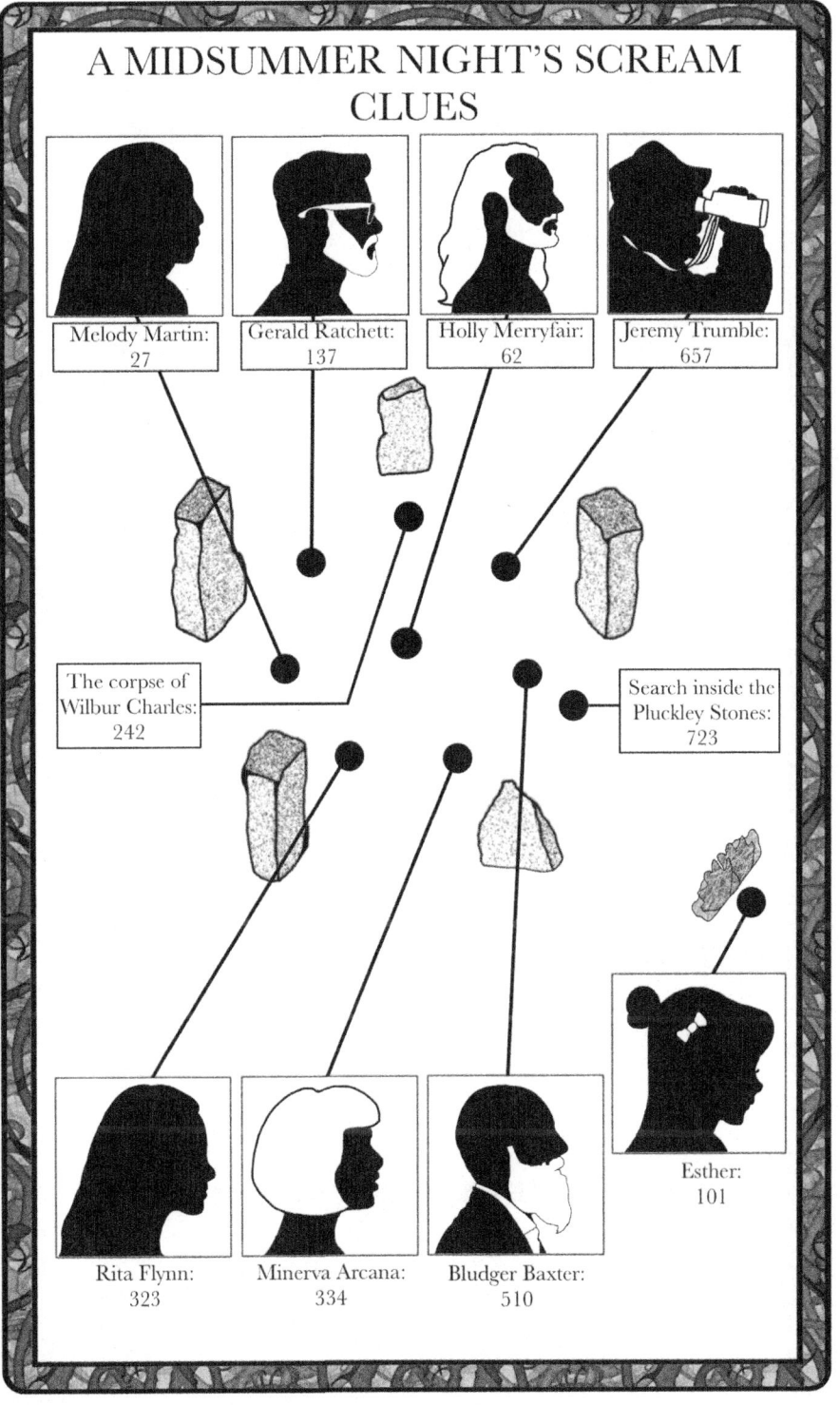

BONUS MYSTERY:
WHO IS ESTHER'S MOTHER?

For this mystery, you must use the information and clues you have gathered so far and use them to guess who Esther's mother is.
If you are not correct in your first guess, keep trying until you get it right.

DN RTQK TLZITK,

O QD NGXK DGZITK,

NGXK YQZITK VQL QF QDTKOEQF LGSROTK. O DTZ IOD OF WKOULZGVT QFR VT VTKT LVTHZ QVQN OF Q KGDQFET. O YTSS HKTUFQFZ QFR IT YSTR IGDT VITF IT STQKFTR ZIT FTVL.

DN IGDT VQL RTLZKGNTR OF ZIT WSOZM LG O AFTV O EGXSR FGZ KQOLT NGX, LG O EQDT ZG HSXEASTN UKTTF QFR STYZ NGX QZ ZIT RGGKLZTH GY LZQLOL IGXLT. O ZIGXUIZ DOLL YQCTKLIQD VGXSR WT AOFR ZG NGX WXZ O VQL VKGFU.

O IQCT HKGXRSN VQZEITR NGX UKGV YKGD QYQK QFR VGXSR RTQKSN SGCT ZG DTTZ NGX. OY NGX VGXSR SOAT ZG AFGV DN ORTFZOZN, DTTZ DT QZ ZIT LZQFROFU LZGFTL QZ LTCTF HD GF ZIT YOKLZ GY PXSN.

- DGZITK. BB

The encrypted note from Esther's mother.
Clue: **TYPEWRITER**

26. PERRY GULCH'S LAST STAND

Sunday, 24th of June, 1956

Perry Gulch awoke on Sunday morning at 10am with a pounding head. As usual, he had fallen asleep on a bench in the church's graveyard. An empty bottle of whisky was still clutched in his hand and his well-thumbed copy of King Lear acted as his makeshift pillow.

The morning service was underway inside the building. The congregation must have filed past him whilst he was still sleeping. Perry could hear the voice of Reverend Amos Harper, who was giving a sermon on how it was the duty of all Christian people to care for their fellow man.

Perry didn't have any friends in the village but everybody knew him. Most regarded him as a nuisance and an eyesore but Reverend Harper tolerated him; Dexter Maybrick - who had served alongside him in the army - would stop to talk on occasion. Sometimes Cuthbert Crookshank and his wife Eloise would toss insults his way like confetti, whilst villagers Isaac Peters, Phoebe Burgundy and Millie Costa would laugh or hold their noses as they scurried by.

This morning however, something was different. Somebody had left an unopened bottle of red wine beside his bench. A gift!

Without hesitation, the man pulled the cork from the bottle with the aid of his trusty corkscrew and took a gulp of the wine.

He convulsed and fell unconscious almost immediately. His near-dead body was not discovered until the end of the church service.

Who poisoned Perry Gulch?

PERRY GULCH'S LAST STAND CLUES

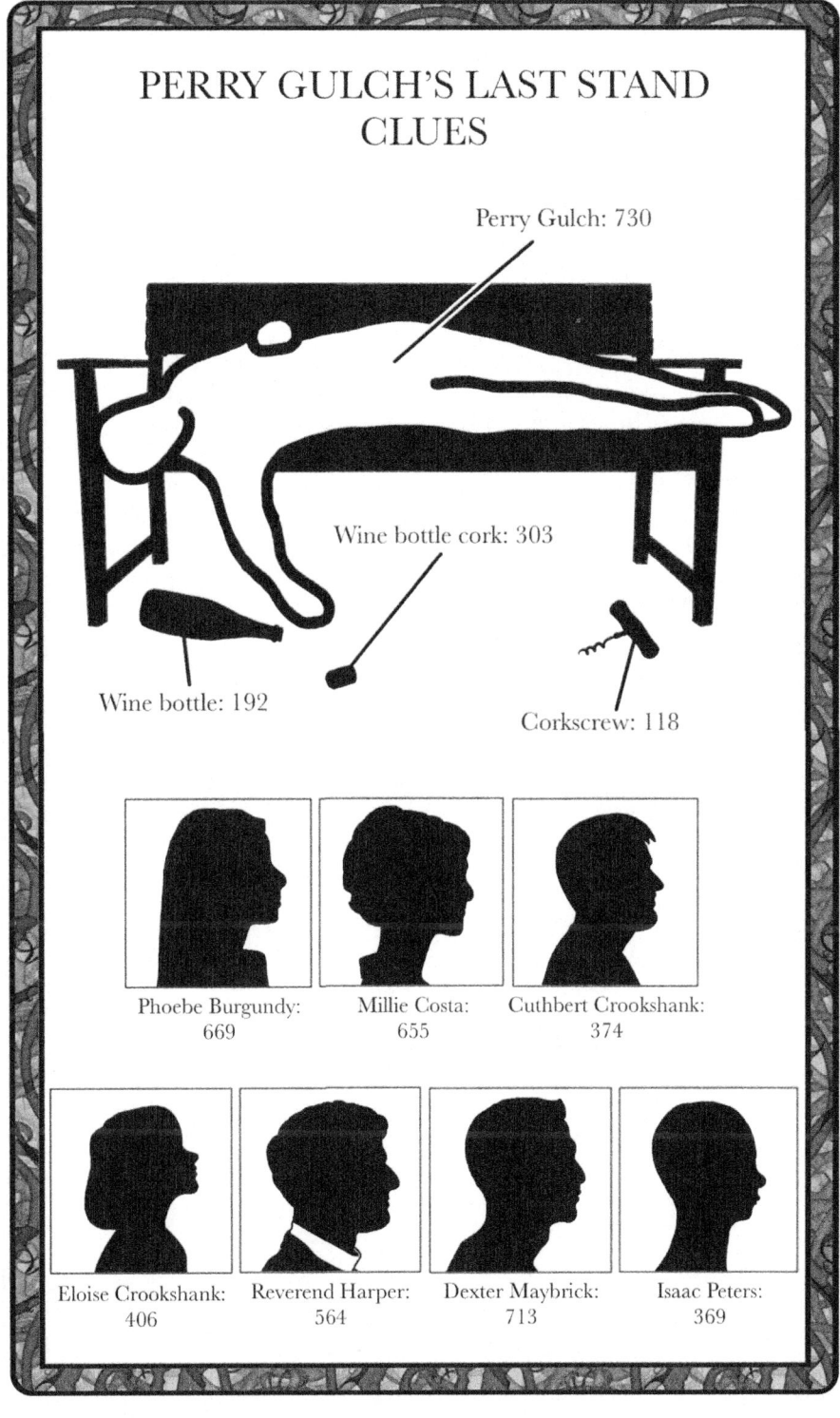

- Perry Gulch: 730
- Wine bottle cork: 303
- Wine bottle: 192
- Corkscrew: 118
- Phoebe Burgundy: 669
- Millie Costa: 655
- Cuthbert Crookshank: 374
- Eloise Crookshank: 406
- Reverend Harper: 564
- Dexter Maybrick: 713
- Isaac Peters: 369

27. THE SUMMER FETE: PART ONE

Saturday, 30th of June, 1956

Pluckley Green looked truly magnificent in all of its finery for the first day of the summer fete weekend. Cheerful bunting fluttered high on the breeze, flowers cascaded from baskets and pots along the streets, the smell of sizzling foods billowed from market stalls and the park's bandstand revelled with the sound of the local brass band. The sun beamed down from a cloudless sky. The summer fete was about to commence.

This year, the fete was to be declared open by the popular author Conrad Cutlass. Cutlass had found enormous success with his "Piddly Glen" series of mystery novels - all of which contained thinly-veiled and not always flattering caricatures of Pluckley Green and its residents.

The hero of the "Piddly Glen Mysteries" was postman Lawrence French - clearly modelled on Pluckley Green's jovial and dependable postman Larry Finch. His assistant in sleuthing was the local scientist Wilhelmina Rudders - a rather fanciful depiction of botanist Wilma Rogers. Meanwhile, the recurring antagonists of the novels were the feared and hated judge John Trangle and the snooty historian September Wheatley - better known to the village as Judge Jan Treagle and August Barley.

The books proved to be so popular that the village's librarian, Stacey Weedle, struggled to keep them in stock. Meanwhile, villager Kathy Wilkes founded the "Conrad Cutlass Fanclub". This popularity had made Cutlass (and his literary agent Jay Towers) enormously wealthy.

Following tea and cakes at the village hall, the residents gathered before the ribbon which had been draped across the high street.

After a short speech, in which Conrad Cutlass praised the village, he was handed a pair of scissors and said "I now declare this summer fete open!"

The instant the metal scissors cut through the red ribbon, there was an enormous white flash. Conrad Cutlass had received a massive electric shock and now lay dead on the ground.

Who murdered Conrad Cutlass?

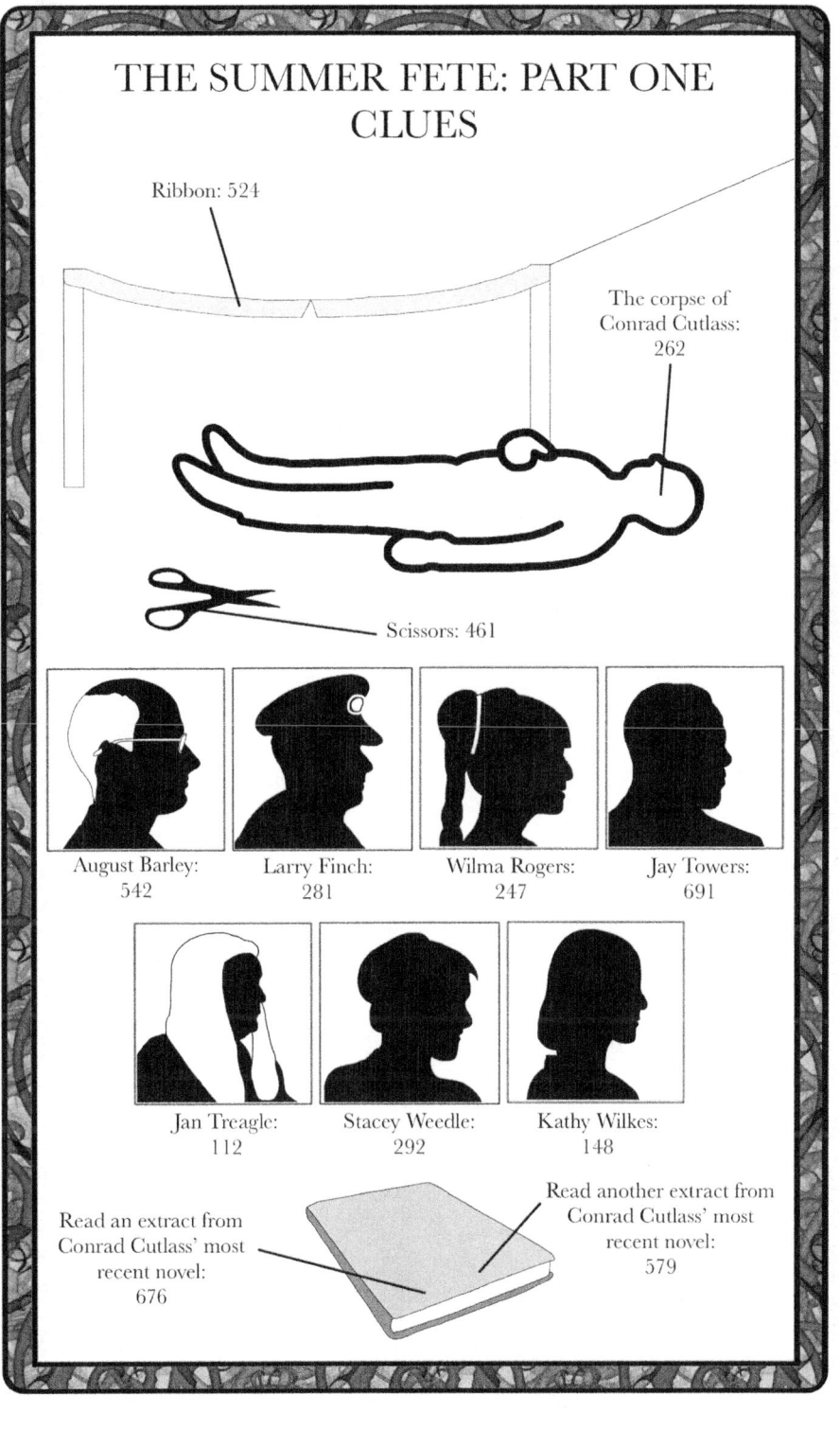

28. THE SUMMER FETE: PART TWO

Sunday, 1st of July, 1956

Every year, the closing event of the wildly popular Pluckley Green summer fete is the beauty contest - and 1956 was no exception.

A platform had been erected in the centre of Pluckley Green Park and a huge crowd had gathered to witness the spectacle of local women parading in front of a panel of judges until one was deemed the most desirable in the village.

By 6pm the contestants were now taking part in the talent portion of the competition.

Della Dempsey - last year's winner - was first upon the open-air stage and had defended her crown by singing a piece from a Gilbert and Sullivan operetta. She was followed by Penelope Gannet, an accomplished dancer, who performed an elaborate (if lengthy) ballet routine in front of the three judges.

The judging panel was made up of Lord Pendergast, Diana Spiff and, quite surprisingly, conservationist Jeremy Trumble.

The climax of Penelope Gannet's routine was an intricate pirouette, in which the dancer spun four times upon the toe of a single ballet slipper.

Suddenly, yet entirely silently, an arrow which had been launched from a bow pierced through the woman's neck. She dropped dead upon the stage.

Where was the arrow fired from?

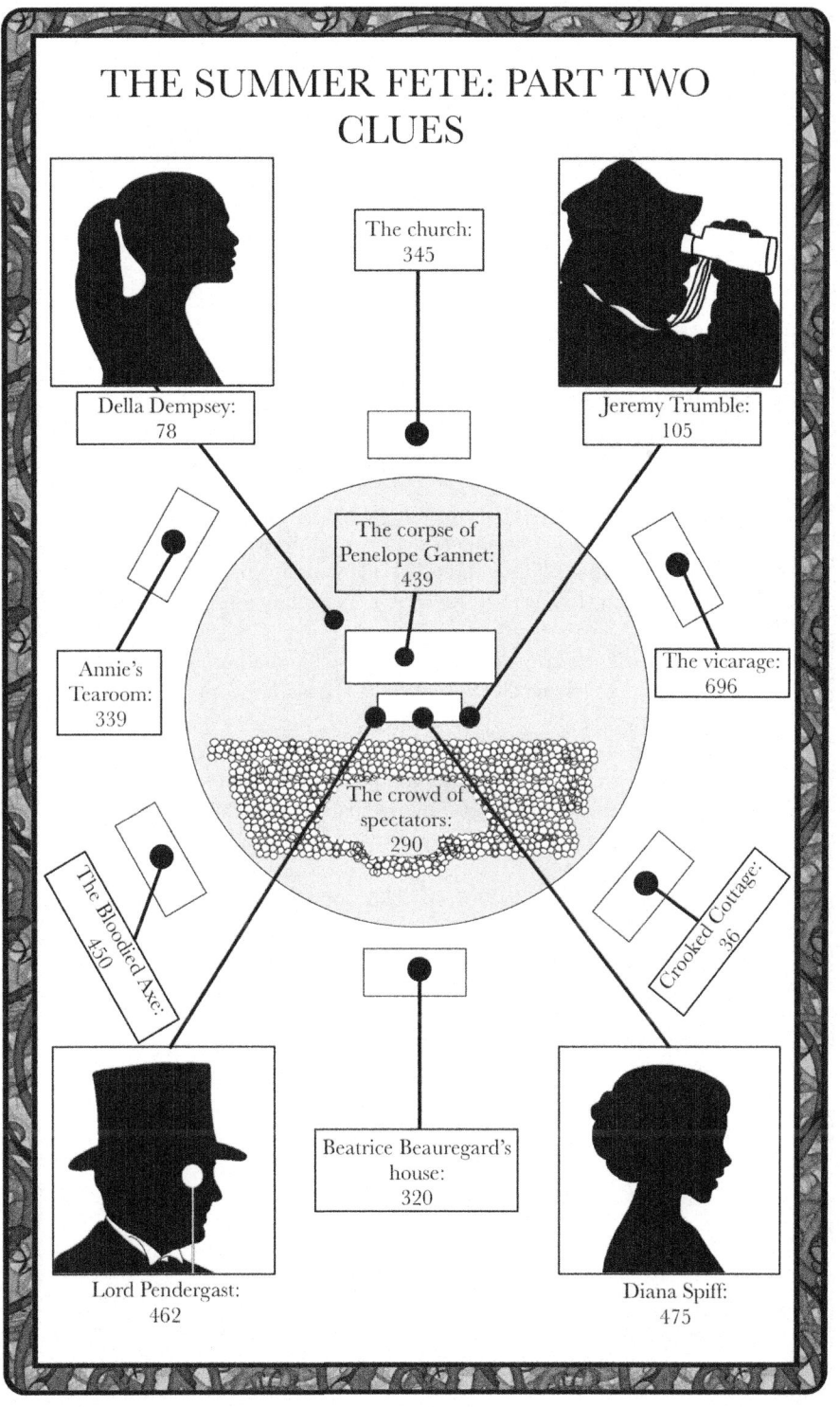

29. MURDER ON THE PLUCKLEY EXPRESS

Wednesday, 4th of July, 1956

One of the most pleasant aspects of life in Pluckley Green is how easy it is to escape the confines of the picturesque, murderous village and explore other parts of our fair nation.

As beautiful as the bucolic setting may be, the lure of the seaside may often become overwhelming for the villagers, which is why twice a week a train departs from Pluckley Green Station to the coastal town of Worlebury-on-Sea. The village's residents can enjoy a day of sun, sand, buckets and spades and sticks of rock before returning home for the evening.

On Wednesday morning at 9am, the train pulled out of the village station with six Pluckley Green residents - who had opted to share a cabin together.

These residents were; Dorothy Halcyon - a somewhat snobbish and unpleasant retired haberdasher; Reverend Amos Harper; Mavis Davis; Miss Faversham and best friends Colin Carnegie and Alvin Luft.

The conversation in the hot cabin was jovial and friendly but the moment the train entered the pitch black of a tunnel, there came a blood curdling scream from Dorothy Halcyon.

As the train left the tunnel, the cabin was flooded by sunlight and it became immediately apparent that Dorothy Halcyon was dead. There was a deep wound in her chest, from which blood was gurgling and spurting.

The reverend hastily pulled the emergency chord in the cabin and the train rolled to a stop at the next station - which is where the investigation will begin.

Who murdered Dorothy Halcyon?

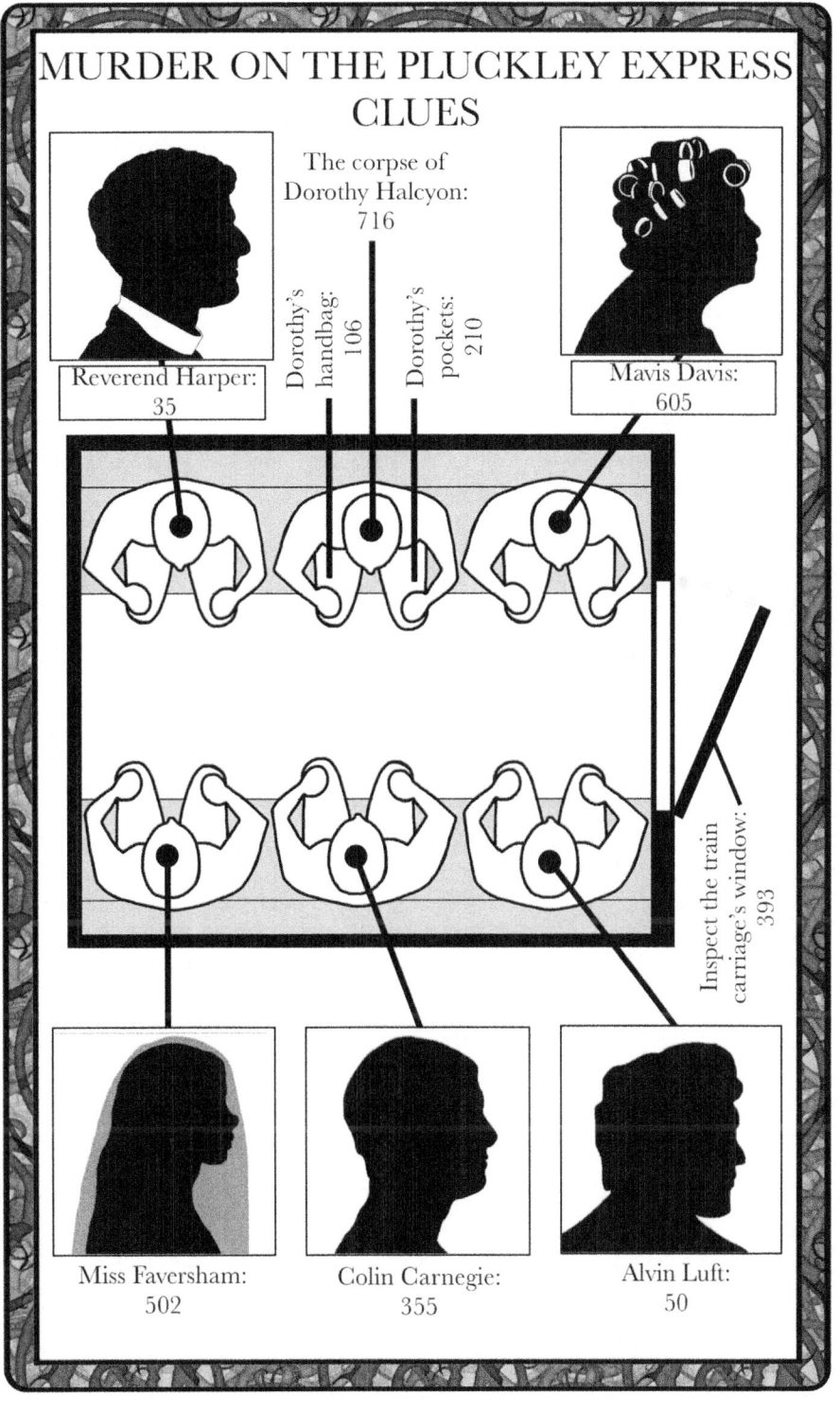

30. THE FEARLESS FIVE

Thursday, 12th of July. 1956

The Fearless Five are a team of young mystery solvers who travel around the English countryside (during their school summer holidays) sleuthing the solutions to perplexing rural mysteries.

The gang consists of four youths; the oldest, Jonathon; his younger brother Rick and their sister Fran. The three siblings are joined by their cousin Henrietta "Henry" and her loyal dog Jimmy.

The Fearless Five have travelled to Pluckley Green after finishing their final year at school and intend to investigate reports of mysterious lights seen upon the heath at night.

The fivesome spent their first night on the land of the farm belonging to Milo Kidder and his wife Tamsin. The boys slept among the hay of a disused barn whilst the girls camped in a tent outside. Despite a torrential downpour of rain, Jimmy slept outside - acting as guard dog to the four youths throughout the evening.

At about midnight there was a tremendous bang - the sound of a gunshot. Milo, the farmer, had been shot through the head outside his farmhouse.

A note had been dropped near the man's body. "Jonathon, I can't take this anymore. I want to leave the Fearless Five and get on with my life. We are not children anymore!"

Who killed Milo Kidder?

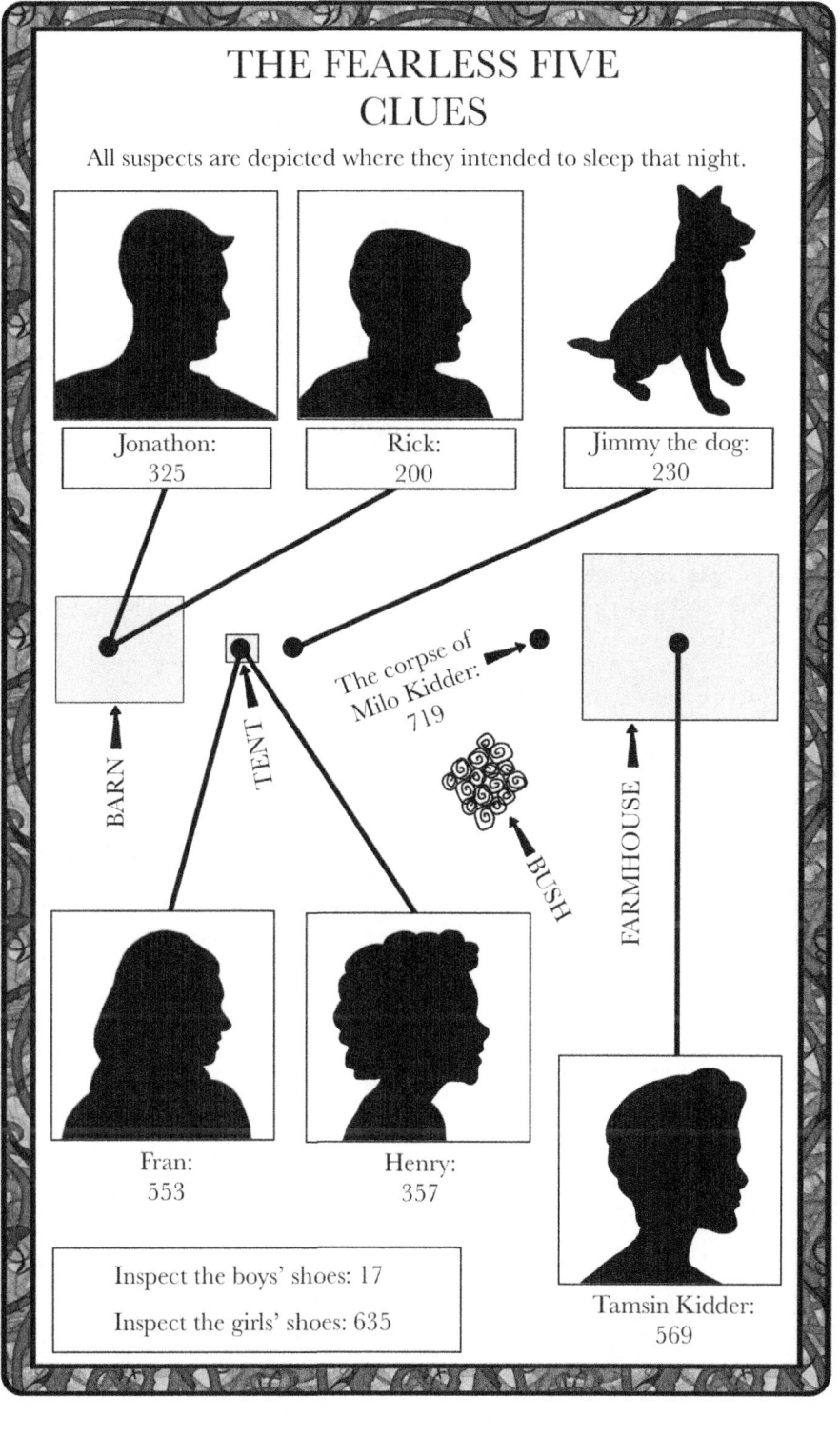

31. TCHOTCHKE'S REVENGE

Monday, 16th of July, 1956

Toby Tchotchke has escaped! The world-renowned archaeologist was a member of the Tchotchke Triplets (until he murdered both of his brothers at the start of this year). He was reported missing from his cell in Brigstowe Prison last Tuesday.

Over the past six days there have been multiple reports of a man matching Toby Tchotchke's description being spotted in and around the village of Pluckley Green.

At 8pm on Monday evening, the man - now drenched in blood and still clutching a bloody butcher's knife - was finally captured by police officer Randall Jorgen in the Western Woods.
"I have claimed my revenge and killed August Barley", he grimly informed the police as they led him away in handcuffs. "And you will never find his body."

August Barley is indeed nowhere to be found but his diary details how he had several chores and engagements to fulfil today. These included lunch at the Bloodied Axe, visiting cobbler Sidney Snell for shoe repairs, demonstrating beekeeping to Beatrice Beauregard on his farm, repairing an old well near the canal, writing reports about the Western Woods and the caves along the river and finally an evening meal with judge Jan Treagle.

Where is the corpse of August Barley?

TCHOTCHKE'S REVENGE CLUES

Toby Tchotchke: 398

Beehives: 56

Bludger Baxter: 426

Bloodied Axe: 24

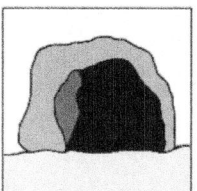
Caves: 384

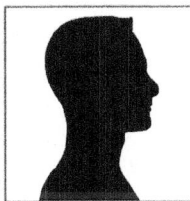
Beatrice Beauregard: 515

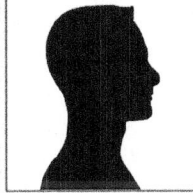
Randall Jorgens: 166

Well: 718

Sidney Snell: 34

Western Woods: 519

Judge Jan Treagle: 232

Read August Barley's diary: 114

32. A MURDER OF CROWS

Friday, 20th of July, 1956

When farmer Maxwell Furrows awoke at dawn, he almost immediately knew that something strange was afoot.

The scarecrow which stood in the centre of his lush and bountiful cornfield did a poor job of deterring the crows at the best of times but this morning it seemed to be actively attracting them.

Dozens of the birds were circling the scarecrow (which had been made by the farmer's wife Sandra) and some were even swooping down to peck pieces off it.

When Maxwell went to investigate, he discovered - to his great horror - that the scarecrow was actually the corpse of tree surgeon Benjamin Hellman, who lived across the field with his wife Juno, an aspiring actress.

Maxwell's immediate course of action was to run to the Hellman's neighbours, Pierce and Paulette Green. Pierce was a policeman and he and his wife frequently visited Maxwell's farm with their 19 year old son, Ash.

Sandra Furrows had only made the scarecrow the day before, so it must have been replaced with the body of Benjamin Hellman during the night. There was a track leading through the corn where someone had dragged the body into the centre of the field.

Who murdered Benjamin Hellman?

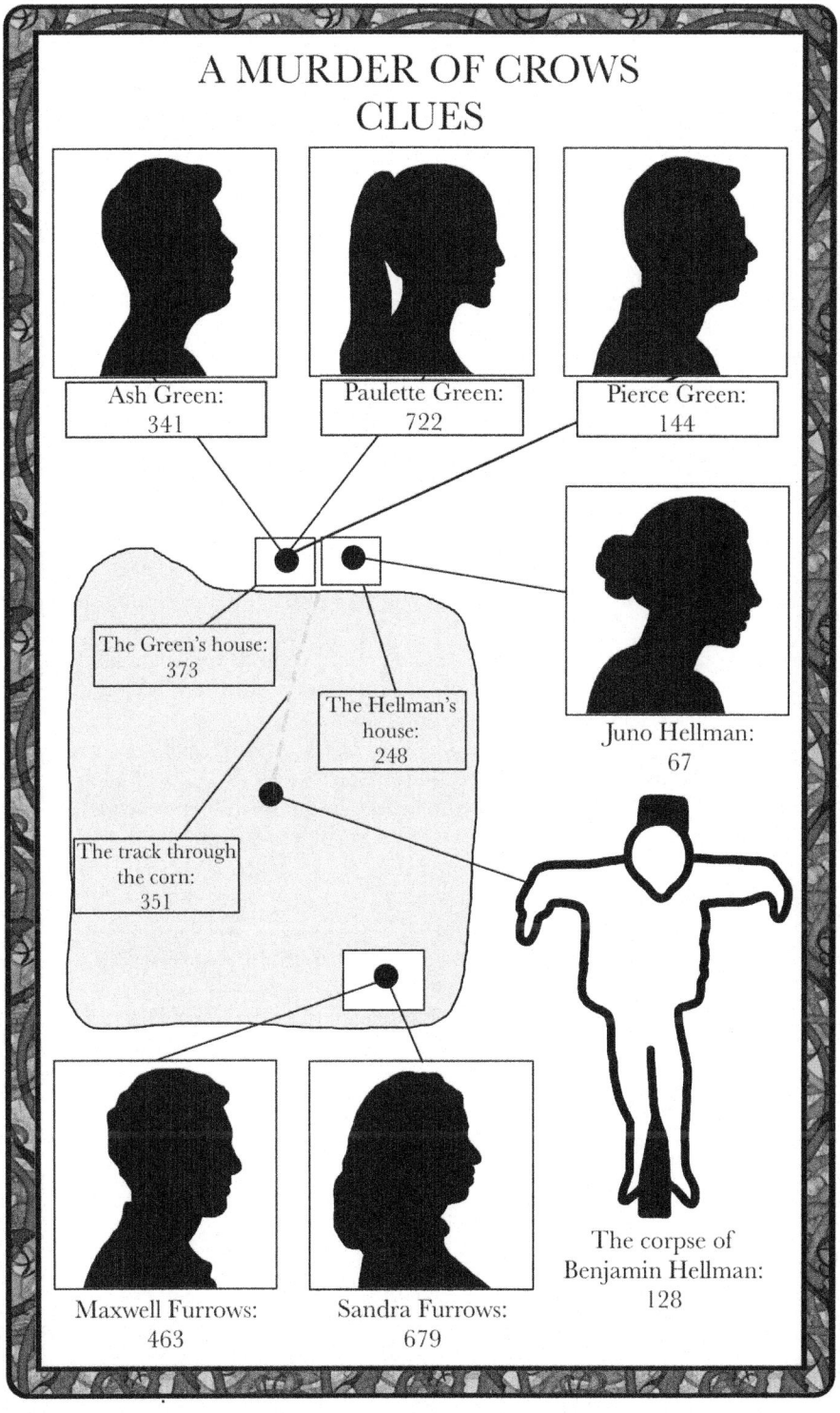

33. THE GHOST OF PLUCKLEY CASTLE

Saturday, 28th of July, 1956

Pluckley Castle is the huge and ancient fortification which sits high on a hill just outside the Pluckley Green parish boundary.

Built between the 12th and 15th centuries, the castle is a popular attraction for tourists with an interest in history. It has also proven to be quite a draw for those with a love of the supernatural.

The keep, which is set within the castle grounds is said to be haunted by a figure in a grey dress with long, bedraggled hair. "The Grey Lady" is rumoured to be the tormented soul of a heartbroken duchess, who hurled herself from the castle keep's tallest tower sometime during the 18th century.

As a result, the castle will occasionally be hired out at night to so-called "ghost clubs" - paranormal investigators who are hoping to experience a ghostly encounter for themselves.

One such group are "The Pluckley Green Ghost Club" - a five member team of ghost hunters who were given permission by Bethany Torrance (the castle's manager and head tour guide) to spend the night within the castle's walls. They were even permitted to lower the castle's portcullis to prevent anybody from being able to enter or exit the castle during the paranormal investigation.

All five members - Jules Myers, Becca Loomis, Marty Voorhees, Denzil Bates and lead investigator Arabella Krueger - had decided to split up and explore different sections of the castle keep by night. Just as midnight struck, there came a terrible scream from the tallest tower and Arabella Krueger was seen plummeting down to the courtyard below. The four surviving members of the club rushed to the courtyard, which is where they found her broken body.

Who murdered Arabella Krueger?

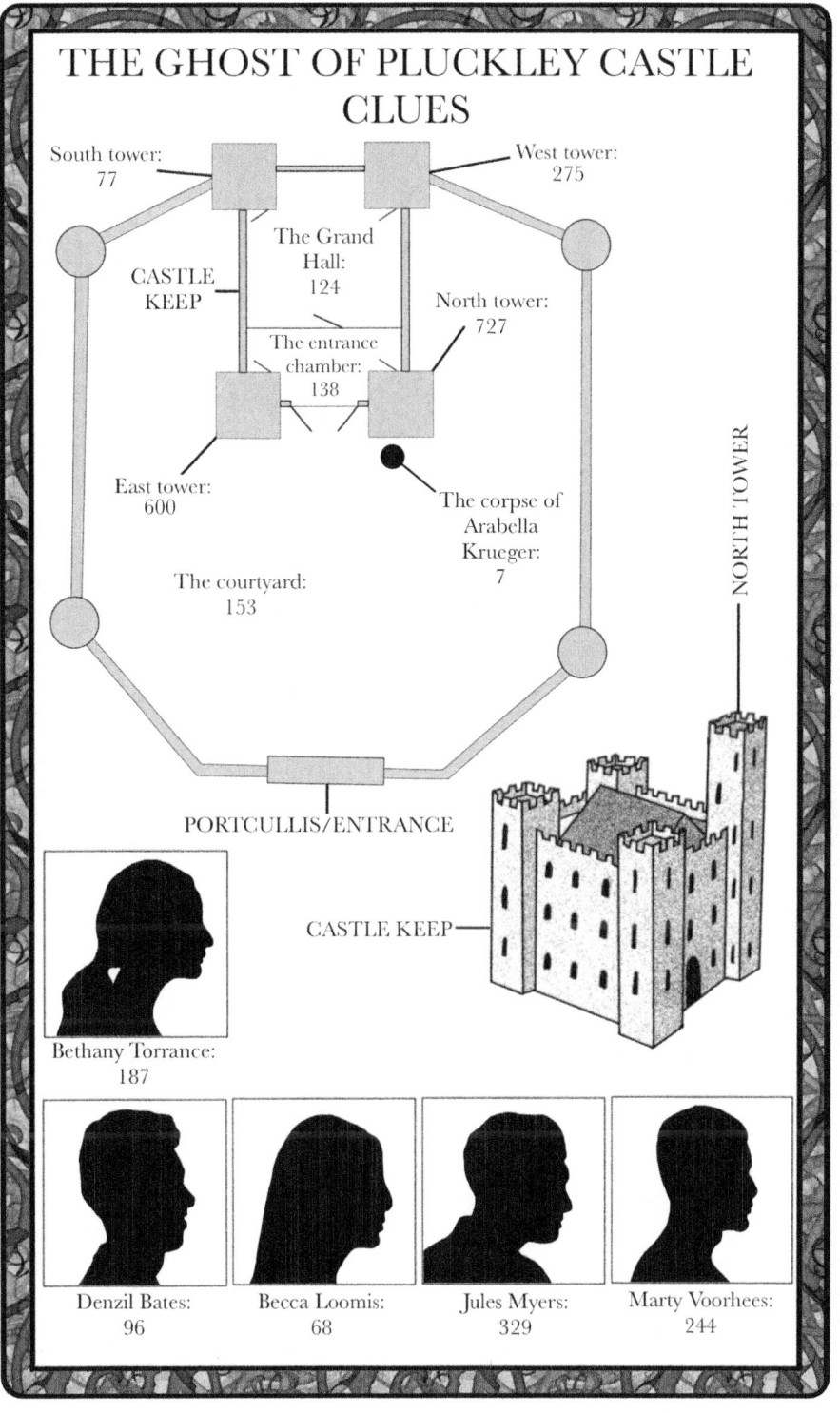

34. SUNDAY IN THE PARK WITH GORE

Sunday, 5th of August, 1956

It was a beautiful Sunday afternoon when Phineas Flitter's face exploded.

The residents of Pluckley Green had been enjoying a sunny bank holiday weekend and many of them had gathered in a small, tranquil park alongside the river to while away the perfect afternoon.

Much of the chatter among the sun-soaked villagers was about the mysterious letter which had been hand delivered to the letterbox of the Pluckley Green Press - supposedly from the serial killer nicknamed "The Ghost".

Phineas Flitter himself worked for the Pluckley Green Press, as a journalist working on the newly introduced gossip column. Nicknamed "The Tittle-Tattle", every Friday his tawdry article repeated salacious rumours about the village's residents and had become the most hated, yet widely read in the weekly publication.

Phineas Flitter, was known to spend every Sunday afternoon of the summer relaxing by the river, writing his latest, sensationalist headline whilst smoking a cigar. His latest column - due to be published on Friday - was rumoured to be his most jaw-dropping and scandalous so far and it promised to expose one of Pluckley Green's most beloved residents as a liar and a fraud. The villagers had, predictably, become very anxious over what this column might contain.

At 1pm precisely, Phineas Flitter removed a cigar from his jacket and lit it. He took one puff and then, with an enormous bang, the cigar - and the man's face - exploded like a bomb. He was killed instantly.

Who murdered Phineas Flitter?

35. TRAGIC MAGIC

Friday, 10th of August, 1956

The Doll's House Theatre is a small entertainment venue on the western outskirts of Pluckley Green.

Although the theatre (owned and managed by retired actor Thelwyn Olivers) is home to only 48 seats, the small business' audience enjoys the performance space for its varied roster of entertainers.

Once a month, Thelwyn hosts a variety night at the theatre, in which performers from around Somerset are invited to demonstrate their talents in the intimate setting. Although the monthly event may have seen audiences dwindle in recent years, it still remains the most popular night in the theatre.

On this evening, the first performer onto the stage was "The Great Illusio", a magician local to Pluckley Green whose routine included pulling a rabbit from a hat and producing a bouquet of flowers from his sleeve.

Next up was comedian Bernie Hastings, whose somewhat hackneyed stand-up routine was accompanied by only polite, sympathetic chuckles from the audience.

The final act of the evening was Captain Conjuro and his glamorous assistant Mesmerelda - another magical act. Their sleek and polished routine had won them audiences and larger stages across the county.

The routine reached its climax with the duo's most famous illusion - the guillotine trick. The trick was always the same. A near full-sized guillotine was wheeled onto the stage and Mesmerelda would lay down in place at the bottom. The blade would drop when Captain Conjuro pulled a rope and - seemingly miraculously - Mesmerelda's head would not be severed from her neck.

However, this evening Mesmerelda decided (seemingly on a whim) to suggest that Captain Conjuro and she should swap places.

Captain Conjuro - not wanting to spoil the show with an onstage disagreement - reluctantly agreed and laid down in place at the foot of the guillotine.

To the horror of the audience (which included Judge Jan Treagle and Captain Cunjuro's wife Anita Cryer), when Mesmerelda released the rope, the blade fell and sliced the magician's head clean off.

Who murdered Captain Conjuro?

36. THE MURDER OF MR MOANER

Tuesday, 14th of August, 1956

There is nothing in this world Humbert Miner enjoyed more than complaining. Day after day, the man would sit at his desk, writing letters of complaint about the most piddling of gripes.

The pavements of Pluckley Green were too hot in the summer. Postman Larry Finch was wearing shorts on his delivery round instead of the regulation trousers. The pound cakes Eveline Topham sells in the corner shop used to be much sweeter. The birds in Irving Putters' pet shop sing too loudly.

The man had no friends but many enemies and the lonelier he became, the more pointless, time-wasting letters he produced.

His favourite form of complaint was opposing planning applications to the council. Just this week he had learned that Tilly Millman had applied to build an extension to her home in order to house her elderly father, Art Millman. Meanwhile, Grover Ramsay and his wife Peggy had asked for permission to build the village's first ever private swimming pool in their back garden. Humbert Miner intended to oppose them both.

On Tuesday morning, postman Larry Finch arrived to deliver mail at Humbert's cottage and discovered that yesterday's post was still in the letterbox.

Larry immediately informed the authorities, who broke through the locked door, only to find Humbert slumped dead at his writing desk - midway through writing his latest round of complaints.

Who murdered Humbert Miner?

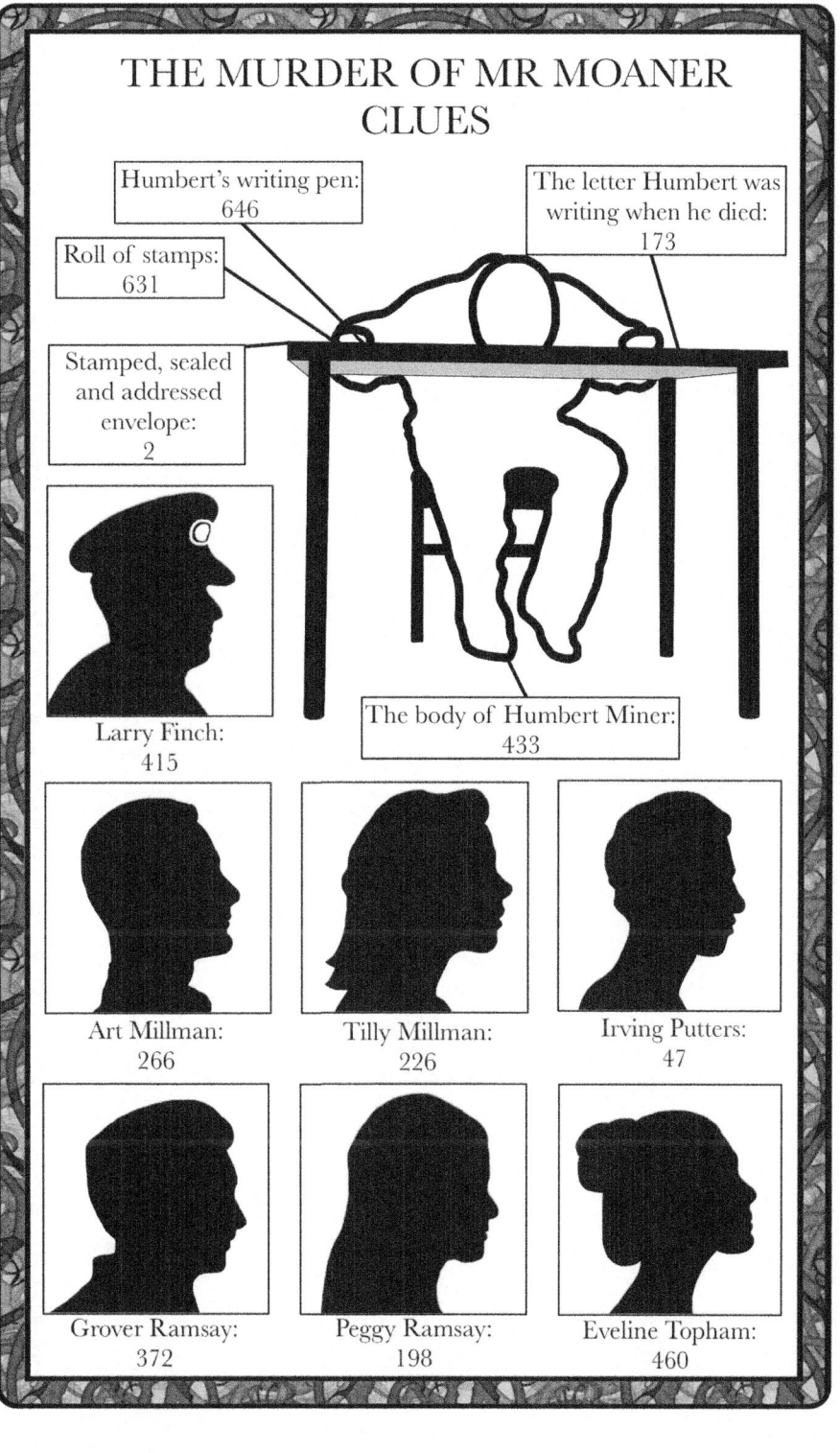

37. THE ASSASSINATION SITUATION

Wednesday, 29th of August, 1956

The last Thursday of August was election day in Pluckley Green. Villagers were expected to vote for a representative in the parish council and whichever candidate won was predicted to do so with only the narrowest of margins.

At 7pm, on the evening before election day, the three candidates met in the village hall for their final session of hustings - in which they would each answer questions from an audience of voters.

These candidates were; Cuthbert Crookshank, the incumbent parish councillor who was fighting to be re-elected; Diana Spiff, who wished to represent Pluckley Green on behalf of the newly-formed Third Realm Party, who pledged that more schools for elite students like her daughter, Judy Spiff, would be built and finally; historian August Barley, whose platform as an independent candidate focused strongly on preserving the historic value of the village.

Also on the stage that evening was Constance Tomlin, editor of the Pluckley Green Press, who served as host for the evening.

The first to speak at the hustings was Cuthbert Crookshank, who stood up from his chair to address the sparse audience. After his pre-prepared speech, in which he outlined his plans for Pluckley Green to become a tourist hotspot, he got into a fiery exchange of words with Bludger Baxter, who was in the audience. Bludger was very unhappy with Cuthbert's plans for another pub to be opened in the village.

So incandescent with rage was Bludger that he stormed from the hustings into the balmy summer night.

At 8pm, Cuthbert was halfway through answering a question from villager Michelle Whittle when an almighty bang echoed through the village hall.

Cuthbert Crookshank clutched his neck, fell to the ground and died. He had been shot.

Who murdered Cuthbert Crookshank?

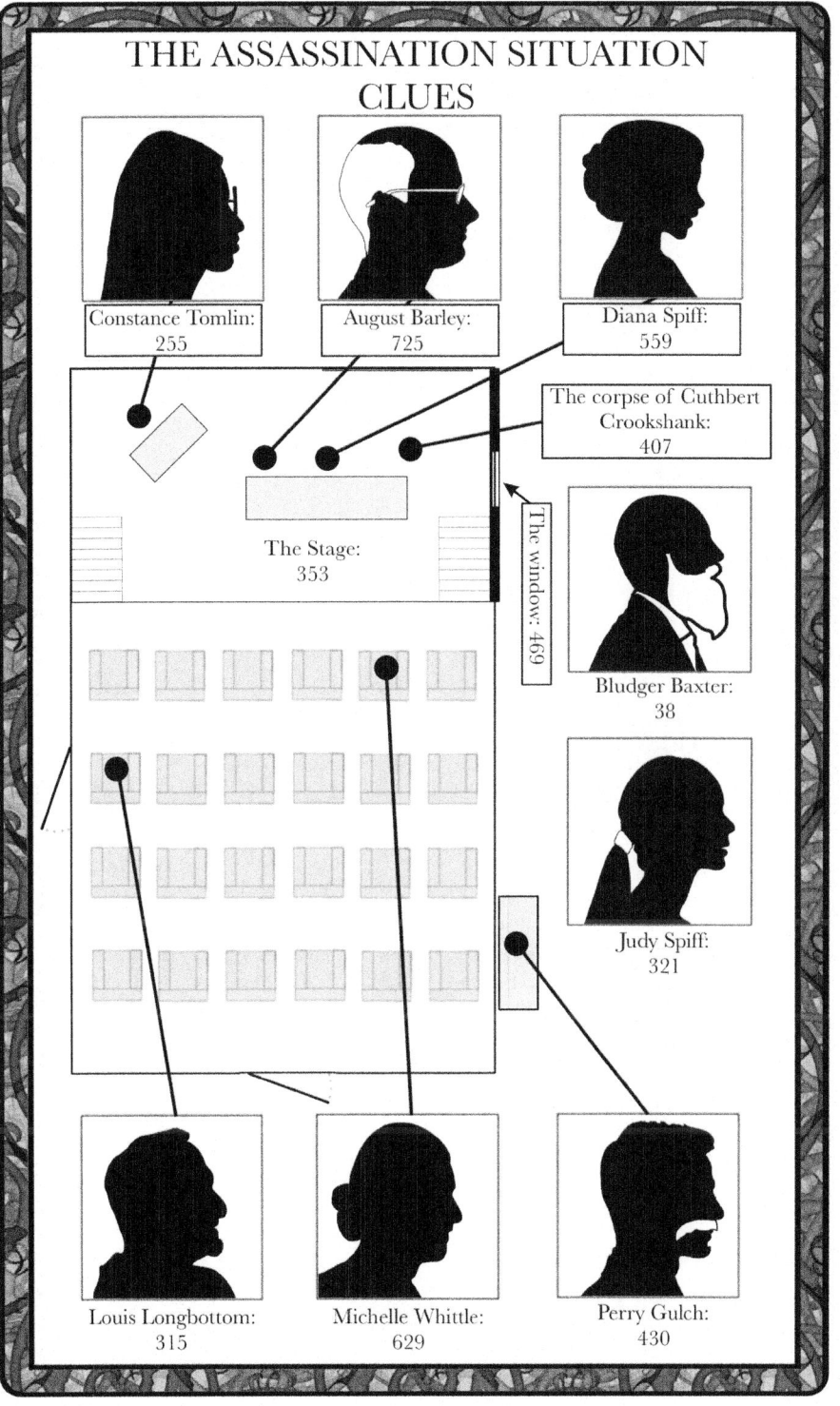

38. SIN AND TONIC

Friday, 7th of September, 1956

The 50th birthday party of the Second Lady Pendergast was due to be one of the highlights of the Pluckley Green social calendar.

In a rare act of community spirit, Lord Pendergast threw open the doors to his manor house and everybody in the village was invited for a night of revelry.

Lucien Pendergast may be widely despised throughout Pluckley Green but his wife remains a popular member of the village (possibly even a figure of pity) and as a result, many residents came to wish her well.

Partygoers attended the soiree in their finest attire and wished Lady Oxania Pendergast a happy birthday upon arrival, before indulging in the rare opportunity to snoop around the Pendergast's achingly huge mansion.

At 10pm, Lady Pendergast brought her husband his favourite drink - a double gin and tonic with ice and a slice of cucumber.

Lord Pendergast, who was seated in his enormous armchair in the smoking lounge, took a sniff of the drink's bouquet and noticed something strange - the unmistakable smell of cinnamon.

Incandescent with rage, he threw the glass to the floor and bellowed "SOMEONE IS TRYING TO POISON ME WITH WHIPPER SNAKE VENOM!"

The only people known to have gone into the kitchen where Lady Pendergast prepared the drink that evening were; Mavis Davis, Bludger Baxter, Reverend Amos Harper and Lady Pendergast herself.

Who attempted to murder Lord Pendergast?

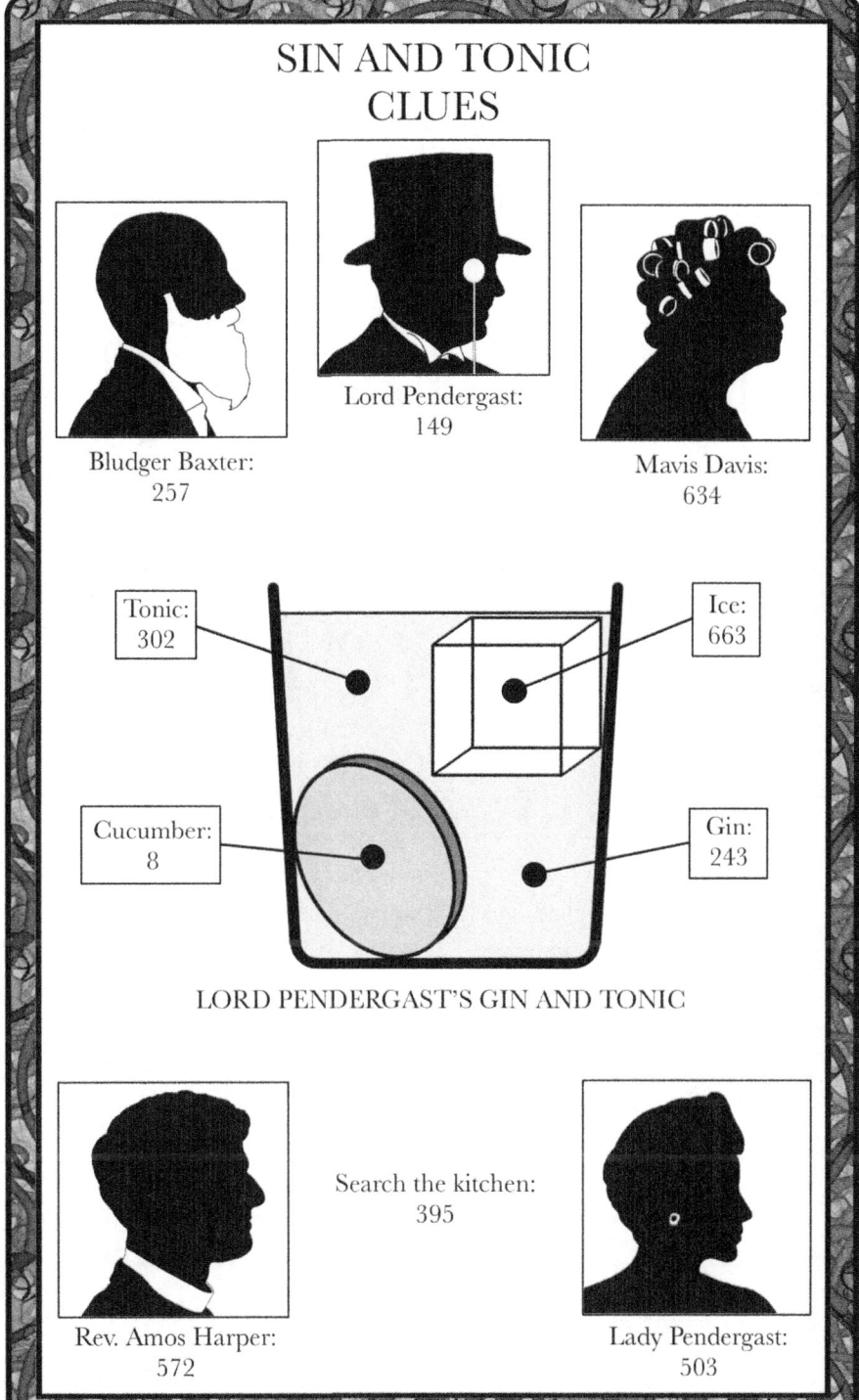

BONUS MYSTERY: WHO MURDERED LORD PENDERGAST?

After shooting Lord Pendergast, the mysterious figure fled into the night - but accidentally dropped a note at the doorstep of Pendergast Manor.

To my sweetest love,

The poison plot has failed this evening.

I am devastated and now my husband is more furious with me than ever.

I fear for my safety and my life.

Back in March, I gave you my mother's silver watch as a symbol of my undying affection and love for you. I hope that you will look at it this evening and reflect upon what I ask of you.

Please murder Lord Pendergast. It is the only way I can ever be free - and after his death, you and I can fully embrace this love which has blossomed between us.

L.O.P.

Use the information you have gathered so far and select who you think is the murderer.

Bludger Baxter:
429

Reverend Amos Harper:
535

Mona Prim:
60

Wilma Rogers:
528

Jan Treagle:
570

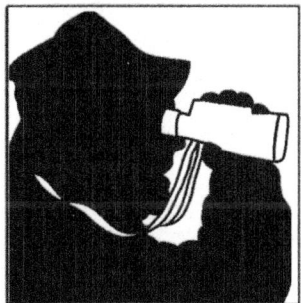

Jeremy Trumble:
637

39. A WALK IN THE WESTERN WOODS

Saturday, 15th of September, 1956

The Western Woods are a dark and mysterious forest at the edge of the village. Some say they are haunted, others say they are cursed. Almost everyone says they would rather avoid the perpetually dark place at all costs.

However, this does not deter the Pluckley Ramblers, a walking club who meet every Saturday morning to walk through the foreboding forest.

The five members of the rambling club are; supposed clairvoyant Minerva Arcana; hospital matron Bathsheba Sharpe; university student Artemis Baird; general practitioner Doctor Henery White and his friend, surgeon Paris Montgomery.

As usual, the group of five set out on the footpath through the forest at 10am. The six mile route formed a large circle which encompassed most of the dense woodland. A small, abandoned cottage marked the halfway point of the moderate walk.

Bathsheba was the first to arrive at the end of the walk. She was followed by Minerva Arcana and then Artemis Baird. Paris Montgomery was the next to complete the ramble and after some impatient waiting, it became clear that Doctor Henery White was nowhere to be found.

The group of four hastily retraced their steps and at 12.30pm, the body of Henery White was discovered behind the abandoned cottage. His throat had been slashed and a cutthroat razor had been abandoned beside him on the forest floor.

Who murdered Doctor Henery White?

A WALK IN THE WESTERN WOODS CLUES

The cutthroat razor: 592

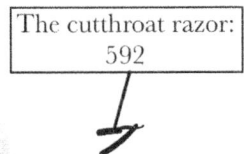

The abandoned cottage: 563

The corpse of Doctor Henery White: 710

Bathsheba Sharpe: 577

The first person to complete the walk

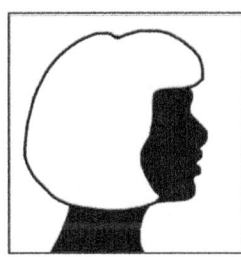

Minerva Arcana: 236

The second person to complete the walk

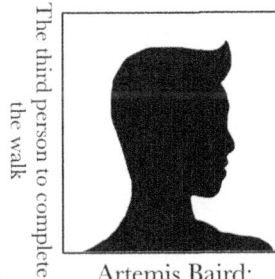

Artemis Baird: 608

The third person to complete the walk

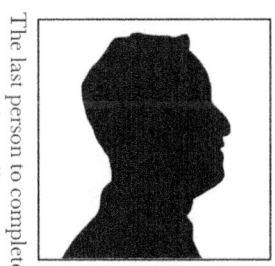

Paris Montgomery: 401

The last person to complete the walk

40. THE GHOST IN THE FIRE

Thursday, 27th of September, 1956

At 5 o'clock in the morning, the charming cottage on the edge of Pluckley Green Park belonging to Mr Bertrand Mallard burst into flames.

Bertrand Mallard had spent his working life as a tax inspector but in retirement had taken on the position of umpire for the village team's many cricket matches.

There would be no more cricket matches for Bertrand Mallard though. For he had been burnt to a crisp within his own home.

The first person at the scene was postman Larry Finch, who had just begun his delivery round. He had not only noticed that the cottage was aflame but that poor Bertrand was trapped inside.

He called for help from Perry Gulch, who was napping on a bench in the park and the two men tried valiantly to break into the house.

It was to no avail and the screams from the man inside the cottage ceased as he collapsed from smoke inhalation and fell into the flames.

Upon arrival, the local firemen broke open a window to gain access to the home and extinguished what was left of the fire.

Mr Mallard lived alone in the cottage and was the only fatality of the blaze. His house appears to have been fully secured with locked windows and doors.

How did the fire start?

41. THE CIRCUS OF BLOOD

Thursday, 7th of October, 1956

Just as surely as the leaves turning brown, autumn brings the annual arrival of Bostwicke's Travelling Circus to Pluckley Green.

Founded in the late 1800s, the circus draws huge numbers of villagers over the course of a week, who enjoy watching acrobatics, lion taming, clowning and general merriment inside the big top.

The ringmaster of the circus is Bartholomew Bostwicke - a role he inherited from his father.

Other acts at the circus include; Polo the Clown (performed by Dominic Tell); trapeze acrobat Dazzle (real name Wanda Highsmith); strongman Chip Burlington and lion tamer Leonard Price.

As always, a huge audience of hundreds was in attendance for that evening's show. Among the crowd was Miss Faversham, who continues to bewilder the people of the village with her newfound love of entertainment and whimsy. Also in attendance was Curran Cornwell, who (until a year ago, when he was fired) was the circus' clown.

After the ringmaster's introduction, strongman Chip Burlington took to the sawdust-strewn stage for his show of strength. However, midway through his routine - and in view of hundreds of spectators - Polo strode onto the stage and fired a bullet directly into the strongman's skull, killing him instantly. The clown then fled the scene.

Polo/Dominic was wrestled to the ground in his caravan by lion tamer Leonard Price. However, the entertainer insists that he did not kill the strongman.

Who murdered Chip Burlington?

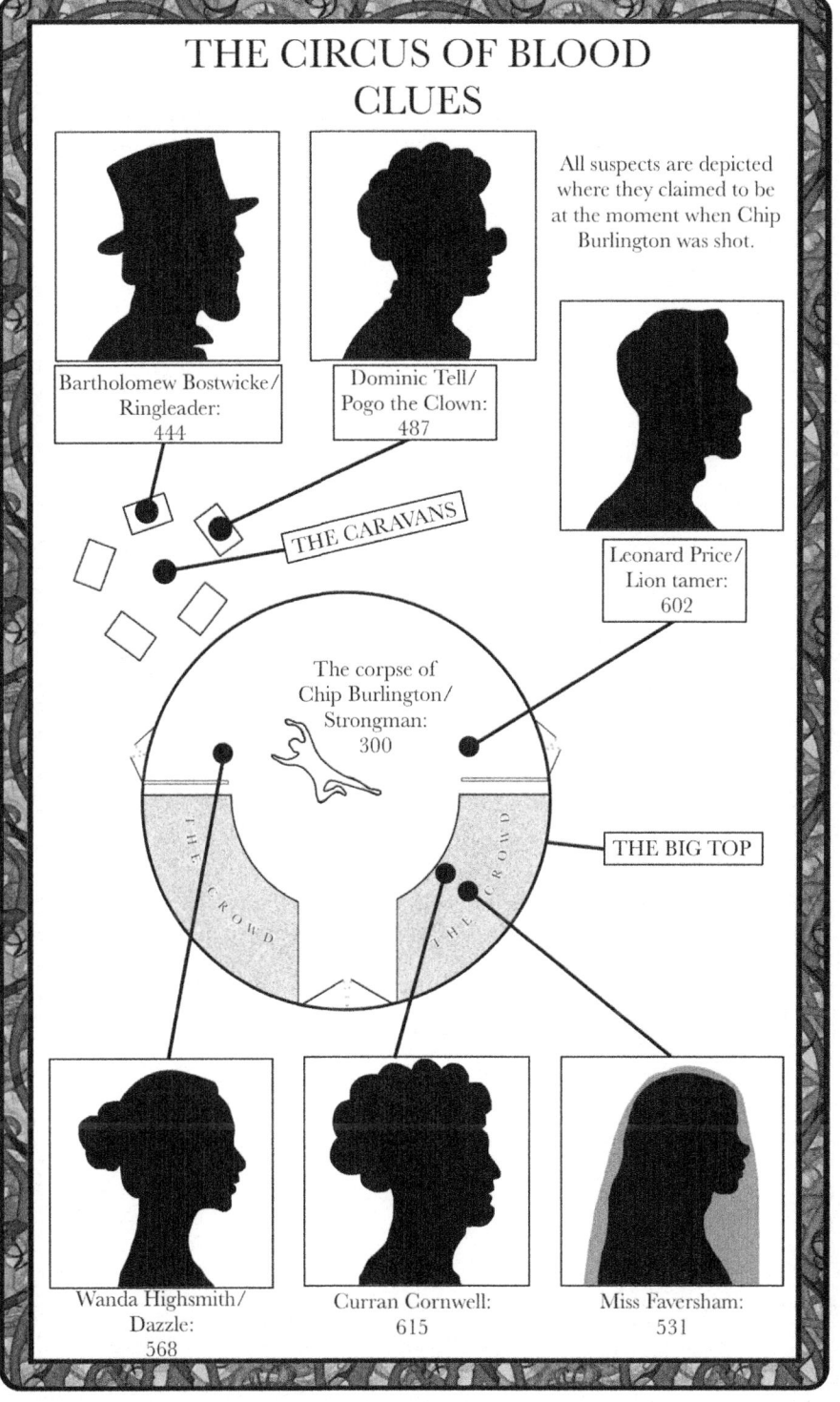

42. MURDERING ABOUT ON BOATS

Wednesday, 17th of October. 1956

Since leaving boarding school, friends Karl Danvers, Ryan Moon and Herb Mudgens have made it a tradition to meet-up every October for an autumnal boating holiday.

They hire a narrowboat and lazily drift along the waterways of England, admiring the understated beauty of the season and watching the migratory birds arrive in advance of winter.

Now in their tenth year of this tradition, Karl and Herb have brought their wives along for the excursion, leading to an enjoyable (if cramped) adventure on the water.

On the second morning of their holiday, the friends were moored along the canal where it passes through the village of Pluckley Green. The five of them had just finished breakfast in the boat's small dining room/kitchen and had retired to different parts of the boat in preparation for the rest of the day.

It was at this time that a terrible scream came from Cabin 3 - Ryan Moon's tiny onboard bedroom. It was a scream which was also heard by Mona Prim, who was taking a morning stroll along the canal path.

Herb Mudgens was the first to enter the cabin, where he found his friend dead on the floor.

Who murdered Ryan Moon?

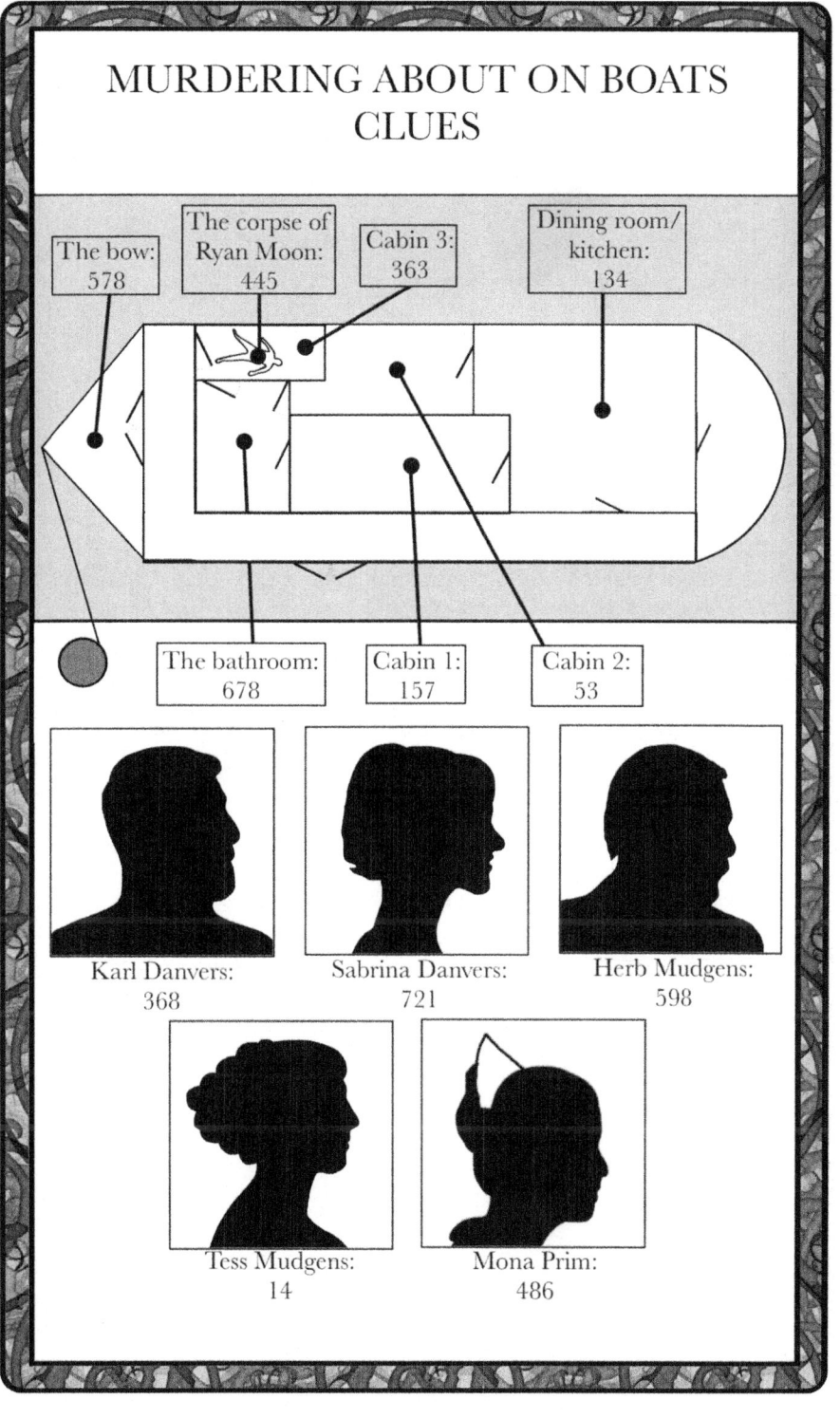

43. HALLOWEEN: PART ONE

Wednesday, 31st of October, 1956

For most of the villagers of Pluckley Green, Halloween was a non-event, a night just like any other.

However, for a handful of friends, the occasion is the cause of a rather joyous party.

Every 31st of October, undertaker Dorian Moribund and his wife Sheila invited guests to their house (a house which also served as a funeral home) for a spooky night of thrilling games and spine-chilling ghost stories.

Each year, the interior of the funeral home was decorated with fake spiderwebs and flickering candles and the guests were encouraged to wear Halloween costumes.

The guests this year were; Atlas Moribund, a bookmaker and the brother of Dorian; Stanhope Jones, junior assistant to Dorian at the funeral home, and Scott Mallard, a solicitor whose father had recently been buried by Dorian Moribund. The other party guests were Mavis Davis and August Barley.

Mavis Davis was the first to arrive at the party. She was about to ring the house's doorbell when she spotted something frightful through the window. In the kitchen of the funeral home, Sheila Moribund at first seemed to be apple bobbing in a bucket which sat upon the kitchen table but Mavis then noticed that a figure dressed in a long, black, hooded cloak was stood behind her and was actually forcing her head underwater.

Mavis pounded at the door just as the figure in the cloak fled from the kitchen via a backdoor. The other guests (and Dorian Moribund) arrived at the house as Mavis Davis managed to break open the door but it was too late. The woman had been drowned in the bucket.

Who murdered Sheila Moribund?

HALLOWEEN: PART ONE
CLUES

Check the kitchen's back door: 623

Inspect the kitchen: 44

The body of Sheila Moribund: 720

August Barley: 151

Mavis Davis: 432

Stanhope Jones: 496

Scott Mallard: 115

Atlas Moribund: 632

Dorian Moribund: 380

44. HALLOWEEN: PART TWO

Wednesday, 31st of October, 1956

Meanwhile, at the Pluckley Standing Stones…

Halloween may not have been an important date for most of the village but for the Ancient Order of Pluckley Pagans, Halloween - or Samhain, as they knew it - was one of the most sacred nights of the year. It was when the group welcomed the darker half of the year and venerated the (many) people who had died in the village during the previous twelve months.

All eight members of the Pluckley Pagans were in attendance for the grand ceremony. As was customary, they wore white robes and face masks.

After the Samhain ceremony, the masks were removed and Holly Merryfair - the Grand High Wizard of the Order - invited his fellow Pagans to join together in performing a binding spell. The spell was intended to stop The Ghost from being able to kill again.

Two members of the Order turned down this invitation. Minerva Arcana had plans with her mother and Bludger Baxter wanted to play no part in it.

The five who joined Holly in the binding ritual were; plumber Gerald Ratchett; conservationist Jeremy Trumble; retired secretary Melody Martin, dog walker Helena Turner (who had recently returned to the village after attempting to murder Holly Merryfair in January) and her husband, market porter Bert Turner.

As Holly took to the centre of the circle, each of the five other members stood by one of the standing stones.

Holly spoke some incantations to the gods of the sky and then produced an apple from a jar of spiced honey water.

As the members knew well, an apple soaked in spiced honey water was a vital part of any binding spell. On a small plate, Holly sliced the apple into six equal parts with his ceremonial dagger and then ate one piece himself.

He then took the plate of apple slices to Melody Martin, who ate a piece. Holly then moved anti-clockwise around the stone circle, reaching Helena Turner last. She took the final slice of apple, ate it and then promptly dropped dead.

Who murdered Helena Turner?

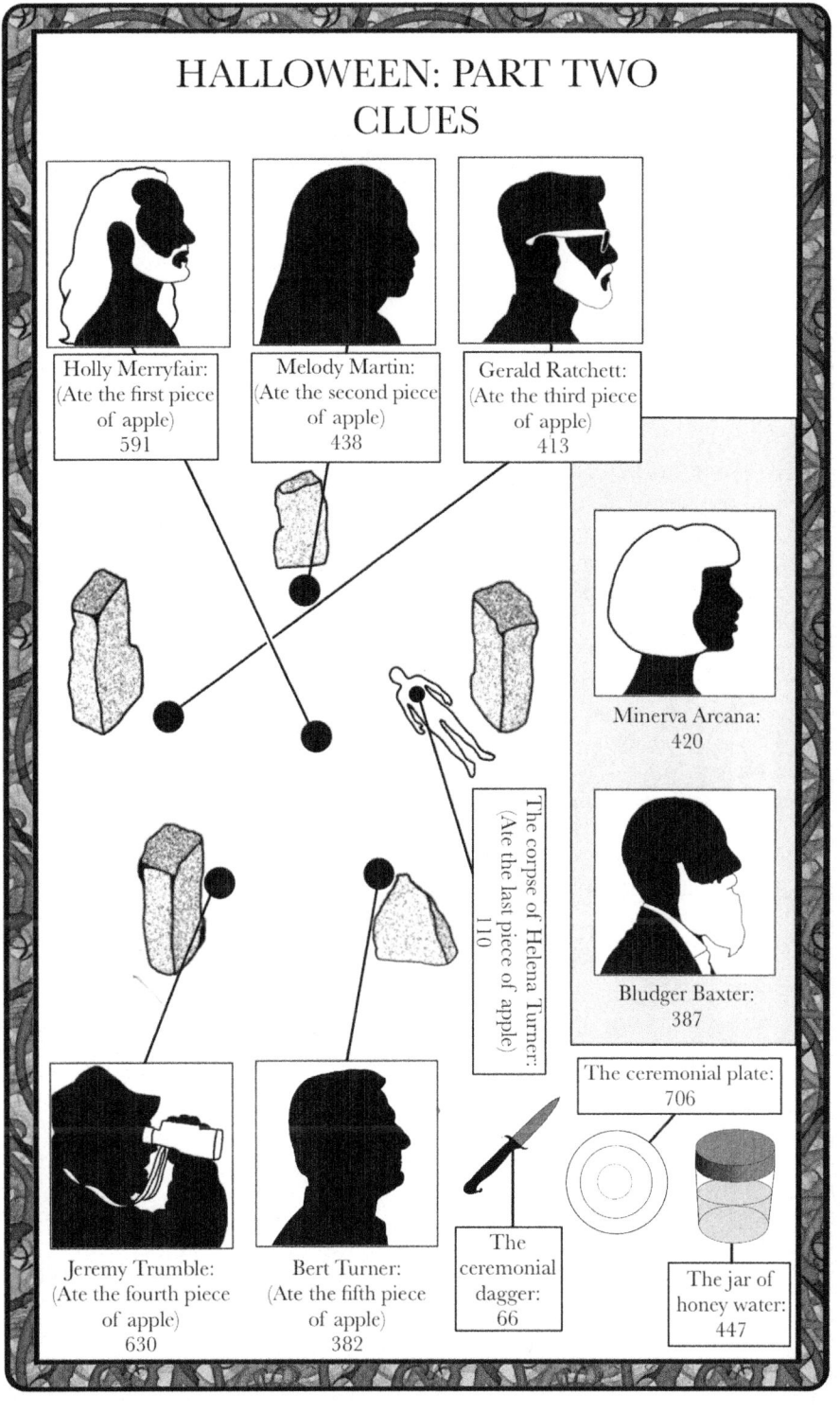

45. THE FALL OF THE HOUSE OF SPARROW

Sunday, 11th of November, 1956

At 4am on a chilly November morning, Professor Reginald Sole stepped out of a taxi in the middle of Pluckley Green and unlocked the door to his new home.

Mr Sole had brought Crooked Cottage in order to live closer to his fiancee, Daisy Doyle. The couple intended to live there together after they were married.

He opened the door, lit a cigarette and he, along with the entirety of Crooked Cottage were blown to bits in an enormous explosion.

The only people who were in possession of keys to the house were Daisy Doyle, Beatrice Beauregard (who lived next door to Crooked Cottage), Mavis Davis (who had taken it upon herself to regularly water the many houseplants in the cottage) and Mabel Witherspoon (who had been asked to cook a cake in advance of Reginald's arrival.)

Daisy had spent the night before the explosion with her sister Wilma Rogers, in the houseboat they share.

Who murdered Professor Reginald Sole?

THE FALL OF THE HOUSE OF SPARROW CLUES

Beatrice Beauregard:
135

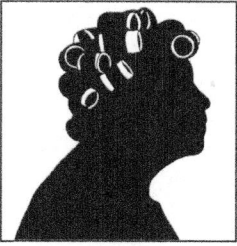

Mavis Davis:
604

Daisy Doyle:
687

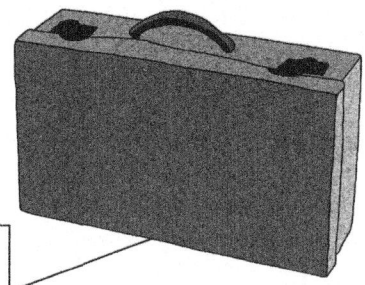

Inspect Professor Reginald Sole's suitcase:
661

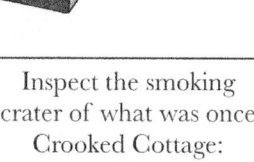

Inspect the smoking crater of what was once Crooked Cottage:
61

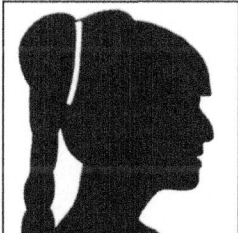

Wilma Rogers:
421

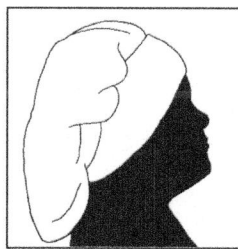

Mabel Witherspoon:
537

46. A STEP IN THE WRONG DIRECTION

Tuesday, 27th of November, 1956

In August, Bludger Baxter applied to the council with plans for an extension to the basement of the Bloodied Axe Tavern. As soon as this proposal was approved, the landlord employed the services of Manville Builders Ltd. and work was due to begin in late November.

Manville Builders was founded in the aftermath of the Second World War by Oliver Manville and over the following decade, the process of rebuilding a war-torn nation proved to be very lucrative.

The five builders employed to work on the basement extension were; Oliver Manville, who would serve as foreman of the project; his son Douglas Manville; Michael Doncaster; Edgar Minster and Richmond Reed - all of whom were long-term employees of the business.

The five men arrived at the door to the Bloodied Axe Tavern at 9am and were met by Bludger, who let them into the pub. Oliver was the first to enter the basement and the moment he did so, he let out a bellowing scream.

Bludger and the four other men rushed to the top of the steps which led to the basement. Oliver Manville lay dead upon the stone floor of the basement in a pool of his own blood.

Who murdered Oliver Manville?

A STEP IN THE WRONG DIRECTION
CLUES

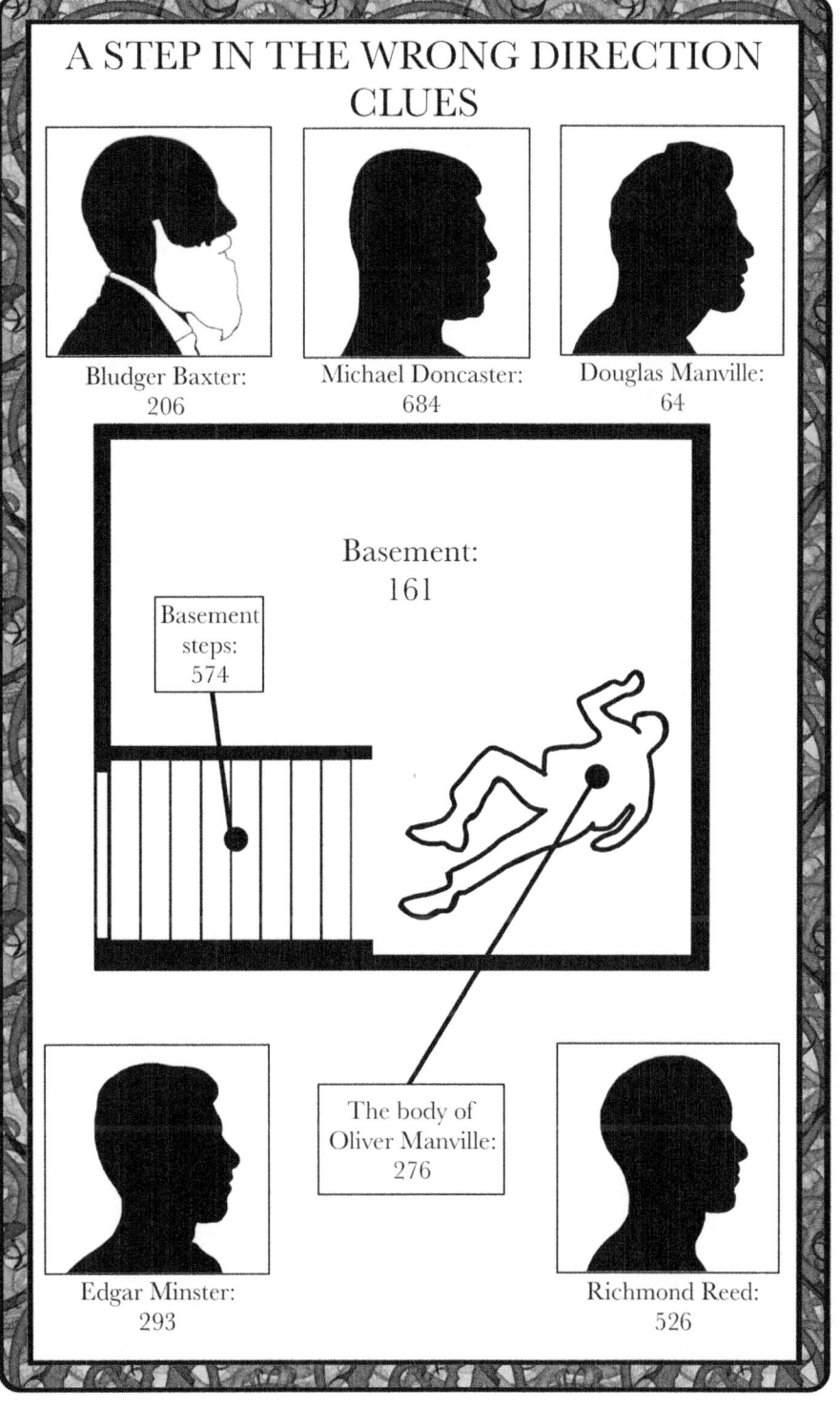

Bludger Baxter: 206

Michael Doncaster: 684

Douglas Manville: 64

Basement: 161

Basement steps: 574

The body of Oliver Manville: 276

Edgar Minster: 293

Richmond Reed: 526

47. THE BLOODIED AXE

Friday, 8th of December, 1724.

By the time Christopher Aurelius arrived by foot in Pluckley Green, the clock upon St Julian on-the-Edge church informed him that it was 9pm. The snow had started to fall in fluttering flakes.

He smiled to himself. His trusty leather boots had served him well - he had made it on time for his appointment with Fenton Hughes at the Feathered Cap (the only tavern in the village).

As Christopher approached the inn, he spotted a beggar shivering in the cold. The man was barefoot and his fingers were turning blue. Christopher dropped a gold coin into the poor man's trembling palm - after all, what did money mean to him anymore?

Inside, the pub was warmed by a roasting fire. Songs were being sung and the ale flowed liberally.

Christopher was served a pint by the barmaid Alice Page and then sat with his friend Fenton in the snug.

"I have the treasure," said Christopher - who was unaware that their conversation was being eavesdropped by farmer Gregory Barnes, who was seated nearby. "It is more wonderful than I could ever have dreamed!"

Fenton searched his friend's satchel. Inside it was a single metal cup. A chalice. The man could not quite believe what he was seeing.

"Now that I know it is real, I'm prepared to make a substantial offer. Meet me at dawn in the church and tell no one of your plans." The man left in a hurry and a daze.

At closing time, Christopher enquired with the jovial landlord, Peter Slender, about accommodation for the night and was shown to a room.

But in the morning, there was no sign of Christopher. Just a huge puddle of blood upon the bed where he had slept. There was a bloodied axe abandoned amongst the gore.

Who murdered Christopher Aurelius?

THE BLOODIED AXE CLUES

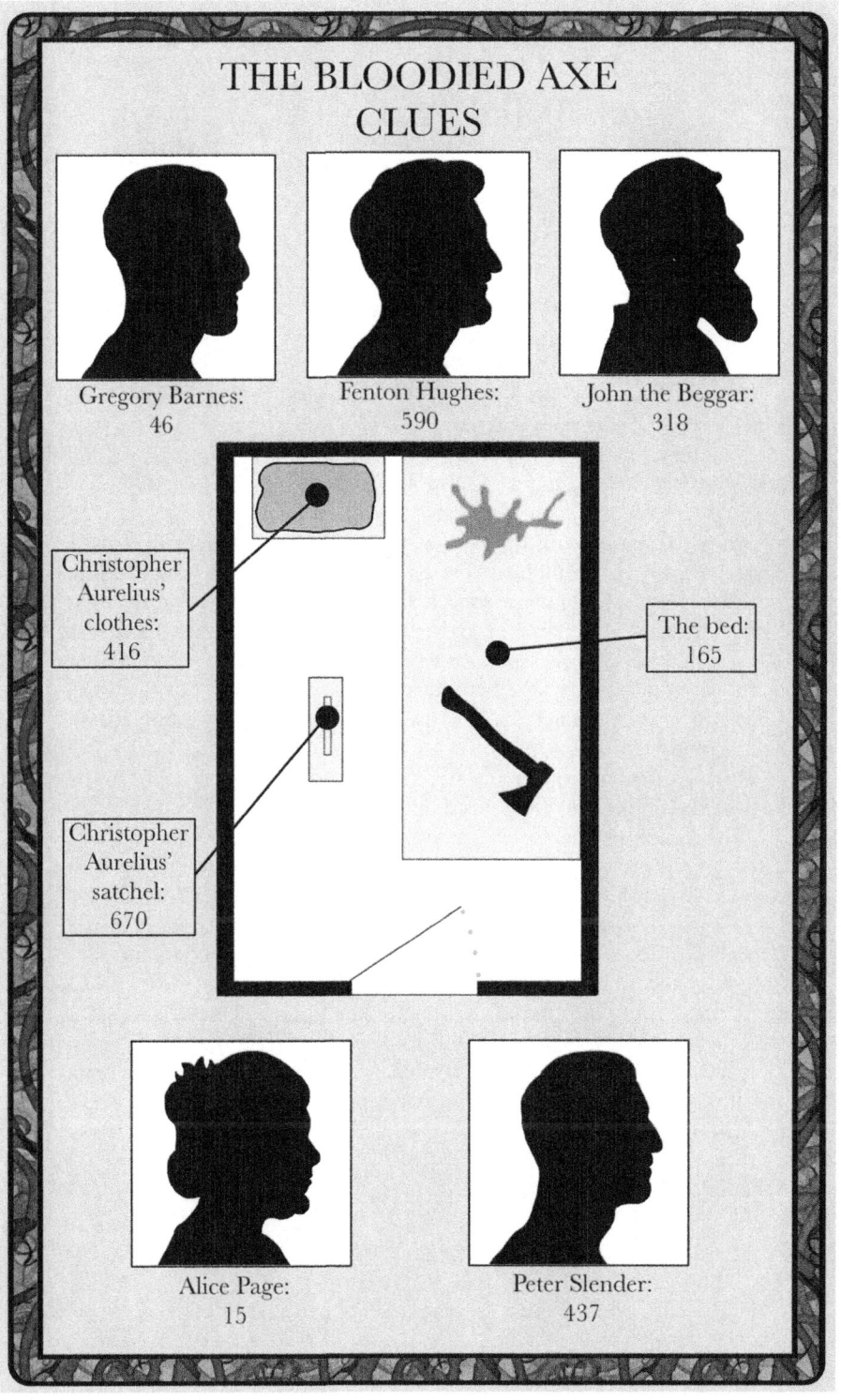

Gregory Barnes: 46

Fenton Hughes: 590

John the Beggar: 318

Christopher Aurelius' clothes: 416

The bed: 165

Christopher Aurelius' satchel: 670

Alice Page: 15

Peter Slender: 437

48. BRIDE AND BOOM

Monday, 24th of December, 1956

Christmas Eve was a day filled with even more cheer than usual in the village of Pluckley Green as it was the wedding day of Miss Faversham and her handyman Winston Lampeter.

The pair were married by Reverend Amos Harper in a small church service which was followed by a grand reception at Stasis House - to which every villager was invited.

The dining hall of the (thoroughly cleaned) mansion house was filled with guests for the banquet and the bride and groom were seated at a large table in front of everyone.

After the meal, Winston gave a speech in which he thanked Miss Faversham for her kindness. Miss Faversham (dressed in a new white wedding dress) then gave a speech in which she declared she would henceforth go by the name of Genevieve - in honour of her maid who was still missing. She also took the opportunity to remind everyone that decades of hiding her face behind a veil had protected her from the ageing effects of the sun, which is why she looked 20 years younger than people might expect.

During the speeches, a multi-tiered wedding cake was brought to the back of the dining hall and placed upon a table.

The guests were then encouraged to sip champagne and mingle. These guests included Mabel Witherspoon (who had been tasked with baking the wedding cake); Hilda Faversham (the estranged sister of Miss Faversham); Phoebe Parks (Winston Lampeter's former girlfriend) and Kirsten Caldicot (Winston Lampeter's previous wife) who had with her Steven Caldicot, her husband.

It was during this period that one of the guests, Hamish Kingston, took the opportunity to surreptitiously sample the wedding cake. With a knife he cut a small slice into the corner of the three-tiered extravaganza and it - along with Hamish Kingston - were blown to smithereens by an explosion.

Who killed Hamish Kingston?

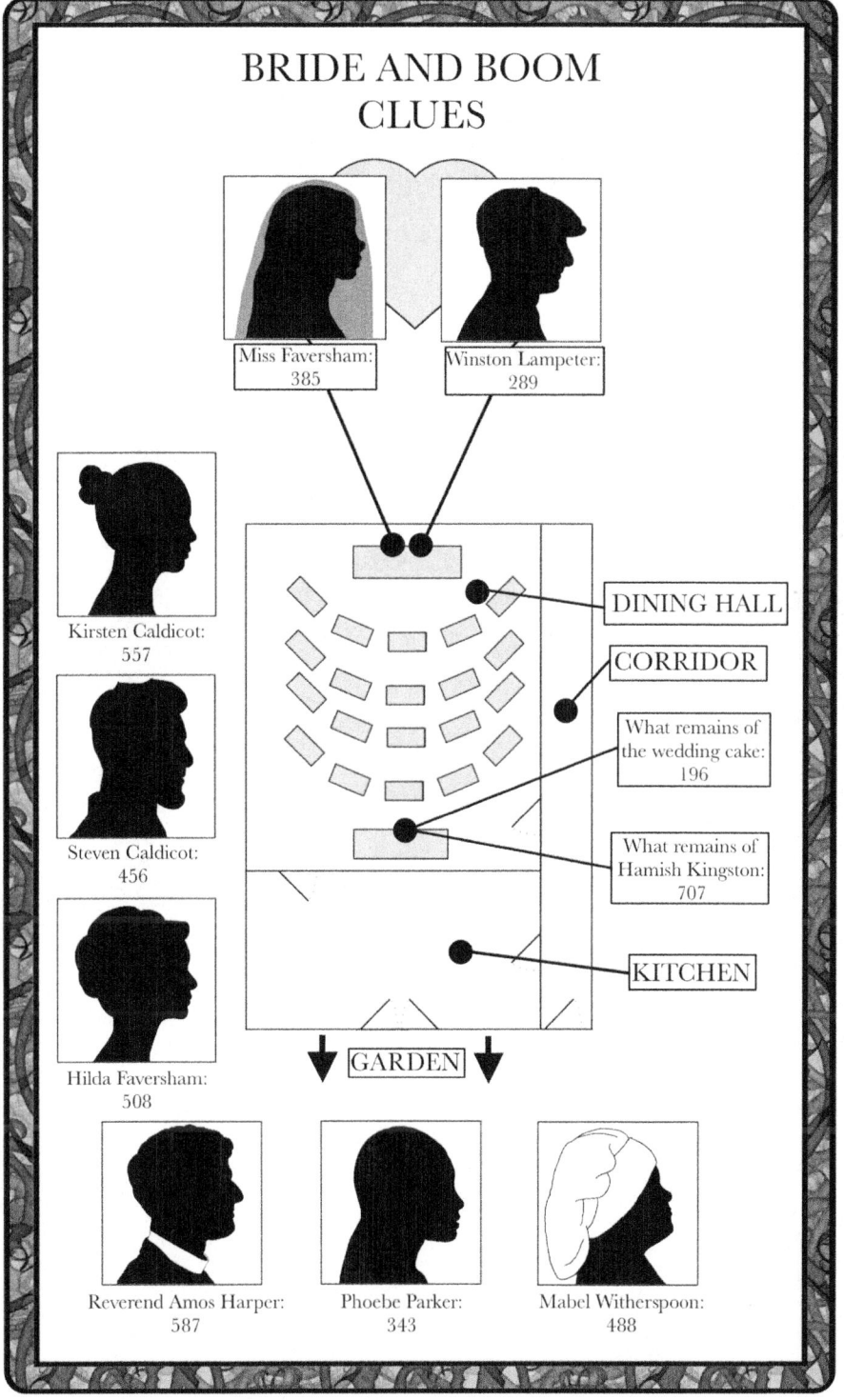

49. BOXING DAY BLOODSHED

Wednesday, 26th of December, 1956

It was a tradition in Pluckley Green that Boxing Day was the day when a group of volunteers would go door-to-door through the streets of the village and collect donations of money. These donations would then be passed on to those in need.

This annual charity drive was led by the newly engaged Reverend Amos Harper. Joining him were; fashion designer Colin Carnegie; estate agent Dante Finn; his wife, landscape artist Wendy Finn and retired policewoman Bethany Parker.

This year had proved to be an unbridled success. In the early hours of the evening, the group stopped at the end of Harlow Terrace where the home of Prudence Rosehip was located.

There seemed little reason to ring the doorbell of the notorious miser who had moved to Pluckley Green in January but Reverend Harper argued that perhaps the spirit of the season would encourage an ounce of generosity from the woman.

The reverend rang the doorbell and when there was no response, he peeked through the keyhole. Through it, he saw a terrible sight. Prudence Rosehip lay on the floor of her hall in a pool of blood.

Reverend Harper kicked the door open but it was too late to save the wretched woman. She was dead - and it appears she had been for quite some time.

Who murdered Prudence Rosehip?

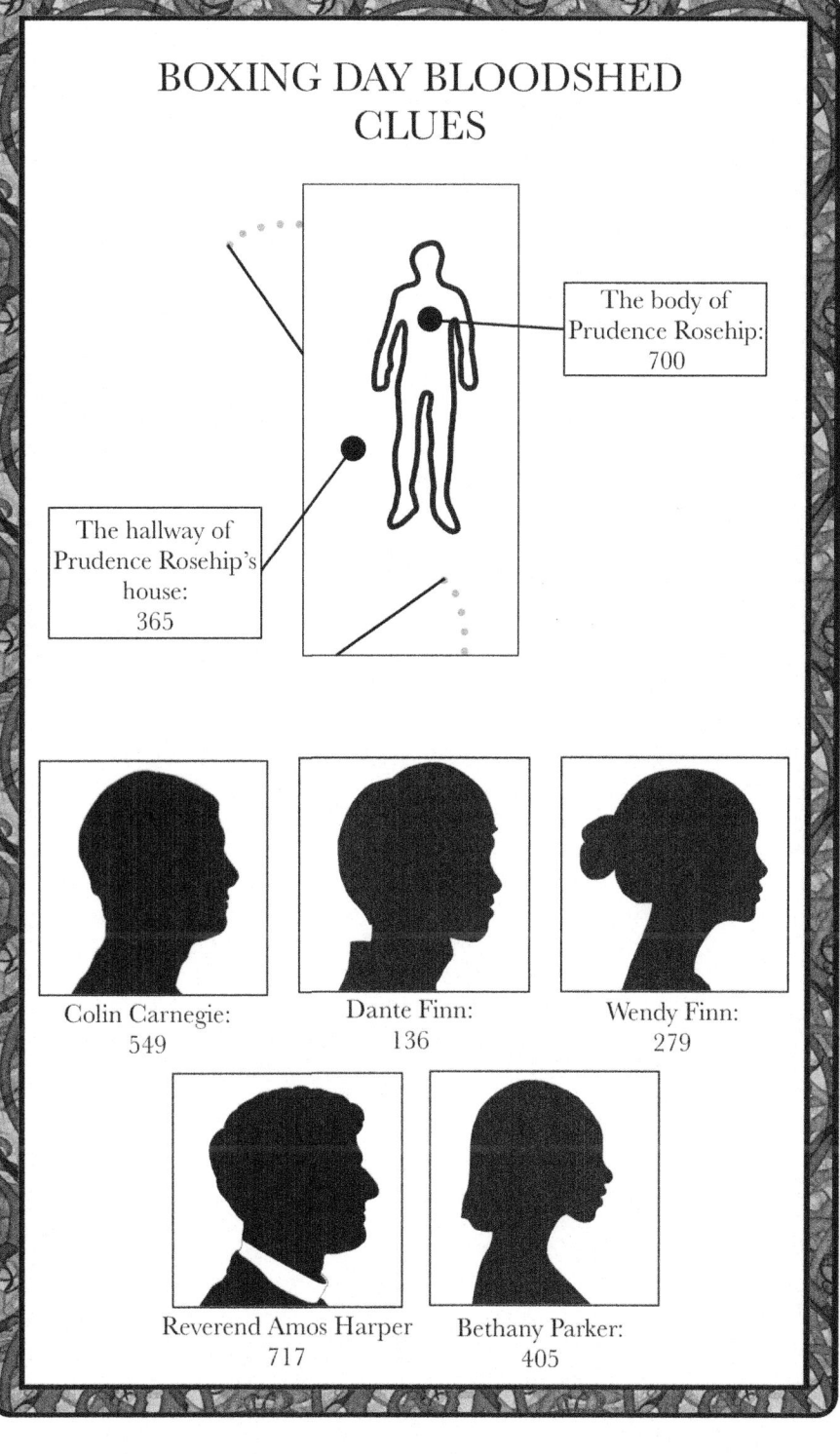

50. NEW YEAR'S EVIL

Monday, 31st of December, 1956

It was 5pm and Jenny Carter - the barmaid of the Bloodied Axe Tavern - was eagerly anticipating the arrival of tonight's revellers.

New Year's Eve was always the busiest night of the year for the tavern and Jenny expected tonight to be no different. 1957 would surely be another wonderful year for the safe and pleasant village - and that was certainly worth celebrating.

Jenny had just finished decorating the pub with streamers and bunting when the door burst open.

Larry Finch, the village postman, was stood in the doorway, his hand clutching his bleeding neck. "The Ghost has slashed my throat!" He gargled before collapsing to the floor.

Jenny called for an ambulance and then ran to the door of the pub. In the street outside, Beatrice Beauregard was stifling a scream, Holly Merryfair gawped on, confused in his white robes and Perry Gulch was yelling for help - blood was dripping from his paperback copy of "King Lear."

"IT IS THE GHOST!" Jenny screamed. " WHOEVER THEY ARE, THEY ARE NEARBY!"

Many of the villagers within earshot ran to their homes - and then knocked upon the doors of their neighbours.

Within minutes, a mob of hundreds had flooded into the moonlit streets of Pluckley Green. Villagers were brandishing flaming torches and pitchforks - ready to hunt down the serial killer in their midst.

Where was Larry Finch when his throat was slashed?

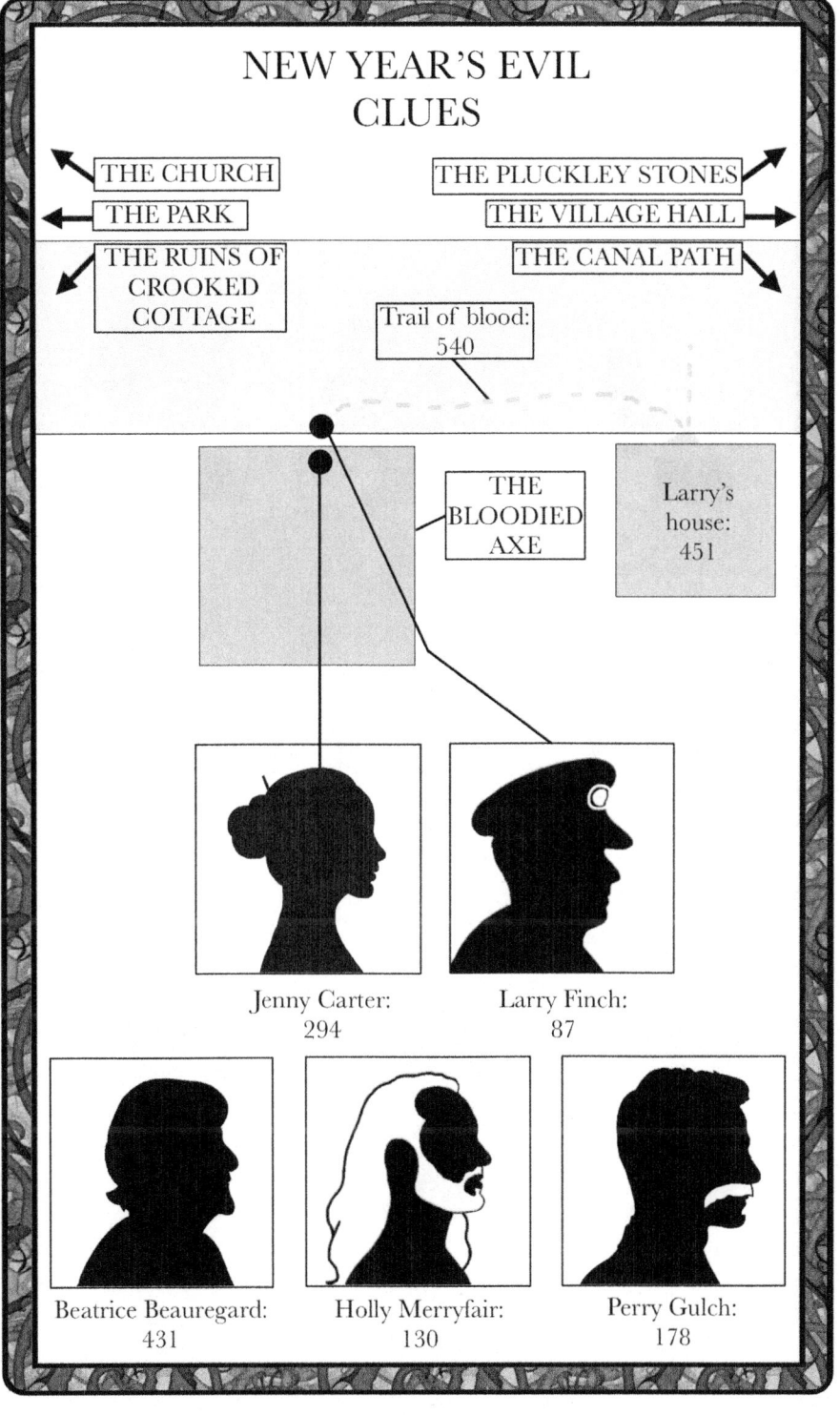

WHO IS THE GHOST?

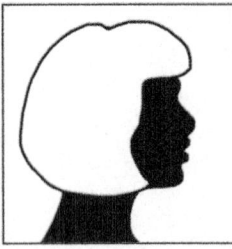
Minerva Arcana:
375

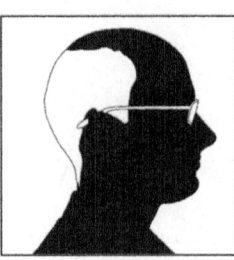
August Barley:
455

Bludger Baxter:
28

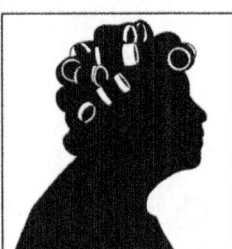
Mavis Davis:
677

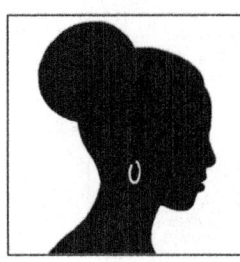
Daisy Doyle:
296

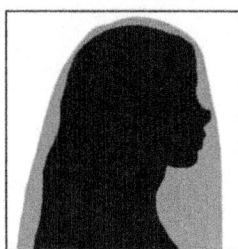
Miss Faversham:
214

Larry Finch:
596

Perry Gulch:
703

Reverend Amos Harper:
40

Use the clues and information you have gathered over the course of this book to deduce who you believe to be the serial killer who has been plaguing the village throughout the year.

Holly Merryfair:
690

Lady Pendergast:
190

Mona Prim:
239

Gerald Ratchett:
571

Wilma Rogers:
392

Judy Spiff:
140

Judge Jan Treagle:
622

Jeremy Trumble:
109

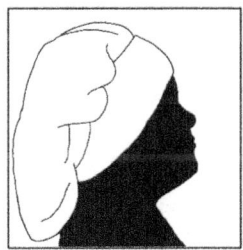

Mabel Witherspoon:
349

THE EVIDENCE FILE

1: St. Julian on the Edge is a dusty, draughty ancient church - the kind you will find in quaint villages across the nation. Named after the patron saint of innkeepers, musicians and murderers, for centuries it has been the spiritual heart of the village. Despite the horrific incident, the church looks much the same as it always has and nothing seems out of place.

2: There is a sealed envelope on the desk beside Humbert's dead body. It is addressed to the local council. Inside it is a long-winded letter in which he opposes the construction of the Ramsay's swimming pool. There is nothing unusual about the envelope.

3: The letter is from Fenton Hughes. It would have been delivered from Pluckley Green to Glastonbury via horseback - at enormous cost. *"Mr Aurelius, I am delighted to hear that your search has been successful. As you know, I am an honest man who has always kept his word. Meet me at the Feathered Cap in Pluckley Green at nine o'clock. If I judge this treasure to be authentic, I shall reward you with my entire fortune and estate."*

4: "Oh it was simply *ghastly!* Somebody - I can't say whom, as it happened so fast - leapt from the shadows and pushed that poor man in front of the train. He or she was dressed all in white. I'd seen the victim earlier, he was in the waiting room reading a newspaper. Before that, I had seen him leaving the pub."

5: In the library, Stacey Weedle has set up a small memorial to Lucy Sparrow - who was murdered by The Ghost inside Crooked Cottage. She was a librarian at Pluckley Green Library. The memorial consists of a collection of photographs and heartfelt messages of condolence from her colleagues.

6: "Marvin took me out to a restaurant on the evening of the 31st of January. He was rather splendid company and I was sure that we hit it off well but when I was talking to a friend the following morning and I mentioned his name, she showed me an article from the local paper. I was shocked by what I read and have avoided answering the phone since then." *To read the article, go to entry **582**.*

7: The body of Arabella Krueger lays broken and splattered across the courtyard. She has clearly fallen from a tremendous height before hitting the ground. She does not seem to have any wounds which suggest she was injured before the fall. She was a small, slim woman and it would not have taken a great deal of strength to lift her up to throw her over the castle ramparts.

8: There is a single slice of cucumber in Lord Pendergast's gin and tonic. It has a slight smell of cinnamon. *To look for the rest of the cucumber in the kitchen, go to entry **356**.*

9: At the stroke of midnight, Adriana Arcana and her daughter Minerva attempted (but failed) to contact The Ghost via a seance. The pair of them firmly believe that the Pluckley Green killer is a supernatural entity who is exacting revenge upon the village for past misdeeds.

10: "Beatrice and I shared a magical evening together, strolling along the canal path. We talked about the village, our hopes and our mutual love for the sport of archery. I walked her home and she kissed me goodnight at 10pm. As I was walking back to my house, I spotted Mabel Witherspoon in Crooked Cottage. She was wearing a white apron and was turning off the cooker in the kitchen. She left shortly afterwards. Later, I passed another woman. She was walking in the direction of Crooked Cottage. I didn't get a look at her face but she had a set of keys in her hand. She was whistling a jaunty little tune, which I recognised from the film "Kiss Me, Kate". She seemed to be awfully happy about something!"

11: Larry and his wife Rose keep the door to their home locked at all times. His clean and well-ordered house is free of any evidence of violence. On a shelf is the trophy his team won at last year's pub quiz. The trophy is a metal cup mounted onto a piece of wood. Bludger Baxter made the trophy a few years ago with items he found in the pub basement. The walls are decorated with Wendy Finn landscape paintings. There is a note in the kitchen. It was written by Larry's wife. *"Larry, just a reminder that I will not be home when you finish your shift. I am going to Brigstowe so I can get you-know-what! I am so thrilled about it! Rose. x"*

12: That evening, Mavis Davis took a bunch of white roses to the cemetery of St Julian on the Edge church and stood before her sister's grave. Tearfully she placed the bouquet and softly whispered, "I am so sorry".

13: "Lord Asquith-Hulme has always been a proud man and he has been very good to me over the five years since I became his assistant. Over the course of this weekend I have been running errands on his behalf throughout the village and beyond. Last night I was invited to the home of Doctor White and spent much of the evening discussing Lord Asquith-Hulme's ongoing struggles with gout. I do wish he would eat healthier and drink less". *To read more about gout, go to entry* **41.**

14: "This is the second holiday I and my husband have taken this year with Sabrina and Karl. The first was to Cornwall in July. Sabrina and I were feeling daring so the pair of us wore rather scandalous bikinis on the beach that I had bought from Paris. We were innocently walking by the breakwater together when we spotted that disgusting pig Ryan Moon behind a rock. He was photographing us. Ryan hadn't even been invited on holiday with us - he must have followed us down. My husband got very angry with *me* when I complained - saying the pair of us were being immodest and how it wasn't Ryan's fault that he had a wandering eye. I was in the dining room/kitchen with Karl Danvers when we heard the scream. The pair of us were studying a map of the waterways and deciding where we would like to go today."

15: "I spoke to Christopher Aurelius only once. He was clutching to his satchel as if t'were a newborn! He spoke to that wealthy man for the rest of the night. I left at 11pm, by which time Christopher was talking to Peter. I went to the orchard near the heath after that. I usually keep it as a secret but I am a member of the Ancient Order of Pluckley Pagans. We were conducting a ritual - the Winter Wassail - led by our Grand High Wizard Albany Merryfair. His family have been Pagans for generations!" *To speak to Albany Merryfair, go to entry* **458.**

16: The second victim of "The Ghost" - Pluckley Green's newest serial killer - has already been selected and is due to go on a blind date with a former surgeon this evening. She will later become a suspect in this surgeon's own murder.

17: Jonathon's shoes are caked in wet mud. Rick's shoes are clean and dry.

18. "The cause of Lester Pratt's death was not immediately apparent but on closer inspection I discovered the unmistakable bite marks of a whipper snake upon his hand. I would suggest that the man died at approximately midnight - that was around the time my wife and I were hosting Carl Turpin for a dinner party. He is a longtime friend and we spent much of the evening discussing Lord Asquith-Hulme's malady - as well as Carl's new, rather fancy pair of round spectacles!"

19: The wall stands at chest height. Against this wall on Helen's side is a beautiful and well-maintained rose bush - the only part of the garden she diligently cared for herself, rather than her gardener, Giles Greenham.

20: Mrs Tipple's gun is cold. There are no bullets in its chamber.

21. The guillotine has been the duo's greatest magic prop for more than a decade. As the audience has learned all too well, the guillotine is fully functional and capable of beheading a person with ease. The trick comes from a single pin - small enough to be nearly invisible to the audience - which is pushed through the stocks at the bottom of the guillotine to prevent the blade slicing all the way down to the ground. However, this life-saving pin is missing and nowhere to be found - rendering the guillotine and its abilities all too real… Before Captain Conjuro and Mesmerelda's performance this evening, the guillotine was stored backstage.

22: The wardrobe contains part of Lady Pendergast's vast collection of fur coats. At the back of the wardrobe is a small hole, less than an inch in diameter. The hole continues through the wall. On the floor is Lord Pendergast's pistol - he usually keeps it on his bedside table in the master bedroom.

23: "My wife and I see a great deal from Pendergast Manor - Holly Merryfair doing his ludicrous rituals; August Barley tending to his bees at his apiary; Judy Spiff training her horse and Beatrice Beauregard practicing archery - but never once have I seen a devil dog! Shortly after midnight I heard screams from the heath. It must have been those five campers. The moon really is quite something to behold when it is full upon the heath but the mire makes the place dangerous at night. I suspect this whole tragedy was no more than a simple misunderstanding. The imagination really can wander in the dark and they were probably startled by something like a fox which spooked them into a panic. One of them presumably ran into the mire and some kind of creature has pecked at his corpse. This ridiculous legend has haunted my family for generations. My first wife claimed to have spied the hound and I believe this supernatural hogwash contributed to her downward spiral into death. She was convinced she was doomed!" *To learn more about the First Lady Pendergast, go to entry **258**.*

24: The pub is looking very much the same as it always does. Nothing seems out of place or unusual - although Bludger has noted that a large knife went missing from the pub's kitchen this morning.

25: Harry lays dead on his lawn. He is on his back with a pitchfork standing upright in his chest - it must have entered his body with an incredible force. He lays about five feet away from the disputed wall and has no other injuries. *To inspect the pitchfork, turn to entry **245**.*

26: At 92 years of age, Holly Merryfair is one of the oldest residents of Pluckley Green. He has been a member of the Ancient Order of Pluckley Pagans since he was born as both of his parents were key members. It has been said that his mother birthed him among the Pluckley Stones. As a result, he has never seen any reason to hide his religious affiliation and is proud to openly celebrate his faith - much to the shock and concern of many of the villagers. He has been the High Wizard of the Order for several decades and has no plans to step down from this position.

27: "I have been a member of the Pluckley Pagans throughout all of my adult life but now I am in my twilight years, it has come to mean so much more to me than a simple belief. Holly and I are the oldest members of the Order and I believe we are both ready to return to the soil from whence we came. Perhaps it was simply Wilbur's time too. When the God and Goddess call upon us on our final day, then we must hear the call. I do however wish that the God and Goddess saw fit to alleviate my arthritis. It is at the point where I can no longer even lift a pencil in my trembling hand!"

28: It may have appeared that Bludger Baxter was killing the residents of Pluckley Green as part of an ancient sacrifice ritual, but the pub landlord was away from the village when Penelope Gannet was murdered. You can either guess again or go to THE GHOST: THE SOLUTION at the back of this book to learn the full story...

29: "Now, I'm not one to gossip but I'll tell you why my neighbour Della Dempsey did not leave her house all night. It is because shortly after 8pm Lord Pendergast knocked on her door - and the pair were occupied all evening. The walls along this terrace are paper thin, so I think you can guess what I mean! Della acts as if she is pure as the driven snow. Let me tell you this, it is not even the first time Lord Pendergast has spent the night with her - I feel so sorry for the Second Lady Pendergast."

30: "I was looking at Mrs Tipple when Lord Pendergast got shot. I have been dreading this eviction. I dislike all of them but this one felt particularly dire. When I was a nipper, Mrs Tipple was my English teacher. She believed I could amount to something

- she was the only person who ever thought I could. When the shot was fired I was begging her to put the gun down and to leave the property quietly. She was just so upset - I hate to think what she must think of me now. She had such high hopes for me and all it amounted to was spending the past two years as a servant to a tyrant, running around the village, making people homeless and waving a gun around. I hope he doesn't survive!" *To check Lenny's gun, go to entry **251**.*

31: The wardrobe in Room 1 contains two changes of clothes and a bag of digging tools. The back panel of the wardrobe sounds hollow, as if there is empty space behind it.

32: The filing cabinet has alphabetised records of each of Scott Mallard's clients. The file concerning Dorian and Sheila Moribund contains their last will and testaments. As the couple had no children, Sheila named her husband as the sole benefactor following her death - and then a local charity should her husband die before her. Dorian had done the same for his wife but should she die before him, his wealth and his business would go to whoever was the most senior assistant at the funeral home at that time.

33: Dressed in his white, hooded robe, Holly Merryfair was struck once in the forehead, possibly with a rifle as there are no footprints in the snow (other than the victim's own), suggesting that the shooter was quite some distance away. He now lies on the blood soaked snow in the centre of the stone circle. Quite astonishingly, he still has a faint pulse - at 92 years of age, the High Wizard manages to surprise (and infuriate) many with his absolute refusal to die. *For further information about Holly Merryfair, go to entry **26**.*

34: "August Barley - men's size 9, wide, was at the cobblers first thing this morning. I carried out some repairs on his walking boots and we chatted for a while. He had plans to visit some of the locations he was writing about for his book on the history of Pluckley Green and also had some repairs to do on his farm. It seems that there had been an incident of vandalism there. The poor man had no idea that he had a maniac on his tail. I hope that Toby Tchotchke swings for this crime!"

35: "Can't the people of this village just enjoy one day of pleasure at the beach without it being tarnished by bloody murder? I was kept up late last night due to unforeseen and rather harrowing business involving one of my parishioners and I was very much in the mood for a day of relaxing by the seaside! Everything had been going well until we entered the long tunnel. Dorothy was sat right next to me and let off an ear piercing scream as she was stabbed. Once the train left the tunnel and we saw what had happened, I immediately reached for the emergency chord and the train came to a halt. Who could do such a thing - and where did the knife which stabbed her go?" *To search the reverend's briefcase, go to entry **188**.*

36: The door to Crooked Cottage has been locked since the murder of Lucy Sparrow. One of the windows on the side of the house which faces the park has been smashed but the window is far too small for a person to climb through.

37: "I'm still in shock. Colin and I went fishing with him just this morning and we were all happy and excited because Dickon actually had plans to propose to Lana on this very day. He was nervous about it, so the pair of us were trying to give him encouragement. Poor Lana must be heartbroken."

38: "I was *livid* with Cuthbert Crookshank! For as long as anybody can remember there has only been one pub in Pluckley Green. Another pub would halve my business! I was so irate that I was yelling at the man on the stage and to prevent myself from thumping him, I had to leave the village hall via the back door and go for a pint at my pub. I don't think I've ever been so angry. Hopefully, now that he's dead, the plans for a second pub will have died with him!" *To check Bludger's alibi at the pub, go to entry **534**.*

39: "Well, I'm not one to gossip but… well, if truth be told I'm afraid I have nothing to gossip about Lucy Sparrow anyway. If anything, the only remarkable thing about that woman was how unremarkable she was - not a hint of scandal or secrets - just an ordinary person living an ordinary life. Crooked Cottage has been in her family for centuries but Lucy has been the first Sparrow to live there in living memory - you see, it is said that there is a curse upon the cottage and that any member of the Sparrow family who lives there will die an untimely death…"

40: The Reverend has attempted (and failed) at murder only once - when he tried to kill Lord Pendergast. None of those present at the wedding of "Miss Faversham" and Winston Lampeter is The Ghost. You can either guess again or go to THE GHOST: THE SOLUTION at the back of this book to learn the full story…

41: Gout is a painful inflammation of the joints - most commonly that of the big toe. It can be caused or aggravated by a poor diet or the overconsumption of alcohol. The swelling will often occur intermittently and will lessen with time. Sufferers may have to walk using a cane and pain can be alleviated by wearing shoes two sizes larger than the patient's usual measurement.

42: "It is a terrible shame about that young man but the attempt at life was clearly aimed at Cuthbert Crookshank. I don't think anybody even knew that Cuthbert had been routinely lending his car to Tommy Tomlinson until the crash this morning. Hopefully that will be enough of a signal to the chairman that the theme of the fete must be changed to something more traditional. The ghastly, crass and classless American theme would have bought shame upon the village! As for me, I was at my home last night with my wife and sons."

43: On the evening following the murder of Phineas Flitter, Mavis Davis paid an unexpected visit to the Second Lady Pendergast at her home. Word had reached the woman that Lady Pendergast had been attempting to hide a bruise around her eye. "*Please!*" Mavis pleaded with her. "You *must* leave your husband. My sister lived with a man who beat her and I encouraged her to stay to avoid the scandal. And now she is dead!"

44: The kitchen is a simple room with one window facing the street outside. There are two doors. One is the entrance to the kitchen from the street and the other is a backdoor which leads to an alley behind the funeral home. There is a large table in the centre of the room with wooden chairs around it.

45: This stone, which is made from a darker rock than the others, is known as the Demon Stone or the Cursed Stone. According to legend, the stone was once a demon who had been summoned to the heath by the High Wizard during his ceremony. The demon, along with all of the other sinners, was turned to stone by the Christian God. The stone is believed by many to be cursed and few villagers are brave enough to even touch it.

46: "As Peter Slender's most trusted and loyal friend, he has given me the keys to the tavern - so that I might enter the property if it is ever necessary. There is no need for keys to the rooms upstairs as there are no locks on the doors. Yesterday evening I had been chopping wood on my farm near the pub and decided I'd earned a pint, so I went to the Feathered Cap. Later that evening, I found myself eavesdropping on the conversation between Christopher Aurelius and Fenton Hughes. They were discussing something utterly preposterous. What they were saying was more fairytale than fact. It was as if the two men had lost their minds! After the evening at the pub, I retired to my farmhouse and did nothing more with my night but sleep."

47: "Most people in Pluckley Green enjoy the chitter-chatter of the birds in my pet shop but not Mr Miner. In fact, Humbert had lots to complain about here. The gerbils were too greedy, the goldfish were too lazy, the stick insects were too difficult to spot.

My pet shop has been here for more than 50 years and Humbert has been a thorn in my shoe for at least 20 of them! Putters' Pets has had a good few months of sales. Birds, fish, rodents have all been popular. Why, even a few days ago a lady bought a whipper snake. We don't sell many of those!"

48: Stanley Slavsky of the Pluckley Players is currently in the rehearsal stage of the latest play he is directing - an ambitious production of "An Inspector Calls" in which he himself will be playing all the roles. "Yes, Douglas Manville was here yesterday evening from 7pm until midnight. He volunteers his time and labour for free whenever we stage another play. He does so because of his love of theatre. I do believe he may be a budding thespian himself!"

49: The newspaper is the Pluckley Green Press. The front page is mostly concerned with the various murders which have struck the village in the past week. Evidently, the victim brought this newspaper from home, as the paperboy who delivered it wrote the man's address at the top of the page. *To visit the victim's home, go to entry 342.*

50: "Dorothy was a mean and rather spiteful old bat. She said some dreadful things to Colin and me - but that doesn't mean either one of us did away with her. I was desperately looking forward to a day by the sea - and a certain pub I'd heard stories about. Such a change from Pluckley Green!" *To inspect Alvin's pockets, go to entry 595.*

51: "I feel awful. You see, the party was my idea and I was the one who organised it, I even managed to get a discount at Pluckley Parties Supply Shop. I can't help but feel it's my fault - if it hadn't been for the party, that poor girl would still be alive." *To visit Pluckley Parties Supply Shop go to entry 371.*

52: The Finns live next door to Prudence Rosehip - or at least, they did when she was alive. The house is a delightful, thatched cottage which enjoys a stunning view of the surrounding countryside.

53: Cabin 2 is shared by Herb and Tessa Mudgens and is the second largest cabin on the boat. Most of the room is taken up by a double bed. Clothes have been neatly folded into a chest of drawers. The room is very neat and looks as if it hasn't been used much this morning.

54: "I was backstage and chatting to Thelwyn when it happened. Poor Christopher - but also poor Jane. The thing about the role of "the glamorous assistant" is that she is almost always just as talented and skilled as the magician himself. It was certainly true of Mesmerelda. Jane is a magician, a contortionist and an escapologist on top of being a master of misdirection. She was working just as hard on that stage as Captain Conjuro. That's the problem with being the assistant - all the effort but none of the limelight. I know Christopher's wife, Anita was worried about how much time he spent with Mesmerelda rehearsing but she need not have worried. Their relationship was purely professional - I should know as I was at most of their rehearsals too - Jane has been my girlfriend for two years!"

55: "As a member of the Ancient Order of Pluckley Pagans, nights of full moons are sacred nights and it is not uncommon for me to join Holly Merryfair at the Pluckley Stones for a ceremony. However, last night I retired to bed before midnight and slept the sleep of an exhausted man. This week has been busy as much of the village is still without running water following the storm. The only peculiar thing I have noticed is that my axe has gone missing from my toolshed. I was certain it was there the last time I checked." *To investigate Gerald's toolshed, go to entry 72.*

56: As always during the summer months, August Barley's hives are abuzz with activity as the busy bees turn pollen into honey - like the wonderful little alchemists they are. August moved to the farm ten years ago and his honey-making business has expanded greatly in that time. The apiary now consists of six hives which operate like miniature factories, producing huge quantities of honey to be enjoyed across Somerset. There is no sign of August anywhere and his hives show no sign of being visited by him today.

57: Immediately behind the stage is an open area with tables where props are held. Alongside these are racks of costumes on hangers which actors are expected to find between acts - with the assistance of stagehand Colin Carnegie. All of the prop daggers and knives used in the play are theatrical ones with harmless, retractable blades. The rack of clothes features costumes from previous plays, including "Lysistrata" - in which the cast wore black robes and theatrical masks.

58: "Peter Pickle was a rather strange man. He arrived yesterday evening and asked about lodgings for the night. Later on I saw him in the bar. He sat in the shadows, away from the glow of the fireplace and managed to make one pint of beer last all evening. He must have left very early because I saw no sign of him this morning. He wore large spectacles and had a rather extravagant, bushy moustache."

59: There are two entrances/exits from the stage to backstage and two sets of steps which lead to the body of the hall where the audience will sit during a performance. There is a small pool of blood around the corpse of Leon Cribbage. He has been stabbed in the back with a dagger.

60. Lord Pendergast was not the only person in Pendergast Manor to be conducting an extramarital affair. Unbeknownst to him, his own wife and her maid, Mona Prim, had fallen in love and desperately wanted to build a life together. This abiding love was cemented earlier this year when Lady Pendergast gifted Mona a silver watch. The only way that the pair could truly be together would be for the abusive and tyrannical Lord Pendergast to die. So when Lady Oxania Pendergast's plan to poison her husband failed, she asked Mona to murder him that evening - and Mona did not hesitate. Disguised under a hooded cloak, she took a shotgun to Pendergast Manor in the dead of night - and blasted Lord Pendergast's head to pieces. Now with Lucien dead, Oxania and Mona are free to live their lives in the manor - raising Oxania's two sons. The murder will become yet another secret the two women share together.

61: Crooked Cottage is no more! The oldest house in the village is now just a smouldering crater in the centre of the village. The explosion was so huge that it upturned nearby cars and blasted out the windows of surrounding properties. There is nothing left of Reginald Sole except for a few charred bones which are strewn across the street.

62: "I had my back to Wilbur and my gaze was cast to the sky when he was murdered. I heard the scream and when I turned, he was dead at the Demon Stone. I hope that this does not mean a return to the bad old days. According to legend, many centuries ago the Pluckley Stones were the scene of human sacrifice to the God and Goddess. Each of the five stones would require a sacrifice throughout the year. I have no idea if the myths are based on truth but nowadays our sacrifices come in the form of offerings; we leave a book at the Reader Stone, a bottle of port at the Drunkard Stone. Much more respectable. I cannot imagine who would have had anything against poor Wilbur."

63: Jessica has a noticeable pink handprint upon her cheek - which she refuses to elaborate on. "It was no surprise to us that we were elected the May King and Queen. Our wedding was such a romantic affair that we captured the hearts of the village. Yes, Jack and I were courting for a while last year but then I met Kevin and we were married within months! The party had been a dream until the murder. Kevin was a perfect gentleman of course. Taking everyone's coats and jackets at the door and fetching me drinks whenever I was thirsty."

64: "My poor father! It is such a tragedy that he died due to an unforeseeable accident! The business was doing exceptionally well and he had plans to relocate to London. I was excited by the move and this new opportunity for Manville Builders Ltd. I suppose my father's business belongs to me now? My first decision shall be to fire that good-for-nothing Michael Doncaster! Last night, I spent my evening at the village hall. I was building sets for the Pluckley Players latest production". *To visit the Pluckley Players, go to entry **48**.*

65: Behind the circus big top - near to where Leonard's lions are kept in a cage - the performers' caravans are parked in a circle. These horse-drawn caravans serve as the performers' means of travel, their living quarters and their dressing rooms. Leonard's caravan looks perfectly normal and nothing seems out of place.

66: There is nothing out of the ordinary or unusual about Holly Merryfair's ceremonial dagger.

67: "My husband works… I mean worked as a tree surgeon. From time to time he is called upon late at night when a tree is in imminent danger to a property. Last night I got home just before 11pm - I am currently starring in the lead role of the Pluckley Players' Hedda Gabler and last night was my third performance. After getting home and discovering that my husband was not here, I went to bed upstairs. There seemed to be a terrible row going on at the Green's house next door at that time but I was so tired that I promptly fell asleep. The next thing I knew, it was morning and Paulette Green was tearfully knocking on my door. She then shared the terrible news. How shall I ever cope? My husband had his shortcomings but I loved him dearly." *To check Juno's story with Stanley Slavsky of the Pluckley Players, go to entry **254**.*

68: "Don't worry about us. In fact, I do believe that the Pluckley Green Ghost Club will continue to thrive without our lead investigator. In fact, we are likely to become even more prominent in paranormal circles without a disbeliever in charge. Every creaking floorboard or flickering candle had a rational explanation in her eyes - where's the fun in that?! Obviously Arabella's rational mind wasn't enough to save her because, believe it or not, I saw the ghost! I was on the roof of the east tower and saw the Grey Lady through the windows of the north tower - the tallest tower - I couldn't see what happened when she reached the roof as the tower is so much taller than the others but I saw Arabella fall and heard the sickening sound of her hitting the courtyard. I do believe that the Grey Lady herself may have murdered our leader!"

69: "I must be honest, my sister and I were very worried about what might be contained in Phineas Flitter's latest gossip column. On the night of the storm a few months ago, something happened and the pair of us faced no consequences for it. I'd hate for something as dreadful as that to become public knowledge. According to rumours, his latest column was set to be his most explosive yet - although it seems as if the only thing that was explosive was his cigar… My sister and I had just reached the park by the riverbank after a woodland stroll. We settled down on the grass and then the cigar detonated. Neither of us have spoken to Phineas today."

70: There are six red apples bobbing around Sheila's head in the bucket of water. There is nothing unusual about the apples, the bucket or the water.

71: Dickon was a healthy young man in his twenties with no known health conditions and yet he died in an instant as certainly as if he'd been struck by lightning. His body lays among the crocuses with the engagement ring upon his finger."

72: The unlocked toolshed is in sight of the mire. There is no sign of Gerald's axe to be found. There is a pot of half-used phosphorous paint in the corner of the room. *To ask Gerald about the paint, go to entry **518**.*

73: "Charles Willis was indeed at the church all morning. He asked for my advice in helping to quell the dispute between neighbours but unfortunately, I could offer no solutions."

74: According to legend, this stone was once a dancer who performed a provocative dance upon the heath - so that she might entrance the men of the village. For the sin of dancing on a Sunday, she was turned to stone by the Christian God. There is a fresh, still warm bullet embedded in the stone.

75: In the damp earth around Doctor White's body there is one set of bootprints which match the boots he is wearing. There is another set of bootprints which lead from a nearby bush to the spot where the doctor was standing. These bootprints then lead back to the footpath. The prints are from a medium sized walking boot.

76: "Oh thank heavens! It is such a relief to read that note as I thought I was the only who wanted to get the hell out of this useless club! The Fearless Five haven't solved a proper mystery in years and all we do now is traipse around the English countryside looking for something to do. I'm almost nineteen and still get bossed around by my older brother and I'm sick to my back teeth with it! Nowadays, we're just trying to re-capture those brief days of glory we once enjoyed. I just want to work in banking and get a mortgage!"

77: The door to the south tower is in the grand hall. The south tower consists of little more than a stone, spiral staircase which opens to a roof which is surrounded by ramparts. The tops of the east and west towers are visible from there but the top of the north tower is not as it is much taller than the others.

78: "What happened was awful, but at least people got to hear my singing before the murder. I was simply mesmerising! Penelope was standing on one foot and pirouetting around like a spinning top. Then she just dropped down dead! Arrow right through her neck. I imagine that the pageant will be cancelled this year and as the reigning championing I shall be declared this year's winner by default?"

79: "Bertrand Mallard has been coming to the Bloodied Axe for years but I have never once seen him take even a sip of alcohol. He was a dedicated teetotaller. I knew him well and he was always in good spirits - even though he suffered poorly from back pains. Apparently it got so bad he had taken to sleeping in his armchair at night."

80: The kitchen is a small room adjacent the dining room. There is nothing unusual about it. There is a waste bin under the sink. *To look in the bin go to entry 585.*

81: Perry Gulch enjoys reading "King Lear" not just for the story and beautiful writing but because the character of The Fool - much like Perry himself - is the only one to speak the truth at all times.

82: The ring is a simple, yet handsome gold band. There is nothing about it which seems unusual and no poison or any other substance has been painted upon it.

83: "I am still furious about the fete's theme this year. America? Does nobody believe in English values anymore? Last night, my mother unwisely took me to see the latest abomination from the Pluckley Players. I am studying "Hamlet" at my school - incidentally I am head girl of Unity Mitford Girls' School, I don't know if I have mentioned that. My father has learned from past mistakes with the Pluckley Players and chose to spend the evening alone at home."

84: "Phineas Flitter smoked a brand of cigar called Woodsman Robusto. I had to get them delivered just for him. He purchased two packs of them from me last week but I also sold a lone Woodsman Robusto cigar to a young woman. This might sound barmy of me but she was the spitting image of Genevieve Jensen. I'd seen photographs of her in the newspaper but for obvious reasons it couldn't have been!"

85: Holly Merryfair was born and raised within the Pagan world and both of his parents were notable members of the organisation. With no children of his own and the 92 year old refusing to name a successor, the usually harmonious Ancient Order of Pluckley Pagans has become a hotbed of rivalries, gossip and speculation as to what will happen when the High Wizard is no more - all of which will no doubt continue now that Holly has survived the attempt upon his life.

86: The real Miss Faversham has been dead since March of this year. The woman who has taken her name, home and life is her maid Genevieve Jensen. As a child, Genevieve always dreamed of a better life but opportunities were few and far between. She had to settle for a life of servitude to a tyrannical and wicked woman and to abandon all hope of a life filled with adventure. Becoming Miss Faversham has given Genevieve a second chance at life and it is a chance she intends to fully embrace.

87: Larry Finch is losing a lot of blood and has already fallen unconscious. As she waits for the ambulance to arrive, Jenny Carter is holding a tea towel against the gushing wound on Larry's neck. The wound is alarmingly deep and death seems almost guaranteed. *To search the pockets of Larry's jacket, go to entry* **260**.

88: The trivia quiz which is held at the Bloodied Axe Tavern every New Year's Eve is regarded as the toughest and most fiendish in all the county. Teams (who are limited to no more than five members per team) travel across Somerset to compete and yet nobody has been able to win against the Pluckley Bird Brains. Teams do not enter the pub quiz for financial gain - the top prize is temporary ownership of a trophy, a free pint at the bar and a day trip to Pluckley Castle. The real prize for all involved is the prestige and admiration which result from winning.

89: Most of the body of Lucy Sparrow is sitting upright in a chair beside a writing desk, whilst her severed head rests upon her lap. It is a hideous and terrifying sight which has evidently been staged to maximise the horror for anyone witnessing the scene. There is almost no blood present in Crooked Cottage, suggesting that Lucy was murdered somewhere away from her home and her body was brought here.

90: Dickon is wearing a purple velvet jacket, which he obviously reserves for special occasions. In the right pocket there is a jewellery box. Inside the box there is a gold engagement ring. Inscribed inside the ring are the words *"My wife. I will love you until the stars turn cold."*

91: The section of code Miss Faversham has brought with her reads *"ZXC=TUV"*.

92: The dark and shadowy corner where the killer hid is near the end of the station platform. There is nothing on the ground and no trace of the murderer.

93: The judge who presided over the trial of Silas Marsten is named Jan Treagle and may be second only to Lord Pendergast to claim the title of "Most Hated Man in Pluckley Green", owing to his wicked, callous nature which favours the wealthy and privileged in all of his rulings.

94: "Good heavens! I knew Lucy to be a good and caring neighbour but I do believe she liked to keep to herself. She was a rather quiet lady. I hadn't seen her in more than a week so I assumed she must have been away visiting friends or family. I haven't seen anyone coming or going from Crooked Cottage, nor did I hear anything - and that includes screams of bloody murder!"

95: "Miss Faversham is not my mother and has never pretended to be. She is a tyrant and nothing more, I haven't even seen her all morning. She raised me only because she needed a plaything to toy with. Then she grew tired of me and now wants me to rot in this house alongside her. She will not even let me listen to my records - even with the volume turned low - and will hardly ever let me go outside. I was abandoned as a baby outside the church and for some reason it was decided that it would be good for that harridan to raise me. This morning I awoke to the sounds of screaming as yet another row broke out. Then there was a smash like china breaking and a scream of pain from the maid - Miss Faversham must have scolded her again. I do hope Genevieve is safe."

96: "While the other members of the Pluckley Green Ghost Club explored the four towers, I was left downstairs in the grand hall. After snooping around the room for a while, I sat at the table and waited for the investigation to be over. I was facing the door which led to the entrance chamber and I can assure you that nobody came through the door or entered the hall whilst I was there. As the newest member of the club, I am always at the bottom of the pecking order when it comes to investigations. Arabella *always* gets to visit the most sensational or spooky locations herself - even though she simply dismisses anything paranormal she experiences there. I'm usually left to explore the most boring places with the least amount of paranormal activity reported. As always, I saw nothing inexplicable or strange this evening, although I did hear Arabella scream as she fell from the tower!"

97: Bill's hide contains a pad of ornate sketches of birds enjoying their natural habitat, as well as an easel which holds a half-finished watercolour of the estuary. The oblong storage box in his hide contains nothing but art supplies.

98: "I believe I was the first onto the stage after I heard Thalia scream and I saw Leon collapse. As a stage hand it is my duty to pass props and costumes to the actors in the dark of backstage - with the help of my trusty torch. It had been much like any other rehearsal - and just like any other rehearsal, Thalia was strutting about like a prima donna and being unreasonable. She was standing in the wings at stage right throughout Macbeth's soliloquy. Just as Leon took to the stage, I am certain that I heard someone rifling through the clothes rack - as if they were looking for something but in the darkness I couldn't see who they were. As for me, when I'm not helping out with the Pluckley Players, I like to think I have a good eye for fashion and hope to be a designer in London one day."

99: Mabel's family home was destroyed during the Brigstowe Blitz - which also killed much of her family. She moved to Pluckley Green shortly after the war to begin work at the vicarage - and so that she could watch her daughter grow under the care of Miss Faversham. She had left the baby on the doorstep of the church in 1943 (as she had fond memories of childhood holidays in the village). It was decided by the parish council that the wealthy but childless Miss Faversham would offer the foundling girl a loving home and upbringing. They did not know that Miss Faversham was a wicked, vindictive tyrant.

100: Gerald Ratchett is the village's most trusted plumber. Day or night, he will be at the scene of any busted water pipe or an overflowing drain. His father, Gabe Ratchett (who was earlier this year, crushed beneath the weight of a falling church bell) was a plumber before him and taught him all he needed to know about the trade. Gerald's work necessitates him being inside the homes of many of the villagers and has given him unfettered access to their private lives. Over the years he has spied many sordid secrets throughout the genteel village of Pluckley Green.

101: "I desperately wanted to visit the standing stones on the solstice, just to see what all the fuss was about. People say such crazy things about human sacrifice so I was very disappointed to discover that all the Pagans do is chant in a circle and shout at the sky! To think, I snuck out of Stasis House after my bedtime just for this nonsense! I was looking at Minerva towards the end of the ceremony - I have thoughts and inklings about her. She was standing next to the landlord of the Bloodied Axe Tavern and both of them had taken down the hoods of their cloaks and were looking upwards with their arms outstretched. From behind the bush I couldn't see anyone else. I was getting very bored and then I heard a woman scream... Now, if you don't mind, I am close to finishing decoding this letter and would like to get back to the task." *To look at Esther's notes on the code, go to entry **337**.*

102: Lana's lipstick is a muted crimson colour. She purchased the tube from the Pluckley corner shop. It has not been tampered with and no substance or poison has been applied to it.

103: "This week it was my turn to buy the box of doughnuts. We take it in turns because it is more fair that way. I purchased five doughnuts from the bakery this afternoon - Mavis is on a diet and Miss Faversham does not care for them. I arrived at Penelope's home at 7pm precisely. I was the first of the guests to arrive and put the box of doughnuts in the kitchen, which is where they stayed until 9pm, when they were brought to the dining room by Penelope for all of us to enjoy - my favourites are the custard ones! I must be honest when I say I was no friend of Beverley Potter. That vile woman said awful things about my fiancée Sebastian and had refused to attend our upcoming wedding. I am not the least bit sad that she has passed away…" *To visit the bakery where Daphne bought the doughnuts, go to entry* **667.**

104: There is a tree in the front garden of the cottage. In the past, Bertrand Mallard allowed children to climb it after school. Freshly carved into the bark of the trunk of the tree are the words "I AM THE GHOST AND I HAVE CLAIMED MY FOURTH VICTIM".

105: "I don't even really know why I'm here. Every year the fete organisers choose the pageant's judging panel from the village "elite" but every so often they like to toss in a commoner like me - just to make it seem fair and unbiased. To be honest, I rather wish I hadn't agreed as I've been bored throughout. I wasn't even watching the ballet as I got distracted by a honey buzzard which was flying high overhead. As I was gazing upwards I saw the arrow - directly above me and darting at a tremendous speed towards the stage." *For further information about Jeremy Trumble, go to entry* **209.**

106: In the dead woman's handbag there is a half-eaten tube of mints, a small makeup kit with a mirror and a writing pen filled with green ink.

107: The latches on all of the windows around the cottage have been glued shut from the outside with superglue. Whoever did this must have taken quite some time and evidently did not want to allow Bertrand any hope of escaping.

108: "When we arrived at the park, I saw Rowf and was hoping that friendly dog would come over to say hello but unfortunately, he was distracted by the smell of something around Phineas' jacket. A few minutes later, I was looking at Rowf just as the explosion happened and my mother - Mabel Witherspoon - shielded my eyes so I didn't see what was left of that journalist. Thankfully, I have no secrets and nothing to hide, so I wasn't the least bit concerned about that newspaper column!"

109: The avid birdwatcher and conservationist was a member of the judging panel for the beauty contest when Penelope Gannet was murdered. He saw the arrow pass overhead and therefore is not The Ghost. You can either guess again or go to THE GHOST: THE SOLUTION at the back of this book to learn the full story…

110: Helena lays dead at the foot of the Watcher Stone. She is dressed in her white robes. Her ceremonial mask is beside her on the ground. *To inspect the mask, go to entry* **544.**

111: Randall Jorgens is currently on the front desk of the police station. "Last night was very quiet here - rather boring in fact. It was so slow that I suggested Pierce Green leave earlier than scheduled, at 10pm rather than midnight. He left promptly after that and, as expected, the rest of the evening was entirely uneventful."

112: "The character of John Trangle - the heartless and villainous judge of the Piddly Glen mysteries is such a slanderous caricature that I once sought legal advice to sue Cutlass. I am not ashamed to say that I am glad that there will be no more books assassinating my character! As for me, I have spent all of this morning far away from the opening ceremony so that I do not risk meeting that author face to face!"

113: Alastair's pistol is fully loaded with six bullets in the chamber. It is cold and has not been fired recently.

114: August Barley's diary helpfully lists his engagements for the day by time: *"9AM - Boot repairs at the cobblers. 10AM - Visit the caves for research. Midday - Lunch at the Bloodied Axe. 2PM - Repair the old well bucket. 3PM - Visit the Western Woods for research. 4PM - Beekeeping demonstration for Beatrice Beauregard. 6PM - Dinner at Jan Treagle's house."*

115: Scott is dressed as Dracula. "Dorian Moribund did a tremendous job last month with my father's funeral. Nothing can bring my dear father back - and the pain of knowing that his killer is still out there and walking the streets of Pluckley Green is an endless torment - but I knew I could rely on Dorian to give him the sendoff he deserves. He really is the best in the business, although I don't quite know how he manages it - he is notorious for always leaving things to the very last minute! I was working at my office earlier this evening and had to leave in a hurry to make it to the party on time. When I arrived, Atlas, Scott and Stanhope were already outside the funeral home and Mavis was beating on the door and trying to force her way inside. Dorian was walking up the street with a case of wine in his arms. Such an awful shame for all involved. *To visit Scott's office, go to entry **193**.*

116: Larry Finch has served as the village postman for more than forty years. Jovial, friendly and earnest, the much-loved member of the community is also in a unique position. As postman he is privy to all kinds of secrets - who is sending love letters to whom, who is in financial difficulties with the bank. However, Larry regards his job with utmost respect and guards each of the villagers' secrets with his silence. It has also led to the postman developing a deep-seated distrust of many of his villagers - which explains why he keeps his home locked and secured at all times.

117: Bernard Baird is, posthumously, one of the most decorated soldiers in Pluckley Green. For his service to his nation - and for making the ultimate sacrifice during the Second World War - the man is regarded as a true hero who died saving many lives. He was known to be a praiseworthy husband and father.

118: Perry's corkscrew is much the same as it always has been. There is nothing unusual about it.

119: Lester Pratt is dead. His body lays on its back upon the floor of his hall. He is dressed in pyjamas and a dressing gown. His face is fixed in an expression of agonised shock. It is not apparent how he died but there are two small pin-prick holes on the palm of his left hand. There is an empty tube of salted peanuts on the floor beside him. *To inspect the tube of peanuts, go to entry **513**.*

120: The clothes are the kind of overalls you'd expect a tree surgeon to wear. Benjamin Hellman's name has been stitched into the lining. In one of the pockets is a handwritten note, it reads: *"Tonight must be the night when we finally succumb to our urges. Come to my door at 8pm, please. All I think of is you! P. X"*

121: On the ground directly outside of the window, a small pistol has been dropped. It is the same kind of handgun which several villagers own for protection. There is a large bush outside the window in which somebody could easily hide.

122: Judge John Treagle is a feared and hated man throughout the village - indeed, throughout the county. He has never been afraid to let his innate snobbery interfere with his sentencing and will always show leniency towards wealthy, educated or upper class criminals, whilst subjecting poor or lower class offenders to the most severe of punishments for even the smallest of crimes. When he sentenced Toby Tchotchke to a short stay in a minimal security prison, it was widely seen as an act of leniency based on the fact that the double-murderer was a learned man.

123: Perry Gulch was once celebrated as a hero for his unwavering loyalty to the nation during the Second World War. As a soldier, he took part in conflicts around Europe and was heavily decorated for his service. However, upon his return to England Perry Gulch struggled to find work and was haunted by the memories of what he had witnessed. As a result, he took to the bottle and gradually slid into homelessness and alcoholism. To much of the village he is seen as an embarrassing nuisance and is likely to be barred from the Bloodied Axe Tavern any day now. He is often seen sleeping on benches around Pluckley Green - always with a bottle by his side and a well-thumbed paperback copy of "King Lear" serving as his pillow. He has sold most of his wartime medals to pay for his addiction.

124: The grand hall is a huge banqueting hall with a high, vaulted ceiling and an ostentatious dining table which is laden with candelabras. There are no places in the room in which anything could be reliably hidden.

125: Mabel is diligently cleaning the headstones and clearing away the chunks of Reginald Sole which have landed in the graveyard of St Julian on the Edge church. One grave has fresh, white roses upon it. The grave is for a woman named Katherine Sole (1910-1954).

126: A note has been folded and placed between the first and second pages of the reptile book, it reads: *"The third digit of the code is the number of pubs in Pluckley Green"*.

127: Pluckley Green has used the same maypole for over one hundred years. There is nothing unusual about it - except for the dead body dangling from it.

128: The corpse of Benjamin Hellman is mounted on a pole and faces the Green and Hellman homes. He is in a terrible state. His eyes have been pecked away by crows - as have his lips and tongue. It is not immediately clear how the man died but upon closer inspection, he has a deep knife wound in the middle of his back. The man is dressed in the same tattered clothes which were once worn by the scarecrow.

129: "My sister and I have lived together since her divorce last year. Jarvis was a good, kind man but grief can sometimes be too huge for even a marriage to contain. I have lived on my narrowboat on the canal since becoming a widow during the war - which is why we sought shelter during the storm this night. The soup was delicious but evidently not to Mr Marsten's taste as it promptly killed him. Oh well, I suppose when you're as rich as him just a taste of commoners' food can finish you off. I assisted Mabel during the evening but was not involved in preparing or serving the soup. Neither was my sister. I wonder how it is that we all ate the same soup yet he was the only one to die?"

130: "I was passing by the Bloodied Axe after an early evening visit to the Pluckley Stones and saw Larry stumbling towards the pub. I was going to joke that he must have started his New Year's Eve drinking early but then I saw the blood... At the standing stones I did not see anything unusual but I did pass Bludger - who had also chosen to enjoy the evening with a walk."

131: The name of the Bloodied Axe Tavern and the motive of the serial killer who will come to be known as "The Ghost" are connected.

132: After a thorough search of rows A-C, there is nothing unusual or suspicious about any of the first three rows of audience seating.

133: "I arrived earlier this morning to help Agnes pack the last of her meagre possessions. How can a man be so cruel? Agnes missed just one payment and he evicts her without question. What truly sickens me is that Lord Pendergast seems to *enjoy* making people suffer - it is all just a game for him, other people's lives always have been. When I heard the gunshot, I was looking at Mr McDonald across the road. Poor man is almost blind but I shall be taking him to the hospital on Monday for his cataract operation." *For more information about Mabel Witherspoon, go to entry **223**.*

134: The dining room/kitchen is a small space with a window along one wall and a skylight in the ceiling. There is a round table with chairs around it. A map has been unfurled on the table and is held in place with paperweights. There are dirty cereal bowls in the sink. There are several thin knives in a drawer below the sink.

135: "I was out for the evening last night with my boyfriend Heathcliff Mandelbrot. The pair of us have been seeing each other for quite some time and he took me for a romantic autumn stroll along the canal path. I recall seeing Wilma Rogers and her sister Daisy Doyle in a houseboat. Poor Daisy seemed awfully distressed! Heathcliff walked me to my door for 10pm and then left. I went to bed shortly afterwards but was awoken at 4am by that dreadful explosion. It rocked the whole house and destroyed the windows. I thought at first that it been an H-bomb! I looked out of my shattered bedroom window and saw a crater where Crooked Cottage used to stand." *To speak to Heathcliff Mandelbrot, go to entry* **10.**

136: "I can't say I'll miss Prudence one bit. She's a nasty, fork-tongued woman who has caused nothing but misery for her neighbours. My wife and I are unfortunate enough to live next door to her and she revels in being mean and unpleasant to everyone. That said, I didn't kill her! As a matter of fact, work has taken me away from the village for quite considerable amounts of time these past two months. I suspect it is the work of The Ghost - in which case, I would gladly shake the hand of whoever he or she is and say thank you!" *To visit Dante and Wendy Finn's house, go to entry* **52.**

137: "Wilbur was to my direct left during the ceremony. When I was gazing skywards I did not see or hear anything untoward until the scream. I have known and liked Wilbur for many years. Like me, he always liked to keep his involvement with the Order a secret - unlike some people I could mention. People make assumptions about Pagans. We are peaceful people who simply believe that nature itself is a conscious spirit."

138: The entrance chamber to the castle keep is a rather bare, unfurnished room where the doors to the north and east towers can be found. There is nowhere in the entrance hall where anything could be reliably hidden.

139: The hedgerow is spattered with white icing and sponge. Miniature figures of a bride and groom have been cast aside on the ground.

140: The head girl of Unity Mitford School for Girls and four-time red rosette winning Somerset Junior Trials dressage champion may have the hate in her heart required to become a serial killer but she and her mother were away from the village in India when Larry Finch was murdered. You can either guess again or go to THE GHOST: THE SOLUTION at the back of this book to learn the full story…

141: "I don't know what came over me when I grabbed my late husband's gun. This cottage has been my home for decades and I suppose I just panicked. I did not fire the gun though, of that I am certain. Mabel was trying to calm me down and I was about to drop the weapon when I heard the shot. I had been looking at young Lenny Goon. Believe it or not, that man has the heart of a poet." *To check Agnes Tipple's gun, go to entry* **20.**

142: "My wife and I have never had any interest in sport and yet without fail trivia quizzes will have a round on the subject. That is why we thought it was prudent to learn something on the matter. After the gunshot rang out I immediately ran to Wilma - she was screaming and Eustace was dead. From a humanitarian perspective it is of course a tragedy but every cloud has a silver lining. A chain is only as strong as its weakest link and Eustace was without a doubt the weakest link in our quiz team. I think we already know who is best to replace him."

143: Prudence's garden is overgrown with weeds and littered with various balls which have been accidentally kicked or batted over the wall. There is a row of rapidly growing bushes along the eastern edge of her garden. In the shed there is a large collection of tools. Her garden enjoys a beautiful view of the countryside to the west.

144: "I was working a shift at the police station in Brigstowe last night. I was scheduled to work until midnight so I wasn't home until gone 1am. Benjamin Hellman has always been a good neighbour and I have never had any trouble from him. I have no idea who could mean him any harm." *To check Pierce's alibi with the police, go to entry **111**.*

145: Jack Quick is young, healthy man - albeit a rather scrawny one. It would not have required a great deal of strength to overpower him. The fingermarks around his throat suggest that he was strangled to death and then hung from the maypole with ribbons tied around his neck. He hangs about a foot above the floor and there is a sticky, sweet smelling liquid dripping from his face. *To check the pockets of his jacket, go to entry **468**.*

146: As well as playing cricket as part of the same team for many years, Bertrand Mallard and Larry Finch have been good friends for as long as either of them can remember. They spent much of their time together enjoying evenings at the Bloodied Axe Tavern.

147: On the afternoon of New Year's Eve, Esther decided to begin reading the book Reverend Amos Harper had gifted her as a Christmas present. It was a book about the folklore, myths and legends of Somerset. The book was written some years ago by the Tchotchke Triplets.

148: "I am simply enraptured by Conrad Cutlass. In fact, you could call me his number one fan! Sadly, the membership of the fan club has been dwindling but us loyal devotees still get excited for each new instalment of the Piddly Glen Mysteries! I met him first thing this morning. I was dazzled that he even remembered my name or wanted to talk to his biggest fan. There was a lot of coming and going in the village hall as things were getting arranged. Then the ceremony began and... oh dear, it really is tragic to think there will be no more stories from my beloved author!"

149: "It is hard not to be offended that someone would try to murder me in my own home! Such a dreadful lack of manners. The evening had been going marvellously - particularly the fireworks display. I did get into a rather heated debate with Mr Baxter. The man is not pleased that I have been financially backing these plans for a second village pub. The argument blew itself out though. I went into the kitchen only once earlier. For some reason, my wife was pouring a sackful of perfectly good ice cubes into the sink. Right up until the attempted poisoning happened, I'd say the evening was going delightfully."

150: "The party had been a joy until we found Jack's body. It had started out well. I met Jack, Aria, Judy, Kevin and Jessica at the door and then we spent the rest of the evening dancing. At about 10pm I saw Jack reading a note. After that he just stared at me, smiling. It made me feel nauseated! I remember him being a letch earlier this year at my Valentine party. I have no idea who even invited him there as it was supposed to be a ladies only event!"

151: August Barley is dressed as an Egyptian mummy. "I have known Dorian and Sheila Moribund for many years and I also knew his father - Dorian Moribund Snr. My good friend, John Jones is the most senior assistant in the funeral home and knows Dorian and Sheila to be the kindest, most loyal couple he knows. Dorian would never do anything to harm his wife. Poor John, he suffers with his health and he really should have retired years ago. I arrived at the party at 7pm, just as the guests were rushing into the kitchen. Sheila was already dead by that point."

152: "I visited Nagatha at about 2pm, after I'd cleared the table. She was in good spirits - well, as good a spirit as an old horse her size can be. I gave her a pound of kibble and a sugar cube as her afternoon treat. She attempted a stroll around her paddock sometime afterwards but she looked woozy and unsteady on her hooves. At first I thought she was just being lazy but she almost had to drag herself back to her stable. That is where we found her collapsed."

153: Much of the courtyard is spattered with Arabella's blood. At the bottom of the tallest tower - the one from which Arabella fell - a long, dark wig has been wrapped up in a grey dress and tossed into a hedgerow, as if it were haphazardly thrown from the roof of the tower in an attempt to hide it in a hurry.

154: The Tchotchke brother has been stabbed through his neck but no weapon is present at the scene. The corpse of the man is in bed and wearing pyjamas. He has an expensive looking ring on his ring finger. The man's wallet (which contains no identification but a good deal of money) is untouched on the bedside table.

155: Jeremy's hide is a rather chaotic mess of scattered books on local wildlife and notes of sightings scrawled across loose pieces of paper. In an oblong storage box in the hut there is a collection of ordnance survey maps and a book of tide times.

156: "I suppose I have always been more invested in this past time than my husband. It is kind that he humours me and joins in though. I would dearly love for him to become the head of our little society but I fear that it is far too early to start enquiring about that?"

157: Cabin 1 is the largest of the three bedrooms on the boat but it is still a rather cramped space. A double bed takes up much of the room. On the bedside table, there is a copy of the book *"A History of Pluckley Green"* by August Barley - he successfully published his labour of love just two days ago. The cabin is the temporary bedroom of Karl and Sabrina Danvers. There is a small wardrobe in which the couple have hung a few of their clothes upon wire hangers and there is a pair of binoculars hanging from a hook on the wall. The only window in the room is built into the ceiling. There are two doors, one which leads to the corridor and the other leads to the shared bathroom.

158: Since the death of his wife two years ago, Harry has maintained a beautiful, traditional English cottage garden. It was his pride and joy, however, it was becoming rather overstuffed with bountiful flowers and he was eager to expand his land to accommodate them all.

159: "Now, I'm not one to gossip but… if you ask me, Sebastian Turner is not a man to be trusted. It's no secret that he's been seen several times with the church cleaner - and she was doing more than just dusting his mantel, if you know what I mean! Her husband must be distraught, people say he's taken to walking around the village late at night. Scandalous!" *To learn more about Mavis Davis, go to entry* **427.**

160: "Obviously, everybody knew that I was going to win the race - because that's what I always do, it's never even close. Of course it's partly due to my natural abilities but I also train far harder than anyone else. Even with a bad foot I was still the clear winner. Usually I lead right from the start but this year was a little different. Bruno was ahead of me until we started the approach to the Western Woods. He must have burned himself out from that initial push."

161: The basement of the Bloodied Axe Tavern is a rather small, cramped space with barely enough room to fit the many barrels of beer the pub requires to operate. In the floor, there is a trapdoor which leads to the web of tunnels which run beneath the village.

162: The meeting between Esther and Mabel Witherspoon at the standing stones went exceptionally well. So much so that once the tears had dried, the pair vowed to go away on holiday to Brigstowe together, so that they might become better acquainted with one another. They will be gone from the village for two weeks.

163: "My ex-husband's behaviour is no longer of any interest to me. I turned my back on him the moment I learned of his affair with that strumpet. I'm not in the least bit surprised that his womanising would lead to his downfall, nor am I surprised that the man was tacky enough to invite his date to Pluckley Green Park - me and he used to go there all of the time when we were courting."

164: "I shan't be able to get the image of that poor man being squashed like a tube of toothpaste out of my head. Still, when you think about what could have happened instead, I suppose you could think of it as being tremendous good fortune…"

165: The bed is a gruesome mess with blood soaked all the way down to the mattress. The axe has been tossed upon the sodden bedsheets - it too is drenched in blood. There is nothing beneath the bed.

166: "That vile Tchotchke man was spattered with blood when we found him in the Western Woods. He even had that bloodied butcher's knife in his hand! He may think of himself as a clever man but we found him camped out precisely where he was after the first murders back in January. It was August Barley who reported him to the police back then and that maniac murderer has been hellbent on revenge ever since!"

167: Crooked Cottage is without a shadow of a doubt, the oldest building in Pluckley Green. It was built sometime during the 11th century and there have always been strange stories about it being haunted or cursed. It is said that at some point it was used to store illegal goods - boats would bring barrels of rum up the river which were intended for Brigstowe, but the crew would secretly unload them at Pluckley Green and claim the cargo had been stolen by pirates. However, nobody has been able to explain how these smugglers would have been able to haul the barrels of rum from the river to Crooked Cottage without being spied by the villagers. Perhaps the stories are no more than legends.

168: At first glance, the wardrobe seems to contain only a change of clothes but upon further inspection, it is revealed that the back panel to the wardrobe is actually a door - opening to Room 1 and allowing free movement between the rooms.

169: The note sent to Esther appears to be a gibberish jumble of letters. Nevertheless, she has so far managed to decode: *"Your father was an American soldier. I met him in Brig…"* In the margin of the note, Esther has written *"ASD=KLM"*.

170: Reverend Amos Harper was born in Pluckley Green and has every intention of one day dying there too. A friend to all the village and a discreet ear to those in need, he has been the vicar of Pluckley Green for over 25 years. He is also somewhat blind to the affections of others - which is why he has remained oblivious to the fact that Mabel Witherspoon (his live-in cook) has been madly, desperately in love with him for many, many years.

171: Perhaps it is due to his prowess as a former bare-knuckle boxer that makes Bludger Baxter so invested in competitive events but he enjoys challenges of all sorts - be they of the body or mind.

172: Rowf is Lord Pendergast's loyal gun dog. Owing to years of training, Rowf is fearless around loud bangs and enjoys the smell of gunpowder.

173: The letter Humbert was in the midst of writing when he died was one of complaint (of course). In it, he opposed the construction of Tilly Millman's extension to her home on the grounds that it would spoil the view of the heath when viewed from Dorset Street.

174: The bookcase is laden with books. Lucy seems to have a particular interest in British folklore, nature and beekeeping. All of the books are in alphabetical order according to title, except for one - a book about British reptiles which seems conspicuously and intentionally out of place. *To look inside the book go to entry **126**.*

175: Judy Spiff and her mother Diana both detest British winters. On the day following the murder of Benjamin Hellman, Diana Spiff booked tickets so that her family could spend December in India.

176: The Pluckley Players production of Macbeth uses several daggers - all of which are props with retractable blades. However, the dagger in the back of Leon Cribbage is most definitely real. It is very ornate and has a gold handle.

177: The serial killer who murders under the guise of The Ghost was invited to the wedding reception but chose not to attend.

178: "Yes, I have blood on me but I promise it's not what it looks like! I was returning from the village hall - where I'd been dealing with some personal business - when I saw Larry Finch stumbling about on his doorstep. I thought he was simply looking for his keys but then I saw the blood and how rapidly he was turning pale. I tried to help him by stemming the blood-flow with my book - it's a trick I learned from my time in the army. The poor guy was delirious and pushed me away. He then wobbled along to the pub - which was wise of him as there is a phone in there." *To visit the village hall, go to entry **338**.*

179: The latex gloves are very stretchy and could easily fit any size of hand. Their stretchiness also means that taking fingerprints from them would be impossible. They are freely available from Brigstowe Royal Infirmary but can also be purchased from the pharmacy in Pluckley Green.

180: Poor Nagatha rests on her side in the hay of her stable. Her breathing is laboured but regular. The reverend has placed a warm, damp cloth upon her head. She has vomited up the last meal she ate.

181: The letter reads: *"My dear Daisy, I have dreadful news for you. The man you are engaged to marry is a terrible monster. He beat and later murdered his first wife. He does not deserve you. He does not deserve to live. I wish I had done something to save her but now it is too late."*

182: "I do enjoy my little games but not when they end in cold blooded murder! Poor Charlotte has been my friend for many years. She was a good woman but also impulsive with her heart and made poor decisions. I was at the foot of the staircase when I heard the gunshot go off. I knew at once something terrible must have occurred." *To learn more about Lady Pendergast, go to entry **336**.*

183: "I was not in the library at the moment the gun went off as I had gone to the lavatory. I'm sure the girl at the table saw me, as did Stacey on the reception. I complained to her about one of the books being in the wrong place in the art section - this never would have happened when Lucy Sparrow was alive! Unlike other members of the Pluckley Green Brights, I have no areas of weakness in my knowledge so intended to spend the afternoon drifting between various sections of the library - starting with art." *To check the misplaced book in the art section, go to entry **698**.*

184: "It was fun while it lasted but I was under no illusion with Marvin. Married men will promise you the world but when it comes down to it, none of them will leave their wives for their mistresses. It was me who broke things off. As soon as he was fired from his job and no longer had the income to keep me in the lifestyle to which I had become accustomed, I moved onto the next wealthy man I could find. People still blame me for what happened during that operation, although I hardly think it's my fault for keeping the man up all night!"

185: The archaeological finds from the triplets' recent Glastonbury excavation are in a tin box and are an unsorted mix of wooden and stone trinkets. The items do not appear to be valuable and a hand-written inventory of the items reveals that none of the Tchotchke brothers' finds are missing.

186: Outside of the village hall there is a gravel path which runs from the entrance of the hall to the carpark. It also passes the hall's exit door (which opens onto the backstage). Dumped unceremoniously amongst the shrubbery at the side of the path is a long, black robe and a theatrical mask.

187: "I left the ghost club at the castle at 6pm and spent the evening in my cottage with my cat. I was very excited to meet the members of the Pluckley Ghost Club. I subscribe to their monthly newsletter and find it fascinating - if a little too sceptical for my tastes! As a writer, Arabella can be rather dismissive of paranormal activity but

I suppose that is the best approach - eliminate the explainable so that all that remains is the unexplainable. I first met the group the afternoon before the investigation when they joined the tourists for a guided tour of the castle. They returned in the evening and before I left them for the evening, I checked all of their bags - we've had problems with groups bringing alcohol into the castle and I didn't want there to be any trouble. I didn't see anything unusual in any of their bags, just notebooks, cameras and torches. I rather hoped they'd let me join the ghost hunt but they pulled down the castle portcullis from the inside so, despite having the keys to the property, even I wouldn't have been able to get in once their investigation began! Now that their lead investigator is dead, I wonder if they're looking for new members to join their club?"

188: Reverend Amos Harper's briefcase contains a copy of the bible, the latest (and final) mystery novel by Conrad Cutlass and a collection of tiny flags on cocktail sticks - which were intended to be put atop the many sandcastles the reverend hoped to build today.

189: Merlin is a very large, very friendly black bloodhound/mastiff cross. He is the descendant of several generations of dogs which have lived with Gerald Ratchett and before that, his father Gabe. There are dried flecks of strangely coloured paint around the hound's eyes.

190: Octavia Pendergast may have played a role in the murder of her husband - but her reasons were entirely justified. She has no motive for becoming The Ghost. You can either guess again or go to THE GHOST: THE SOLUTION at the back of this book to learn the full story...

191: "I only conversed with one of the brothers - named Todrick, if I recall. He had some rather hair-raising yarns about his exploits around the world - including how he survived a crocodile attack in Egypt some years ago. After seeing the scar, I reckon he was lucky to have escaped with his life - and his leg!" *For further information regarding Perry Gulch, go to entry **123.***

192: The bottle of wine was dropped on the floor of the graveyard when Perry collapsed but it did not break. The wine is a rather inexpensive looking cabernet. *To visit the village off-licence go to entry **240.***

193: The solicitor's office of Scott Mallard is situated in the heart of the village. On his desk there is a framed picture of Bertrand Mallard with his friend Larry Finch. The rest of the desk is messy and chaotic. A nearby filing cabinet looks much more organised. *To check this filing cabinet, go to entry **32.***

194: "After a delightful holiday with Esther in Brigstowe, I invited my daughter to live with me at the vicarage - with Reverend Harper's permission, of course. We have been having a lovely time of it! In the past, I would have been petrified that Phineas Flitter's column would be about me and Esther but now that the secret is out in the open, I have nothing to hide. As soon as the explosion happened, my only thought was for Esther's wellbeing, so I shielded her eyes with my hand. What was left of Phineas was an awful mess."

195: When Mona Prim mentioned that she had won the Pluckley Green summer fete beauty pageant five years in a row during the war, she also spoke of how the title required the winner to be free of scandal or moral impurity. Being an unwed, pregnant woman would certainly have ruled her out of the competition in the eyes of the conservative village. She is not Esther's mother.

196: Evidently, the cake was not a cake but an elaborate explosive device covered in pink icing. The bomb must have been made to detonate the instant somebody slid a knife into the cake - and poor, greedy Hamish was the first to do so. After the speeches, Miss Faversham and Winston were due to cut the cake together. The cake is now nothing but streaks of pink icing splattered around the dining hall.

197: In Mavis' handbag there is a change purse, a book of crossword puzzles and the remains of a note which has been torn to pieces. The note is impossible to read but has been written in green ink.

198: "Our friends in Hampshire just got a swimming pool installed and my goodness, it was heaven! I hope it can go ahead now. I don't wish to speak ill of the dead but Humbert Miner - or Humbert Moaner as I called him - was a deeply unpleasant man who will not be missed one bit."

199: "My grandmother is an elderly widow who is flailing under her late husband's debts. My parents and I struggle to make ends meet as it is but we help with her rent whenever we can. When we heard last week that Nanny Tipple was going to be evicted, me and my friend Alvin thought that maybe we could block the door - stop the bailiffs from coming in. I held onto the frame with my right hand and locked my left arm with Alvin's. He in turn held onto the frame with his left. Neither of us had a free hand to fire a gun!"

200: "Oh what a smashing time we were all having! Fran had promised she would prepare and pack our six daily picnics and Jonathon and I were going to go fishing in the river for breakfast! This dreadful business has really put a damper on things but I shan't allow it to ruin our hols! I was woken up by the sound of that shotgun - I'm usually quite a heavy sleeper but the sound of that blast was incredible! Jonathon wasn't in the barn for some reason. I also noted that the shotgun which had been mounted on the wall of the barn was missing." *To show Rick the note, go to entry* **76**.

201: The bread was freshly made this morning and purchased by Mabel Witherspoon from the local bakery. It has not been tampered with and is perfectly edible. There is also no trace of poison to be found on the butter smeared across the slices of bread which were served with supper.

202: Miss Faversham sits upon her armchair in the living room as if it were a throne. "My maid? Genevieve was called back to London this morning. She has family there and said that her mother is very unwell. She also said that she won't be returning and we shouldn't bother trying to search for her or even wonder about where she went. As for the mess in the kitchen, I'm afraid I accidentally cut myself while opening the mail - no more than a slight paper cut. It caused me quite a fright though and I accidentally spilled my soup!" There does not appear to be a cut on her hand but there are what look like fresh burn scars on her forearms.

203: "Yes, I'll admit it, ever since the race started up again after the war I've been collecting bets upon the run. Yes, it's illegal gambling but it is small scale and nobody gets hurt. It's just a means to up the tension of the big day". *To view the betting odds and see who has placed bets on the runners, turn to entry* **685**.

204: Recent events in the life of Lady Pendergast have left her feeling neglected and unhappy in her marriage. Since the beginning of the year, she has been seeking ways in which she might escape from her terrible circumstance and the tyrannical husband she both fears and detests.

205: "I do not normally post mail on a Sunday but yesterday I missed a letter for Lester Pratt at the bottom of my mailbag, so chose to deliver it today on my own time. I arrived at Lester's home at around 9am. The front door was open and through the doorframe I could see into his house - which is where I spied the corpse. I ran from there at once and did not stop until I reached the police station. I haven't noticed anything out of the ordinary this morning but yesterday I did notice a man I didn't recognise heading out towards the wetlands. He was wearing round spectacles and had on a pair of leather gloves - which I thought unusual given the mild weather we have been enjoying."

206: "I hope the death of Oliver Manville isn't going to delay work on the basement too much. The extension down there will increase the amount of space I have to store beer barrels, so I - and the rest of the village - can enjoy even more ale! This morning I awoke at 7am. I had expected that I would have to make breakfast for the man who was renting one of the guest rooms but when I checked in on him, he had already left. He was a rather peculiar man who gave his name as Peter Pickle. At 9am I met the builders at the door. Oliver went straight to the basement and died. It's all very annoying!" *To ask about the guest who stayed overnight at the Bloodied Axe, go to entry **58**.*

207: "That Hilda Faversham is a game one for a posh lady! She had been giving me the eye throughout the reception and when I went to the garden to collect some glasses, Hilda was upon me! She pulled me into a bush and... well, you can use your imagination. I saw the strangest thing from inside the bush. A woman marched out of Stasis House holding the enormous, white wedding cake which had been in the kitchen. She just tossed it into the hedgerow and then went back inside. About five minutes later is when Hilda and I heard the explosion." *To inspect the hedgerow, go to entry **139**.*

208: "I was surprised that posh Steadman boy had proposed to our lovely Saucy Sally but the heart wants what it wants, does it not? I had been drinking in the park for most of the evening - as Bludger Baxter has barred me from the pub - and fell asleep on a bench. When I woke up, the clock on the church said it was 1.30 in the morning and it was then that I heard a series of loud bangs coming from the pub. Sounded like gunshots to me."

209: Jeremy Trumble is a nature lover, conservationist and campaigner on behalf of Pluckley Green's many areas of outstanding natural beauty. At all times, the gentleman (who lives in a shack at the edge of the wetlands) can be seen with a pair of binoculars around his neck and is almost always involved in a campaign to save a vital piece of the wilderness or lobbying on behalf of a rare species. He is well-liked among the villagers, who generally see him as a kind-hearted oddball. He is noteworthy for his honesty and integrity - Jeremy Trumble will always keep his promises. Like most of the residents of Pluckley Green, he harbours a deep and abiding hatred for Lord Pendergast.

210: One of the pockets of Dorothy Halcyon's summer jacket is empty but the other contains a neatly folded, handwritten note. It reads: *"I have been spending your money well and enjoying myself greatly. Your financial contributions these past three months have certainly helped keep my tongue from loosening. However, if you do not pay me the next instalment of hush money, I shall have no choice but to let the whole village know about your terrible secret and what you did to your poor sister. You have until the end of today to pay."* The note is written in green ink.

211: The most recent diary entry is from the 1st of November, 1956. It reads: *"There were two more murders last night. What is going on in this dreadful village? I only moved here in January and since then there have been countless murders. The really strange thing is that nobody behaves as if this is unusual. They are either all taken by some kind of delusion, bewitched by a curse, or (as I suspect) all too thoroughly stupid to notice that anything is wrong. I met my gormless neighbour today - the estate agent. He is a frightful bore and still enraged with me! Oh how I enjoy toying with these fools! He was at the train station and seemed close to tears with me! Apparently he is going to Cardiff for a month. I despise him - along with this weird little village and its ridiculous residents."*

212: "The dart which killed Wilbur was undoubtedly from my pub - it says so on the flight - but that doesn't mean I killed him! Last night at the Bloodied Axe, a handful of the Order were in attendance. Wilbur Charles - may he rest in peace, Gerald Ratchett, Rita Flynn and Minerva Arcana. This morning I was doing a spot of reorganising and I noticed that one of the pub's darts was missing from beside the dartboard. Obviously, I didn't think much of it at the time…"

213: Lady Pendergast has an angry and fresh black eye on her face, which she has attempted to mask under layers of foundation. "My husband and I had a terrible argument last night but he has assured me that his infidelity is over. We were both very scared that his affair with Della Dempsey was about to be exposed and I did not want to become the laughing stock of the village. I believe that the explosion was caused by Phineas Flitter's cigar. Somebody could have easily replaced his regular cigar with an explosive one whilst his back was turned. I myself am rather familiar with cigars as my husband smokes them - he buys them from the tobacconist Mr Willow in the village."
To visit Mr Willow, go to entry **84.**

214: Miss Faversham - or Genevieve Lampeter as she is now known - is not the Pluckley Green serial killer. None of the people present at her wedding reception are The Ghost. You can either guess again or go to THE GHOST: THE SOLUTION at the back of this book to learn the full story…

215: "The bride proposing to the groom is not what I would have chosen for my daughter, but I suppose I'm old-fashioned like that. My husband and I were aware that Dickon had intentions to propose to Lana himself as he had asked my husband's permission three days ago. Thwarted love - it breaks my heart!"

216: "I was due to start work at 2pm today - much like every other Saturday, so I mercifully did not witness the bodies or the bloody scene. It is all such a pity in so many ways. I've cared for the Dubois garden for thirty years and they and the Willis family were once great neighbours to each other. So much so that many years ago I installed a gate in the wall so that the children of the families could play in each other's gardens. All of that changed only relatively recently - grief can turn people so bitter."

217: "I was there at the start and the end of the race. I had no idea that once he darted off from the Bloodied Axe Tavern, that would be the last time I ever saw my beloved Bruno alive. Last night he spent a good amount of time at my cottage near the canal. He was understandably anxious but was keeping himself busy and distracted by sorting through my toolbox (I am an upholsterer, you see). He left shortly after 8pm but I did happen to spy him on the canal path at dawn. Maybe he was performing some last-minute exercises, so I didn't want to disturb him."

218: The window of Room 1 cannot be opened as the frame has been repainted so many times. The window to Room 2 can be opened but a dusty spider web across the latch suggests that it has not been done so in quite some time.

219: The Master Stone is the largest of the five Pluckley Standing Stones and is also known as the Reader Stone. According to legend, the stone was once a man who was reading books on the heath (rather than attending church) and for this sin was turned to stone by the Christian god.

220: "I can't help but feel I've had a rather lucky escape. You see, Gabe always rang the first bell but this evening he asked if we could swap so he may have a try of the fourth bell. He was like that - always liked to change things up and try something different. I suppose there are a fair few in this village who'd rather it had been me getting squashed beneath that bell…"

221: "I was rather pleased with my hiding place - the cupboard under the stairs. Indeed, I do believe that I would have won had the game not come to such an abrupt end. That's me, I suppose, I know how to keep things hidden - unlike my buffoon of a husband. I heard the gunshot midway through the game and the resulting hubbub made me leave my hiding place. That's when I heard the scream. It's such a shame - because it probably would have been the first time I'd ever won hide-and-seek at a Pendergast party!"

222: None of the four people responsible for poisoning Lord Pendergast's drink were the person who later murdered him that night.

223: Mabel Witherspoon will be turning 50 this year. The cook moved to Pluckley Green following the war - the Brigstowe Blitz had destroyed her home and killed most of her family. Mabel's wizardry in the kitchen led to her serving as a cook for American soldiers stationed in Brigstowe during the war. Shortly after peace was declared, Mabel moved to Pluckley Green (a village she fondly remembered from childhood holidays) and found work as a live-in cook for Reverend Harper. Over the years, her affection for the kind-hearted holy man has turned into an abiding and deeply felt romantic love, which she has kept a closely guarded secret.

224: As Lord Pendergast plans for his wife's birthday party in September, at least two people are planning his murder at the very same event.

225: Harry's daughter is distraught. She is the one who called the police at 12.05pm to report the double murder. "I arrived at noon on the dot, as I do every Saturday and it was me who found the bodies... It wasn't always like this. Both families were so close when I was growing up. I just can't believe that this idiotic rivalry has escalated to this."

226: "Humbert Miner was nothing but a nuisance by reputation alone! I work as a receptionist at the doctor's surgery and he once wrote a letter complaining that the lights in the waiting room were too bright. When we changed them, he wrote another saying they were now too dim! As soon as I submitted my application to the council for the extension to my house, I knew Humbert would oppose it. I just hoped that the council would have grown weary of his nonsense and would rule in my favour."

227: "My wife and I had decided to clear the air after an almighty row last night. My wife was upset by some of my extramarital activities but I assured her that the affair was over - for good this time. Yes, I was worried that the gossip column this week might be on the subject of my affair, but I was also rather concerned that it might be about the details of my first wife's death. I assure you, I shall be making up for my wandering affections by throwing my wife an almighty party for her 50th birthday in September. I'd even ordered fireworks for the celebration. They were being stored in one of the gatehouses on the estate - which reminds me, a couple of nights ago there was a break-in at that very gatehouse and a few of those fireworks were stolen."

228: From The Pluckley Green Press. 20th of July, 1955: *"The Pluckley Green Fishing Competition ended in upset yesterday when local man Dickon Paisley protested the result. According the him, the winner Alex Kendrick was a cheat, who used bait which had been outlawed in the contest. Kendrick, whose record-breaking red herring secured him victory refused to comment. Paisley's tantrum was deemed so excessive that the judging panel ruled that he should be banned from competitive fishing for the rest of the year."*

229: Pluckley Castle features a guestbook in which visitors to the castle are invited to sign. The guestbook includes signatures from Robin Richard Pascoe, Lucy Sparrow and Penelope Gannet. All of whom visited the castle this year.

230: Jimmy is a young and friendly dog. He has very little to say for himself or evidence to provide.

231: Wilma is a botanist who lives in a narrow boat on the canal with her sister Daisy Doyle. As a woman in the male dominated world of science, Wilma has had to work twice as hard for half the recognition of her male peers and yet she persists, owing to her love of the subject. Headstrong and independent, Wilma became a widow aged 30 when her husband was killed during the Second World War. She had no children with him and has no plans to ever marry again.

232: "I was due to meet August Barley at my home for dinner this evening. I have been an acquaintance of the man for quite some time and he wished to discuss some of the details of his upcoming book about the history of the village with me. However, he did not attend my house at 6pm as agreed and now I learn that he has been murdered. Most inconvenient! Toby Tchotchke must have been nurturing his hatred and lust for revenge since January when August reported him to the police! I was the judge of Tony Tchotchke's trial and I fully expected that a fine upstanding citizen such as that learned man would be a better behaved prisoner than he has proven to be!" *For more information about Judge Jan Treagle, go to entry* **122.**

233: "I usually have a kind word to say for everybody but let me tell you that Miss Faversham is an irredeemable monster and nothing more. I walk past that decrepit old house every morning and the way she screams at her maid is something else. I'm quite certain she beats her too - judging from the sounds I hear. This morning was something different though. There was a loud quarrel and then the sound of crockery breaking, followed by a bloodcurdling scream of agony - and unbridled rage. I'm certain that it could only have come from that poor maid who has gone missing."

234: The first note is from Bludger Baxter. It reads *"Just thought I'd post this note through your letterbox to remind you to bring the cup back to the pub - it's been a whole year! Bludger."* The other note is written with exceptionally neat handwriting. It reads: "*Larry. I have discovered something remarkable about the death of Bertrand Mallard. Meet me by his grave in the churchyard at 4pm and I will tell you more. Perry Gulch."*

235: On Saturday night of that Easter weekend, Reverend Amos Harper was called to Stasis House by young Esther. She was deeply distressed over a coded letter which had been sent anonymously to her. The letter came from a resident of the village who claimed to be her mother.

236: Minerva Arcana wears a sensible looking pair of walking boots. "When we started the walk, Bathsheba, Artemis and Doctor White were ahead of me. The three of them are a lot more competitive than me as I enjoy a much more casual stroll through the beauty of the woods. I chatted to Paris Montgomery for a while but he really is a rather slow walker and I eventually got ahead of him. The thing with the Western Woods is that they are so dark that you cannot see further than about 20 feet ahead or behind you. The eeriness is quite thrilling! It was me who discovered the doctor's body behind the cottage. What a terrible tragedy. He was a kind man." *For further information about Minerva Arcana, go to entry* **324.**

237: "Of course I'm shocked by what happened but I can't say I'm upset. Pip Longfellow was a terrible chauvinist. Not only did he proclaim that birdwatching was strictly a men's pursuit, he often took my photographs of the rarest and most beautiful birds and claimed that he himself was the photographer. As for my whereabouts, last night I left half way through a play at the village hall and headed home by myself. I was in bed before 10. The thing I can't quite get my head around is that when we met at dawn, not one of us was brandishing a rifle. Where did the gun come from and just as pertinently, where did it go?"

238: "Yes, I wrote that note and I meant every word of it. I was going to give it to Jonathon at supper but I knew he would make a terrible fuss about it. Perhaps I was a little anxious about how the others would react too - so I had planned just to silently leave in the morning and get the next train back to London. I wonder how this note could have ended up in the muddy field? I probably dropped it from my pocket as I was tying Jimmy up for the night."

239: The former maid of Lord and Lady Pendergast (and now "close personal companion" of Lady Pendergast) witnessed The Ghost on the morning of the murder of Robin Richard Pascoe. She is not the serial killer. You can either guess again or go to THE GHOST: THE SOLUTION at the back of this book to learn the full story…

240: Carter Conway runs Pluckley Green's only off-licence. It sells a limited selection of wines, beers and spirits. However, with it being a Sunday he is not working today. "Business hasn't been that robust of late. People are spending far too much time in the pub for my liking, rather than drinking at home as I'd prefer! Yesterday I had only two customers. One was Dexter Maybrick, who purchased a bottle of cabernet. The other customer was a lady who I had not seen before. She bought three bottles - two chardonnays and a cabernet."

241: The kitchen of Stasis House is a bloody mess - literally. Blood is sprayed and splattered across the cobweb laden table, the floors, walls and even the ceiling. A blood covered letter opener has been cast amidst the gore on the floor. There is also a broken china bowl on the floor, in a pool of chicken soup. There is a small pile of blood splattered envelopes - opened and unopened on the table.

242: Wilbur was a 70-something former teacher who had been a member of the Ancient Order of Pluckley Pagans for over 50 years. Most people in the village had no idea of his involvement in the group. He is slumped on the ground in his ceremonial garment of a long, hooded cloak. A dart is protruding from the front of his neck. *To inspect the dart, go to entry 536.*

243: Lord Pendergast favoured an expensive and hard to find brand of gin named "Old Sarum Opal". Lady Pendergast bought the bottle of the gin for her husband just yesterday. There is no sign of the rest of the bottle anywhere.

244: "I don't know what to think as I can't believe my own eyes! Just before Arabella screamed and fell from the tower, I saw the Grey Lady! I could see her through the windows of the tower as she made her way up the spiral staircase. She was just as described - grey dress, messy hair and carrying a candle to light her way! It was quite a climb to the top of the castle but once I got there I was enjoying the view. I think I briefly saw Jules at the top of the west tower but my attention was completely stolen by the ghost! As the founder of the group, Arabella was rather frustrating sometimes - always having to find a rational explanation rather than take a leap of faith into the unknown. I can't explain what I saw. If the Grey Lady was one of us in a grey dress and wig, how could we have smuggled such items in? Bethany Torrance searched all of our bags before we entered the castle this evening."

245: The pitchfork is intact and is a standard garden implement. There is nothing unusual about it and no fingerprints can be found on the handle.

246: Adriana Arcana may be a fraudulent medium but the spirit board, belonging to her daughter Minerva, has been known to be uncannily accurate in predicting the future.

247: "I've certainly enjoyed the "Piddly Glen Mysteries" in the past but I can't help but think that in taking inspiration from me for the character of Wilhelmina Rudders, he might have focused a little too much on a certain attribute of mine... Poor Conrad was happily enjoying a cup of tea in the village hall earlier. He was sitting alone and was kind enough to sign a copy of his latest book for me. I must have been one of the very last people to speak to him."

248: The Hellman's home looks much like any other quaint cottage you would find in Pluckley Green. In the bedroom, only Juno's side of the bed appears to have been slept in last night.

249: There are five tiny glass bottles of tonic in the kitchen - all of them unopened. After a brief search, a sixth, empty bottle is found. For some reason it has been put into the bread bin. It has a tiny pin-hole sized prick in the bottle top - as if a needle has punctured it.

250: During her wretched, miserable life, Miss Faversham did come to learn who the biological mother of Esther was - a woman in Pluckley Green who had abandoned her baby out of desperation. This woman still lives in the village and would dearly love to contact Esther. This was the reason why Miss Faversham chose to keep Esther almost imprisoned in Stasis House for all of those years.

251: "I don't have my pistol with me. Ordinarily, Lord Pendergast likes us to carry guns as it offers us and him protection but this time I decided to leave mine at home. I really didn't want to frighten Mrs Tipple."

252: The article kept in the extensive church archives is from the Pluckley Green Press and is dated May 8th, 1955. *"There was outrage outside Brigstowe Crown Court yesterday when Silas Marsten was found not guilty of death by dangerous driving. The historian is said to have been speeding through Pluckley Green when he struck and killed 13 year old Rosemary Billings, who was on her way home from school. Her father, Jarvis Billings commented "My poor daughter was killed by that man's reckless actions and yet a judge has deemed her death no more than a tragic accident. Where is the justice in that?""*

253: At the sewing circle, Daisy mentioned that she had spent her war years in Pluckley Green and her husband had not been conscripted as he was a farmer. This would have made an affair (and pregnancy) with an American soldier very hard to keep secret. She is not Esther's mother.

254: "Juno Hellman was really rather splendid last night. In fact, every performance from her in this production has led the audience to believe the impossible - that the Pluckley Players have actually managed to unearth a talented actor! I'm as shocked as anyone but looking at the audience, she had them enraptured - particularly young Ash Green, who seemed mesmerised from the front row throughout the play. Juno left at about 10.30pm but Ash joined some of the remaining cast for a lock-in at the Bloodied Axe. He didn't leave until past 1am, the same time as me!"

255: "According to an opinion poll, Cuthbert Crookshank was likely to win the election with a reduced majority. Diana Spiff and her… lively party were in second place. I am not supposed to show bias as host of these public debates, but I rather thought we had defeated ideas like Diana Spiff's a decade ago… I was looking at Cuthbert when the shot rang out. He was answering a question and using a map on the wall to do so. I am certain I glimpsed some movement outside of the window just before the gunshot."

256: The spirit board was originally gifted to Minerva during the war. In 1943, Minerva was working for a magician and entertainer at the social club for American soldiers in Brigstowe. An admirer thought she could add a spiritualist component to her act.

257: "Let me tell you one thing about parties. You can never have too many ice cubes. That is why I brought a sackful of them from the pub with me tonight - despite people's worst assumptions about me, I can be rather considerate. I was in the kitchen looking at the fancy bread bin just as Lady Pendergast took that gin and tonic to her husband. Reverend Harper had clearly had one too many, as he accidentally knocked the bottle of Old Sarum Opal gin onto the floor where it smashed. He did say this afternoon how he wanted to relax and enjoy himself tonight."

258: Sometime in the late summer of 1934, the First Lady Pendergast was taking an evening stroll on the heath when she spotted the hideous gurt dog - with glowing eyes and monstrous fangs. She fled to her mansion and was convinced that the dog was an omen of her death. She took to her bed shortly afterwards and during the course of the following week, grew progressively weaker and eventually succumbed to whatever mysterious ailment had bedevilled her.

259: "I have just heard word that the man who was blown up in that explosion was a rather terrible person and I do not believe anyone should grieve him. Last night, Mavis and I caught the train into Brigstowe. We had not shared an evening together for quite a while and we had a marvellous time! We went to dinner and then to the pictures to see a film. We were back in Pluckley Green by 10pm." *To visit the cinema in Brigstowe, go to entry **714**.*

260: Larry's jacket pockets contain some cough drops and two handwritten notes. There is no wallet or house keys. *To read the notes, go to **234**.*

261: In all of the wills written by all of the victims of "The Ghost", the only people who stand to inherit any money are each of the victim's immediate next of kin. Inheritance is not the motive for murdering any of the people "The Ghost" has killed so far.

262: Conrad Cutlass lays on his back on the street. Smoke is billowing from his boots and around his collar. His hair is standing wildly on end. His death must have been instantaneous.

263: "What ghastly business! I have known the Tchotchke Brothers for years. Their dedication to history and archaeology is unmatched - so much so that I fear it may have come at the expense of their private lives. You see, only one of the triplets ever married."

264: "Back in my day, the Pluckley Green Run was a far smaller event - but I still excelled in it. Perhaps I did not fully realise my sporting ambitions but I am very content as a trainer for aspiring runners (although Milton is currently my only trainee). Milton and I were out training just last night, which is when he sustained an injury to his foot. I suggested he not run on it but he was determined." *To ask about the previous night's training event, go to entry **418**.*

265: The copper wire was folded into the nylon ribbon. The path of the wire continues beyond the ribbon and through an open window of the village hall. Inside the hall, the wire is plugged into an electric socket on the wall. The socket is switched on.

266: "A couple of weeks ago, I got trapped behind him in the post office queue. He was there for over an hour, complaining about absolutely anything and the cost of everything. I've never seen a man buy so many stamps in my life! I went to school with Humbert. Believe it or not, he was once a friendly, outgoing chap. Old age changes some people for the worse. I try to stay positive, even though I have the aches and strains of age. Hopefully this extension to my daughter's house will allow me to live a more comfortable life."

267: Leon was stabbed in the back and then dropped to his knees, which is when he delivered his clumsy final words. He then fell forwards and died. His body is still slumped upon the stage in a puddle of blood. There is writing upon his hands which, upon closer inspection, are the lines of dialogue which the actor repeatedly forgot. When he was not acting with the Pluckley Players, Leon Cribbage worked as a carpenter. *To inspect the dagger, turn to entry **176**.*

268: Michael's toolbox contains all the regular implements one would expect of a builder. However, one would probably not expect to find a fake moustache and pair of oversized glasses hidden amongst the tools. "How in the world did they get in there?" said Michael, "I've never seen them in my life!"

269: "After we saw the hound come bounding out of the darkness, the five of us screamed and fled into the night. I found myself in a thicket of trees. I am certain that I heard voices nearby. One of them said "I can see the tent this way, follow me Gary". It was a man's voice. I try to stay out of that business as best as I can but I think it's fair to say that Benjamin, Donny and Gary have all been in love with Tamara for years. It has caused a terrible strain on our friendship group."

270: Padlocks are rarely seen in Pluckley Green. In a safe and pleasant village, people leave their bicycles on the pavement without protection and their sheds and doors are rarely locked. The padlock not only stopped Bertrand from escaping the inferno but also prevented Larry and Perry from gaining entry.

271: Barney and Tanya's hide is a carefully arranged hut with books on a shelf in alphabetical order. The hide was built as a wedding gift from the couple's friends, so that they could enjoy their mutual hobby together. In a storage box there are two half eaten cheese sandwiches.

272: "Sally was a lovely girl and I was happy that she was to become my daughter-in-law - I'd never stand to hear a bad word said against her. Donny has always had a kind heart - something I believe he inherited from my late husband - and that heart has sometimes led him in surprising directions. My son is absolutely devastated that the wedding will not be going ahead."

273: On the morning of the 1st of January, Minerva Arcana was certain she spotted Toby Tchotchke. The archaeologist (and wanted criminal) was talking to someone she could not see. The pair were at the edge of the Western Woods. "It's not just a legend!" Toby excitedly explained to the unknown person. "All those years of research just to discover it here in this village!"

274: The village fete holds a raffle every year and the prizes are taken from donations given to the church on the Sunday before the celebration. Members of the congregation place their donation onto a table before the service begins. Donations include a cake, a ticket to Pluckley Castle and a bottle of chardonnay.

275: The door to the west tower is in the grand hall. Most of the space within the west tower is taken up by a stone, spiral staircase which leads to the roof where beautiful views of the surrounding area can be enjoyed. At the bottom of the staircase, tucked away in a dark corner, is a wooden trunk. Inside it there is nothing but a few strands of what looks like long hair from a wig.

276: Oliver Manville lays dead upon the basement's stone floor. His head has been split open and a huge amount of blood has formed a puddle around the open wound. In any ordinary village, this death would be ruled as a simple, tragic accident - but Pluckley Green is no ordinary village…

277: "When I heard the gunshot, I at first thought it had something to do with the storm. It really is lashing at the mansion and making some frightful sounds! I was hiding under the bed of the first guest bedroom. Shortly after the game began Lady Pendergast came into that room and discovered the maid in the wardrobe but didn't find me. The gunshot came a little while after that but it was only when I heard a scream that I knew the game must be over."

278: "Just because a man was poisoned whilst eating a soup I prepared, suddenly suspicious eyes are upon me! For shame! Well, answer me this. I served the same soup from the same saucepan to Mr Marsten as I did all the guests - along with the Reverend and I had some myself too. If the soup was poisoned, how can it be that the rest of us are still alive?"

279: "Oh Prudence was a *dreadful* woman! I have never known anyone take so much pleasure in being so unpleasant and mean of spirit. Children in the village would call her the wicked witch! I hadn't seen Prudence in weeks and had rather hoped it had meant the old bat had left the village for good. On Christmas Eve my husband and I went out for an evening with Colin Carnegie and Alvin Luft and we spent much of the evening laughing and gossiping about what a nasty creature she is!"

280: "The seance was one thing but I did not like the sound of that spirit board - that is dark magic stuff - but Adriana Arcana assured us that we'd be safe. We asked the board who The Ghost was but the planchette did not move. Then we asked who the next victim would be and it spelled out two letters - I am sure the first was "P" but the horror of the murder has clouded my mind. I was holding hands with Adriana and Horace throughout the seance and neither one moved, which is why it was such a shock to see him dead when I opened my eyes. Horace and I were not friends, owing to his plans to level the old orchards to build holiday homes - but I didn't kill him!

Those orchards are my life blood. Where else am I to get the apples for my award winning cider? Settle for inferior? Not I!"

281: "I must say that I have found it enormously flattering to have the mystery-solving, dashingly handsome hero postman of the books be based upon me! Lawrence French is such an admirable and brave character and I always look forward to finding out what my literary twin will get up to next! It is dreadful that there will be no more books. I got to meet him briefly this morning. Tea was being served in the village hall. It was quite a hustle and bustle and as I was leaving I managed to trip over a ginger-haired young man who was under a table near the door. I have been walking with a limp all day because of that stumble!"

282: "Obviously, I wanted something dreadful to happen to Leon - that way my boyfriend Melvin could take over as Macbeth. That's why whenever Leon was about to step on stage I always told him to "break a leg" - but I didn't want him to be murdered! Every play we do, Stanley *has* to cast Leon in the lead. It's quite pathetic really, so at least that will come to an end. I was watching Leon from stage right when that lunatic in the mask stabbed him with a dagger. Whoever that was then fled from the village hall. I was so distraught that I screamed and then burst into tears. When I'm not acting I work at the museum in Bigstowe but acting is my true calling."

283: The cause of the First Lady Pendergast's death has never been found. However, rumours persist that because his first wife was infertile, Lord Lucien Pendergast murdered her rather than suffer the public shame of divorce. He was then free to remarry and sire an heir with another woman.

284: The box of doughnuts contained one jam doughnut, one custard doughnut, a chocolate doughnut, a doughnut topped with hundreds and thousands and one topped with icing. All of the doughnuts have been wholly or partially eaten.

285: "Frank Greenburg asked me to talk some sense into Lester Pratt and I had every intention of visiting him last night but there was something of a crisis in Stasis House which I had to deal with at short notice. Lester targets the church most years as a form of transgressive rebellion but I do believe him to be a Christian at heart. The pranks have no doubt been escalating over time. Ten years ago it was nothing more than spring-loaded, fake snakes in a can but last year it was rotting fish in the font. Something had to be done to stop him but it should never have been murder." *To learn more about Reverend Amos Harper, go to entry* **170.**

286: "The canal path is the last refreshment stop before the finish line. I became a spotter three years ago following my retirement. I've never been very sporty but it gives me something to do and I enjoy the excitement. At the canal path, Milton West was the clear lead and Lyle Carmichael was behind him. I did not see a trace of Bruno Brown."

287: "Being the winner of Pluckley Green's summer fete beauty contest comes with certain responsibilities, one of which is to remain a morally pure, upstanding citizen and of course, to abstain from certain behaviours - until marriage, at least! It is a beauty contest, after all and nothing is uglier than loose morals. Last night I went to bed early - at about 8pm. Even someone as naturally radiant as I needs her beauty sleep! I think my neighbour Mavis Davis can attest that I did not leave my property at all last night." *To check Della's story with Mavis Davis, go to entry* **29.**

288: Tucked down the side of one of the seats in the back row of the auditorium is a small, metal pin. There is nothing unusual about any of the other seats.

289: "Poor Hamish. I went to school with him and he has always had a love for all things sweet. When my bride was giving her speech, I was facing the door to the kitchen where the cake was being kept. I saw someone bring the cake out but I didn't have my glasses on so all I saw was a blur of blue!"

290: The crowd of onlookers had expected little more than a gentle competition and the opportunity to admire some young ladies. They were instead all witnesses to a murder. Among the startled throng of people is Esther. "The arrow *can't* have been fired from here, the crowd is dense and somebody would have seen them with a bow! I only stopped here for a minute and now I must leave - I need to do something important at the Pluckley Stones!"

291: Adriana Arcana's seances are always preceded by a consultation of the spirit board. It is a wooden board upon which the alphabet has been etched. Guests are invited to place their hands on a planchette (a small triangular piece of wood) which then moves around the board, seemingly of its own free will. According to Adriana, it has proven itself to be accurate at predicting the future many times before.

292: "There was a time when we couldn't keep Conrad Cutlass' books in stock at the library as they were so popular they were practically flying off the shelves! Cutlass has always been a prolific author - at least one new Piddly Glen mystery every year but I have to admit, they have become rather stale and routine of late and his popularity is nowhere near what it used to be - Lawrence and Wilhelmina are always in pursuit of John Trangle and solving mysteries along the way and it's just become a bit… dull. It's no wonder so many of his readers are moving onto other writers, especially Tarquin Taggers and his action-packed "Chase Slater" books!"

293: "I had decided that I wanted to quit Manville Builders. I have enjoyed every aspect of working for that company - except for that odious, work-shy toad Michael Doncaster - but the proposed move to London… well, I just don't want to go. Pluckley Green has my heart and I am certain that one day it will have my bones. Cities are scary, dangerous places! I spent last night at my house in the village. I was organising my toolbox. I know that doesn't give me a very firm alibi as I live alone." *To inspect Edgar's toolbox, go to entry* **498**.

294: "Larry just burst through the door and was bleeding profusely and clutching his neck. He looked so scared! Tonight is meant to be the busiest night of the year but this afternoon has been as quiet as a library. So much so that Bludger went out for a walk earlier. Larry said yesterday that he wasn't going to participate in the pub quiz this year but he would drop by in the evening to return something. He must have been attacked elsewhere and stumbled here so that somebody could call for an ambulance." *To learn more about the pub quiz, go to entry* **705**.

295: Each of the performers in Bostwicke's Travelling Circus has their own horse-drawn caravan which serves as their dressing room, living quarters and means of travel. Polo's caravan is locked whenever he is away from it. Next to his makeup mirror there is a signed, glossy headshot from Wanda Highsmith. She has added a note which reads *"My dearest Dominic. You will always have my heart. I love you."* Inside Dominic's makeup kit, it is clear that several pots of face paint are missing.

296: The assistant to the village baker has only killed one person - the man whose dangerous driving led to the death of her daughter. She is not The Ghost. You can either guess again or go to THE GHOST: THE SOLUTION at the back of this book to learn the full story…

297: "These evictions are always high drama. Ever since the war ended I've been looking for that adrenaline rush - and to be able to boss people around! I've been working for Lord Pendergast since 1945 and it's been dependable employment - plus he gives us pistols to carry for protection! Alvin and Colin were blocking the door. I was looking at them when I heard the gunshot. I hope Lord Pendergast pulls through. I need this work - jobs are hard to come by at the moment." *To check Alastair's pistol - which is on the passenger seat beside him, go to entry* **113**.

298: "I've been a spotter at the Pluckley Green Run for more than a decade now and know all of the runners well. To my surprise, the first runner to appear at the Pluckley Stones was Bruno Brown. I gave him a beaker of orange squash and recorded his time. The next runner was Milton West. He looked rather pained and his stride seemed less mighty than usual."

299: "I knew Jack but didn't like him well. It boils my blood that he and Jessica were once an item. Still, that's all in the past now. My work with the army takes me away quite often but days like today remind me why I love this village so much - such a tight-knit community. The party was all going so well until we found Jack hanging there." *To ask Kevin about the army, go to entry* **476.**

300: Chip Burlington was shot once through the temple at near point-blank range. Blood, skull fragments and brain matter are splattered across the sawdust covered floor of the big top. The gun was dropped beside the strongman's body when the clown fled the scene. *To inspect the gun, go to entry* **457.**

301: "I thought a Leap Day proposal from Lana was an enchanting idea. Lana and Dickon were such an adorable couple and I just knew they were going to make the most wonderful bride and groom. I didn't see Dickon all morning, nor did I see his friends Colin and Vernon as they all went fishing in the wetlands first thing - I know Lana worries about them out there, what with all of those whipper snakes about at this time of the year."

302: The tonic which was used in the drink came in tiny glass bottles - each bottle being a single serving of tonic. *To check the other bottles, go to entry* **249.**

303: There are two holes in the wine bottle cork. One was made by Perry with his corkscrew but the other is an imperceptibly small pin prick - it looks as if needle or syringe has been pushed through the cork.

304: Underneath Pluckley Green runs a manmade tunnel. During the 18th century it was used by smugglers to hide their goods. Only a handful of the village's residents know of its existence. It is filled with secrets…

305: August Barley is a highly respected historian who has documented the history of the village throughout much of his sixty years of life. Stuffy and academic, it is said that he prefers the company of his honey bees, which he farms at his apiary on the southwest outskirt of Pluckley Green, to that of any people. The honey he sells is regarded as the finest in all of Somerset.

306: "Yes, I was due to marry Alice Faversham 20 years ago. A gentleman's options are rather limited in the village so I believed I had to settle for what I could find. Following the death of my first wife, I was eager to find myself a second Lady Pendergast and plans were afoot for us to wed but I got rather cold feet and ended up eloping with her maid of honour, Oxania - who remains my wife to this very day."

307: "Terrible business. I knew the man well enough as he spends a good deal of his time at this station. We would chat occasionally but I never once saw him catch a train. No surprise that he'd be here on this day - shame he never got to see it. I believe his name was Robin."

308: "Daphne arrived at my home at 7pm and put the box of doughnuts in the kitchen - which is where they remained until 9pm. She remembered my favourite - topped with hundreds and thousands - yummy! I was in and out of the kitchen all evening, as a good hostess should be. I only spoke directly to Beverley once. She was very happy that the summer fete committee had decided that she would be arranging flowers this year, which understandably, has caused some tension in the sewing circle."

309: Minerva Arcana did work at a social club for American soldiers stationed in Brigstowe during the war, however, a few days ago she shared the detail that she is infertile and has never been pregnant. She is not Esther's mother.

310: St Julian's has only one entrance - a large, wizened, wooden door which is countless centuries old. The only people with keys to the lock are Reverend Amos Harper, cleaner Daphne Robinson and her husband, organist Humphrey Robinson.

311: The trapdoor in the basement of the Bloodied Axe Tavern which leads to the tunnels underneath the village has not been opened in over a year.

312: "I am devastated and beyond heartbroken. People said that Sally would never settle down and abandon her loose ways but with me I think she found happiness. It took three proposals for her to say yes. People thought I was mad because of her reputation but none of us choose who we fall in love with."

313: "From where I was in the darkness, I could see where everyone ran when the gurt dog appeared. Gary and Donny went east along with Gustav but he fell into a thicket. Tamara ran due south and I fled after her. She's a fast woman and I could not keep up. I met her at the tent and Gustav appeared soon afterwards with scratches from the thicket and twigs in his hair! I don't want to sound disrespectful but Tamara is now an available woman again. Perhaps I stand a chance with her!"

314: Mona Prim is now the romantic partner of Lady Octavia Pendergast. For obvious reasons, the two women have chosen to keep this secret. However, tongues are freely wagging across the village. Before finding love with Lady Pendergast, the maid had enjoyed whirlwind romances with women across Somerset and beyond. Despite appearing very demure and passive, Mona Prim burns with a passionate hatred towards the village of Pluckley Green (and for society at large) for the way it treats women like her.

315: "Yes, I brought a pistol to the hustings. What of it? I take it everywhere for protection in this village. It doesn't mean I fired it - even though Diana Spiff and her vile beliefs deserve a bullet. I was here because I wanted to counter her extremism with some common sense. To be honest, Cuthbert Crookshank was of no interest to me and my vote was going to go to that August fellow."

316: The Pluckley Green Run begins outside the Bloodied Axe Tavern. It also serves as the finish line for the circular race. On the night before the race there had been a good number of people coming and going to the pub - none of whom seem to have stopped for a drink. *To talk to Bludger Baxter, go to entry **203**.*

317: "Of course I don't believe in any of this nonsense but as a historian I am deeply interested in the folklore and beliefs of the village. As sceptical as I may be, I wanted to take the seance seriously and held hands with Preston on my left and Helga on my right and closed my eyes. I did not feel either one of them move during that time. I wonder what will happen to the orchard now? My honey bees rely on all of that blossom nectar." *To learn more about August Barley, go to entry **305**.*

318: "Peter is a good man but he has a rather weak constitution for a pub landlord! The man was kind enough to offer me a chair by the warm fire for the night. The pair of us had a few drinks but Peter got a little bit tipsy and fell asleep in the snug. I awoke at dawn and left the tavern before Peter stirred from his sleep. Being a beggar is a dangerous occupation and one only for the desperate. As a result, I sleep lightly and with one ear open at all times. If anyone had opened the door to the Feathered Cap as we slept, I would have heard it. I can assure you that nobody entered the pub all night. Now, if you will excuse me, I must move on to my next village. When all you own can fit into one bag, you are free to travel as you please!" *To look inside John's bag, go to entry **550**.*

319: Gerald is currently out at work but through the glass door a wet and muddy dog can be seen sleeping on the floor of the hall. Four windows of the house face the stone circle.

320: Beatrice Beauregard has a bow and arrow proudly mounted upon the wall of her living room. "It belonged to my late husband. He competed nationally in archery tournaments. I was rather good myself too. During the pageant I was busying myself around the house with chores. I find competitions for beauty to be rather self indulgent and in poor taste. I did not witness the event but I am certain I heard the sound of glass breaking just before the crowds began screaming."

321: "I didn't want to go to the stupid hustings and I knew it would be boring and stuffy inside the village hall, so I asked mother if I could wait outside during it. It went on for ages so I went for a walk around the village. Mother has some marvellous plans for Pluckley Green. People like us will no longer have to live alongside the undesirables - like that drunk man on the bench over there - he'll be the first to go! After the hustings, mother was going to take me to another horse trial."

322: The small fireplace in the cottage has not been used since the snowfall last month. The chimney is far too narrow for for a person to climb through.

323: "I am the newest member of the Order. As a physiotherapist I have to be discreet about my involvement as people make terrible assumptions about Pagans. I am certain that the old myths about human sacrifices at the Pluckley Stones are just lies and slander from the Christians of the village. I became a member after Melody Martin introduced me to the Order - I had been helping her with her arthritic pains. I do wish Holly were more guarded when talking about the group - he makes life so much harder for the rest of us. I believe I was the first person to see that Wilbur had collapsed, that is why I screamed."

324: Just like her mother - Adriana Arcana - Minerva Arcana works as a spiritualist medium and clairvoyant. However, Minerva is not above employing fraudulent means to "prove" the existence of supernatural powers. This is only because she is so eager for others to believe in a spiritual realm. Minerva is a member of the Ancient Order of Pluckley Pagans but is also quite content in forging her own spiritual path alone.

325: "We were all so *thrilled* about spending another spiffing summer hols together! What a wizard time we always have and to think, this time we were going to solve yet another mystery together! I heard about the lights on the heath from a friend who camped here once and I just knew the Fearless Five had to investigate! At about midnight I awoke in the barn and quite desperately needed to relieve myself, so I left the barn, said "hello" to Jimmy, who was doing a super job as guard dog and then headed towards a bush. It is then that I heard the gunshot." *To show Jonathon the note, go to entry* ***701.***

326: "I must admit that I was rather surprised to see Mr Marsten in the church. His name has been met with scorn since the dreadful incident last year and given the company in the church this evening, it is no wonder his presence was unwelcome. I was concerned that an argument might break out - especially as Wilma is so protective of her sister. In fact, Wilma discreetly requested to me that Silas be seated as far as possible from Daisy during supper. I had put word out on Thursday that the church would be open tonight for those seeking shelter from the storm. Of course, I had no idea beforehand who would be here tonight. I have spent this evening attempting to keep spirits in our group high but the presence of Silas Marsten has brought dark clouds over the church just as surely as this storm has." *To read a newspaper article in the church archives about the incident last year, go to entry* ***252.***

327: At the library, Wilma Rogers mentioned seeing a girl seated at a table. She did not recognise this girl nor know her name to be Esther. She is not Esther's mother.

328: "I've never really believed in any of this ghostly mumbo-jumbo but I have enough of an open mind to be curious about these things and I thought it might be worth attending the seance just in case it really did unmask The Ghost. I didn't much like the spirit board - especially what it spelled out - but the seance was much less frightening. August was on my right and Adriana on my left. Both of them held firmly onto my hands and neither one moved. When I opened my eyes, Horace was dead. I heard rumours that Horace was going to sell the farm - that would've made all of us workers unemployed. I suppose that won't be happening now."

329: "The ghost investigation didn't fully get underway until about 11pm - and we expected it to last all night. I explored the west tower alone. There wasn't much to see from the lower levels of the tower, so I made my way up to the top and enjoyed the view. Just before I heard the scream I saw Marty Voorhees on the south tower and Becca Loomis on the roof of the east tower. I waved at them both but I don't think they saw me as they had startled expressions on their faces - as if they'd both seen a ghost! I liked Arabella and shall miss her. I think it is good for a paranormal group to take a scientific approach and she always wanted to find the logical, rational explanation for anything we investigated."

330: "I have been best friends with Colin for two years and his grandmother has been very kind and understanding to us. One day soon, Colin and I are going to move to London, where we'll be great roommates… At school, Mrs Tipple was my favourite teacher. I couldn't bear to see her made homeless, so that is why Colin and I tried to do *something*. The shot was so loud and immediately afterwards I heard what sounded like something metal falling underneath the car." *To check under the car, go to entry* **376**.

331: The calendar hanging upon the wall features monthly illustrations of picturesque Somerset villages. On the previous Wednesday, Lucy had a social engagement to "Meet A to talk about B". The only other date highlighted in the calendar is the 13th of June, which she has circled in red and added the words "MY BIRTHDAY - drinks with the PBBs!"

332: The interior of Bertrand Mallard's cottage has been burnt to a crisp. The mantelpiece above the fireplace is little more than charcoal and a nearby armchair is nothing but ash and metal springs. It is a terrible sight. *To inspect the contents of a cupboard in the cottage's living room, go to entry* **728**.

333: The sparse contents of the wardrobe reveal that Lucy Sparrow likely lived alone in Crooked Cottage. Amongst her clothes hangs a long, white hooded robe. Evidently Lucy was a secret member of the Ancient Order of Pluckley Pagans. *At the bottom of the wardrobe, there is a hatch. To open it, go to entry* **554**.

334: "I have been a member of the Order since before the war. As a very young girl I underwent an emergency operation. It saved my life and yet it meant that I would never have a child of my own. I bless the God and Goddess for my life and yet I do hope that they might grant me a miracle one day. I remain hopeful that they will. My interest in all things occult and spiritual have been with me throughout my life. I deeply love the Order and all of its members. Wilbur will be hugely missed and I do not believe whoever killed him intended to do so."

335: "I am distraught! Who would ever do this to my poor horse! The last time I saw her well was just after noon - that dressage girl was the first of my guests to arrive and she asked to visit Nagatha. I just pray that she pulls through!"

336: Octavia Pendergast has been married to Lord Pendergast for twenty years but will forever be known as "The Second Lady Pendergast" by everyone (including her husband) as the first Lady Pendergast died many years ago - under suspicious circumstances. She is a quiet, shy woman who is rarely seen without her husband. Recently she has taken up archery as a hobby and has shown an interest in reading about poisons and their effects.

337: The note Esther has with her shows part of a code she has deciphered. It reads: "*QWE=ABC*".

338: A meeting for alcoholics who have decided to go sober was being held in the village hall earlier this afternoon. On the register of those pledging to quit booze for life is the signature of Perry Gulch - written in his regular, scruffy handwriting.

339: In the village's quaint little tearoom, Lady Pendergast and her maid Mona Prim had been watching the pageant through the open window. Annie May, who owns the tearoom couldn't help but eavesdrop on the conversation between the two women. It seems that Lady Pendergast is more than just suspicious of her husband's fidelity. Annie says that neither woman stood up from the table during the pageant.

340: The living room is as untouched and unclean as it has been for two decades. A carpet of cobwebs covers the floor. Last week's newspaper - The Pluckley Green Press - is beside the armchair where Miss Faversham sits in her yellowed, veiled wedding dress. *To read the newspaper, go to entry **485**.*

341: "My poor head is hurting me today - I had a little too much to drink last night! I have known Benjamin Hellman and his wife Juno all my life as they have been my parents' neighbours since before I was born. I've never wished harm to come to either of them. Last night I watched Juno Hellman in Hedda Gabler. She was magnificent. What an astonishing talent - and such radiant beauty... After the performance, I went to a lock-in at the Bloodied Axe and didn't get home until 1.30am!"

342: Most residents of Pluckley Green never lock their doors but the victim was clearly more vigilant and cautious than most. Through the window, bookcases laden with books about historic trains and the history of England's railways can be seen, alongside a few on general knowledge and trivia. The letterbox has the name "Pascoe" written upon it.

343: "It was bold of Miss Faversham to invite me to this reception as she is fully aware that Winston and I were courting many, many years ago. The reception was going marvellously. I was seated among the crowd and then a little while afterwards, kaboom! That greedy, impatient man had been blown to smithereens. I'm just glad that I didn't choose to wear the same peach dress as Kirsten Caldicot. That would have been an embarrassing faux pas!"

344: "I thank the Lord that I did not witness this dreadful calamity. I was in my study when I heard the enormous crash. I have no idea why the Almighty would see fit to take such a decent man by such a gruesome means but they do say he moves in mysterious ways. To think that Sebastian owes his life to that last minute change of order!"

345: Despite being a Sunday, Reverend Amos is nowhere to be found in the church. The church is empty and the door has been left ajar. The entrance to the building faces the park and the stage where the pageant is being held.

346: Captain Conjuro - real name Christopher Cryer - is most definitely dead. His head was sliced clean from his body when the blade fell and it was propelled across the stage by a fountain of blood. It is quite an unpleasant sight...

347: The timetable shows all the regular trains which are scheduled for that week, including the 9.50 to Bigstowe. It also notes that *"This Friday, Pluckley Green Train Station will be visited by the world famous Flying Welshman. The historic train will not be stopping in the village but trainspotters will not want to miss out on this remarkable event at 9.52AM."*

348: Bludger Baxter always keeps a loaded shotgun behind the bar for "personal reasons" and for protection - should the man's past ever catch up with him... The gun is still loaded with two dusty shells.

349: Mabel Witherspoon was away in Brigstowe with Esther when Penelope Gannet was murdered. She is not The Ghost. You can either guess again or go to THE GHOST: THE SOLUTION at the back of this book to learn the full story...

350: "Last night I was at Pendergast Manor with Lady Pendergast and her sons. She was rather upset, if I am to be honest. Her and the lord's marriage has come under a bit of stress recently. I have no idea where he was last night. I do love the fete and I can understand why this year's theme was met with such disdain. However, Mr Crookshank was *determined* we go with "American Dreams". Did you know that during the war I won the fete's beauty contest five times in a row! To be honest, they only awarded it to me as I was young and slim and tried to live a quiet life that was bereft of scandal." *To check Mona's story with Lady Pendergast, go to entry **702**.*

351: A track has been made through the corn by somebody dragging the body of Benjamin Hellman to the centre of the field. The track begins at the northern edge of the cornfield, where two houses - one belonging to the Greens and the other belonging to the Hellmans are situated.

352: The maid's bedroom is small but clean and well kept, unlike the rest of Stasis House. The mattress on the double bed has two depressions in it - suggesting that two people have recently shared the bed overnight. None of the maid's clothes or belongings are missing.

353: At the back of the stage, behind where each of the candidates and the host sat, there was a large map of the village on the wall.

354: Inside the photo album are many images of Bertrand Mallard playing and umpiring cricket. There are also pictures of him at the Bloodied Axe with his friends. The final image in the photo album is of him celebrating some sort of victory. Larry Finch is seated beside him and cheering.

355: "Alvin and I were looking forward to a day by the seaside. Moreover, we'd heard word that there is a pub in Worlebury-on-Sea which caters to… men like us… I was sat directly opposite Dorothy Halcyon. She kept on giving Miss Faversham a very peculiar look. I don't think the two like each other very much. However, I do know that neither Miss Faversham nor Alvin murdered her. The compartment was cramped and I was shoulder to shoulder with them both - neither one of them moved whilst we were in the tunnel." Colin has no jacket pockets or a bag of any kind to inspect.

356: In the kitchen there is a smear of what looks like a crushed cucumber on the floor. It appears to have been squashed underfoot.

357: "I was so excited to be on yet *another* adventure with my cousins - instead of spending the summer on my own private island with its castle, golden beaches and crystalline blue waters. Investigating these lights would surely make us as famous as that time when we caught those smugglers in the abandoned lighthouse - right? We were all over the newspapers then - the crime fighting children who can solve any mystery! Jimmy woke me and Fran up at about midnight with his barking but I almost immediately fell back asleep once I heard Jonathon's voice calming that dog down - then the shotgun went off and Fran was yelling at me from outside the tent and telling me to get up!" *To show Henry the note, go to entry **551**.*

358: "It is a rather unique gift, I must confess but I have an encyclopaedic memory for the shoe sizes of all my customers. It comes in handy for my work as a cobbler. For instance, Doctor White wears a size 10, whilst Reverend Harper is a surprisingly hefty size 14. Lord Asquith-Hulme is a slender size 9, whilst his assistant Carl is a size 11 - people come from miles around for my services and I remember their exact measurements every time."

359: "I believe my wife and I were the final guests to arrive. It's rather a shame that all of this frightful business occurred because I was hoping that I could bend the reverend's ear and gain his support for the housing development I am planning in the northeast. I think I should abandon my hope of winning support with the other guests present, my temper rather did get the better of me over lunch." *To learn more about Lord Lucien Pendergast, turn to entry **666**.*

360: On the weekend of the Summer Fete, Bludger Baxter had been away from the village in London with his brother.

361: "This is devastating! I am shocked beyond belief. I had hidden behind a rack of coats at the bottom of the staircase. Earlier I had spied Matilda hide in the cupboard under the stairs, where she remained concealed throughout the game. I could see that Lady Pendergast was about to discover me when the shot rang out. I immediately leapt out of hiding and formed a search party with the other players. What followed was a frantic hunt for several minutes before the maid discovered poor Charlotte's body and screamed. Whatever shall I do? How will I ever replace her?"

362: The most recent diary entry was written on the evening of the 12th of February - yesterday. *"I heard Genevieve and that handyman at it again last night, the filthy creatures - how I despise them both. I'd do away with them if I believed I could. The mere thought of love and romance, even happiness finding a home in Stasis House turns my stomach. If I myself should be denied joy then no one should be entitled to it."*

363: The cabin in which Ryan Moon slept (and was murdered) is unfeasibly tiny - barely the width of a wardrobe. His bed is a narrow shelf. There is a small, round window which peers out to the canal. There is a door which leads to the communal bathroom and another which leads to the bow of the boat. Beneath Ryan's bed is a camera and a folder containing an extensive collection of photographs of women in various states of undress. Among the photographs are images of Sabrina Danvers and Tess Mudgens wearing bikinis whilst on a secluded beach.

364: "I suppose suspicion must be upon me for this crime as the pair of us were seen as rivals in our field. While it is true that Mr Marsten and I failed to see eye to eye on several issues regarding local history, I regarded him more as a colleague. It is correct that both of us were working on books about the history of Pluckley Green but surely that is no grounds for murder? I arrived at 6pm along with most of the other guests and did not leave the church once - nor did I see anyone else leave. As far as I am aware, nobody present could have known who any of the other guests would have been."

365: The hallway of Prudence's house is an ordinary space and is unadorned by any decorations. It seems that she was dressed for bed but walking towards the front door of her house when she was killed. Blood has splattered across the walls and has dried into brown streaks. The front door to Prudence's house was always locked at all times of day. A note has been folded and placed through the letterbox. *To read this note, go to entry **621**.*

366: "I was watching from the audience seats and can safely say this was Captain Conjuro's worst show ever... Admittedly, everything was going well up until the beheading. Yet again, Captain Conjuro and Mesmerelda are going to get all the headlines tomorrow and I'll be overlooked. It's so unfair. I've been in the entertainment business for just as long as those two but because they have all the glamour, I just get ignored. Maybe that will change from now on..." *To inspect The Great Illusio's magic box (which he uses to store his props and tricks for his shows) go to entry **466**.*

367: Helen's garden is an immaculately symmetrical regency-style garden. Giles Greenham has performed a marvellous job in ensuring that not a leaf is out of place in the formal, manicured space.

368: "I have to admit, I was getting rather tired of Ryan and his roaming eye, especially the way he stared at Sabrina - like a thirsty man looks at a glass of cool lemonade. But what was I to do? I didn't want to start any trouble or risk fracturing our friend group. This morning, Tess and I were in the dining room (which also serves as the boat's kitchen) and we were planning the day's route with the help of a map. My wife was in the shower and Herb and Ryan were going about their own business. We were staring at the map when we heard that dreadful scream. By the time we reached Ryan's cabin, Herb was already there and Ryan was dead!

369: "I have heard word that Perry Gulch is a decent man but I have yet to see any evidence of it. He drinks, he stinks and the village would be a far better place without him. Back in January he wasn't as bad as he is now but I haven't seen him without a drink in his hand for months now! Perhaps the rumours that he was The Ghost's next intended victim are true... Yesterday I called upon my neighbour for advice about wine, as I was due to attend a dinner party with my girlfriend Millie that evening. I don't have a clue about wine but my neighbour was not only helpful but she gave me a bottle of chardonnay to take with me! This morning I saw Perry Gulch outside the church. He was sleeping and already had his next bottle of wine at his side."

370: Mesmerelda's real name is Jane Brown. "It is all my fault! If I hadn't suggested that we swap places, he'd still be alive! My decision was made purely on a whim - I thought that maybe our audience had seen the guillotine trick so many times that swapping roles would be entertaining for them! Our most recent reviews have complained that our old routine is getting a little stale and forgettable. Well, we certainly gave them a show they won't be forgetting soon... It is a horror beyond words. His poor wife." *To read a review of the magic duo's most recent show, go to entry* **499.**

371: Pluckley Parties Supply Shop is the foremost (and only) party supply shop in the village. From gift cards to wrapping paper, balloons and gas tanks, banners and party favours, all are here at low, low prices. The establishment was founded by husband and wife Daniel and Delia Steadman, although, since Daniel's death, the widow has run the company by herself.

372: "I have taken to turning around and walking the other way whenever I see Humbert Miner approaching in the street, as I know I will be trapped listening to his gripes and complaints if I don't. We submitted plans for our swimming pool last week. It will be truly marvellous if it does get built. As soon as we submitted, we knew full well that Humbert would oppose the plans. What a petty, miserable man!"

373: The Green family lives in a very pretty yet indistinct rural cottage adjacent to that owned by the Hellmans. Inside it is cluttered yet homely. The sheets on Pierce and Paulette's bed look freshly cleaned. Some clothes have been stashed down the back of the bed. *To look at the clothes, go to entry* **120.**

374: "If you ask me, whoever poisoned Perry Gulch is a hero and I would dearly like to shake his hand! Perry is an unsightly, unclean embarrassment to the village. The fete is just a few days away and Pluckley Green needs to look its finest for the celebration. I think we all know who was responsible for his demise - The Ghost! This morning my wife awoke me at 7am with a breakfast in bed. We were at the church by 9am. That wretch was snoring on a bench as we passed him by. There was an unopened bottle of red wine on the floor beside him."

375: The supposedly clairvoyant and deeply spiritual daughter of Adriana Arcana genuinely believes that The Ghost is a supernatural entity - which is why she attempted to contact it at Halloween. She is not the killer. You can either guess again or go to THE GHOST: THE SOLUTION at the back of this book to learn the full story...

376: On the ground under the car is a warm pistol. A single bullet has been fired from its chamber.

377: "Mrs Tipple is a fine, upstanding neighbour and was an esteemed teacher to boot. It is shameful that Lord Pendergast is able to stomp around this village like a tyrant, leaving good people like Agnes Tipple homeless and afraid. That snivelling little creature boils my blood - and I am quite certain that I would have shot him if I had been able to. Unfortunately, my cataracts prevent me from successfully aiming at anything farther away than the edge of my front lawn!"

378: Pip Longfellow has been shot once through the head. Evidently he was peering through the opening of the hide when the shot entered his forehead and exited through the back of his skull. As a stationary target, the shot would not have required the killer to have been a particularly skilled marksman. *To visit Pip Longfellow's house go to entry **472**.*

379: Last month, Conrad Cutlass received a letter from someone claiming to be "The Ghost". The Ghost wanted Cutlass to go public with the revelation that the Pluckley Green murderer was not a person but some kind of supernatural entity. Cutlass ignored the letter, assuming that the writer was a harmless attention seeker.

380: Dorian Moribund is dressed as the Grim Reaper in a long, dark, hooded robe. "My darling wife is dead and I am shattered. What am I supposed to do? She was my world! At 6.50pm I left my house to buy some wine from Carter Conway's shop at the end of the street. As I exited my home via the front door, I saw a figure in the street dressed in a similar way to me. I assumed he or she was a guest at our party (which annoyed me slightly, because I made sure *everyone* knew I was going to dress as Death for the party - so that nobody else had the same idea!) Whoever they were, they must have been the one who drowned my poor wife. The wine shop was close by so I was back home by 7pm. Mavis was hammering on the front door and Atlas, August, Stanhope and Scott were staring at me shocked. It is then that I saw my wife through the window." *To check Dorian's story with Carter Conway, go to entry **422**.*

381: Billy "Bludger" Baxter is the fearsome landlord of the Bloodied Axe Tavern. He took ownership of the pub in the years following the war and earned himself a formidable reputation as a no-nonsense landlord. Liked by few and feared by all, Bludger's story is shrouded in mystery. Some say he was once a member of a London gang, others claim he was a bare knuckle boxer. Most people are certain that he has murdered in the past. Whatever the truth, Bludger Baxter remains secretive and tight-lipped when it comes to his story.

382: "My poor, dear wife. Yes, we had our issues - not least that she disappeared for months after attempting to murder Holly Merryfair - but she was still my wife and we have raised a beautiful Yorkshire terrier together! I was the penultimate member of the Order to receive a piece of apple - as I am slightly older than my wife. Once Holly had spoken his incantation, I ate my piece. Holly then took the plate to Helena, my wife took the last slice, ate it and died. It doesn't make any sense - unless it was something other than the apple which killed her."

383: The front door to Bertrand Mallard's house has been padlocked shut from the outside. If the man had tried to escape this way it would have been impossible. *To inspect the padlock, go to entry **270**.*

384: The caves are a naturally occurring feature along the north side of the river at Pluckley Green and are of great interest to geologists in the region. There is a trail of size nine boot prints in the mud leading to and from the mouth of the cave as well as size 11 shoe prints heading in all directions from, to and around the cave and alongside the adjacent riverbank.

385: "Of course, one always hopes that nobody will die of a cakesplosion at your wedding but these things do happen. Right up until Hamish was blown to pieces the day was going really well. I was happy to be reunited with my long-lost sister Hilary - I mean Hilda! However, I do think it was rather gauche of her to wear white for my wedding! I don't know how her dress managed to get quite so muddy later on in the day…"

386: "I had gone to this venue simply for a night of diverting entertainment. Today is the day I sentenced my one hundredth criminal to execution, so I felt as if I deserved a reward to celebrate my achievement. The chemistry between Captain Conjuro and

Mesmerelda was quite something and she certainly brings a degree of glamour to the proceedings. It is a shame that this was their final performance as a double act... Also, it is an even greater shame that the guillotine never became an execution device over here - that beheading was really quite spectacular!'

387: "I wanted to have no part in the binding spell and made my feelings very clear. Not one person there knows why The Ghost is doing these murders and for all we know, he or she could have a very reasonable motive. Who are we to stand in the way of someone completing a task which they have clearly put a lot of time and effort into!"

388: "Where did the gun go? We've looked everywhere in the library and cannot find it! I had wanted to replace Eustace for some time - that's why I have been bringing Calvin with me to these meetings. He's dreadful at trivia - worse than useless because he actually has the ability to talk people *out* of the correct answer. Whenever we lose it's because of him. When I heard the gunshot I had my back to Eustace and was looking at that strange girl at the table. She was writing something odd on a piece of paper. Now with Eustace dead, Calvin can replace him and we can beat the Pluckley Bird Brains at the Bloodied Axe quiz!" *For more information about Wilma Rogers, go to entry **231**.*

389: The soup is a very simple yet very delicious vegetable broth made with a mixture of seasonal veggies which were available at short notice from the village greengrocers. The soup was served from a saucepan and ladled into plain bowls. Both the saucepan and bowls came from the church's kitchen. The soup has not been tampered with in any way.

390: In the library, there is an extensive collection of books on the history of trains and the railway. The most popular of them all is a book on Richard Trevithick - inventor of the steam train.

391: Blood is smattered and sprayed across the inside of the wardrobe doors. At the back of the wardrobe there is a hole - less than an inch in diameter. It is about head height and continues through the wall behind the wardrobe.

392: Aside from having no motive for becoming the Pluckley Green serial killer, it was said that the explosion of Crooked Cottage woke The Ghost from his or her sleep. Wilma and her sister Daisy Doyle were both awake on their houseboat at that time. You can either guess again or go to THE GHOST: THE SOLUTION at the back of this book to learn the full story...

393: As it was a warm day and the train cabin was rather stuffy, the window to the compartment was open to let a breeze in. It would be very easy for somebody to toss a knife through the window into the blackness of the tunnel after stabbing Dorothy Halcyon...

394: "Marvin took me out to the Bloodied Axe Tavern on the 11th of February - a place I am already familiar with and as a result, had rather low expectations for the evening. He was amiable enough but I think - like many men - rather intimidated by my intellect. I also wasn't happy that I could hear a fair amount of whispered gossip around us from the other patrons of the pub - clearly Marvin was the subject of a good deal of rumour in the village..."

395: There is nothing suspicious about the state of the kitchen - it is simply messier than usual because of the party going on. In the sink, there is a wet potato sack, surrounded by melting ice cubes. *To inspect the kitchen bin, go to entry **603**.*

396: Lana is clearly and understandably devastated. "I can't believe that this has happened. I planned this day for weeks in advance, so that it would be magical for us both - instead it has become a tragedy! The only people who knew about my plan beforehand were my parents and my dearest friend Petra. I didn't tell Vernon or Colin anything, they're both dreadful at keeping secrets!" *To inspect Lana's lipstick, go to **102**.*

397: "Marvin took me to a cafe on the 2nd of February. To be honest, I found him quite a boorish pig who claimed I looked old for my age and fatter than I'd described in my letter to him. I was glad to see the back of him - but I didn't wish him dead."

398: Toby Tchotchke is drenched in blood and handcuffed in the back of a police car, waiting to be brought back to the prison. "As soon as I broke free from Brigstowe Prison the only thing on my mind was revenge against that man! I would've gotten away with murdering my brothers if it hadn't been for August Barley going to the police in January! I succeeded in my mission and now August is dead. You will never find where I have hidden his body!"

399: Before retiring to bed, Christopher Aurelius had become increasingly anxious about his treasure. How many people knew he had it? What if Fenton could not wait until dawn to possess it? What if he was discovered with it? To alleviate his worries, he hid the chalice in the basement overnight. He slept safe in the knowledge that only he knew where it was hidden among the cluttered shelves. He had planned to collect it before he left the pub in the morning…

400: Bludger Baxter at the pub sighed and said "Yes, he was here this morning. He wanted to settle his bill from last night. He was a regular but I never knew his name because we all just called him "Railway" on account of his love of trains. His whole family were obsessed with trains - he once told me his father gave him his middle-name because it was the Christian name of the man who invented the steam engine. Can't remember for the life of me what that name was though!"

401: Paris wears a simple pair of loafers. "I have never been much of a competitive walker. I like to take my time and enjoy being out in nature. I have known Henery for many years and have been proud to call him more than just a work colleague, he was my friend. It did not even trouble me when he became engaged to my ex-girlfriend Angela. In fact, I wished them both well and was looking forward to being Henery's best man at the wedding. I believe I was the last to finish today and my arrival at the end of the walk made it apparent to the other members that something must have happened to Doctor White." *To speak to Angela, go to entry **704**.*

402: "Unfortunately our plans for a rather sedate luncheon have gone awry. I was simply hoping that the afternoon would be spent hobnobbing over tea and cakes - and perhaps I could explain to the vicar the perilous state our nearby wetlands are in. Sadly, it was not to be. I really hope that horse pulls through - Nagatha is a lovely old mare." *To visit the wetlands, Turn to entry **548**.*

403: Helen lays dead on her back upon her lawn. She has deep red handprints around her throat, indicating a truly savage strangulation. She is wearing rubber gardening gloves and a pair of secateurs lies in the grass nearby.

404: "Oh the news of Tommy's death is simply frightful but it will not dissuade me and my husband in our campaign against the theme of this year's summer fete. Honestly "American Dreams" could not be more out of keeping with our village's rustic aesthetic. Last night, my daughter Judy Spiff - head girl of Unity Mitford School for Girls and three-time red rosette winning Somerset Junior Trials dressage champion - and I, went to a production of "Hamlet" by the Pluckley Players. I don't know what we were expecting but it was dire, even by their low standards. We were there from 7pm until midnight - their performances really do drag on. My husband was wise and opted to stay at home instead." *To speak to Judy Spiff, go to entry **83**.*

405: "As a policewoman in Pluckley Green, I have seen more than my fair share of crime scenes and it is my estimation that Prudence Rosehip has been dead in her hallway for about two months - which would mean that the night of her murder was about the same time as a shotgun went missing from Alivin Luft Snr's woodshed. I am not in the least bit surprised that nobody has found her body in all this time - it is because nobody cared about her enough to visit. I live across the street from her and the last time I saw her was when my grandson accidentally knocked a cricket ball into her garden. I knocked on her door to ask for it and she just laughed in my face and refused. An evil woman if you ask me - you'd have more luck getting blood from a stone than a charitable donation from her! I swore I would get revenge on her somehow but I promise I did not kill her!" *To inspect Prudence Rosehip's garden, go to entry **143**.*

406: "Of course I try to be civil with Perry Gulch but everybody has their limits and that man is a blight upon this village. Over this coming weekend we are expecting visitors from all over Somerset so Pluckley Green should look its finest. I truly hope that Mr Gulch does not survive the poisoning so he cannot befoul the event! Yesterday, my next-door neighbour visited briefly to ask about wine for a dinner party and I very generously gave him a bottle of chardonnay. My husband and I went to bed early in the evening and I was up just before him - I made him breakfast in bed. Then we were at church for 9am - for we are decent, Christian people."

407: Cuthbert Crookshank was standing on the stage when he was shot. The bullet appears to have entered the right side of his neck. The bullet did not exit from the other side, suggesting it lodged in a bone there. Death would have come almost instantaneously.

408: Only the first few pages of the album of wedding photographs contain any pictures and show a young Miss Faversham and her boyfriend courting and smiling for the camera. She is pretty and he is sharp of features and wears a monocle. Another picture shows Miss Faversham on the morning of her wedding day, looking radiant in her immaculate, white wedding gown with a veil drawn across her delicate face. There are no more photographs of that day. *To speak to Lord Lucien Pendergast go to entry **306**.*

409: "Of course I had been warned about Lester Pratt throughout my weekend at the vicarage. I will not stand to be humiliated in public and was rather concerned to learn that the village has failed in previous attempts to thwart that odious prankster. I do not deserve to me made a fool of - especially in my condition. However, I must admit that Reverend Harper has been very accommodating of me and my cane as I recuperate."

410: The ropes from which bells 1-3 hang are in good condition and seem well maintained. However, the rope to bell 4 appears to have been cut with a penknife about 3/4 of the way through - the weight of the swinging bell would've been enough to snap the remaining chord. A ladder leads to the bell tower from where the ropes hang.

411: There is nothing unusual about the table. It is a standard, circular table and is used for all of Adriana Arcana's seances. There is nothing hidden underneath it.

412: "I'm afraid that I lost my temper with Jessica earlier. She had promised that she would vote for me to be May Queen - as did Kevin and Jack. Then when I saw the ballots, they *all* voted for Jessica! I lost by just one vote! Everybody knows it has been my dream to be May Queen and I *always* get what I want! I shan't miss Jack one bit. He was a dreadful man who turned my stomach - that was why I threw my lemonade in his face. My only hope is that the maypole isn't damaged!"

413: "A binding spell is a truly ancient form of magic. It prevents someone from being able to commit acts of evil or from causing harm to others. In this case, we were trying to bind the elusive Ghost. How has he or she managed to evade capture for so long? I received a piece of apple after Melody - as I am the next oldest after her. Once I took my apple, Holly performed a brief incantation and then I ate my slice. The apple itself was rather delicious as it was seeped in honey and spiced with cinnamon. I don't understand how Helena's slice could have killed her." *For further information regarding Gerald Ratchett, go to entry* **100**.

414: The book, *Archaeological Studies of England* is a highly respected academic text which was written by the triplets. On the opening page, Toby Tchotchke dedicated the book to his parents, Todrick Tchotchke dedicated it to his cat, Hieronymous and Tony Tchotchke-Vale dedicated it to his wife, Deborah.

415: "The number of letters Humbert would write in a week was truly staggering. Sometimes I'd open the pillarbox on the corner of his street and every letter in it would have his handwriting on the envelope. The money he spent on stamps must have amounted to a small fortune! I believe he became somewhat of a pest at the post office. I don't understand how anyone can become so bitter. I once tried befriending him by inviting him to the Bloodied Axe but he almost seemed offended by the suggestion! I do believe that complaining was his only source of joy in life. There are certainly more things in this world to be thankful for than to complain about." *To visit the post office, go to entry* **556**.

416: Neatly folded upon a chair beside the bed is a pile of clothes. The clothes were the ones Christopher had been wearing the day before and no doubt were what he intended to wear today too. The pile of clothes consists of snug socks, extensive underwear, trousers, a vest and a woollen gansey. A large overcoat has been hung upon the back of the door.

417: "I did not know Mr Scrub at all but I am dreadfully shocked by what happened to him. I greeted all of the guests at the door and led them to the drawing room. I promise you I had nothing to do with the murder."

418: "Last night, Milton and I conducted a practice run. At 8pm he set off along the regular route and I am quite certain he would have broken his own personal best time were it not for someone (I suspect maliciously) scattering rusty tacks along the canal path. One of them went right through the sole of his plimsoll and this morning his foot looked infected - which explains why his time today was so much worse than was expected."

419: Each of the circus performers travels in a horse-drawn caravan which also serves as their dressing room and also their living quarters. These caravans are parked in a circle behind the big top. There is a flaming metal barrel in the centre of this circle where the performers dispose of their rubbish. Inside Dazzle/Wanda's caravan it is clean and neat. There is a note beside her makeup mirror which reads: "*My love, my darling Wanda. Come back to me! Everyday my heart aches for you. I adore you and I promise that if you give me another chance, I will treat you right. All my love, L.*"

420: "I left the Order before the binding ritual began as I had promised my mother that I would be home before midnight to join her for a seance. Halloween is the night when the line between the realms of the living and of the dead is at its thinnest. I knew Helena well, I suppose I would even refer to her as a friend but I had not forgiven her for trying to murder Holly. Her husband had not forgiven her either as when she returned to the village last month, he had begun divorce proceedings. Bert and Helena chose to keep the divorce quiet but they were having an awful time deciding who should get their beloved dog Crowley once they had separated."

421: "I had been overjoyed by the news of my sister's engagement. I was so happy that I paid for an announcement note in the Pluckley Green Press! The wedding had been set to go ahead in the new year but yesterday evening an anonymous letter was delivered to our houseboat with some terrible information. I was up all night consoling poor Daisy. Now that Reginald has been blown to smithereens, I don't know if I should be distraught or relieved!" *To read the note, go to entry* **181**.

422: "I was very pleased to see Dorian Moribund in my shop. He is an extremely wealthy man who likes to purchase only the finest wines. He arrived at 6.52pm and bought a case of Malbec. I can see his home from my shop and as he was leaving, I was certain I saw someone in the alleyway behind his house. The person ran from the alley to the front door of the funeral home. I couldn't tell you who they were but I knew from their frame that the person was a man. Whoever he was, he reached the front of the house just as Dorian was arriving there."

423: "I took over as editor of the Pluckley Green Press when my sister was arrested for the murder of Marvin Makepeace. Since then I have attempted to increase circulation of the paper by publishing columns I know will get people talking. Yes, Phineas Flitter's *"Tittle-Tattle"* column infuriates some but it is also the first page everybody turns to when they get their latest edition of the paper. To be honest, his latest revelation was not quite as sensational as Phineas made it out to be and in light of events, I doubt we will publish it anyway. The newspaper has been doing very well with its extensive coverage of The Ghost. It was only last week that we received and published a note delivered to the Pluckley Green Press offices. It was posted through the letterbox late at night and written by hand. We've checked the handwriting against everyone who works for the paper and it doesn't match anyone." The note reads: *"Three bodies down and two more to come. Do not come searching for a mortal man, for I am a supernatural being, a demonic spirit, who is taking vengeance against this squalid little village of fools."*

424: "I went to bed at about 1.30am, at which time Saucy Sally had started cleaning up after the party - I've always trusted Sally to clean up, lock the pub and go home after a night. I'm embarrassed to admit that I was rather worse for drink and fell asleep on the landing at the top of the stairs. I awoke at about 7am and was desperate for water, so I went downstairs to the bar, which is when I found the body. Such a shame, everyone loved Saucy Sally. It had been a very merry party. Perry Gulch tried to enter the pub at one time but I've barred him for being too much of a drunken liability. Last time he was here he got so drunk he claimed he'd once been served wine from the Holy Grail. The poor man is succumbing to addiction and I will not support his downward spiral." *For more information about Billy "Bludger" Baxter, go to entry* **381**.

425: There is not much left of the murdered man to inspect. The remains look much like someone has poured a gallon of minestrone soup onto the tracks.

426: "August Barley came into the pub at noon for his regular ploughman's lunch and a pint of beer on the side. We chatted briefly but there was nothing about his demeanour to suggest he was worried about being stalked by a killer! This morning I opened up as usual. It was just me in the pub but after checking the barrels in the basement, I discovered that a butcher's knife had been taken from the kitchen. It must have been that dastardly Toby Totchke who swiped it from me!"

427: Mavis Davis is the village busybody. Always peeking through the net curtains or spying through keyholes, she is privy to the private lives of all the village's residents. This information she freely shares with anyone who will listen and whilst this makes the retired librarian unpopular with many, Mavis Davis' gossip is a treasure trove of information for any investigation.

428: The Tchotchke Triplets had been light and jovial throughout the New Year's Eve celebration. That was until the midnight hour approached and there was a distinct change in the brothers' demeanour. They sat together quietly, almost conspiratorially as they spoke in hushed tones. They did not cheer the winning pub quiz team, nor herald the dawn of 1956 with a toast. Something had altered the course of the night, something which had disturbed their celebrations and one by one they calmly retired to bed.

429: As much as the intimidating landlord of the Bloodied Axe Tavern may have despised Lord Pendergast, he was not responsible for his murder. None of the people who poisoned Lucien's gin and tonic that evening was the mysterious figure who later shot him.

430: "In the past, I have voted for Cuthbert Crookshank but I do not think I will this time. I like his plans to build another pub in the village but I am not a fan of his wife attempting to murder me two months ago. I heard quite a commotion inside the village hall and saw Bludger storm out just before 8pm. Obviously tempers were boiling. I didn't see where he went but I did hear some rustling in the bushes by the open window just before the shot was fired."

431: Earlier this this afternoon I left my house to go for a wintry, dusky walk. As I left my home I saw that Bludger Baxter was posting something through Larry Finch's letterbox. A little later, as I returned to the west end of the high street, I noticed something peculiar. There was a person, dressed in white - a man or a woman - skulking through the shadows and bushes. I recognised the white outfit they were wearing but I could not tell you where from. There was also something familiar about the figure's gait. When I got back from the park is when I saw Larry stumbling to the pub. He was leaving a trail of blood behind him."

432: Mavis Davis is dressed as a black cat. "I arrived at the party a little bit early - at about 6.55pm. I knew Sheila wouldn't mind and maybe I could assist with some last minute party preparation. What I saw instead was the poor woman being drowned. She was seated at the table and the figure in the black robe was standing behind her and holding her head under the water! A man dressed as Frankenstein's Monster (who I have subsequently learned was Atlas Moribund) appeared beside me and he also witnessed the drowning. I beat upon the front door and the man in the black robe fled the kitchen through the backdoor. Now, I'm not one to gossip but I've heard that Dorian and his brother Atlas despise one another! I was surprised to hear that he was due to be among the guests for the party."

433: Humbert is slumped face-down at his desk. Unsurprisingly, he was midway through writing a letter of complaint. On the desk is the letter, a pen, a roll of stamps and a sealed and stamped envelope which is addressed to the local council.

434: According to legend, the Watcher Stone was once a notorious voyeur of Pluckley Green who was spying upon the provocative moves of the dancer. For this sin, he was turned to stone by the Christian God.

435: "I'm not one to gossip but Mrs. Goodyear at the greengrocers told me that she overheard Lana and some other man who wasn't Dickon quarrelling in the tearoom. Lana was adamant that she had feelings only for Dickon and wanted the love letters to stop at once - or else she'd tell her father to intervene."

436: "This has all been a ruse. That note was clearly just a means to get us all out into the wetlands so that Pip could be murdered - as there is no trace of the rare warbling snow dipper to be found. If you ask me, his death is no more than good riddance to bad rubbish. That man almost ruined my marriage - my husband doubted my fidelity for months after that dreadful business last year."

437: "I'm afraid to say that I will not be much help in regards to recalling last night! I let that poor beggar in for the evening - it was snowing and I did not want him to freeze to death - and the pair of us ended up drinking and talking until the midnight hour had passed. I was so taken by spirits that I fell asleep in the snug. I do recall Christopher Aurelius. He is a Cornish chap who collects rare treasures. He has been to the Feathered Cap many times over the years. He asked for a room for the night - which is where I found that blood this morning. I remember that just before Christopher went to bed, I saw him go down to the basement. I have no idea why, there is nothing there but bricks and cement as I am halfway through building some walls to reinforce the cellar. I chop wood for the fire down there too - so it is where I keep my axe... *To visit the cellar, go to entry **482**.*

438: "My slice of apple was delicious and not poisonous at all. Perhaps the binding spell was simply too powerful and someone as nasty and ill-willed as Helena was knocked dead just by the strength of the magic. All five of us watched Holly slice the apple into six parts and he did not remove or replace any slices. Before the ritual began, he performed an incantation - which is sort of a prayer which is spoken to the sky - and then he took a slice himself and ate it. After that, he approached me with the slices, as I am the next oldest in the group following him."

439: The arrow entered through Penelope Gannet's throat and is now jutting out of the back of her neck. Because she was spinning at the time the arrow struck, it is impossible to tell from which direction the arrow came from.

440: "My mother was once a remarkable woman. A sportswoman, if you can believe it and a pioneer for specialising in field events, especially the discus and javelin. It was the death of my father which destroyed her spirit. We scattered his ashes in the garden last year - by his favourite rose bush. She's cared for that rose bush every day since. As for me, I have been at the church all morning and was witnessed by dozens of people there, you can check with Reverend Amos if you want an alibi." *To speak to Reverend Amos Harper, go to entry **73**.*

441: "I was out for the whole morning at work - three people can vouch for my whereabouts. I was called early to do some emergency car repairs for a villager and was at the scene promptly at 7.30am. I've been a member of the Order for almost 30 years and regarded Holly as a masterful leader - and more importantly, a friend. I don't know who will take over now but one thing I am certain of is that it won't be me - I'm already busy enough with work as it is."

442: One window of the pub is ajar by no more than six inches. Presumably, Sally opened it to allow the cigarette smoke to clear. No other windows are open and were locked shut throughout the evening.

443: When the bells of St Julian rang for Twelfth Night, the sound of the fourth bell crashing to the floor was heard throughout the village and beyond. One of the villagers was disturbed from their evening task - compiling a list of the names of five Pluckley Green residents. After returning to their work, they wrote at the bottom of the page "First murder. 9.50am, TOMORROW."

444: "After opening the circus with my introduction, I retired to my caravan, so I missed the murder altogether. The role of ringmaster is rather more complicated than head showman. It is I who organises everything from scouting locations, to providing spare costumes for forgetful performers and even arranging what we shall eat each evening. The ringmaster is basically the captain of a big, disorganised ship! The murder of Chip Burlington is a tragedy and a travesty for the circus. Every circus needs a strongman - the audience simply expects it and now we must find a replacement. I am truly disgusted that I employed Dominic Tell for this past year. I never should have replaced Curran - so what if he was a drunk, at least he wasn't a murderer!" *To visit Bartholomew Bostwicke's caravan, go to entry **494**.*

445: Ryan Moon worked as a gardener on various grand estates around the country. It was a job he was frequently fired from. His body is wedged between the bed and the wall of the small cabin. His only injury is a deep and deadly stab to his right eye. His eyeball has burst and blood and goo has poured from the empty socket onto the cabin floor.

446: "I was asleep on a bench in the park and heard Larry shouting to wake me. By the time I reached Bertrand's cottage it was already an inferno and the poor man was screaming inside. There is no doubt in my mind that this was arson - and murder - as the door to the house was chained and padlocked shut from the outside. Earlier in the night I had seen a figure dressed all in white from head to toe and with something covering his or her face. Whoever they were, they were doing something strange to the windows of the cottage... Whatever outfit or costume the person was wearing, it looked somehow familiar, as if I'd seen it somewhere before. I fear I may have witnessed The Ghost!"

447: The jar is about half filled with a mixture of water and the finest honey from August Barley's apiary. The mixture smells strongly of the spices which have been added to the honey water.

448: "Miss Faversham only lets me inside the house if there is work to be done but I see quite a bit through these grimy windows. She could have had that house cleaned anytime that she wanted to but she keeps it in this tumbledown mess as nothing more than an affectation. This morning I saw Gen in the kitchen and Miss Faversham was in an even more foul mood than usual and threw her hot soup at the poor maid. Next thing I know, Gen has gone missing. The rest of the morning I have spent caring for this flowerbed. It's been well fertilised so in a few months time it should be a blooming marvel."

449: Library records indicate that Harry was correct all along and that the boundary of his garden really is three feet into Helen's garden.

450: The Bloodied Axe is unusually quiet as almost all of the regulars had been watching the pageant when the murder occurred. The barmaid Jenny Carter explains that "It's been dead in here all afternoon. Not that I'm complaining. I've just been doing my nails and listening to the radio" Several windows and the door to the pub all face towards the park. There is no sign of Bludger Baxter. The trapdoor in the basement of the Bloodied Axe (which leads to the network of tunnels beneath the village) is covered in cobwebs and has not been opened in some time.

451: As always, the door to Larry's house is locked. There is a good deal of blood on the doorstep.

452: Pluckley Green Park, with its manicured lawns, ample seating and beautiful ornamental fountain is the pride and joy of the village - and the meeting place for friends, lovers and rivals for many decades. The park is carefully and lovingly managed by gardener Giles Greenham.

453: The ornate dagger which has been plunged into Horace Scrub's throat is the same one Adriana Arcana uses in all of her seances. A very thin fishing line has been tied around the handle of the dagger. *To find out where this line leads, go to entry* **610**.

454: Lord Pendergast is the most hated man in the village and he is also thoroughly despised by someone living very close to him too - somebody who would gladly see him dead and is planning a means to murder him before the year is out.

455: Impressive work. You have successfully managed to track down the killer. You can now turn to THE GHOST: THE SOLUTION at the end of this book for the full story.

456: "I was rather shocked when the cake exploded - so much so that I spilled my glass of champagne over the cook's dress. Thankfully she was wearing a floral print so it wasn't that noticeable. My wife and I were sat beside one another during the speeches and holding hands. In fact, she was holding my hand so tightly that I was worried she might break it. She was also grinding her teeth - I suppose that means that she was really happy for her former husband and his new bride."

457: The gun is a standard pistol. It has five bullets remaining in the six chambers of the barrel. The words *"Property of Leonard Price"* are written on the gun's handle in black pen.

458: "The Winter Wassail is an ancient tradition. We sing and make merry music for the trees in the orchard in hope that they will bear blossoms in the coming spring. I was joined by the barmaid Alice Page. Farmer Gregory Barnes was also there - although I probably shouldn't have said that. He likes to keep his involvement with the Order a closely guarded secret!"

459: "If anything, Lester Pratt's so-called jokes have become even more elaborate with each passing April Fool's Day. From itching powder in the choirboys' robes to whoopee cushions on the pews, he targets church events almost every April 1st. It was inevitable that he would attempt to stage something at the Easter parade this year. Something had to be done to thwart his plans, so I enlisted Sidney Snell's help in hopes that he would distract Lester throughout the morning. I also asked that Reverend Harper visit him the night before to talk some sense into him. I myself was out for dinner with my wife last night and was witnessed by many people."

460: "The slander against my pound cake was an absolute outrage! That recipe has been in my family for generations. Yes, I may have skimped on a few ingredients of late, but times are hard and sugar is expensive! I never actually met the man - he was far too reclusive and unpleasant to socialise. It's a good job I never met him as I'd have felt compelled to throttle him myself!"

461: The scissors are made from copper and are the same pair used for all ceremonial events held in the village.

462: "I had grown a little tired of that overlong ballet routine and by the time Penelope began her pirouette, my eyes had become distracted by Della Dempsey at the edge of the stage. She really is very talented indeed... I'm certain Della would have won the pageant - Penelope was a skilled dancer but she was rather plain and long of face."

463: "Living on the outskirts of the village like this means that one becomes very close to what few neighbours they have. My wife and I have been good friends with both the Greens and the Hellmans for many years and found them to be decent and trustworthy neighbours. I first knew that something was wrong when I saw the crows circling the scarecrow and then I noticed that he had been turned to face the other direction. It was horrible seeing poor Benjamin like that."

464: The kitchen is kept clean to an impeccable standard by Miss Witherspoon - who always manages to stay spotless despite only ever wearing her white uniform and apron. In the kitchen are the empty teapot and untouched Victoria sponge.

465: "The Second Lady Pendergast has rather trifling interests and these childish games do keep her amused - and compliant. That is the only reason I choose to indulge her in them. I hid in the easiest place possible for her to find me - mere feet away from where she was counting and as a result, she discovered me first. A little while later, after Mona had joined me at the dining room table, we heard the gunshot and then discovered poor Charlotte in the wardrobe. I have no idea how this could have happened but I fear it will harm our reputation as party hosts..."

466: The Great Illusio's magic box is a wooden trunk in which he keeps all of his props for his conjuring tricks. There is nothing unusual or suspicious about its contents. Before The Great Illusio's act, it was stored backstage alongside all the other performers' props.

467: "This was my first time as a spotter for the Pluckley Green Run. I'm actually from Brigstowe but am a fan of all sports. I didn't recognise the runners by face but I recorded the numbers the runners wore on their vests. The first to appear at Stasis House was number 0120. I handed him an orange squash, as I did with all the runners."

468: In the breast pocket of Jack's jacket is a handwritten note. It reads: *"Jack, why have you never noticed me? Please meet me at the maypole at 10.30pm so that you might steal my first kiss. Virginia. X."* To speak to Virginia Day about the note, go to entry **681**.

469: "The window at the side of the stage had been opened to allow for a breeze to enter the village hall on the warm evening. *To look outside the window, go to entry* **121**.

470: "I think Marvin wanted to impress me, as he knows I am an aspiring actress, so he took me to see a play by the Pluckley Players at the village hall on the 26th of January. As always, the cast was dreadful and the actors could barely remember their lines - Marvin was so bored that he fell asleep. Needless to say, we have not had a second date."

471: There is nobody in Pluckley Green quite as spoilt as Judy Spiff. Born into enormous wealth, the daughter of Diana and Oswald Spiff has never wanted for anything. She wears her privilege as a badge of honour and truly believes that her bloodline makes her a better person than almost everybody else. She is outspoken in her repellent political beliefs and shares her family's opinion that the wrong side was victorious in the Second World War.

472: Like most of Pluckley Green's inhabitants, Pip kept his house unlocked (this is a safe, sleepy village after all, not a dangerous, scary city). Inside there are bookshelves heaving under the weight of books upon books on ornithology. There are display cases lining the living room, featuring rows of colourful bird eggs, which Pip has collected by hand over the years. The eggs are trapped behind glass and the bird chicks inside have long since died.

473: Eustace has been shot through the temple and lays dead on the floor. In his hand is the book on European cities he was reading while standing in the geography section of the library.

474: The wall (where it is currently situated) has been in place for over a hundred years. According to Harry, the wall - which stands at chest height - was originally built in the wrong location and the legal and historic boundary is actually three feet within Helen's garden.

475: "There was no contest really. Della Dempsey was clearly going to win again - that kind of beauty is exceptional and rare - and no amount of pirouetting can beat that. I didn't see where the arrow came from but just before it struck Penelope I distinctly heard the sound of glass smashing but couldn't tell you in which direction it came from. I'm only serving as judge so that it might encourage my daughter, Judy Spiff - head girl of Unity Mitford School for Girls and three-time red rosette winning Somerset Junior Trials dressage champion to compete next year."

476: "On occasion, I am called up to go to East Berlin - to make sure the Russkies aren't up to their usual shenanigans. It doesn't amount to much action beyond checking passports and filling out forms but last time I was there it was for three months. As if the war itself hadn't gone on long enough - now it's a war against paperwork!"

477: In the pocket of the victim's shredded winter overcoat there is a notebook. Inside this, there is a handwritten list of all the world's most famous trains, including the Orient Express and the Royal Scotsman. All of the names have been crossed out, except for that of the Flying Welshman - the last on the list.

478: "I had one doughnut from the box, topped with icing, as usual. I was the third person to arrive at Penelope's house. At one point we began sharing stories of our experiences during the war. I spent those years working in the greengrocers and raising my dear daughter Rosemary with my husband Jarvis - as a farmer he was not conscripted. I did not dislike Beverley as much as others did. She could be curt and rude but that's not reason enough for murder. I remained seated at the dinner table throughout the meeting."

479: "I became the editor of the Pluckley Green Press soon after the death of my father. He had never cared for trivial things such as a lonely hearts column but as soon as I instigated it, it became a hugely popular feature of the paper. People reply to the classified ads by writing to the Pluckley Press and I pass the communications onto the lonely hearts themselves. We did it this way in hopes that it would ensure the privacy and safety of all parties involved - but it was clearly not enough to prevent something like this from happening."

480: "I am still rather shaken by that explosion. It was just so loud! I had been enjoying a sunny afternoon by the river - although I have been somewhat anxious about this upcoming newspaper column. The rumour had been that this latest piece would be his most salacious yet and… well, there is a detail about my identity which I would like to keep to myself. I have never liked Phineas Flitter and his column is nothing more than a stream of mean-spirited drivel. All he ever does is sit by the river, writing his venomous prose and smoking those obnoxious, foul-smelling cigars. I had been eavesdropping on the conversation between Jeremy Trumble and Phineas Flitter in hopes that I might discern what his latest column could be about. When he produced his cigar, I very politely asked him not to smoke it around me but he ignored my wishes and then… boom! It seems he should have listened to me after all!"

481: "I have been the owner of the Doll's House Theatre since it opened in 1948. Since then it has established a name for itself as premier entertainment venue. They say there is no such thing as bad publicity but this is not what I would have wanted - people will be scared to perform here if they think it is unsafe! I saw the whole thing from backstage and it was horrible. I was talking to Bernie Hastings and then the blade fell and… it was so gruesome! My duties this evening have been to take everyone's tickets and then show them to their seat according to the seating plan." *To inspect the seating plan, go to entry* **711.**

482: In the centre of the subterranean room there is a pile of bricks. Peter Slender has been busy building walls around the basement. Most of these walls are half finished and stand at waist height. One wall has been fully completed and the cement between the bricks is still wet. In a corner of the basement there is a cluttered set of shelves. There is no sign of an axe.

483: Dickon is wearing a purple velvet jacket, which he obviously reserves for special occasions. In the left pocket there is a small bottle of breath freshener spray.

484: A theatrical review of the Pluckley Players' "Romeo and Juliet" from the 2nd of February, 1956. *"Never has there been a story of more woe than that of the Pluckley Players latest crime against theatre. Leon Cribbage - once again cast in the lead role (and we all know why) may very well be the most abysmal actor to ever tread the boards. His interpretation of Romeo was so wooden that I began to wonder if a tree had somehow gained sentience and decided to become an actor (although a tree might actually do a better job of remembering its lines). Once again it is only the minor cast who show even a glimpse of talent but thanks to nepotism, the star of the show always has to be Cribbage, who shares top billing with his almost equally terrible stage partner - Thalia Jones as Juliet."*

485: The headline article is from the 3rd of February, 1956 edition of the Pluckley Green Press. *"MISS FAVERSHAM SAYS NO TO CHILDREN'S PLAYGROUND: The mysterious and reclusive Miss Faversham of Stasis House made a rare public appearance on Wednesday, when she visited a meeting at the village hall where a proposal to build a children's playground in an area of the heath near to her house was being debated. When asked what the children of the village should do for recreation, she retorted "Are there no prisons? Are there no workhouses?""*

486: "I happened to be strolling along the canal path when I heard an earsplitting scream from the narrowboat. There was a man smoking on the bow of the boat and he must have heard the scream too - as he dropped his cigarette and ran inside. I have always enjoyed my morning walks but they are rarely this dramatic. I heard the name of the murder victim is Mr Ryan Moon - a name I know only too well - he was the man employed at the Pendergast Estate to do some gardening and then was promptly fired for attempting to take photographs of Octavia as she sunbathed on the patio. A vile, lecherous peeping Tom!" *For further information about Mona Prim, go to entry **314**.*

487: "I swear on all that is holy that I did not kill Chip Burlington! I was in my caravan throughout Chip's performance as I needed to put my clown makeup on. I wish somebody could vouch for my whereabouts but I was in the caravan alone. After Chip did his strongman routine, Wanda was due to take to the trapeze for her acrobatic routine. I was hoping that I could see that as she is my girlfriend and it fills me with happiness to see her perform. I was supposed to go on stage immediately after her. I had struggled to put my makeup on as it seems that some of my face paints have gone missing. The next thing I knew, Leonard was at the door to my caravan and he wrestled me to the ground and accused me of murder!" *To check Polo/Dominic's caravan and makeup kit, go to entry **295**.*

488: "I know people will suspect me of hiding a bomb in the cake - after all, I was tasked with baking one for the happy couple - but I swear, it was not me! In fact, the cake I made was a tasteful, white one with adorable little figurines of the bride and groom on top - not that pink monstrosity which was in the dining hall. I left my cake in the kitchen and after the speeches, we turned around and that pink eyesore was on the table at the back of the dining hall. I was very happy for the newlyweds. Yes, Winston and I were once courting when I was a young woman but that was aeons ago and I am now resigned to the fact that I shall die a spinster. When the explosion happened, I was chatting to Gerald Ratchett - the plumber. The bang was so loud and startled us so much that some buffoon managed to spill champagne all over my lovely dress! Poor Hamish. Nobody deserves to die in a cakesplosion, even if they are exceptionally greedy." *To visit the kitchen, go to entry **545**.*

489: "Our date took place five days ago. We went for a snowy walk to the Sinners' Stones - as he knew I had an interest in mysticism. The date went very well in my opinion and we had a pleasant afternoon together. He gave me his phone number at the end of the date but whenever I've tried to call it, the number isn't recognised - he must have written it down incorrectly."

490: "On New Years Eve I hosted the annual Bloodied Axe Pub Quiz. The Tchotchke Brothers did not participate but seemed to be in good spirits all evening. As I was closing up for the night I happened to notice that a knife had disappeared from the kitchen but did not think anything of it until I discovered the bodies in the morning."

491: The trunk of Gary Grimpen is submerged up to its waist in the thick and murky mire. His arms and head have been sliced from his body and are half sunken in the mud around him. The wounds at his neck and shoulders suggest that his arms and head were sliced off with a weapon rather than torn off by a beast. *To search the area for a weapon, go to entry **588**.*

492: Wilbur is at his home and holds a coffee in his trembling hand. He was up late celebrating a friend's birthday at the Bloodied Axe the night before and says he is hungover rather than anxious. His garden overlooks the Pluckley Stones in the distance.

493: "Oh it was awful. I have known Bertrand for most of my life. He was a fine and honest man with a fierce intellect. He was a terrific cricketer as well and made a laudable umpire in retirement. I had just started my delivery round when I happened to see flames from Bertrand's home. Naturally, I was there as fast as my legs could carry me. I called for help from Perry Gulch and the pair of us tried breaking in but we couldn't - you see, someone had chained the door from the outside. It has to have been murder!" *For further information about Larry Finch, go to entry* **116**.

494: The circus performers each have their own horse-drawn caravan which serves as their means of travel, dressing room and living quarters. The caravans are stationed in a circle behind the big top. There is nothing unusual or out of place with Bartholomew Bostwicke's caravan.

495: "I'm afraid I find it very hard to stay interested in sport and get very easily distracted. When the gunshot rang out I was staring enviously out the window at the sunny village outside. I still don't understand the purpose of these meetings - are we really supposed to revise all the knowledge in the all the world? Impossible! When I turned around, Cosmo was already running to Eustace's aid. I liked Eustace and shall miss him but he really should have been replaced on the team a long time ago but none of us were prepared for the social awkwardness of telling him. What bothers me most though is… where is the gun? We have searched the whole library for it and can find no trace."

496: Stanhope is dressed as a werewolf. "I only started working at the funeral home a few months ago and I am currently only a junior assistant. I had hoped that I would be working for Dorian for a long time and would rise through the ranks. I arrived at the party just as Mavis Davis was battering at the door. I could see through the window that Mrs Moribund had her face in a bucket of water. When Mavis broke the door open, we all rushed in at once but it was clear that the poor woman was already dead. Who would do such a thing?"

497: The body of Sally Carter lays on the pub floor, surrounded by the mess of the party from the night before. There is no blood around her, nor are there any wounds indicating how she died. To all the world it appears that the woman has simply dropped dead. There is a single dart in her hand.

498: Edgar's toolbox is neat and well organised. It contains the usual array of work tools a builder would require. There is nothing unusual about the toolbox or its contents.

499: From The Somerset Spotter's review of Captain Conjuro's show at the Theatre Royal, Brigstowe on the 1st of August. "*As always, Captain Conjuro and his rather magnificent assistant, Mesmerelda have provided a highly competent and audience pleasing show. However, after all of these years of dusting off the same old routine, their act is starting to show its age. All of the illusions, the asides and the misdirections are precisely where they have always been. If you have seen their show before then there are no surprises in store for you at all. I am loathed to admit that at times I found myself more bored than spellbound.*"

500: Beverley Potter is slumped back in her chair. Her mouth is agape and inside is a half-chewed piece of jam doughnut. The rest of the doughnut has been dropped to the floor.

501: Tiffany's hide is immaculately tidy and ordered. On the wall there is a chart recording all the times the avid photographer has visited the hide and the wildlife she spied with each visit. It is evident that she visits the hide about three times a week - usually in the evenings or mornings. Her previous visit had been on Monday, the 20th of February, when she was accompanied by the rest of the ornithologist club. In an oblong storage box there is a flask of coffee which has gone cold.

502: "I never liked that foul-mouthed, fork-tongued woman and I shan't miss her one bit. That said, her demise was a frightful, messy thing to witness. To think, all I wanted was a restful day beside the sea! I do hope this matter is resolved swiftly so that we can get to our destination soon." *To look in Miss Faversham's handbag, go to entry* **533**.

503: "Yes, it was me who prepared my husband the drink and I suppose that in itself makes me look rather guilty. However, please let me assure you that the only component of the drink I supplied myself was the Old Sarum Opal gin. The other ingredients - the tonic, ice and cucumber were all on the countertop when I entered the kitchen - I don't even know who put them there. Before the party, I had been visiting some friends at Annie's Tearoom - we wanted to have a less raucous celebration of my birthday together."

504: Mona Prim, the Pendergast's loyal maid has recently taken to wearing a rather expensive looking silver watch. "I found the body in the wardrobe. It was a grisly sight. She must have been shot at close range because her face was a gruesome mess. I hid in the wardrobe of the first guest bedroom and was the second player to be found. Shortly after joining Lord Pendergast in the dining room, I heard the gunshot and went in search of the source. It is then that I found the body. I know it may seem trivial to mention now, but during the meal Lord Pendergast dropped a fork onto the floor and when I bent low to pick it up, I saw that Mr Nolan and Mrs Merton were playing footsie under the table. Perhaps those rumours of their affair are true?" *To inspect the wardrobe where Mona was hiding, go to entry* **22.**

505: This stone leans at a precarious angle and according to local legend, it was once the village drunk who made himself intoxicated on a Sunday. For this sin he was turned to stone by the Christian God.

506: The note is written in a style which closely resembles Gordon Nolan's penmanship but is not identical. It reads: *"My Dearest Charlotte, the danger and excitement of this storm is making me feel amorous. When Lord and Lady Pendergast suggest we play hide-and-seek, please go to the wardrobe in the second guest bedroom and you and I can hide in the dark together! Show nobody this note. G."*

507: "My poor husband! Yes, I had my concerns about Christopher and Jane, Captain Conjuro and Mesmerelda have such great onstage chemistry that it's hard not to worry about all of those late nights they spent together rehearsing... But I never wanted anything bad to happen to him! I took my seat when the doors opened and did not move from there throughout the evening."

508: "I hadn't seen my sister in almost 20 years, so it was quite a surprise to discover how different she looks to how I remember from all those years ago. I was not at the reception for the speeches as I was, well, in a bush. I had lost something there and one of the friendly waiters at the reception was helping me find it..." *To speak to Lance Masters, the waiter, go to entry* **207.**

509: Brigstowe Royal Infirmary is (as the name suggests) located in the city of Brigstowe. It employs a good number of the villagers of Pluckley Green. Matron Bathsheba Sharpe works on the E Wing alongside many nurses - including Angela Baird. Hospital employees frequently take small, surplus hospital supplies home with them.

510: "People are surprised to learn that a man like me has a spiritual side but I have been a Pagan for many years, even before I moved to the village - although I have the good sense to keep my involvement to myself, unlike Holly Merryfair! I am very much of the belief that the stones really were once the site of human sacrifices. I am not arguing that we should return to those days but I am certain that the stones are hungry for blood and if we were to satisfy them, perhaps a lot of this village's problems would disappear... I did not see who threw the dart but I assure you it was not me." *To ask Bludger about the dart, go to entry* **212.**

511: "When Sally broke up with me, it hurt a good bit. I thought we were having fun but the thing to remember when you're going with a girl like that is it's probably going to end in tears, so I knew it wasn't going to be a lasting thing. I'm just glad we managed to stay friends - she'd even slip me the odd pint for free! She'd found herself a good chap in Donny."

512: The body of Charlotte Merton lays slumped on the floor of the wardrobe. She has been shot in the head - with the bullet entering through the forehead. There is a handwritten note clutched in her hand. *To read the note, go to entry 506.*

513: The cardboard tube of salted peanuts is about five inches tall and about the same in diameter. The brand is a popular one which is available in the village corner shop - and throughout the nation. The lid lays on the floor beside the tube. Lester did not have a peanut allergy.

514: "I do not say this with any hyperbole but I do believe that my husband loved that car more than me. The only person he trusted to drive it - other than himself - was Tommy Tomlinson and even then it was only if it was to be used for official committee business. This morning Tommy was at the door at 7am and asked to borrow the car to go to Brigstowe to organise entertainment for the fete. The poor man would have had no idea that the car had been tampered with. The sabotage must have happened when we were out last night. We went to Marley's Restaurant in the village. Dunstan's birthday is approaching and we wanted to say thank you to him for all the work he has done on the committee. When we got home at half past midnight there was a little puddle of liquid under the car but it didn't look like anything serious to me."

515: "I had been hoping that August Barley would teach me a little about beekeeping. He used to live next door to me and would frequently give me jars of the most delicious honey! He has always been very generous with his time and expertise in the past so it was my intention that I could learn some of the basics from a true master! Unfortunately, he was nowhere to be found at 3pm, which is when we arranged to meet at his apiary. Now I learn it is because he has been murdered. How utterly devastating."

516: The man's wallet has been torn apart by the force of the train and most of the contents have been destroyed. There is a partial scrap of what had once been a library card. *To visit the library, go to entry 390.*

517: Daisy Doyle had been enjoying the perfect life with her husband Jarvis and their daughter Rosemary. Everything changed when Rosemary was struck and killed by a dangerous driver. The couple's grief drove them apart and they divorced soon afterwards. Daisy now lives with her sister in a houseboat on the canal. She has a part-time job in the village bakery. The unimaginable pain from her loss has led her to do some unspeakable acts in the past.

518: "Very well, I admit it! The gurt dog is nothing more than my bloodhound/mastiff cross Merlin. At night I paint luminescent paint around his eyes and let him wander the heath. I have been doing it for more than twenty years with several generations of dog and my father, Gabe Ratchett did it before me. You see, the mire is deathly dangerous at night and people are prone to drowning there. I let Merlin roam the heath so that he will drive people away at night - I just wanted to keep people safe! It may seem like a dreadful ruse but the paint washes off and causes Merlin no harm and I do believe it has prevented many an unnecessary death in the mire! The only people to know about it are my fellow members of the Pluckley Pagans."

519: Just off of the main path leading into the dark and foreboding Western Woods is a small shelter made from branches and leaves. Presumably this is where Toby Tchotchke has been staying for the past six nights. There are size 11 shoe prints in the soft mud around his encampment.

520: Larry Finch's name is stitched into the front of his wallet. In his effort to stumble to the front door he must have accidentally dropped it. Inside the wallet is a key to his house. *To use this key on Larry's front door, go to entry 11.*

521: Before his retirement five years ago, Gabe Ratchett had worked as a plumber but had been a member of the Pluckley Green Ringers for over 20 years, becoming the head of the society in 1954. He was regarded as a fine, upstanding and well-liked gentleman but is now just a puddle of goo.

522: Like almost every other room in Stasis House, Miss Faversham's bedroom is covered in dust and cobwebs and the windows are thick with grime. Beneath her canopy bed, the sheets are unmade and on the pillow there is a diary. *To read it go to entry **362**.*

523: "It might seem like a strange thing to confess at a time like this but I do believe I was the only person in the village who actually liked Cuthbert Crookshank's theme for the village fete. Something modern and glitzy! It is a moot point regardless as it is certain to change - Mr Crookshank must know that the sabotage of the car was meant for him. It is my 25th birthday later this week and Cuthbert and Eloise offered to take me out for a slap up meal at Marley's Restaurant in the village. We were there from 8 until midnight, after which I walked home, which was westward from the restaurant whilst the Crookshanks headed east on foot. I was in bed by 12.30am."

524: The red ribbon is made of nylon and has almost been cut in half by Conrad Cutlass' scissors. Folded inside of the ribbon is a thin wire made of copper from which sparks are snapping. The nylon ribbon would have insulated the copper until the metal scissors made contact with it. *To find the end of this copper wire, go to entry **265**.*

525: Holly Merryfair is on the heath, walking a large dog. "I have asked Gerald Ratchett for use of his dog Merlin this morning. As a bloodhound/mastiff cross I was hoping he might be able to find the scent of the killer but unfortunately he is more interested in chasing rabbits than solving crimes! I met the five youths just before midnight last night. The only one I recognised was Donny - he is the newest member of the Ancient Order of Pluckley Pagans. I was attending the standing stones for a full moon ritual - I always like to give thanks to the goddess. They were very enthusiastic about seeing the moon in her full glory upon the heath." *To look at Merlin, go to entry **189**.*

526: "The boss is dead and I am truly heartbroken. I'm not very good at expressing my emotions, so you will have to take my word for it when I say that I am devastated! This morning, we were all outside the pub and on time for our first day of work on the basement. The landlord let us in and Oliver rushed to the basement - he is always eager to get started before anyone else. Then he screamed out and died! Last night I had a couple of pints at the Bloodied Axe with my friend Larry Finch. We were discussing The Ghost, the village and the possibility of relocating to London." *To speak to Larry Finch, go to entry **726**.*

527: "I'm still so shocked that it hasn't even turned into grief yet. Lana's proposal to Dickon was a fabulous surprise but Vernon and I had known for more than a week that Dickon intended to propose to Lana himself on this very day - he'd bought a ring and everything. This morning Dickon was rehearsing his lines for the proposal and I was giving him advice. Vernon gave him a breath freshener, so that he could be minty fresh when he kissed Lana after the proposal."

528: Pluckley Green's intrepid botanist most likely despised Lord Pendergast as much as anyone else in the village but she did not murder him. Wilma and Lady Pendergast have yet to interact in any meaningful way together.

529: "I should apologise to all those present for my husband's outburst over lunch. He and that dressage girl had quite the disagreement over certain equine practices. You see, my husband breeds thoroughbreds for racing and does not regard dressage as a sport at all. Unfortunately the sugar-free diet he is following has given him a rather short and irritable fuse. And that girl… well, she's a spoiled brat and nothing more."

530: The Western Woods are the setting for many ghost stories and folk tales. Perhaps the most fanciful story of them all is the legend that King Arthur himself once owned the forest and frequently spent time there when away from his castle in Glastonbury.

531: As always, "Miss Faversham" wears her old and tattered wedding dress and hides her face behind a veil. "I have always adored the circus! As a small girl it was my dream that I would one day become an acrobat but alas, life was not to lead me that way… I was having a wonderful time watching the show - until the murder happened. At first I thought it was a rather bizarre and tasteless part of the act. Polo the Clown just marched onto the stage and shot that poor strongman in the head! I struggled to see everything as I was unfortunately seated behind a man with the most ludicrous orb of ginger hair! Imagine going round in public looking like that!" *For more information on Miss Faversham, go to entry* **86.**

532: Lord Pendergast has been shot through the right shoulder. There is a good deal of blood on the seat beside him, suggesting that the bullet came from the direction of Agnes Tipple's house.

533: In Miss Faversham's handbag there is a note, written in green ink. *"This is the THIRD time I have asked for hush money from you. I know you are not truly Miss Faversham but instead an imposter - her own maid! If you do not pay the sum I have demanded I shall expose you to all the village!"*

534: Several regulars at the Bloodied Axe Tavern say that they saw Bludger Baxter enter the pub just before 8pm and angrily order a pint from the barmaid. He had just started drinking it when the shot was heard from the village hall across the road.

535: Evidently, being a man of the cloth was not enough to dissuade Reverend Amos Harper from attempted murder - as he had unsuccessfully attempted to poison Lord Pendergast that very evening. However, none of the people responsible for poisoning the gin and tonic was the one who shot Lord Pendergast.

536: The dart was travelling at quite some speed when it entered Wilbur's neck as it had imbedded itself deep into his throat. On the flight of the dart the words *"Property of the Bloodied Axe Tavern"* have been printed. The dart has a distinct smell of cinnamon.

537: "Daisy Doyle had asked me if I would bake a cake to celebrate her fiancée moving permanently to the village. Because of his work commitments, Reginald Sole was due to arrive at Crooked Cottage in the early hours of the morning, so I suggested to Daisy that I could cook a cake in the cottage - that way it would be waiting for him when he arrived. I was actually very excited about using a gas cooker for the first time in my life! Crooked Cottage was the first house in the village to have gas installed and… well, I can see how the explosion happened now… I swear that I did not leave the gas on. I checked and double checked. I was at the cottage from 8-10pm last night. The sound of the explosion rocked the vicarage and woke me with a horrible start. Today, I am going to tend to some of the graves in the churchyard and later I shall be going for a walk with my daughter Esther." *To visit the churchyard, go to entry* **125.**

538: There is a serial killer in Pluckley Green and he or she has already begun their operation. Their first victim was Robin Pascoe, the trainspotter who was pushed in front of a train. This killer is acting alone and without help from anyone else.

539: "Earlier this afternoon, we were strolling through the trees, of this small suburban park and discussing what this upcoming column could be about. Everyone in the village is convinced that the scandal in the paper will be bigger and more damaging than anything Phineas has published before. We were both concerned that the column could have something to do with us… After leaving the shade of the trees, we sat down in the grass. Phineas was about ten feet away from us. Neither of us had spoken to him today. Almost as soon as we sat down, the explosion happened."

540: There is a trail of blood where Larry stumbled to the pub and collapsed. This trail begins halfway up the high street - to the east of the Bloodied Axe Tavern. Most likely, this was not where he was slashed - just the point where the blood started to flow far enough to reach the ground. Larry appears to have made an attempt to reach his house - which is situated next to the pub - but was unable to get inside, so instead stumbled on to the Bloodied Axe. A wallet has been dropped on the ground close to where the trail of blood begins. *To inspect this wallet, go to entry 520.*

541: From the *"Big Book of Poisons"* in the vicarage library: *"One of the most popular toxins favoured by the modern poisoner is whipper snake venom - extracted from the rare and highly dangerous snake, which can now only be found in wetlands around the Somerset area. Despite the difficulty in obtaining this venom, it remains highly recommended by skilled practitioners in the art of poisoning as, when dried, even a minuscule dose can be enough to kill a small horse and remains almost undetectable in the body. It does however have a slight scent, akin to cinnamon."*

542: "I may work in the field of non-fiction and history writing rather than mystery fiction like Conrad Cutlass, but I still know how hard it can be to get words onto paper - that said, Conrad Cutlass was a no-talent hack who couldn't write an original character to save his life! He just chose a real person from the village, slightly changed their name but kept that character's description identical to their real-life counterpart! Ever since Tarquin Taggers perished in that dreadful car accident, Cutlass' book sales have been in the doldrums - people *love* an author when he's dead! If you ask me, the literary world is better without him! As for the murder itself, has anyone questioned Larry Finch about why he's suddenly walking with a limp?"

543: "It was harrowing to find poor Gary in pieces like that. The pair of us didn't always see eye to eye - especially in regards to Tamara. A love triangle is one thing but a love square is quite another - but I shall miss his friendship. Last night, after we saw that horrifying dog, we all scarpered. I believe I fled east and had to make my own way back to the tent."

544: The mask Helena had been wearing for the Samhain ceremony was placed on the grass beside her during the binding ritual. The mask is completely white with holes where the eyes, nose and mouth are placed. There is nothing unusual about the mask and no poison has been applied to it.

545: There is no sign of any cakes - pink or white - in the kitchen. A door leads from the kitchen to the back of the dining hall. The backs of all the wedding reception guests were turned when the cake was brought out from the kitchen - as Miss Faversham was giving her lengthy speech.

546: The incinerated car was a 1954 American built Hudson Hornet and had been the pride and joy of Cuthbert Crookshank. It would appear the car's brakes have been cut.

547: "This will be frightfully bad for business! During my seances I ask that all present hold hands so that we form a circle around the table and they close their eyes so that they may focus their psychical powers upon the dagger. Usually they open their eyes to see that the dagger is floating mid-air but this time it was stabbed through Horace Scrub's neck! We really should have continued with the spirit board as we had some success with it. We asked the board who would be the next victim and it provided us with the initials. Something… "G" - I wish I could remember the first letter."

548: The wetlands are a vast, flat boggy expanse which has been left for nature to thrive in abundance. Nestled outside of the northeastern corner of Pluckley Green, this wetland has become a breeding ground for many of England's rarest species.

549: "My days of living in Pluckley Green are coming to an end. My friend Alvin and I are moving to London to open a fashion boutique! As for Prudence, I can't say I enjoyed her company very much - she never seemed to like anyone and was always filled with spite. To be honest, I had not really noticed her absence from the village these past few weeks as she is far too unpleasant to spend any time thinking about." *To speak to Alvin Luft, go to entry* **729**.

550: John's bag contains a copy of the Bible, a change of socks and underwear, a pair of leather shoes, a map of Somerset and a purse which holds a few gold coins.

551: "I didn't write this but my God I wish I'd had the guts to do so! It's about time one of us stood up to Jonathon and told him that this has to stop. I'm sick of deluding myself into thinking that this piddling nonsense with the lights will make us famous again. Nobody cares, we all know the lights are just Pagans from the village doing some sort of ritual. Hopefully this will be the end of us as a group. Did you know this isn't even the original Jimmy? The first one died of old age - that's how long we've been stuck doing this crap!"

552: "Now, I am not one to gossip but I knew Silas Marsten fairly well. Not that I liked him, of course - nobody did after what happened. I actually knew that Silas Marsten would be here this evening as he said as much when I spoke to him in the bakery. I just *had* to tell absolutely everybody. The sheer *nerve* of that man pretending that he can act as if nothing happened last year. He still speeds around this village like a madman in that car - that just shows how little remorse he feels and how, if you're rich and well connected, you can get away with anything. What he did was enough to end the marriage between Daisy and her husband. Something like that changes people - and their marriages."

553: "Oh I so enjoy being a member of the Fearless Five. Every summer hols I look forward to the thrill of preparing endless picnics for these greedy, thankless brats and having to wash all of their clothes in a stream. In case you hadn't guessed, I am being sarcastic. I vowed to myself that this is the final summer I put up with being treated like this. Can you believe the boys didn't even let us sleep in that cosy barn after they showed us around? We had to sleep in a tent on the boggy ground! That manic dog barking woke us up in the tent at midnight and then Henry fell back to sleep - that is when I heard the shotgun blast." *To show Fran the note, go to entry* **238**.

554: The hatch at the bottom of the wardrobe opens to what is unmistakably a trapdoor. It is large enough for a person to easily fit through and is possibly as old as Crooked Cottage itself. It is not possible to open the trapdoor as it is fitted with a locking mechanism which requires a three-digit code to open. It is safe to assume that there is a similar lock on the other side of the trapdoor. Judging by the make of lock, it was likely installed in the 1920s - long before Lucy Sparrow moved into the cottage.

555: Among the photographs of Lucy Sparrow on the memorial which was set up by her fellow librarians are images of her partaking in various outdoor activities including rock climbing, birdwatching and flower pressing. In many of these photographs she is surrounded by friends - one of whom was a trainspotter named Robin Richard Pascoe.

556: The queue in the post office is moving smoothly and quickly today in the absence of Humbert Miner. The stamps and envelopes which customers are buying are kept locked away in drawers behind the counter. Only the postmaster or postmistress have access to them. Today, the postmistress is a young woman named Hebe Summers: "Things are certainly operating a lot more efficiently here now that Mr Miner is dead. He spent so much time in the post office complaining that my coworker Margaret nicknamed him Mr Moaner! It wasn't just the post office that he complained about. The sun shone too brightly on the marble fountain in the park, the bees made too much noise, children laughed too much for his liking. A truly sour man who I shall not miss one bit!"

557: "I remember my wedding day to Winston. Reverend Amos said I was the most beautiful bride he had ever seen. I wish nothing but happiness for Miss Haversham and Winston. I mean, just because Winston asked for a divorce because he had fallen in love with Miss Faversham doesn't mean I am still bitter about it. It is not as if I am living every hour of every day wondering what could have been or that I am constantly tortured by the pain of a heart which simply refuses to heal. And of course, I certainly didn't marry my husband within days of the divorce being finalised simply because I had a petrifying fear of dying alone. Oh no, not I! My husband Steven was best friends with Winston - and I can assure you that I didn't choose him just because I thought it would make Winston jealous. I mean, just look at my husband in his handsome blue suit. What a sufficient man I have married!"

558: Lester Pratt's front garden is somewhat of an overgrown mess. There is a patch of mud by the front step to his house. In this mud there is a good number of footprints. Most of these are a mens size 8 shoe, however, one of them is a mens size 11.

559: "Cuthbert was an embarrassing idiot who has brought nothing but shame upon this village. Always focusing on the needs of the many - and not the elite few, who are the only ones fit to govern. On top of that, he was a terrible public speaker. Turning your back on the audience like that? Unprofessional to say the least! I felt quietly confident - regardless of what public opinion may have suggested - that I would comfortably win this election with a landslide. After that, I would make it my mission to eliminate all of those who we deem undesirable from our village."

560: "That wicked Miss Faversham exploited and abused poor Genevieve. She made her work all hours of the day for a pittance and I'm certain she abused her too - scratching with those vicious talons of hers. The scratching and hair pulling was getting worse in recent weeks. I just hope that nothing terrible has happened to that poor maid and that she has managed to escape from that wretched house and that evil woman. She kept that woman locked away most of the time - so much so that I doubt most of Pluckley Green would even be able to recall her face!"

561: Click! The trapdoor opens to a dark tunnel. In the space immediately beneath the wardrobe, Lucy had stored a few of her belongings (Crooked Cottage was far too small even for her meagre possessions). The tunnel continues in one direction - where it opens to the basement of the Bloodied Axe Tavern. In the other direction it opens to a small cave by the Arbon River. It is impossible to tell how old this tunnel is or how (and why) it was made.

562: The thawing of the snow has lead to an unprecedented flow of the river into the wetlands estuary. With the migrating birds just weeks away from their spring arrival, the estuary is currently a rather barren, empty space with little wildlife. Carried here by the torrential rush of the river is a rifle - half buried in the estuary silt. A single bullet is missing from its chamber.

563: The cottage in the Western Woods was abandoned decades ago. It has partially collapsed and has been taken over by the spread of nature. The cottage was frequently used by Doctor White while out walking, as it was a discreet and convenient place to nip behind to urinate. At the back of the cottage - where Doctor White's body is located - there is a spray of blood on the wall, suggesting that the man's killer crept up behind him as he faced the building and slashed his throat.

564: "I allow Perry to sleep on a bench in the graveyard - it seems like the Christian thing to do - but I won't allow him into my home because of the stench. I do wish Perry would have a bath or at least change his clothes! Earlier this year I tried to find him some work, first at Gerald Ratchett's plumbing company and then at August Barley's bee farm but both times he was fired for being drunk at work. I saw Perry outside the church this morning and it would seem that somebody gave him a bottle of wine during the night or early morning. You don't think it was The Ghost, do you? Now, if

you don't mind, I must sort through some of the donations to the village fete raffle."
*To look through the donations, go to entry **274**.*

565: "I am no fool. I knew precisely what was going on with my wife and that man and perhaps I had learned to accept it. I wasn't happy about it, of course - and Matilda was even considering divorce. I suppose that situation has resolved itself but I am nevertheless devastated. I shall miss her dearly. I hid behind the curtains of the second guest bedroom. I wanted my wife to join me there but she insisted that she hide in the wardrobe of that room instead. During the game, I had a good line of sight and I swear that I saw nobody enter or leave the room throughout. When the gunshot went off, I knew at once that something dreadful had happened because I heard Charlotte drop to the floor in the wardrobe." *To check behind the curtain, go to **671**.*

566: "To be honest, I only joined the Pluckley Players so that I could be closer to Thalia. I saw her in Romeo and Juliet last month and I thought she was so beautiful. I don't think that she's too happy with me being the understudy because she keeps on talking about how my nature is too "full of the milk of human kindness" and how if some sort of accident happened, I could take the lead role. I think her part in this play might be driving her quite mad. If I'm honest, I'm going off her a bit. As for me, I was in the dressing room with Eric. We were smoking and laughing again about that dreadful review of the last play. That's when we heard Thalia scream from the wings. It was dark backstage but we managed to make our way to the stage, which is when I saw Leon's dead body. I really hope this doesn't mean that I'm going to have to be Macbeth now…"

567: The guests had their lunch at the dining room table - overlooking Nagatha's paddock and stable. Tea was brought out just after Judy's arrival and was poured from a bone china teapot with matching cups, plates and a bowl of sugar cubes. The cake was a Victoria sponge but it was never served, as all the guests witnessed Nagatha's unsteady wobble back to her stable through the bay windows.

568: "I was due to go onto the stage once Chip finished his act - so I was waiting in the wings when Dominic shot Chip. How awful! To think, the man I loved is a murderer! Dominic and I had been a couple for about a year. Before that, I had been in a rather dreadful relationship. I had fallen madly in love with Dominic and I believe he did the same - although I don't know what to believe from him now! Nobody in the world could ever want to kill Chip Burlington. Despite being the largest and strongest man I have ever sen, he had a sweet and gentle heart. Nobody could hate him. What was Dominic thinking?" *To visit Dazzle/Wanda Highsmith's caravan, go to entry **419**.*

569: "Obviously my husband and I had heard of the Fearless Five before - who hasn't? To be honest, I thought they'd all gone their separate ways years ago but no, it seems that they are desperate to reclaim those glory days when they were capturing smugglers during their summer holidays. My husband and I humoured them as they seemed kind hearted and rather pathetic. That is why we let them stay in the barn and camp outside. The lights are no mystery to anyone - it's just the Pluckley Pagans doing something at the standing stones. Now it would seem that one of those little monsters has murdered my poor husband! We were just about to head to bed when we heard the dog barking. Milo went outside to see what the matter was and that is when I heard the gunshot. I hope all of the Fearless Five hang for this!"

570: The ferocious and feared judge did not murder Lord Pendergast. As a man who respects power, money and the social elite above all else, Judge Jan Treagle would have seen nothing wrong with the ways in which Lord Pendergast was behaving.

571: There is no evidence linking the village plumber to the Pluckley Green serial killer. Moreover, Mabel Witherspoon mentioned conversing with Gerald at the Christmas Eve wedding - no guests at the wedding reception are The Ghost. You can either guess again or go to THE GHOST: THE SOLUTION at the back of this book to learn the full story...

572: "Lord Pendergast is a *wicked* man. Just last night I was trying to console yet another poor lady who has been evicted from one of his properties. It may sound unchristian of me to say, but this village would be a far better place without him in it! Aside from the tyranny of that awful man, I have been very much enjoying our change of circumstances at the vicarage. Esther has been settling in wonderfully. I have been teaching her how to grow plants and today was the day that my crop of cucumbers was ripe for the picking. I actually brought one along this evening, as Lady Pendergast mentioned this afternoon at Annie's Tearoom how much her husband likes a slice of cucumber in his gin and tonic."

573: The explosion of Crooked Cottage was so loud that it awoke villagers across Pluckley Green. Among those who were jolted from sleep was the elusive person who has become known to all as The Ghost.

574: The staircase which leads from the ground floor of the pub to the basement consists of eight steps. On the second step from the top, a line of fishing line has been tied from the bannister to the wall at ankle height. This almost invisible tripwire is undoubtedly what caused Oliver to fall to his death.

575: "I have been attending these sewing meetings for the past four weeks. It is good to get out of the house, to make friends and enjoy the sunshine - although this old wedding dress is rather hot and stuffy, alas, I can't take it off... I was telling the ladies about Esther's ongoing struggle with the coded note from her mother. I even brought part of the code with me in hopes that the ladies might be able to decipher it. As for Beverley, she was a rather old-fashioned, unpleasant woman - although I suppose people would have said the same about me in the past. I was the second guest to arrive at Penelope's house and I sat at the dining table throughout the evening. I did not have a doughnut as sweet things are not to my taste." *To look at the section of code, go to entry* **91**.

576: "Nobody wanted to see Pip Longfellow dead more than I. Last year he wrote a love letter to my wife, suggesting that the pair elope to Brigstowe together. That ugly, sweaty lech claimed that he sensed an unspoken bond between them. All nonsense, of course, and my wife informed me at once. Nevertheless it caused something of a rift in our marriage that has only recently healed. I couldn't stand the sight of the man and hated that he was still a member of our group but I did not kill him."

577: "I appreciate this walking group because for the most part, people are not here to socialise or chitchat. We are each free to walk at our own pace. As always, I completed the walk before anyone else. Then came Minerva, closely followed by Artemis. Paris was the last to complete the walk and it was then that we realised that something must have gone awry. Artemis is perhaps the only member of the walking group I have much time for, as I work with his mother at the hospital" Bathsheba wears rugged, men's walking boots. *To visit the hospital, go to entry* **509**.

578: The front of the boat is an open-air space in which it is possible to sit back and nonchalantly watch the world glide by. On the floor of the bow there is a stubbed out cigarette and beside it, a length of metal wire - half of which is coated in blood.

579: From "The Bride Wore Stolen Pearls" - Conrad Cutlass' latest "Piddly Glen" novel. *"Jake Powers, the red-headed agent, looked up from his writing desk as the door opened. Wilhelmina Rudders' magnificent bosom entered the room before the rest of her. "I was correct!" She gasped. "Judge John Trangle was in cahoots with the arrogant historian September Wheatley all this time!". "Indubitably, Miss Rudders," Lawrence French replied. "But where is the Kensington Diamond if it wasn't in the handmaid's jewellery box?". Wilhelmina Rudders smiled, "Ever since the masquerade ball I have had the diamond hidden between my bosoms!""*

580: When she is not acting with the Pluckley Players, Isobel runs an antiques shop on Pluckley Green high street. "It's all such a blur now but I remember being part of the scrambled rush to the stage and then Thalia burst into sobs upon my shoulder. It was then that I saw that Leon was dead. As sad as it is, perhaps it will prove to be a blessing in disguise for the Pluckley Players. Maybe a few of us who get overlooked time and time again might get a chance to shine instead of us only staging plays where Leon gets to be the star."

581: Robin Pascoe will be the first of five victims of the serial killer who will come to be known as "The Ghost". Whilst the slayings may at first seem random, these deaths were carefully planned and each of the victims had one important thing in common.

582: *"Local surgeon Marvin Makepeace has been fired from Bigstowe Royal Infirmary. The Pluckley Green resident was found guilty of professional negligence by a medical tribunal yesterday. Makepeace was said to be tired and forgetful during an operation on the heart of Sir. Peregrine Conley - the editor of this very newspaper. Nurses at the surgery theatre gave testimony at the tribunal that Makepeace had earlier been bragging that he had been "kept up all night" by sordid activities with his misstress."*

583: Owing to his status as a vagrant and an alcoholic, Perry Gulch is often dismissed as a shambling fool and a blight upon the otherwise perfect village. In truth, Perry Gulch is a silent observer to so many events which would otherwise go unnoticed. He knows things.

584: With Humbert Miner dead, people across the village felt emboldened to submit planning applications for all sorts of alterations to their properties. Among them was Bludger Baxter, who applied for an extension to his basement to be built. Unbeknownst to him, Bludger was about to unearth a shocking secret from the village's past.

585: In the bin there is a solitary jam doughnut. It is intact and perfectly ordinary.

586: "Wilma has invited me along to these library sessions for the past three Saturdays. At first I thought she had amorous intentions towards me but now I suspect she has merely been trying to hook me in as a replacement for that simpleton Eustace Leadbetter - may he rest in peace. When the shot rang out I was peering through the bookshelves at Wilma in the geography section. Eustace fell to the floor and we all ran to help him but it was already too late."

587: "I did often warn Hamish Kingston that his sweet tooth would be the death of him. I just didn't know it would happen in quite so dramatic a way… I attended the reception but was not present for the speeches - I have a surprise planned for later and it involves my horse Nagatha Christie, so I was taking care of her. On my way back to the dining hall, I passed a woman in a blue dress who I did not recognise. She was carrying a pink wedding cake and doing so very carefully. I could have sworn the one Mabel baked was white!"

588: The mire is dangerously hard to spot in the windswept landscape - even in the daylight. The lethal bog has claimed countless lives over the centuries, their bodies forever locked away beneath its murky surface. Hikers who are inexperienced with the area have proven particularly vulnerable to its merciless presence. Half submerged in reeds at the edge of the mire is a bloodstained axe.

589: "I am devastated and do not think I will ever recover. That car meant everything to me and was the sum of all of my achievements in life so far. Also Tommy was a fine gentleman. It was the car itself which inspired me to instigate this year's theme for the village fete - "American Dreams". I wanted to go with a theme which felt modern, glamorous and with an eye to the future. The idea did not go down well with the stuffy committee (or my wife) but I forced my idea through - as chairman, my say is final. Last night my car was parked on the drive of my house. From 8pm until midnight I was at a village restaurant with my wife and the committee member Dunstan Lavender. When my wife and I arrived home at 12.30am there was some liquid under the car. It was too late to deal with it then but in reflection it could have only have been brake fluid. Somebody must have crawled under the car and cut the brakes."

590: "Last night I met my friend Christopher Aurelius. I could not have known it would be for the last time. The pair of us spoke of antiquities as he knows I am a collector. He has a proud history of uncovering treasures and I pay handsomely and honestly for them. After a few drinks at the pub, I went to visit Father Bastian at the church." *To speak to Father Bastian, go to entry* **658.**

591: "This really has been a dreadful year for the Ancient Order of Pluckley Pagans - what with so many of our members being murderers, attempted murderers or murder victims. Not to mention my specific suspicions I have about a member of our Order - which I will choose to keep to myself... I was glad to welcome Helena back. Yes, she attempted to kill me but if we were to ostracise everyone who had attempted murder in this village, there'd barely be anyone left! One thing I do not understand is that I split that apple into six equal pieces and we each ate a slice and yet only Helena's was poisoned. How could that be?"

592: The cutthroat razor which was used to slash the doctor's neck is a tool which could be easily purchased from one of several shops in the village. It has been dropped close to Doctor White's corpse. There are no fingerprints on the razor's handle. A pair of latex surgical gloves have been abandoned on the ground nearby. *To inspect these gloves, go to entry* **179.**

593: The front garden of the vicarage is adorned with a row of attractive and incredibly tall leylandii bushes. Inside the house there are several bridal magazines scattered across the kitchen table alongside several of Esther's LPs. The vicarage is decorated with pretty watercolours of the countryside around Pluckley Green.

594: "This is the worst and most exciting thing to ever happen in the library! I was reading an Agatha Christie novel at the reception at 12pm. Shortly afterwards, Xander Meeks approached to tell me of a misplaced book. He then proceeded to the lavatory. At 12.05 I heard the gunshot. Nobody has left the library and yet we cannot find the gun. How thrilling! When the shot was fired I was gazing at that dishy architect. He himself had his hands in his pockets and was standing amongst the periodicals. He was staring at someone through the shelves - how I wish he'd look at me that way!"

595: Alvin's pockets are both empty, except for a small wallet which contains some change.

596: It would have been a clever double bluff for the village postman to have deflected suspicion from himself by pretending to have been a victim of The Ghost. However, Larry and his wife Rose were in the Lake District, celebrating their silver wedding anniversary when Lucy Sparrow was murdered. You can either guess again or go to THE GHOST: THE SOLUTION at the back of this book to learn the full story...

597: "My husband's inheritance from his father was a liberation for us. Neither of us were getting any younger and farming is hard work for very little reward. The money meant that we could buy and develop some of the land around the village and build holiday homes there. Horace wanted us to retire to Brigstowe, which was a nice idea but I would have missed the village. I did not feel my husband even flinch as he died and I did not feel August - on my left - move one bit."

598: "I have known Ryan Moon since we were boys at boarding school and even then he had an eye for the ladies at the next-door girls' school! He was always trying to sneak into their dormitories or spy on them in the changing rooms. Boys will be boys! I know my wife and Sabrina disliked Ryan but they didn't understand that a man needs a hobby. I live in Brigstowe with my wife and work for the council - so the narrowboat holiday is the highlight of my otherwise tedious year! When we heard Ryan scream, I was on the bow of the boat enjoying a cigarette. I rushed to his cabin (there is a door from the bow) and that is where I found him dead in a puddle of his own blood!"

599: The spoons are ordinary stainless steel soup spoons from the church's kitchen - that is except for one of them, which is slightly more ornate and made of silver. It is on the table beside Silas' bowl of soup. It has been coated with a sticky, noxious smelling substance.

600: The door to the east tower is in the entrance chamber. From the roof of the east tower the tops of the west and south towers are visible but the top of the north tower is not as it is so tall. The east tower itself consists of little more than a spiral staircase made of stone.

601: The Ghost is very much anticipating the village fete with excitement, as this is when the killer will claim his or her third victim.

602: "I am rather concerned because I have heard that my gun was found at the scene of the crime. I have no idea how it got there and I hope it does not implicate me in Chip's murder. I use the gun for protection when I am training my lions but I have not needed to fire it in years. After our dress rehearsals this afternoon I returned to my caravan and couldn't find the gun anywhere. At the time I thought I had simply misplaced it but now I know it must have been stolen. It is beyond my imagining why anyone would want to harm Chip Burlington. The man was a literal gentle giant and was liked by everyone. I was due to go onstage last but I like to enjoy the show from the wings and watch the audience's reaction. I spotted my old friend Curran among the crowd and Dazzle was in the wings on the opposite side of the stage. As I was standing there, Polo rushed past me in his full makeup and costume and shot Chip right then and there! I was temporarily shocked by what had witnessed - which gave Polo enough time to flee, but I rushed to Dominic's caravan and wrestled the man to the ground. I must admit that he looked both confused and shocked. Why would he do such a terrible thing?" *To visit Leonard's caravan, go to entry* **65.**

603: Inside the bin are several smashed pieces of a bottle of Old Sarum Opal gin.

604: "The explosion woke me at 4am and like much of the village, I rushed to the scene and saw the sorry sight of that lovely cottage - now blown to pieces. Before Lucy Sparrow was murdered, she gave me the keys to her property. She had quite a few houseplants and asked me to water them whenever she was away from the village. After she was murdered, it felt wrong just to let the flowers die, so I continued watering them - almost as a tribute to her. The last time I let myself into the cottage must have been two days ago. Yesterday evening I met up with my friend Imelda Redberry and the pair of us went into Brigstowe for a night on the town." *To speak to Imelda Redberry, go to entry* **259.**

605: "I am still trembling with the shock and horror of it all. One minute we were all merrily chatting away and the next, Dorothy Halcyon screamed - then we saw her. Oh my word! I must admit that we have not always seen eye to eye, in fact, she was rather a cruel woman - both to me and most of the village." *To search Mavis' handbag, go to entry* **197.**

606: "I was *furious* with Beverley. That woman knew that every year it is ME who arrangers the flowers for the fete and yet she decided to put herself forward this year - and for some reason the organisers decided to go with her instead of me! Outrageous! Penelope had been up and down all evening so I offered to make tea at about 8pm and Mavis helped me bring the tea set into the dining room once it was brewed. We had doughnuts at 9pm and I had my favourite - chocolate. Mr Basingthwaite really is a magician! And then Beverley died. No doubt I shall be back on flower arranging duties now!"

607: "A few months ago there was some rather unpleasant business concerning Lana. That Weathers boy decided that he was in love with my daughter and began a campaign of sending love letters to her through the post. Dickon and Lana were so happy together, so I took a rather unprofessional decision for a postman; whenever I saw a letter addressed to Lana in Vernon's handwriting, I opted not to deliver it to her. I thought it best not to confuse the happy couple with a love triangle and as far as Lana knew, the infatuation was over."

608: Artemis wears a pair of medium sized walking boots. "I joined the Pluckley Ramblers last year as I thought it would be a good way to exercise and give me a break from my university work. I study at Brigstowe University but still live in the village with my mother. Before my father died, he very much enjoyed walking and I thought taking up his hobby would be a nice way to honour him. I was quite surprised to discover that the other members of the group were so… unfriendly. Most of them are more concerned with breaking their personal records than spending any time talking. Nevertheless I have persisted with this group. I am dreadfully sorry about Doctor White - he was perhaps the only member of the group I liked to spend time with." *To learn more about Artemis' late father's go to entry* **117**.

609: The roof of Bertrand Mallard's cottage has a surprisingly shallow incline. The tiles on the roof have been heavily scratched by the branches of the tree in his front garden. The gutters are well kept and the chimney is regularly cleaned.

610: The fishing line is so thin that is almost imperceptible to the naked eye. From the handle of the dagger (where it is tied) the fishing line leads around a hook in the ceiling and then behind a pair of floor-length curtains. Behind these curtains an open window leads to the garden of the cottage. *To ask Minerva about this fishing line and the open window, go to entry* **644**.

611: "On the 10th of February, Marvin and I went for a stroll along the Arbon River. It seemed to be going well but when I lit up a cigarette, he immediately ended the date - claiming that as a surgeon it was his belief that smoking was an unhealthy, disgusting habit. Clearly, we were incompatible."

612: Beneath the rug the floor is solid and all of the floorboards have been firmly nailed in place. There is a folded note beneath the rug and upon it are the words *"The second digit of the code is my birthday month"*.

613: "I was sat very close to Phineas Flitter when his cigar exploded. In fact, my right ear is still ringing. I have to admit that I was rather nervous about this upcoming newspaper column. There was an incident back in February at the birdwatching hides in which… well, I won't go into detail but certain people may have gotten away with a certain crime… I was talking to Phineas earlier and he was surprisingly forthcoming about his latest article. It would seem that the rumours of an earth-shattering revelation from him have been greatly exaggerated. His column was due to be nothing more than some idle scuttlebutt about jam. It was quite a relief to hear that!"

614: "I for one am still in shock, who could do such a thing? I was at home at 8am when I heard the shot. I didn't think anything of it until I left my house around ten minutes later and happened to spot Holly's body in the middle of the Pluckley Stones. I called the police right away. Who would do such a thing? Who shall run the Order now?"

615: "I came to the circus tonight to relive old times and to see my former colleagues perform. Chip was putting on a terrific show - right up until he was murdered. I also managed to spy Leonard waiting in the wings in his lion tamer outfit. I certainly miss working for Bostwicke's Travelling Circus but I suppose I was proving to be more trouble than it was worth. I was rather too fond of gin and Mr Bostwicke was fed up with me putting on poor shows as a result. The final straw came last year when I fell asleep in my caravan before a performance. Mr Bostwicke had to use his spare key to get inside and wake me up. I was fired that very night. As a clown, I went by the name of Dropsy - almost all circus performers have a stage name, even Mr Bostwicke. His real name is Luke, not Bartholomew. I wonder if he'd see fit to employ me now. I have kicked the booze and he will need a replacement when Polo goes to the gallows… I was born to be a clown. See this huge ball of ginger hair on my head? That's not a wig, it's my real hair!"

616: Lucy Sparrow - who was one of the women who went on a date with Marvin Makepeace will be the next victim of the serial killer who will come to be known as "The Ghost".

617: "At first I was just pleased for myself at coming in second place but when I heard that Bruno was missing I got very fearful for him and joined the search. Straight after the starting pistol, Bruno was off like a bullet - I didn't even see him for the rest of the race. Milton was running rather strangely, almost like he was in pain."

618: The Tchotke brother has been stabbed through the neck with a kitchen knife. The knife has been discarded on the floor beside the bed. The man's corpse is dressed only in underwear and he has excessive, jagged scars upon his legs - suggesting a serious wound from several years prior.

619: "Last night my wife and I took my daughter to see a production of "Hamlet" by the Pluckley Players. My daughter, Judy Spiff - head girl of Unity Mitford School for Girls and three-time red rosette winning Somerset Junior Trials dressage champion is studying the play at school. As for the fete, this year my wife and I are seriously considering withdrawing our annual donation if the American theme is not changed. This is a traditional village with traditional values."

620: The door to Room 2 was locked from the inside - with the key still in the keyhole. Bludger Baxter had to force his way in, whereupon he found the body of one of the Tchotchke brothers stabbed upon the lone double bed.

621: The note has been written by hand. It reads: *"I AM THE GHOST AND I HAVE CLAIMED ANOTHER VICTIM!"*

622: There is no evidence linking the feared and loathed judge to the Pluckley Green serial killer. You can either guess again or go to THE GHOST: THE SOLUTION at the back of this book to learn the full story…

623: The backdoor from the kitchen opens to an alleyway. This alleyway leads to the street upon which the funeral home is located. A black, hooded cloak has been dumped in the alleyway behind some bins.

624: "My sister was none too pleased with my choice of boyfriend and has never tried to hide it. She and Jack were courting many moons ago but that was all in the past. Jessica has always been that way - jealous of anything her little sister has. Well, look at how things turned out tonight, I suppose Jessica got what she wanted! The evening had been going well. At about ten o'clock, Jack wanted to get some fresh air but changed his mind for some reason and didn't leave until 10.30. That was the last I ever saw of him. I do forgive my sister for being so *angry* with me earlier, I suppose mood swings are to be expected considering her condition." *To ask Aria what she means, go to entry **683**.*

625: "This is a tragedy and nothing less. Obviously I like to cast Leon as my leading man in every production as he is a very fine actor… well, he's getting better… marginally. The truth is that my nephew was an ambitious actor and I don't think a complete lack of talent should stand in the way of his dreams. I also allowed him to choose his own leading lady for each play and without fail he chose Thalia, I think he was rather smitten with her - although Thalia never had a clue that this was the sole reason for her repeatedly getting decent parts in our plays! Before the hideous event, my dearest nephew was standing on the stage performing the soliloquy. I could see Thalia standing in the wings of the stage. Leon's killer entered stage left and stabbed him from behind. There was a terrible scream from Thalia and then everything else was mayhem. Ghastly! My own nephew!"

626: "I was due to compete in the women's Pluckley Green Run this afternoon. It's just as competitive but never as popular and I fear it may be cancelled altogether this year. Bruno was the first to arrive at the Western Woods - which was a surprise to me. He looked dreadful. Green of skin and he could barely run in a straight line. I begged him to stop for a few minutes to recover but he was determined. He just grabbed a cup of orange squash and continued running."

627: The space at the bottom of the well where August Barley was found connects to the caves along the riverbank - and also to the network of tunnels which run beneath Pluckley Green.

628: The serial killer who will come to be known as "The Ghost" has already claimed their second victim.

629: "I attended the hustings in hopes that somebody could answer a question about the village boundary. I am asking that it be altered so that it includes my husband's farm. Mr Crookshank was answering my question when the shot was fired. He had his back to me and the half-a-dozen other villagers in the audience, so that he could point at the boundary map on the wall. It is a real shame for the village that he has been murdered. I think he was a very reasonable councillor."

630: "We all knew that Holly was planning on doing this binding spell as he suggested it a couple of weeks ago. I scrumped him an apple from the orchards by the heath and he has been talking about the ceremony ever since. I shan't miss Helena Turner one bit. She attempted to murder Holly. Holly may have forgiven her but I certainly haven't. How are you supposed to trust someone after that? I wouldn't even employ her to walk my dog anymore - especially as her own dog, Crowley is *riddled* with fleas!"

631: Humbert Miner recently bought an enormous roll of stamps - which he probably hoped would last him through several weeks of complaint letters. There is an unusual scent to these stamps - much like cinnamon.

632: Atlas Moribund is dressed as Frankenstein's Monster. "Despite what rumours may have you believe, I do not hate my brother - nor his late wife. I simply resent him for being the older brother. When my father died, Dorian inherited everything in his will - his wealth, his home, the business. All just because he is a year older than me! No wonder his business is notorious for nepotism - he will only employ his business partner's relatives - which is just bad practice, if you ask me. As for Sheila, she tried hard for me and Dorian to reconcile our differences - which is why she invited me to this ludicrous party. When I arrived, a woman was standing outside the funeral home and staring through the window. I followed her gaze and inside the kitchen I saw a person in a black cloak fleeing the scene and Sheila was face down in a bucket. I am not surprised that Dorian was at the wine shop just as the party was due to begin - he always leaves his organising to the very last minute! Poor Sheila. She did not deserve such a dreadful fate."

633: "I met the members of the ornithologist club at the pub early yesterday evening. We discussed our birdwatching plans for the following morning and everyone was happy and excited at the possible sighting. Later that night, Bill and Pip were going to head out to the wetlands to watch the breeding rituals of the tawny screech owl and Tiffany was due to watch the latest abomination from the Pluckley Players at the village hall. The rest of us opted for early nights and to head for the hides at dawn."

634: "Now, I'm not one to gossip but rumours are saying that the Pendergast's maid, Mona Prim, has quit her position and moved from the house. That explains why poor

Lady Pendergast was left playing hostess at her own birthday party. Who can blame Mona for quitting? Lord Pendergast is a monster. Any man who beats his wife is beneath contempt. This evening, I brought some single-serve bottles of tonic to the party. As I was saying to the Reverend this afternoon over tea, it is so nice to have a sparkling fresh tonic with every glass - rather than a flat one from a bottle that has been left out all evening." For some reason, there is a strange green sludge on the bottom of one of Mavis' shoes.

635: Henry's shoes are clean and dry. Fran's shoes are muddy and also have bits of hay stuck to them.

636: "I joined the Ringers a few years ago. My wife and I were looking for something to do to pass the time and this seemed as good an activity as any. You just don't expect something like this to happen during a very, very boring hobby."

637: The avid conservationist Jeremy Trumble had as much reason as anyone to wish Lord Pendergast dead. However, he did not murder him. Back in January, Jeremy Trumble made a promise not to attempt to murder Lord Pendergast again - and Jeremy Trumble is a man who always keeps his promises.

638: Larry and Rose Finch are eagerly anticipating their silver wedding anniversary. To celebrate, the couple will be leaving the village on the 4th of March for a one-week holiday in the Lake District.

639: The face of the so-called journalist has been blown clean from his skull and lays in tattered pieces along the riverbank, along with several of his teeth. There are no remains of his cigar left whatsoever.

640: "It may seem rather peculiar but Reverend Amos and I have been friends for many decades. The friction between the ways of old and new will always be there but we have a mutual respect for one another's spiritual paths. I came to the church at 6pm as I was worried about the old trees around my home weathering the storm. I didn't know anything about Silas or his past. In fact, the first time I'd heard from him was when he put in an application to perform some excavations at the Pluckley Stones - an application I opposed, of course. This evening, I was trying to make myself useful and to help our talented cook but Daisy informed me that her sister was setting the table. Everything seemed to be going well throughout the meal - but then Silas dropped down dead."

641: The knife is a standard, stainless steel kitchen knife. There are no fingerprints on the handle.

642: Two windows of Helena's bungalow face the Pluckley Stones. In the hall there is a series of hooks bearing dog leads and the keys to various people's homes. She is currently out walking a neighbour's dog by the nearby river.

643: The Pluckley Press is published every Friday but the paper which is open upon Lucy's desk is dated Friday, 2nd of March. Scrawled across the paper in blood are the words "I AM THE GHOST AND I WILL KILL AGAIN".

644: "Very well, I confess! The seances are a sham! Simple parlour tricks! The floating dagger effect is achieved by me behind the curtain pulling on a fishing line. During the seance I creep in through the open window and we have been doing it for years! But I assure you this… sometimes that spirit board… it seems to tell the truth and things it predicts really do come true. From my position behind the curtain I could only see one person - Mrs Scrub - and I can assure you she did not move at all during the seance."

645: "I may have been the only member of the club to have any time for Pip at all. He was disliked by everyone in the group but I was at least willing to give the man a second, third and even a fourth chance. I had been over to his house a few times and last night we were due to go owl spotting together but I eventually suggested he stay at home instead - I wanted some time to myself and Pip was rather a boring man and poor company."

646: There is nothing unusual or suspicious about the pen which Humbert Miner was using when he died.

647: "I was enjoying a bit of a lazy morning in bed when I heard the gunshot. I can assure you that as much as I disapproved of Holly's ways - flouncing around the village in his ceremonial garbs and setting tongues wagging - it was most certainly not me who shot our High Wizard. I cannot abide guns or violence of any kind. In fact, the only person I know who even owns one is Gerald Ratchett. He says it is for protection but protecting what? It's only him and that mangey dog in that dilapidated old house of his."

648: "My attention was mainly on stopping the train, so I didn't get a good look at what happened but from the corner of my eye, I saw a figure all dressed in white - like a ghost - lurch out of the shadows and push the man in front of my train. It made a frightful sound. I shan't be right for weeks."

649: The corpse of Bertrand Mallard is little more than a burned out pile of ash and blackened bones. His body lays beside what is left of his armchair. A smashed bottle of what looks like vodka is on the rug beside him. *To ask Bludger Baxter about Bertrand's drinking habits, go to entry* **79.**

650: "My wife and I were among the first to arrive at the party. Lorraine and I are not really drinkers, so we don't really know the Bloodied Axe all that well but have been friends with Bludger for years. When we arrived, that poor barmaid and another woman were setting up decorations - regular party stuff; balloons; banners and streamers. There was one other man there. I think he was Bludger's brother. My wife and I left at about midnight."

651: The body of Bruno Brown lays in a ditch at the western end of the canal path, partly obscured by weeds and overgrowth. His vest has the number 0120 printed upon it. He has no visible injuries.

652: There is a good deal of blood and brain matter splattered about the hut. There is an oblong storage box in the hide. It contains a flask of coffee and an uneaten lunch of corned beef sandwiches, as well as a book on identifying birds by their eggs.

653: "At around 10pm I saw the most curious thing. Jessica Waterstone and that maypole dancer were having the most dreadful row outside the village hall. It was so loud that it woke me from my slumber on the bench. I haven't been sleeping well - folks in the village say that I am due to be the next victim of The Ghost, owing to something a spirit board said. I hope they are wrong, I'm not ready for the end yet. The row reached a crescendo when the maypole dancer slapped Jessica in the face. Oh the endless drama of youth!"

654: Mavis served as a land girl during the Second World War. When being questioned at the sewing circle she bemoaned the fact that during those years she barely saw any men at all. She is not Esther's mother.

655: "This morning I was up at dawn to water the impatiens in my hanging baskets. My boyfriend's neighbour was out for a morning stroll and I waved at her. Last night Isaac and I went to a dinner party at our friend Dexter's house. It was an evening of good company and fine wine - Dexter provided a cabernet and Isaac brought a chardonnay with him and the three of us finished them both! - I have really taken to wine recently, Mr Conway jokes that I am his best customer! I was at church for 9am and Perry Gulch was there, snoring like a pig and smelling even worse! It seems like The Ghost has done as all a favour and ridded us of that loathsome creature!"

656: The dressing room smells of cigarette smoke. The small window has been propped open slightly but not enough so that anybody could clamber in or out. The dressing room is the usual mess of scattered greasepaint and empty mugs of coffee. On the table there is a review of the Pluckley Players last production - "Romeo and Juliet". *To read the review, turn to entry **484**.*

657: "I have never encountered any problems with people knowing that I am a member of the Order. In fact, owing to my love for nature, most people have assumed me to be a member anyway. Wilbur was a good man and a good friend. When I was a boy, he was also my maths teacher and was very patient with me. I shall miss him. I did not see any of what occurred as I was gazing skywards when the dart was fired at Wilbur."

658: "I was woken from my sleep at 11pm last night. My friend Fenton Hughes was deeply troubled by something he had seen in the Feathered Cap. We spoke not of what it was but I prayed with him all night until the dawn."

659: Gabe's briefcase contains nothing but a marmalade sandwich and a flask of Earl Grey tea.

660: The corpse of Silas Marsten is still seated and slumped face down in his bowl of vegetable soup. His death appears to have happened very quickly. The man was fit and healthy and had no known allergies.

661: Rather miraculously, Reginald Sole's leather suitcase survived the explosion intact. On the outside of the case, the words "Professor R. Sole" have been embossed. Inside there are a few clothes and a diary. The most recent diary entry reads: *"Once I return from Aberdeen, I shall be moving to Pluckley Green so that I may be with my beloved Daisy. She is so much better than that odious shrew Katherine. I do not know why I even married her in the first place!"*

662: "I was the last of the group to arrive. As always, I complimented everybody on their attire - Daisy's lovely summer dress, Marcy's new straw hat, Miss Faversham's... well, she has certainly chosen a look for herself. I went to the kitchen only once and that was to help Marcy bring the tea set in. I am not one to gossip but Marcy was no fan of Beverley. The pair have never seen eye to eye but Beverley recently usurped her position as head flower arranger at the summer fete - things were certainly frosty between them! I have known Beverley for years, she and I were both land girls during the war. What interesting times they were, do you know, in a strange way I miss them - even though I barely saw a man for years! As for the doughnuts, I refrained from them as I have been on a diet for several weeks."

663: The ice in the glass of gin and tonic are rapidly melting. The individual cubes have an undeniable cinnamon scent.

664: When Bludger Baxter went to rouse the Tchotchke triplets in the morning, he discovered that the door to Room 1 was unlocked and ajar. Inside, one of the two single beds was unmade, whilst on the other he found the brutally stabbed body of one of the Tchotchke brothers.

665: On the morning of Friday, the 6th of January of this year, Mona Prim was taking a walk near to Pluckley Green's train station when she briefly spotted a figure dressed all in white. Whoever it was also had something covering their face. The encounter lasted only a second but she was certain she had spotted something similar before - perhaps at Pendergast Manor? She shrugged off the encounter and continued on her walk.

666. Lord Lucien Pendergast is, without a shadow of a doubt, the most hated man in Pluckley Green. He lives in his achingly large manor on the North Hills and owns (through inheritance) most of the land upon which the village stands - as well as much of its surrounding farmland. This makes him the landlord to most of the village - and as a landlord he is seen as nothing more than a greedy tyrant.

667: Mr Basingthwaite runs the village bakery and lives above the shop. "I was just now about to turn in for the night but this news about poor Beverley Potter has shaken me! This afternoon, Daphne Robinson came into the bakery to buy a selection of five doughnuts. Every week one of the ladies from the sewing circle will do the same and I put the doughnuts into a cardboard box for them - although I do not know all of the members by name. Daphne was fortunate that there was still a jam doughnut left. I'd just sold one to a lady in a straw hat. Daphne came in straight after her and managed to get the last one!"

668: A single bite has been taken out of the jam doughnut, the rest of it now lays on the floor beside Beverley's corpse. The sweet treat has an unusual smell, much like cinnamon.

669: "I suppose if Perry Gulch dies it is for the best really. I understand that he was rather heroic during the war but that was so long ago now and the rest of us hardly even think about it anymore. What's to be traumatised about? We won! I saw that man asleep outside the church - he had a bottle of wine ready for when he woke up, it seems. I couldn't tell you much about wine, that is my brother's area of expertise as he runs the village off-licence. Me, I've never taken to the stuff."

670: There is no sign of the treasure in Christopher's satchel. There is a letter addressed to Christopher. The wax seal upon it has been broken. *To read the letter, go to entry* **3**.

671: Behind the curtains where Damien Merton had been hiding is a large window which is latched shut. Beyond that, the storm rages and flashes of lightning illuminate the night sky. Nothing seems to be out of place or unusual.

672: "I left the party soon after midnight, I had no idea that I'd be saying goodbye to Sally for the last time ever. My sister had quite the reputation in the village for her loose morals - but who is anyone in Pluckley Green to judge her? She was a good-time gal and was adored by everyone who met her. That's how I will always remember her."

673: "Seeing as no one will help me decode this note from my mother, I decided to come to the library to see if I can work out what it says with help from books on codes and cyphers. The note arrived at Stasis House on the night of the 31st of March. Ordinarily Miss Faversham does not permit me to receive mail but that was before she…changed. I was sat here at the table when the gun went off. Earlier a man had walked past me, I think he was heading for the loos. I've never met any of the people in the pub quiz team before and I am too young to go to the Bloodied Axe Tavern." *To see what Esther has decoded so far, go to entry* **169**.

674: Horace Scrub is seated at the table with his head thrown back. The dagger has been plunged deep into his throat - meaning that even if he had tried to scream for help, no one would have heard him.

675: "I believe I was the first among the guests to arrive. I am a city man at heart, so don't have much time for these village people and their trivial, old-fashioned ways and am frankly, rather surprised that my brother has chosen to settle here. I offered to help set up the decorations but my offer was declined. I left at about 1am to drive back to Brigstowe."

676: From "The Bride Wore Stolen Diamonds" - the latest "Piddly Glen" mystery novel from Conrad Cutlass: *"Wilhelmina Rudders' bosom heaved as she pondered the puzzle. Lawrence French puffed on his cigar before concluding "The only person who knew where the Kensington Diamond was hidden was the evil and corrupt Judge John Trangle!". "Him again!" Wilhelmina exclaimed, throwing a hand to her full bosom. "That must mean he was the man seen with the dagger in the museum!". Her bosom trembled with fear. "Indubitably, Miss Rudders," Lawrence replied."*

677: The village gossip may be full of secrets but being a serial killer is not one of them. She has no motive for becoming The Ghost. You can either guess again or go to THE GHOST: THE SOLUTION at the back of this book to learn the full story…

678: The communal bathroom contains a toilet, a shower unit and a sink. The shower is still running. There is one small window which faces the bow of the boat. There are three doors to the bathroom which lead to each of the cabins. All three doors can be locked with a key but they are currently unlocked.

679: "I make several scarecrows for the farm each year. I don't know if they do much good deterring the crows but I enjoy it and it gives the farm a sense of tradition. I use Maxwell's old clothes that are too far gone to be darned. I finished the latest one yesterday afternoon and Maxwell had it affixed to the pole before dusk. Whoever changed the scarecrow for Benjamin's body must have emptied the clothes of all of their hay stuffing and then dressed the corpse in my husband's clothes - and then turned it to face north for some reason. It's just ghastly to think about!"

680: During the seance, when asked who the next victim of The Ghost would be, the spirit board spelled out the initials "*P.G.*", leading most to assume that Perry Gulch would be the next target. However, it seems that perhaps the board meant somebody else.

681: "That note is not from me, I swear! It's not even in my handwriting. In a million years I would never go with a man like Jack Quick. He's a cad and a heartbreaker. I have been framed!" It is true that Virginia's handwriting looks nothing like that contained in the note.

682: "I believe that Wilma and I were the last to arrive at the church this evening - we were running a little late as we wanted to secure her narrowboat as well as we could ahead of the storm. We arrived at about 6.05pm. Poor Mabel was busy with the soup all evening but it was I who suggested she take a short break and allow Wilma to set the table. This allowed me the opportunity to converse with the cook about a personal matter. She and I are both divorcees and as such are the subject of much gossip in the village. I wanted to learn how she has learned to cope with such notoriety."

683: "Jessica swore me to secrecy. At the moment she and Kevin are keeping mum about it all but sometime in the middle of November this year I am to become an aunt!"

684: "I was very excited about the business moving to London. Manville Builders has been so successful in Somerset that it was only a matter of time before the capital started calling! Last night I had a few drinks in the pub. I went to the Bloodied Axe straight after work - as I always do - and stayed until closing. I saw Richmond in the pub but we did not talk - the pair of us do not get along. At 9am this morning, I and the other builders arrived at the Bloodied Axe and Bludger let us in. It was our first day of work on this new job. Oliver went straight to the basement and then just died! What could have happened? *To check Michael Doncaster's toolbox, go to entry* **268**.

685: Unsurprisingly, Bludger (in his role as bookmaker) has deemed Milton West the clear favourite to win. People betting on Milton winning include Reverend Amos Harper, Lord Lucien Pendergast and Dorian Blake. Only one bet has been placed on Bruno Brown - from Mick Nicholson.

686: The body of the 30 year old committee assistant has been burnt to a crisp within the shell of the car. Poor Tommy Tomlinson was generally liked by everybody and seemed to have no enemies in the village.

687: "I had been so happy about my fiancée moving to the village. He was due to arrive at the awkward hour of 4am because he was travelling back from giving a lecture in Aberdeen. I was going to meet him at 8am on my way to work at the bakery. We had been courting for three months and I had been thrilled about him moving - absolutely everybody knew about it! However, yesterday evening an anonymous letter was delivered to the houseboat where I live with my sister. It contained terrible allegations about Reginald. I was up all night in tears - my sister was still trying to comfort me when we heard the explosion." *For more information about Daisy Doyle, go to entry **517**.*

688: Harry's 8 year old beagle Darwin is a happy, friendly and otherwise healthy dog who is unfortunately inflicted by occasional bouts of uncontrollable diarrhoea. Harry has always claimed that this is due to Helen tossing laxative-laced meat over the garden wall.

689: "I am heartbroken and devastated. I loved Gary! Last night we all saw that hideous hound with our very own eyes. Not one of us believed the legend and yet there he was. It seems impossible to believe that the stories could be true but once you eliminate the impossible, whatever remains, no matter how improbable, must be the truth. When we saw the gurt dog, we all just ran in different directions. I was by myself as I ran back to the tent but I was certain I could hear someone running behind me. I made it back to the tent first. Benjamin arrived soon afterwards."

690: The jovial leader of the Ancient Order of Pluckley Pagans is one of the few villagers to have never even attempted murder. He is not The Ghost. You can either guess again or go to THE GHOST: THE SOLUTION at the back of this book to learn the full story…

691: "This has been a devastating blow for lovers of crime fiction - and for me personally - as Conrad Cutlass has been not just a client but a dear friend for many years now. His Piddly Glen books were a publishing sensation and reinvigorated the cosy mystery genre! I can't deny that book sales have been rather lacklustre of late but that is only because the "Chase Slater Mysteries" have experienced such a resurgence in popularity recently. Conrad and I had tea together in the village hall before the ribbon cutting ceremony. Countless people were fussing about in there and getting things organised before the event."

692: "I joined the Pluckley Players for the exact same reason everyone in Pluckley Green does anything - to alleviate the boredom. It's fun doing our productions but most of us are under no illusions, we know they're terrible. There's only one good actor in the Pluckley Players - and it isn't me. Stanley will only cast you in a decent role if you're a member of his family. Me and Melvin were smoking in the dressing room when we heard Thalia scream. I'm certain that as we rushed to the stage I saw the exit door open and someone slip inside. When I'm not trying to act, I deliver papers around the village. It's not much but I'm looking for something better."

693: "I hope that nobody is accusing me - Judy Spiff; head girl of Unity Mitford School for Girls and two-time red rosette winning Somerset dressage trials champion - of poisoning that fat tank of a horse? I saw that elderly whale earlier - I always like to check out the local competition - and it was all I could do to stop myself from laughing in its ugly face!" *For further information about Judy Spiff, go to entry **471**.*

694: The ornate waiting room features upholstered seating and a small tearoom. The victim was seen reading a newspaper, which he left behind when he went to the platform. *To inspect the newspaper, go to entry **49**.*

695: Phineas was rarely seen without his jacket - even in the height of summer. In one pocket he would carry a finest Woodsman Robusto cigar and in the other, his trusty notebook, in which he would outline the details of each of his poisonous newspaper columns. On this Sunday afternoon his jacket had been sprawled out upon the grass beside him. It would have been very easy to sneak something into Phineas' jacket pocket without him noticing. The notebook is in the jacket's right pocket. The outline of his latest article - the one he plans to publish on Friday - is the most recent entry. It reads: "*Although it pains me to expose one of our village's most beloved residents as a fraud, I can exclusively reveal that Mrs Toggitt's prize-winning jam is in fact, not her own concoction. She actually* *just buys the preserve from the village shop in Brockham-Down and spoons it into fresh jars. I first discovered this shocking secret when I followed her to…"*

696: Mabel Witherspoon is alone at the vicarage and is preparing to leave. She seems anxious about something. "I was about to go for a walk to the standing stones to fulfil a prior engagement but before I left I thought there was no harm in watching a little of the beauty pageant from the conservatory. What a dreadful sight it was to behold!" The windows of the vicarage's conservatory are open and face towards the park. There is no sign of a bow and arrow.

697: The body of Marvin Makepeace sits upright on a bench in Pluckley Green Park. He is a distinguished, somewhat handsome looking middle-aged gentleman. He has been stabbed once through the heart and has no other wounds. The knife is still plunged all the way to the handle in his chest. *To learn more about Pluckley Green Park go to entry **452**.*

698: The misplaced book in the arts section of the library is entitled "*Waste Management Solutions in 18th Century Devises.*" Upon opening this book it is revealed that all of the pages have been hollowed out to create a space in which a pistol has been stashed. The book does not belong to the library's collection.

699: On the desk there is a collection of pens and papers alongside a stack of envelopes. Taped to the underside of the desk there is a note upon which Lucy has written the words *"The first digit of the code is the number of standing stones you will find at the Pluckley Stones."*

700: The corpse of Prudence Rosehip is a bloody mess. She has a massive hole in her stomach which can only have been from the blast of a shotgun. The copious amounts of blood around her body has dried and her corpse shows significant signs of decomposition. She was wearing her nightclothes when she was shot. In her dressing gown pocket is her diary. *To read Prudence Rosehip's diary, go to entry **211**.*

701: "What is this? Who wrote this? Who would ever want to leave the Fearless Five? We're famous and get into such marvellous scrapes - like the time we caught those smugglers at Smugglers Cove and again at Smugglers Island and then Smugglers Bay. I'm so shocked and hurt!"

702: "Last night my husband went out for a walk at about 8pm. He did not return until the morning and I daren't ask where he has been for fear of the answer. My maid was with me throughout the evening, giving me comfort and reassurance. It may be a terrible thing to say but oftentimes I truly regret the choices I have made with my life."

703: More sinned against than sinning, Perry Gulch was recovering in hospital when Penelope Gannet was murdered. You can either guess again or go to THE GHOST: THE SOLUTION at the back of this book to learn the full story…

704: "I am devastated! Being a widow, I thought love would never find me again and yet Doctor White proposed last month and I said yes! We had only been courting for a short while but it had been like a whirlwind. And now he is dead! Love has left me once again!"

705: The Bloodied Axe New Years Eve Pub Quiz is the hotly contested annual trivia competition. For the past five years the winning team has been the "Pluckley Bird Brains" - a formidable quiz team who named themselves the Bird Brains when they realised each of them shared part of their name with a type of bird.

706: The plate upon which Holly carved the apple is a simple earthenware dish which he uses for his ceremonies. There is nothing unusual about it. When he carved the apple, all members of the group watched him do so.

707: Poor Hamish has been blown to pieces. Bits of him are splattered over the floor, walls and ceiling. There is nothing left of him which will be of any forensic use.

708: Rose Finch - the wife of postman Larry Finch - will be in Brigstowe for New Years Eve to visit a dog pound. The couple have decided that they would like to adopt a puppy.

709: "I suppose if we must learn a lesson from this awful incident it's that we must treasure every day. Even things which seem stable can come crashing down when you least expect them to. This is why vigilance is important and the rule of order must be followed."

710: Doctor White lays dead in the dirt behind the cottage. There is a good deal of undergrowth around his body. His throat has been slashed with one brisk, deep slice of a cutthroat razor and his blood has sprayed against the exterior of the cottage wall. *To examine the ground around Doctor White's body, go to entry **75**.*

711: Due to dwindling audience numbers, The Doll's House Theatre had only sold tickets for half its capacity this evening. Judge Jan Treagle was in seat A5 and Anita Cryer - Captain Conjuro's wife - was in seat B4. The back row of seats was reserved for entertainers who wanted to watch the rest of the variety show after they had performed their act.

712: "Lester Pratt - mens size 8, wide - has been my neighbour since I moved to the village 20 years ago. That is why Frank Greenburg - mens size 12, slim - asked me to chaperone him throughout the morning. I was dreading it to be honest, as the man was a buffoon and an embarrassment to the village. This morning I called upon him at 9am and saw the postman - mens size 9, wide - running from the house as if in shock. My wife - ladies size 6, slim - says that at about midnight last night she heard a knock upon the door to Lester's house and through the wall could hear a discussion between Lester and another man. The man seemed very enthusiastic about a new prank he wanted to show Lester." *To further test Sidney on his knowledge of the villagers' shoe sizes, go to entry **358**.*

713: "I am praying that Perry pulls through. He may not look it but that man is a bonafide war hero and I am proud to have served alongside him. When the rest of us were coming home in '45 it was men like Perry who stayed behind in Europe, overseeing the liberation - I do believe he witnessed some terrible things. It is no wonder he turned to drink. He has become progressively worse throughout this year too and I fear he may now be too far lost in drink to save himself. Last night I hosted a small gathering - just Isaac and his girlfriend Millie. On reflection, perhaps it would have been kind to have invited Perry… but I'd only bought one bottle of cabernet - that and the bottle of white Isaac brought with him would've been gone in an hour!"

714: There are many, many cinemas in Brigstowe but Mavis and Imelda chose to go to the Small Street Picture House. Last night, the only film screening there was "Kiss Me, Kate" starring Katherine Grayson and Howard Keel.

715: That evening, as the Fearless Five were embroiled in their own mystery, Samantha Stein was walking home along the canal path when she spied a mysterious man in the darkness. He was entering one of the caves by the river, which is where she lost sight of him.

716: The woman is slumped back in the seat with a blood drenched gash about two inches wide in the centre of her chest - it looks as if a large knife has been plunged in and then quickly removed. Upon her head rests a brand new, expensive looking summer hat. Dorothy Halcyon was regarded as a bitter, vindictive woman who had few friends in the village.

717: "I knew the odds of getting a charitable donation from Prudence were slim but I thought we might as well try, besides, there was no harm in at least asking. It was an awful sight to see her body in such a grisly state. That said, I do not think she will be much missed in the village. The last time I saw her was in early October when she came over to the vicarage to take some cuttings from my bushes - without my permission, I should add! When she first moved to the village I invited her around and I am *certain* that she pocketed some of my good silverware…" *To visit the vicarage, go to entry 593.*

718: The well sits at the edge of August Barley's farm. The wooden bucket which is connected to the well with a rope has been completely smashed to bits as if it has been bludgeoned with a rock. In the mud there are size 9 bootprints leading to the well and size 11 shoe prints leading to and away from the well.

719: Mr Kidders has been shot once through the chest. There is a shotgun on the ground about ten feet away from his body. It is Milo's own gun, which he usually keeps mounted on the wall of his barn.

720: Sheila Moribund is still face down in the bucket of water. She had been dressed as a witch and a pointed hat is on the table beside her. Apples bob in the water around her head. Sheila is wearing expensive looking jewellery. *To inspect the apple bobbing bucket, go to entry 70.*

721: "This is my first boating holiday with my husband and his friends and I have enjoyed almost every aspect of it. Autumn is a magical season to enjoy nature in Britain and I always relish spending time with my husband. We live in London, so opportunities to be surrounded by wildlife are few and far between. The only aspect of this holiday I have not enjoyed is the presence of Ryan Moon. He is a lascivious, lecherous and dirty creature. Being trapped in a small space with him and his roaming, groping hands is revolting and I must admit to being happy that he will no longer be a problem. I have begged Karl to say something but he just shrugs it off and puts it down to Ryan being a frustrated, lonely man. After breakfast, I retired to my bedroom and prepared myself for the day ahead. It is then that I heard a scream from Ryan's cabin and everyone - including me - rushed in that direction to see what had happened."

722: "I spent most of last night alone. My son is staying with us for the summer from university but he was out for the evening - goodness knows what time he got in last night! I spent my evening reading the final Conrad Cutlass novel. My husband arrived home from work later that night and the pair of us went to bed. Benjamin was a good man and I shall miss him greatly but it is his dear wife I worry for. What a tragic loss."

723: The Pluckley Stones look much the same as they always have. Nothing seems unusual or out of place with them and nothing has been left inside or outside of the circle.

724: "Such a dreadful shame and a shock. Jack may have had a poor reputation but I do believe there was some good in him. During the party, Judy was quite upset and asked to see the ballots for May King and Queen herself. When she did, it seemed to upset her even further. At about 10.30 she threw a glass of lemonade in Jack's face as he was leaving the village hall. She then spent the rest of the evening sobbing at the edge of the dance floor. I'm afraid to confess that I suspect her to be something of a spoiled brat! The whole village remembers Kevin and Jessica's wedding and that is why they voted for them - it was Christmas and made all the more romantic knowing that Kevin was to leave for Germany the next week."

725: "I hate to speak ill of the dead but as a speaker, Cuthbert Crookshank was a rather uncharismatic figure and I struggled to stay focused as he answered questions from the audience. I do believe that the fact that the hustings are so unpopular has benefited Cuthbert in the past. The fewer people who are present to listen to his monotonous droning, the better for him - I think the only reason he has won so many elections is because the villages have found themselves in a routine where they vote for him without question as he seems like a safe enough pair of hands. When the shot was fired, Cuthbert was demonstrating where the parish boundary lay on a map. I was looking at Louis Longbottom in the audience, the poor man looked as if he might be falling asleep!"

726: "Last night, I met my friend Richmond at the Bloodied Axe Tavern and we had a few drinks. I did spot something rather strange there; a gentleman seated alone in the shadows of the pub, nursing the same pint all evening. He did not speak to anyone but I remember him due to his odd appearance - huge, thick spectacles and an extravagant, bushy moustache. I also spotted Michael Doncaster among the crowd at the pub but I didn't speak to him - Richmond and Michael may work together but they despise one another! Michael always goes to the pub straight after work and is always dressed in his overalls with his toolbox at his side! At about 10pm, Michael Doncaster left his toolbox at a table whilst he went to the gentlemen's room and I saw a very weird thing happen. The man with the moustache stepped out of the shadows and did something with Michael's toolbox. I don't know what it was, as the mysterious man had his back turned to me. The man then strolled away, up the stairs to where I suppose he must have been renting a room for the night. I probably should have said something at the time."

727: The door to the north tower is found in the entrance chamber. The tower is far taller than the other three and the roof opens to a dazzling view overlooking Pluckley Green and beyond to the city of Brigstowe. A candle - which has been snuffed out - has been dropped on the roof of the tower. The spiral staircase on the way to the roof is lined with small windows.

728: Inside the charred cupboard are several items which have been preserved from the smoke and fire. There are many books on the subject of cricket and of sporting history in general as well as a crisp set of cricket whites and a bat. There is a photo album on the floor of the cupboard. *To look inside the photo album, go to entry **354**.*

729: "I do hope this boutique works out. Colin and I have put a lot of time and money into it. I just hope Carnaby Street will be the right location for something so stylish and forward-thinking! He and I were there for a couple of weeks looking for just the right place - we left the village on Halloween. While I was there the most curious thing happened in the village. My father's shotgun was stolen from his shed and then two days later it was replaced as if nothing had happened! Most curious. I am excited about moving but I shall miss this village. On Christmas Eve, our friends Dante and Wendy Finn gifted us one of Wendy's beautiful landscape paintings which she painted from her own garden. That was very generous of them."

730: The man has collapsed upon the bench and is currently awaiting the arrival of an ambulance. His breathing is very shallow and his pulse feels very weak. His death may well be imminent.

SOLUTIONS

1. BLOODBATH AT THE BLOODIED AXE SOLUTION

In the end, it was not the local constabulary who captured Toby Tchotchke - the killer of his own two brothers, Tony and Todrick - but the man's trusted friend, August Barley.

Shortly after midnight, as the revellers celebrated the birth of a new year, Toby Tchotchke took a knife from the pub's kitchen and unlocked the door to Room 1 (the room he was sharing with his brother, Todrick).

He waited in the wardrobe for his brothers to retire to bed and then, with the help of the hidden connecting door between the rooms, stabbed both of the men to death in their sleep.

Escaping through the door to Room 1, he fled from the pub into the darkness of the night.

After several hours of hiding out in the icy wilderness of the woods, he sought sanctuary from his friend August on the afternoon of New Year's Day. Horrified and disgusted by Toby's actions Mr. Barley called the police, who promptly arrested the double murderer.

As policemen dragged him away, Toby screamed like a madman and exclaimed "There is a secret at the heart of this village that is worth killing for - and if I cannot profit from it myself, it is a secret I shall take to my grave!"

2. FOR WHOM THE BELL KILLS SOLUTION

The affair between Sebastian Turner and Daphne Robinson had been one of Pluckley Green's worst kept secrets for almost a year. It didn't help that the pair of them made absolutely no effort to hide their dalliance and were frequently spotted together canoodling in the park, the woods and even the Bloodied Axe Tavern.

Heartbroken and humiliated, Humphrey Robinson had taken to walking the streets of the village at night and it was on one of these jaunts that he hatched his plan to win back his adulterous wife.

With the help of his key to the church and his trusty pocket knife, Humphrey entered the church on the night of the 4th of January and scaled the ladder to cut most of the way through the rope from which bell four was suspended - the bell Sebastian almost always rang.

How was Humphrey to know that Gabe would suggest he and Sebastian should change place that evening? The man's fickleness cost him his life.

Humphrey eventually handed himself in at the police station. His plan had failed, an innocent man had died and now Sebastian and his wife were free to spend their lives together.

If you managed to correctly unriddle this mystery, go to entry 443.

3. 9.50 TO BRIGSTOWE
SOLUTION

What should have been an enjoyable morning of trainspotting instead turned into bloodshed and one man's harmless hobby was to be his undoing.

After settling his bill with the landlord of the Bloodied Axe Tavern, Robin Richard Pascoe walked to Pluckley Green Train Station, eager to see the passing of the majestic Flying Welshman. Unbeknownst to him, a most foul plan was afoot and from the darkened shadows of the railway platform, a mysterious figure in white emerged to push Robin beneath the wheels of the incoming 9.50 train to Brigstowe.

We may never know why Mr. Pascoe's life was ended so abruptly, or who committed this monstrous crime but one thing is certain - something very strange and very frightening is just beginning in the village of Pluckley Green.

If you solved this murder, reward yourself with a bonus clue at entry 581.

4. BLOOD ON THE STONES SOLUTION

Jealousy and ambition have been the downfall of many men - and women - and so it was when Helena Turner attempted to murder her way to the top of the Pluckley Green Pagans.

The gaul to carry out such a shooting is one thing, but the means to do so is quite another, so Helena took advantage of the keys to many houses in the neighbourhood she had - owing to her dog walking business.

She used Gerald Ratchet's gun to fire at Holly Merryfair from the mechanic's house (where she had a convenient and uninterrupted line of sight).

Unfortunately for her, the tenacious Holly Merryfair went on to make a full recovery - whereupon Helena Turner promptly fled the village - and Order - to an unknown location. Her whereabouts are still unknown.

If you cracked this mystery, turn to entry 85.

5. ATTEMPTED MURDER AT THE VICARAGE SOLUTION

It would seem that Nagatha was not the intended victim of this attempted murder but Lord Lucien Pendergast. The perpetrator of this crime was none other than conservationist Jeremy Trumble.

Concerned about the Lucien's plans to develop the Pluckley Green Wetlands into a residential area, Trumble took it upon himself to poison the man, thus saving the precious haven.

On the previous Sunday to the attempted murder, Trumble had noted that Lord Pendergast was the only guest to take sugar with his tea.

Upon his arrival (as the second guest at the vicarage), Jeremy Trumble sprinkled the bowl of sugar cubes with the powdered venom he had extracted from a whipper snake - whilst the reverend and Judy Spiff were outside with Nagatha.

Unfortunately for the aged horse (and unbeknownst to Jeremy), Lord Pendergast had given up sugar as part of his diet, and the poisoned cube was accidentally hand delivered to Nagatha by the cook.

Mercifully, it seems that the horse is likely to make a full recovery. In Pluckley Green, murder may be regarded as a terrible crime but attempted murder is little more than an embarrassing social faux pas.

The two men shook hands and Jeremy Trumble promised not to attempt to murder the lord again.

If you successfully solved this mystery then you may find some additional information at entry 454.

6. LOATHE THY NEIGHBOUR SOLUTION

It seems that those three feet of garden meant a lot more to Helen Dubois than mere additional garden space - for it was there that she cared for the beautiful rose bush where she had sprinkled her husband's ashes.

Losing this rose bush and the ground on which it grew would have meant losing a place which held enormous sentimental value to the widow.

On that Saturday, the simmering quarrel between the warring neighbours finally boiled over into violence when the exasperated and furious Helen Dubois hurled her pitchfork over the garden wall with all the might she had instilled from years of javelin training - killing the man instantly.

It was at that moment that Harry's daughter Sophie arrived for her regular Saturday visit and when she saw what had happened, burst through the gate to Helen's garden and throttled the woman to death upon her own lawn.

A senseless, violent tragedy for all involved.

Sophie was arrested for the crime in the afternoon. She did not resist and confessed to the officers all that had occurred.

If you successfully managed to solve this mystery, there is a bonus for you at entry 16.

7. HATE EXPECTATIONS SOLUTION

A veil can hide a good many secrets and never is that more true than with the woman claiming to be Miss Faversham.

Genevieve Jensen did not go missing, nor did she die at the hands of Miss Alice Faversham - because she, in truth, IS Miss Faversham. Poor Genevieve had suffered years and years of exploitation and violence from Miss Faversham and the abuse had escalated in recent months - once the tyrannical woman discovered that her maid and her handyman had started a secret affair.

Miss Faversham enjoyed tormenting her maid and would even scratch at her face and claw at her hair for the slightest misstep. Things reached an inevitable head on the morning of the 13th of February when, in the process of unsealing her morning mail with a letter opener, Miss Faversham decided to confront her maid over the romantic liaison.

A quarrel erupted into a fight and when Miss Faversham threw scolding hot soup over Genevieve's arms, the maid saw red and fought back - brutally stabbing and slicing the tyrant to death in a frenzy of rage.

Winston the handyman was leaving Stasis House after spending the night with Genevieve and did not pause to help - by burying the body of Miss Faversham in the beautiful new flowerbed.

Genevieve herself has donned the aged and withered wedding dress herself and from behind the veil has chosen to live the rest of her life as the secret (and extremely wealthy) Miss Faversham.

If you successfully unwove this web of lies, turn to entry 250.

8. THE LONELY HEARTS MURDER SOLUTION

Times of woe are no times for woo, so when Sandy Tomlin - the editor of the Pluckley Green Press - discovered that the surgeon who had been responsible for killing her father was in pursuit of love, she knew she needed to take revenge.

Sir Peregrine Conley, the former editor of the paper, died during surgery on his heart and a medical tribunal later decided that his death was the result of negligence on the part of the surgeon Marvin Makepeace.

After inheriting the role of editor from her father, Sandy Tomlin was enraged to learn that this negligent surgeon was happily moving on with his life - and vowed to take revenge.

Using her position as editor, Sandy wrote to Marvin, pretending to be a fellow lonely-hearts resident of the village and arranged a date for the divorcee at the local park. Marvin Makepeace had destroyed her father's heart, so she vowed to do precisely the same to him.

The revenge was worth the punishment - Sandy reasoned - and she handed herself into the police, hoping that the courts would sympathise with her motive for murder.

If you managed to solve this mystery, turn to entry 616.

9. LOCK-IN AT THE BLOODIED AXE SOLUTION

It seems that Delia Steadman was less than honest when she claimed that she was excited to welcome "Saucy" Sally Carter into her family. Evidently, the barmaid with the scandalous reputation was deemed less than sufficient for her son and the only solution was to do away with this nuisance.

Being in possession of a party supplies shop put her method of murder close to hand - balloons.

It does not matter which toxic gas Delia used to poison Sally Carter, nor is it relevant how she filled the helium tanks with this gas but when Delia arrived to help set up the party with gas tanks and balloons, the barmaid's fate was sealed.

The balloons, laden with this lethal gas, floated merrily over the heads of the guests all night long and it was only when the party was over and Saucy Sally set about clearing up the decorations - and popping the balloons with a dart in the process - that the murderous toxin was released.

The gas killed poor Sally instantly and throughout the course of the remaining night, it diffused through the open window.

An ingenious, yet evil plan. Delia Steadman will never be a free woman again.

If you solved this devious murder, your reward is a clue at entry 131.

10. MURDER IS FOR THE BIRDS SOLUTION

There are two types of people who spend their time observing wildlife; those for whom nature is a passing, beautiful encounter and those who seek to suspend that moment forever, to capture it and possess it - like dried butterflies pinned to a displayed board or the taxidermied head of a once wild deer mounted upon a wall.

Pip Longfellow was the latter of these two. A man whose interest in the birdlife of Pluckley Green amounted to a desire to capture and own their fleeting beauty.

When Bill Barr was invited to Mr. Longfellow's house, he was horrified to discover that the man had been collecting bird's eggs for years.

The only solution - to Bill's mind - was to do away with this pillager of nature.

He wrote notes to each member of the birdwatching club, so that the group could be away from the prying eyes of the village when he committed murder.

The night before, he had stashed a rifle into the oblong storage box of Hide 3 and it was from there that he was able to fire a clean shot at Pip in the morning.

In the confusion after the gunshot was heard, he tossed the rifle into the river from the door of his hide, whereupon it was swept into the estuary.

The plan to invite the other birders to the site worked perfectly for Bill, as once the members of the group learned the truth, they began to change their testimonies - each now claiming that they had witnessed Pip Longfellow take his own life.

With no evidence against him, Bill Barr left the investigation as a free man.

If you solved this mystery, go to entry 538.

11. A LEAP OF LOVE SOLUTION

Traditions do not die easily in Pluckley Green. However, the villagers themselves most certainly do.

The murder of Dickon Paisley by Vernon Weathers actually had nothing to do with the decision by Lana to propose to her boyfriend on Leap Year Day.

Instead, it was the result of that oldest of all motives - romantic jealousy, as Vernon Weathers himself was in love with Lana Finch. Lana's affections were not reciprocated - in fact, her own father had to intervene so that she would no longer be harassed by the ceaseless love letters he would send to her through the post.

And when Vernon learned that his friend Dickon had plans to propose to Lana, he responded in the manner so many of the villagers choose when faced with a problem - murder.

On the surface, Vernon seemed happy for his friend, even going so far as to give Dickon a bottle of breath freshener spray, so that the couple's first betrothed kiss would be as fresh as the spring flowers which bloomed around them.

However, the spray was laced with deadly whipper snake venom - and Dickon was fatally poisoned almost instantly.

Following his arrest, Lana expressed nothing but hatred and disgust for Vernon. The man may well hang for his crime and Lana's heart may never heal. What a senseless waste of life.

If you successfully solved this mystery, turn to entry 638.

12. TOIL AND TROUBLE SOLUTION

Whoever coined the term "There are no small parts, only small actors" clearly had never been trapped playing minor roles and background characters with the Pluckley Players.

From an unnamed fairy in a "Midsummer Night's Dream," to an unnamed housemaid in "Jekyll and Hyde", from anonymous crew member aboard the "HMS Pinafore" to a literal cherry tree in "The Cherry Orchard" - and of course, Witch #3 in "Macbeth" - Isobel Chance had played every thankless and forgettable role going.

Unlike the rest of the clumsy, wooden performers who made up the Pluckley Players, Isobel was the sole member of the troupe to show even an ounce of talent - and yet the director, Stanley Slavsky always favoured nepotism over ability and would only ever cast his nephew Leon as the lead in any production (who in turn would always select Thalia Jones to be his leading lady).

Isobel knew that if her dream of performing on the glitzy stages of the West End was to be realised, she needed to first get noticed in a starring role - and in order to do that, she needed to do away with Leon Cribbage.

It was a simple enough task. During the rehearsal of the most famous of Macbeth's soliloquies, Isobel slipped into the black robes and theatrical mask backstage and, with a dagger she had taken from her antique shop, crept onto the stage and stabbed the actor in the back.

Then, once she had fled from the village hall, it was a matter of casting aside her disguise and returning backstage via the backdoor, whereupon she could easily blend back in amongst the startled cast and crew.

When Isobel Chance was arrested, she did not go quietly or easily - she instead screamed to the officers that she was destined for greatness and would live out her dreams to become a star. Let's just hope that her prison has an amateur dramatics programme - one that knows talent when it sees it.

If you correctly identified the killer, go to entry 628.

13. MURDER AT CROOKED COTTAGE SOLUTION

A locked-room mystery is a type of puzzle which has been played out across the pages of detective novels for generations. The impossible scenario in which a victim is murdered inside an enclosed room - with no means of entry or exit - is a tantalising and befuddling source of fascination.

However, upon closer inspection it would seem that the ghastly outrage at Crooked Cottage was actually not a locked-room mystery at all - as the dwelling was home to a secret trapdoor hidden beneath the false bottom of a wardrobe.

Evidently, Lucy Sparrow was murdered and beheaded away from the confines of her home and the body was brought to the cottage. It was then staged in a manner which would lead the residents of the village to believe that something truly supernatural had occurred - and that the curse upon Crooked Cottage was real.

But why Lucy Sparrow? She was a seemingly ordinary woman without an enemy in the world. Moreover, how did the killer know about the trapdoor - and the combination to its lock?

Something is not right about this murder. Aside from the savagery of the slaying itself, the killer remains free and has vowed to kill again. There is a greater mystery here - perhaps one which we cannot yet fully comprehend but one which must be solved if Pluckley Green wants to ever know peace and safety again.

If you know the three digit passcode to the trapdoor, that number is the entry you should turn to for some further information. (If the password is correct, the first word of the entry will be "Click!")

14. THE NIGHT OF THE STORM: PART ONE SOLUTION

Few of us are fortunate enough to have been born with a proverbial silver spoon in our mouth and fewer still are unfortunate enough to die by that very means.

Silas Marsten, however was one such unlucky soul to die in that manner - thanks to a silver soup spoon which had been varnished with poison.

The perpetrators of this crime (as two people were responsible) were sisters Wilma Rogers and Daisy Doyle. The two had wanted to murder the arrogant and wicked historian for quite some time but the opportunity had never arisen until this stormy night.

Silas Marsten had been responsible for the death of Daisy's daughter, Rosemary the year before - owing to his reckless driving. However, the judge had been entirely too forgiving of the perpetrator's shortcomings and Silas had walked free from the court.

The mental anguish was too much to bear for Daisy and her husband Jarvis and their marriage imploded beneath the weight of their grief. It was at this point that Daisy and her sister vowed revenge.

Silas inadvertently signed his own death warrant of Thursday, when he casually mentioned to Mavis Davis that he would be weathering the storm in the church - a detail the local gossip would share to all and sundry, including the two sisters, who now had an ideal location for murder.

Wilma's role in this crime was to spend Friday afternoon coating a silver soup spoon in poison she had extracted during her botany studies (her sister knew that soup would be served that evening as she had seen Mabel buying vegetables at the greengrocer's). This spoon she took with her to the church that evening.

Meanwhile, Daisy's task was to distract the cook with chit-chat so that Wilma could lay the table - including the poisoned soup spoon.

The two women were quite content to go to prison for this crime but once they had confessed all to the police, Mabel suddenly claimed that she recalled seeing Silas choke on bread at the table that evening - and pretty soon, all others present (including Reverend Harper) claimed to have seen the same.

The two women were released without charge. They may have got away with murder but perhaps justice was truly served.

If you solved this mystery, go to entry 93.

15. THE NIGHT OF THE STORM: PART TWO SOLUTION

Extramarital affairs are as commonplace as dandelions in the village of Pluckley Green.

Perhaps it is due to the crushing sense of existential loneliness or the aching, ever present state of ennui which plagues the residents. Whatever the reason, matrimonial vows are broken just as readily as bones in the village.

The affair between Gordon Nolan and Charlotte Merton was a barely concealed secret and both party's spouses were aware of this betrayal. In the case of Damien Merton, he chose to turn a blind eye to the adultery but for Matilda Nolan, it was grounds for divorce.

Out of desperation to keep her family intact, it was Nelly Nolan who murdered her father's mistress.

When the guests were exploring the mansion, Nelly took Lord Pendergast's pistol from his bedside table and stashed it away in the wardrobe of the first guest bedroom - preempting the inevitable game of hide-and-seek which would be played later.

Nelly also forged a note in her father's hand that invited Charlotte to meet Gordon in the wardrobe of the second guest bedroom.

Much to Nelly's annoyance, when the game was eventually played, Mona Prim opted to hide in the wardrobe of the first guest bedroom but as soon as the maid was discovered by Lady Pendergast, Nelly crawled out from under the bed and crept into the now empty wardrobe. She then fired Lord Pendergast's pistol through the wall - killing Charlotte in the room next door.

Perhaps because of her age and her motive, the courts will be lenient with Nelly Nolan. Whether this act of murder will be enough to save her parents' marriage, only time will tell.

If you solved this murder, go to entry 204.

16. EASTER FOOLS' DAY SOLUTION

In the end, the best way to take down a prankster was with a jape so old and hackneyed, only a seasoned jokester could still find humour in it - snakes in a can. Only this time the snake was very real.

Lord Asquith-Hulme lacked confidence that the organisers of the parade would be able to halt Lester Pratt and as a result, he decided to take matters into his own hands.

Of the errands he had assigned to his assistant, one was of the utmost importance - seek out and bring him a deadly whipper snake. Carl Turpin (who knew the lord liked to encounter the local wildlife of wherever he visited) innocently - and carefully - gathered a specimen, which Lord Asquith-Hulme later coiled inside an empty tube of salted peanuts.

At midnight of the night before the Easter parade, Lord Asquith-Hulme visited Lester Pratt's home, with the excuse that he was a fellow fan of practical jokes and wanted to demonstrate his latest prank.

Upon opening the tube of peanuts, the deadly whipper snake pounced from its confinement and bit Lester Pratt upon the hand - killing him instantly.

The lord would almost certainly have got away with it had he not accidentally left an imprint of his shoe upon the muddy path of Lester's front garden - a print of a shoe which was two sizes larger than his regular pair, owing to the man's gout.

With the death of a jester came the inevitable arrest of a lord. The Easter parade went ahead without a hitch.

If you successfully solved this mystery, go to entry 235.

17. SEANCE ON A CURSED AFTERNOON SOLUTION

The mystery of what happens to us after we die is perhaps the most fundamental question any of us can ask. It is a question to which Horace Scrub has now been provided an answer.

After inheriting a good deal of money from his father, Horace Scrub and his wife were eager to retire from their farm. Years of thankless toil came to an end and the pair elected to buy up available property around the village with which they could build a collection of holiday cottages for tourists exploring the picturesque beauty of the location.

One such property was the extensive orchard which had provided the perfect apples for Ashton Egremont-Russet's award-winning cider.

Without apples his business would surely collapse and - not wanting to sacrifice taste for an inferior variety of the fruit - Ashton Egremont-Russet decided that murder was his best course of action.

During the seance (once Adriana Arcana and the other guests had closed their eyes), Ashton Egremont-Russet released his left-handed grip on Horace Scrub's hand and reached for the dagger in the centre of the table. With lightning speed he plunged it into Mr Scrub's throat.

The only member of the group who would have known that Ashton Egremont-Russet had broken the circle of hands was Horace Scrub - and he was in no position to talk…

No doubt Ashton Egremont-Russet will rot away in prison like a cider apple on the ground of an abandoned orchard.

If you successfully unravelled this mystery, turn to entry 256.

18. RUN FOR YOUR LIFE SOLUTION

Money has the terrible power to corrupt and ruin everything it touches - even something as innocent as a race around a rural village.

When Bludger Baxter took a sizeable bet from Mick Nicholson, he no doubt thought that the man from Brigstowe was barmy for wagering his money on the perennial runner-up, Bruno Brown. However, Mick Nicholson was not as foolish as he appeared, as he intended to murder Milton West.

Mick volunteered for the role of spotter outside Stasis House and with him he brought a vial of poison with which he could spike Milton's orange squash before handing it to him.

Being an outsider of the village, Mick did not recognise any of the runners - so simply assumed that whoever was in the lead must be the village's star runner.

Of course, the man from Brigstowe had no idea he was actually murdering Bruno Brown - the very man he had wagered his money on.

Bruno was only in first place during the Pluckley Green Run because the night before (as Milton was practicing the course with his trainer) he had scattered rusty tacks across the canal path, injuring Milton's foot and providing himself with the competitive advantage.

It was an act of sabotage which cost Bruno his life.

Milton has lived to race another day whilst Mick Nicholson will be locked away in jail - or swing from the hangman's noose.

If you successfully solved this puzzle, you can find a bonus clue at entry 171.

19. MAYDAY MAYHEM SOLUTION

May Day is the time of year when people come together to celebrate spring - and the new life which comes in its wake.

Jessica Waterstone was preparing to welcome new life herself - in the form of a baby which was due to be born in November. However, it would not take a mathematical genius to calculate that this birthdate would mean that the conception would have occurred around the time of Virginia Day's Valentine party - when Kevin Waterstone was away in East Berlin.

Jack Quick's years as Pluckley Green's most notorious Casanova had surely caught up with him. He had got a married woman pregnant and there would certainly be consequences.

The only man present at Virginia Day's Valentine party was Jack Quick, so Jessica Waterstone's husband would have been in no doubt as to whom the father of the baby was.

During the May Day dance at the village hall, Kevin surreptitiously slipped a note into Jack's jacket whilst helpfully taking the guests' coats. The note claimed to be from Virginia Day (one of the few young women in Pluckley Green who had so far managed to resist Jack's charms) and invited him to meet her by the maypole at 10.30pm.

Kevin simply had to wait in the shadows until Jack arrived, whereupon the army soldier strangled the man to death and strung his corpse from the maypole.

With the biological father of her baby dead and her husband destined for prison, who will help Jessica Waterstone raise her child? Well, in the words of Reverend Harper himself, "it takes a village".

If you successfully untangled this web of deceit, your reward is at entry 583.

20. THE BODY IN PLUCKLEY GREEN LIBRARY SOLUTION

Curating a successful trivia team is all about refining your group's strengths and rooting out any weakness. The weakness in this case was Eustace Leadbetter - by far the worst and most disruptive member of the Pluckley Green Brights.

In any normal village, the solution would have been to ask Eustace to leave the team, however, this is Pluckley Green, where murder is always an option.

For several weeks Wilma Rogers has offered an alternative member in the form of her architect friend Calvin Copperhead. However, nobody wanted to be the one to dismiss Eustace. In the end it was Cosmo Calder who decided to take matters into his own hands.

In the days leading up to Eustace's murder, Cosmo sneaked a book into the library - a book on such a boring subject he was confident that nobody would open. Inside he had hollowed out the pages to create an empty space in which he could hide a pistol. This he stashed in the arts section of the library - the one adjacent to the geography section.

Much to Cosmo's irritation, Xander had chosen on a whim to study art that afternoon and the plan would have been abandoned had the butcher not left the section for a lavatory break.

Seizing his opportunity whilst his wife's back was turned, Cosmo trotted into the arts section, took the gun from inside the book and shot Eustace through the bookshelves.

It did not take long for the killer to be caught and Cosmo went with the police without a struggle. The Pluckley Green Brights managed to lose not one but two members that afternoon and now stand a worse chance than ever in the New Year's trivia quiz.

If you managed to solve this murder, go to entry 555.

21. THE HOUND OF THE PENDERGASTS SOLUTION

In the case of the murder of Gary Grimpen it would seem that there were two mysteries that needed to be solved.

The first of these was that of the Hound of the Pendergasts. The demonic gurt dog turned out to be nothing more terrifying than plumber Gerald Ratchett's bloodhound/mastiff cross Merlin. In order to keep people away from the treacherous mire, Gerald had (for the past twenty years and more) taken to painting phosphorous around several generations of dogs' eyes and allowing them to roam freely around the heath at night. This ruse was inspired by the centuries old legend of the devil dog which had cursed the Pendergast family and had proven to be very successful at deterring people from the heath at night.

This was common knowledge to the members of the Ancient Order of Pluckley Pagans and one of their members, Donny Holmes was to use this to his advantage.

His four friends were fans of camping so when he suggested a night on the heath, they jumped at the chance.

Donny knew that Merlin would make an appearance at some time around midnight - when he and his friends were admiring the beauty of the full moon and as predicted, the appearance of the dog sent the campers fleeing in separate directions.

Donny simply had to follow Gary where he ran and then, in the half-light, led him across the heath to wade into the mire.

Once his love rival was trapped up to his waist, Donny took the axe from Gerald Ratchett's unlocked toolshed - and hacked his friend to bits.

A ghastly crime committed to end the romance between Tamara and Gary. However, when Tamara learned of this horror, she reacted with such rage and disgust that Donny Holmes fled to the heath, whereupon he flung himself into the mire to drown - never to be seen again.

If you successfully solved this murder, go to entry 283.

22. BAILIFFS AND BULLETS SOLUTION

Sometimes it takes an encounter with our past to jolt some sense into our present.

For Lenny Goon, this came in the guise of his former school teacher, Mrs Agnes Tipple.

Mrs Tipple had seen potential in the young boy as a wordsmith and believed that the aspiring writer had the talent to go far. However, the choices for a young man's future were somewhat limited in a rural village in postwar Somerset and Lenny Goon was begrudgingly forced to take the position of bailiff working for Lord Pendergast.

Perhaps it was seeing Mrs Tipple's sad face at the window, or perhaps it was seeing how his former teacher had friends and family united on her side. Whatever the reason, Lenny acted fast and impulsively. Without even turning his head, the bailiff took the pistol from his pocket and fired backwards into the Rolls Royce - hitting Lord Pendergast in the shoulder.

Lenny then dropped the gun to the ground and kicked it away beneath the car.

When the ambulance arrived, Lord Pendergast had lost a huge amount of blood and was clinging to life. He is currently in a Birgstowe hospital and his recovery is expected to take at least a fortnight.

In Pluckley Green, failing to murder Lord Pendergast is regarded as more of an embarrassing mistake than a crime. It was decided that the former bailiff should be required to pay three months of rent on Agnes Tipple's cottage and then the matter would be settled.

If you correctly sleuthed the solution to this mystery, go to entry 304.

23. A STITCH IN CRIME SOLUTION

In Pluckley Green, even the most genteel and relaxed social groups can be simmering cauldrons of rivalries, jealousies and revenge.

When Beverley Potter put her name forward as the head flower arranger at the upcoming summer fete, she was not only treading on the toes of a woman for whom the position was her pride and joy, she was ensuring her own murder.

Marcy Mayhew took being usurped from her role enormously personally and decided to resolve the situation in the way that so many people in the village do.

Every week the ladies of the sewing circle indulge in their favourite doughnuts at 9pm, with each having a personal preference for one variety over all others. All Marcy needed to do was swap a regular jam doughnut for a poisoned one.

Earlier in the day, Marcy had visited Mr Basingwhaite's bakery (wearing her delightful new summer hat) and purchased a single jam doughnut. With the venom of a whipper snake, she injected the sweet treat, which she then secretly took along to the sewing circle.

Using the excuse that she was helping Penelope Gannet out by making tea for the guests in the kitchen, Marcy swapped the regular doughnut for the poisoned one (tossing the regular doughnut into the kitchen bin).

She then brought the tea set into the dining room and waited an hour for the doughnuts to arrive from the kitchen and for her rival to be poisoned.

A tragic waste of life in the name of jealousy. This act of revenge may have felt cathartic in the moment but it will cost the nurse her freedom.

If you correctly solved this murder, go to entry 601.

24. A FETE WORSE THAN DEATH SOLUTION

Whilst the rest of the nation may be eagerly embracing the changes and possibilities of a post-war world, Pluckley Green chooses to stay firmly and proudly in the past.

Cuthbert Crookshank's plan to theme the village fete around America - a decision as perplexing as it was unwelcome - was met with distaste by the generally conservative village and Oswald Spiff believed that this change was a step too far for his tastes. He decided that the chairman of the fete's committee should pay with his life. Despite claiming that he was at a performance of the Pluckley Players' "Hamlet" last night, his own wife and daughter testified otherwise. Oswald instead spent his time that evening cutting the brake pipes of Cuthbert Crookshank's '54 Hudson Hornet.

However, it was poor Tommy Tomlinson who ended up victim of this sabotage - dying in a fiery explosion when it was he who drove the car this morning.

Oswald Spiff was arrested this afternoon. Alas, owing to his wealth and social standing, it is more than likely that he will be given a light sentence - if the judge overseeing the trial is the loathed Jan Tregeagle.

If you successfully solved this mystery, go to entry 246.

25. A MIDSUMMER NIGHT'S SCREAM SOLUTION

In a predominantly and proudly Christian village such as Pluckley Green - where even the slightest deviation from strict social norms is treated with suspicion - the members of the Ancient Order of Pluckley Pagans have learned that secrecy and discretion are of vital importance.

The majority of the Order's members choose to live private lives of undisclosed religious affiliations and their identities are hidden under hooded cloaks at all of the group's meetings.

Holly Merryfair, however, has proven to be less than tight-lipped regarding the Order and its members and can often be seen strolling around the village in his white ceremonial garb.

One member who had evidently had quite enough of Holly's loose tongue was physiotherapist Rita Flynn, who had decided to do away with the 92 year old Grand High Wizard of the organisation.

During the closing moments of the Summer Solstice celebration, when the group gazed skywards with their arms held aloft, Rita threw a dart (a dart which she had taken from the Bloodied Axe Tavern the night before and soaked in whipper snake venom) aimed at Holly Merryfair's exposed neck.

However, she had to act fast, so that no other members saw the murder and in doing so, completely missed Holly and instead sent the dart soaring straight into poor Wilbur Charles' neck. The scream Rita released was one of horror when she realised to her despair that she had killed the wrong man.

As the sun set at the end of the solstice, Rita Flynn was arrested. No doubt she will miss many, many midsummers in the years and decades to come.

If you successfully solved this mystery, go to entry 273.

26. PERRY GULCH'S LAST STAND SOLUTION

Perry Gulch may have been hailed as a hero 12 years ago but today he is nothing more than an embarrassing wreck of a man to the eyes of much of the village.

Detested by almost all of Pluckley Green, Perry has silently watched the village from afar, drinking away his future and descending into the mire of alcoholism.

It was only a matter of time until one of the villagers decided that Perry Gulch was a blight that Pluckley Green could do without and decided to dispose of him. That villager was Eloise Crookshank.

It didn't take much effort on her part. Just a cheap bottle of Cabernet from the village shop and then the injection of a poison, with the help of a surgical needle, through the cork.

Eloise arose early on a Sunday morning so that not even her husband would be aware of her plan and crept out to the churchyard at dawn to leave the bottle beside the sleeping drunk.

As guilty as she may be, in the hours which followed her arrest a few stories began to change shape. Mr Crookshank now recalled waking before his wife and making breakfast in bed for her. Millie Costa no longer remembered waving to Eloise at dawn and Isaac Peters now insists that his neighbour didn't know the first thing about wine. The case against Eloise Crookshank simply evaporated.

After triumphing over the Nazis, Perry Gulch is now fighting his last stand against another formidable foe - the poison coursing through his veins as he lays unconscious in a Brigstowe hospital bed.

If you correctly solved this mystery, go to entry 680.

27. THE SUMMER FETE: PART ONE SOLUTION

The world of books and publishing is a fickle one. One minute you may be among the most celebrated writers of your generation, the next you are cutting the ribbon at a parochial village fete.

Such was the fate of Conrad Cudass. The once famed author was declining in popularity and failing to recapture former glories. Save for a handful of loyal fans, his fanbase was steadily moving onto other writers. What better way to revive book sales than for the author to die a sudden and violent death? It certainly worked for Tarquin Taggers, whose popularity soared following his death in a car crash.

It didn't take much for Jay Towers to arrange the murder. Sometime early that morning, he discretely ran a copper wire through the ceremonial ribbon and connected it to a plug socket in the village hall. No doubt the hustle and bustle of that morning's pre-fete preparations successfully masked his actions.

The instant the metal scissors made contact with the copper wire, the author was hit by a massive jolt of electricity and died instantly.

It is more than likely that Jay Towers will hang for this crime - particularly if his judge in the murder trial is one Jan Treagle.

What is an undeniable certainty is that Conrad Cudass will go on to have a posthumous revival in his career and his books will be more successful and celebrated than ever before.

If you managed to sleuth your way to the solution of this mystery, go to entry 379.

28. THE SUMMER FETE: PART TWO SOLUTION

It is hard to imagine who would want to kill a talented young dancer, let alone how anybody could have the audacity to do so in front of most of the village.

And yet, that is precisely what happened. There can be no doubt that this was the work of the much-feared Ghost - and that whoever that person is, they intended to terrify the village with this demonstration of merciless power.

The investigation gradually eliminated locations around the village which could have been the source of the arrow, until only one place was left - Crooked Cottage.

Once the padlock on the door was broken by the police, they discovered the words "I AM THE GHOST AND PENELOPE GANNET IS MY LATEST VICTIM" scrawled across a note which had been discarded in the cottage.

The Ghost must have entered Crooked Cottage via the secret trapdoor in the wardrobe and then broken one of the windows in order to launch an arrow from inside the house.

Whoever he or she is, they then managed to disappear without a trace through the web of tunnels beneath the village…

If you successfully solved this mystery, go to entry 162.

29. MURDER ON THE PLUCKLEY EXPRESS SOLUTION

Mavis Davis may be the biggest gossip in the village but that does not prevent her from having a deep, dark secret of her own. In fact, it was a secret so shocking that she would do anything to keep it to herself. Whatever this dreadful secret is, Dorothy Halcyon was aware of it - and very happy to exploit it. The woman had taken to blackmailing Mavis Davis.

Unlike Miss Faversham, who had also been the subject of one of Dorothy's blackmail notes, Mavis Davis had succumbed to the extortion and opted to pay the wicked woman.

However, Dorothy Halcyon had continued to demand more money from her - to spend on fripperies such as a new summer hat - and Mavis could no longer afford this exploitation.

As the train entered the dark tunnel, Mavis removed a large knife from her handbag and plunged it into the chest of the woman seated beside her. She then tossed the knife out of the window before daylight flooded back into the train cabin.

Mavis Davis' secret was evidently something which had troubled her, as the night before she had sought solace from Reverend Harper, whereupon she tearfully confessed her scandal.

Once the murder investigation had concluded, this confession was repeated by Mavis to her fellow passengers in the privacy of the train cabin. All of these passengers took pity on the distressed woman and vowed to keep her secret shame to themselves.

Moreover, each of them went on to tell the police that Dorothy Halcyon had actually died when the train came to a sudden halt in the tunnel - as Dorothy was in the process of showing off her brand new kitchen knife.

In fact, the train lurched so suddenly that the woman fell upon her own knife and in her panicked haste, pulled it from her chest and accidentally tossed it through the train window.

An improbable story but one the police had no option but to accept.

If you successfully solved this murder, go to entry 12.

30. THE FEARLESS FIVE SOLUTION

There was a time when the Fearless Five were famous and celebrated as a formidable mystery solving team but those days were long ago and despite their attempts to reclaim their celebrity, the group had grown tired of their own fruitless and exhausting antics.

Except of course for Jonathon. The tireless enthusiasm from the group's oldest member had led him to force the group to reform every summer holiday - and to endure miserable adventures together.

It was Fran who had finally had enough. Initially, she had intended to hand her brother a note which would declare why she no longer wished to be part of the sleuthing team. However, she later decided that murder would prove a simpler (and more permanent) means of disbanding the group.

After being awoken by Jimmy and hearing Jonathon's voice outside her tent, Fran clearly decided to act on instinct and to kill her brother immediately.

After creeping from the tent without waking the sleeping Henry, she tiptoed into the barn, took the shotgun from the wall and after taking a few steps towards the farmhouse, fired the weapon at a figure she saw in the darkness.

However, unbeknownst to her this was not her brother (who was nearby, urinating in a bush) and was instead the kindly farmer who had allowed the youths to spend the night on his land.

Although killing Milo was a terrible accident, Fran most certainly intended to murder that night - and will be punished by the law accordingly.

The circumstances may not have been what Fran had hoped - but at least she will no longer have to spend her summer hols with the tedious Fearless Five...

If you managed to unweave this web of deceit, go to entry 715.

31. TCHOTCHKE'S REVENGE SOLUTION

After escaping from the minimal security Brigstowe Prison, Toby Tchotchke made his way to Pluckley Green on foot and set up camp in the Western Woods.

Perhaps he knew that he would be caught eventually, so he used his brief spell of freedom to do the one thing he had dreamed of since being incarcerated in January - revenge against his former friend August Barley.

The plan had been fairly straightforward. Smash the wooden bucket of the well on August's farm with a rock and then, when the beekeeper/historian was attempting to fix it, sneak up behind him with a knife in hand, repeatedly stab him and then cast his body down into the depths of the well. That is precisely what Toby Tchotchke did at 2pm that afternoon.

When the police made it to the bottom of the well shaft, they discovered August Barley - but to their great surprise, the man had the faintest of pulses and was rushed to hospital. August may well live to complete his history book after all…

Toby Tchotchke however, will almost certainly now hang for this dreadful act of escape and attempted murder.

If you successfully located August Barley, go to entry 627.

32. A MURDER OF CROWS SOLUTION

Even in the quietest corner of a picturesque village, jealousy and revenge can find a place to blossom.

When Paulette Green wrote a note to Benjamin Hellman, she was giving voice to an unspoken attraction the two had silently shared for years. Her invitation was enough to turn an innocent flirtation into something far more real - and scandalous.

With both her husband and son out for the evening, Paulette invited her neighbour over - knowing full well that Juno Hellman would be on the stage that night.

However, what she did not foresee is that her husband would leave his shift at the police station early and arrive home at 11pm - to catch his wife in the throes of passion with his neighbour.

In a fit of rage and jealousy, Pierce Green stabbed Benjamin in the back. He then dragged the naked, dead man into the middle of the corn field, dressed him in the scarecrow's clothes and mounted him on the pole to be pecked by crows.

For the sake of her marriage, Paulette tried to cover this murder by changing the bloodstained bedsheets and hastily stuffing Benjamin's work clothes behind the bed.

It was the following morning that she saw the scarecrow. It was posed to look at the house as a reminder to Paulette of what her infidelity had caused - and perhaps even as a warning as to what might happen to her if she strayed again...

Pierce handed himself in to the very police station where he worked. Only time will tell if the courts will have sympathy for his motive.

If you correctly solved this murder, go to entry 175.

33. THE GHOST OF PLUCKLEY CASTLE SOLUTION

The plan to murder Arabella Krueger was set in motion not during the ghost hunt but during the group made to the castle the afternoon before - when the members of the Pluckley Green Ghost Club were attending the fortification as paying tourists.

It was during this afternoon visit that Denzil Bates hid a grey dress and a dark, acrylic wig in a wooden trunk at the foot of the west tower staircase in the castle keep.

Later that night, whilst everybody else in the club was busy exploring a different location, he left the grand hall and retrieved the dress and wig from the west tower and donned them to climb the haunted North Tower stairwell - which is where he knew Arabella would insist upon investigating herself.

On the way, he carried a burning candle he had taken from the Grand Hall dining table, so that he would be spotted by other members of the ghost club, which would lead them to conclude that Arabella had been murdered by none other than the Grey Lady herself.

Denzil Bates' motive was partly due to jealousy - Arabella always got to lead the investigations and stake out all of the prime locations, whilst he was relegated to the dullest, most boring ones. However, his primary motivation was that he, much like the other members of the club, found Arabella's relentless scepticism detrimental to the club and its reputation. The Pluckley Green Ghost Club will struggle to survive this dreadful event and Denzil Bates will never get to enjoy another ghost hunt - or his freedom - again.

If you successfully solved this haunting mystery, go to entry 229.

34. SUNDAY IN THE PARK WITH GORE SOLUTION

When you live your everyday life incognito, your own face becomes your best disguise.

Such was the case with Genevieve Jensen, the former maid of Miss Faversham, who assumed her identity beneath a tattered wedding veil after murdering her.

By simply removing this disguise, Genevieve was able to visit Mr Willow at his tobacconist shop and purchase a single Woodman Robusto cigar.

Even if people did give her a second glance, they were far more likely to comment on how much she looked liked that seldom-seen maid who went missing all those months ago, rather than guess that she was in fact that very same woman.

Next, Genevieve needed gunpowder. She acquired this by breaking into the gatehouse on the Pendergast Estate and stealing a few fireworks. She then packed the cigar with gunpowder and - on the Sunday afternoon - surreptitiously replaced this deadly cigar with the real one in Phineas Flitter's unguarded jacket.

All this to prevent her true identity from being exposed to the village. However, when she was seated on the grass of the park, she couldn't help but overhear a conversation between Phineas and Jeremy Trumble in which the gossip journalist revealed that his column that week was actually due to be about some trifling nonsense regarding jam.

Genevieve - in the guise of Miss Faversham - attempted to dissuade Phineas from smoking the cigar but by then it was too late. The man lit up and blew his own face to bits.

Genevieve will once again get away with murder. After all, for all the police know, Genevieve Jensen is still missing and presumed dead...

If you successfully blew this explosive case apart, go to entry 43.

35. TRAGIC MAGIC SOLUTION

Spending a lifetime chasing the limelight can drive a person mad. As talented as you may be, charisma is simply something you cannot learn, it is something you have or you do not.

This is why John Guard AKA The Great Illusio, who was jealous and frustrated by the applause Captain Conjuro and Mesmeralda were receiving (whilst his own career had largely stalled), decided that murder would be his best option.

John Guard knew only too well that the true talent behind the duo's magic act was Mesmeralda - she was equally as skilled as her co-star and brought a touch of glamour to the show that set their routine apart. With the double act out of the picture, he would surely start receiving more bookings from local theatres…

Sometime before the variety show commenced, John Guard took the pin from the guillotine which was kept backstage and pocketed it. After performing his lacklustre act, The Great Illusio then went to sit in the back row of the theatre and tucked the pin down the side of his seat - where he assumed it would not be found.

From there, John Guard simply had to watch the rest of the show until it reached its gruesome climax.

He had no way of knowing that Mesmeralda would make a spontaneous change to the routine and suggest that Captain Conjuro be the one at the foot of the guillotine. Unbeknownst to her, this small change was enough to save her own life - and doom his.

Perhaps The Great Illusio will hang for this crime. If not, he will be sentenced to life behind bars. However, Jane Brown - in the guise of Mesmeralda will no-doubt triumph as a solo magician.

If you conjured up the correct solution to this mystery, go to entry 224.

36. THE MURDER OF MR MOANER SOLUTION

Sometimes the most efficient strike is a preemptive one and such was the case when Margaret "Peggy" Ramsay set out to murder Humbert Miner.

Peggy knew all too well that Mr Moaner (as she had named him at the post office where she worked) would oppose her and her husband's plans to build a swimming pool, so her course of action was to murder him before he got the chance.

Peggy first bought a whipper snake from Putters' Pets. Then, with the poison extracted from the reptile, she painted the reverse side of a roll of stamps.

The next time Humbert was in the post office, groaning, holding up the queue and generally wasting everybody's time, she made sure to hand him this poisoned roll of stamps.

Later that day, as Mr Miner was beginning his latest letter writing session, all it took was the lick of one stamp to kill him.

The police arrested Peggy Ramsay the very same day. Just because a man is an unpleasant irritant it does not provide grounds for murder.

Peggy will never get to enjoy that pool even if it gets built.

If you solved this venomous mystery, go to entry 584.

37. THE ASSASSINATION SITUATION SOLUTION

It is rare that an apple falls far from its tree and it was even more unlikely to happen when it came to Judy Spiff.

Born and raised into enormous wealth, Judy had no reason to ever question the terrible morality her parents had imprinted upon her - nor did she want to. Judy Spiff truly believed that she was better than others simply because of a fluke of birth - and sadly, many others believed this too.

The Spiff family were used to getting whatever they wanted, and for mere commoners to bow to their name with respect. However, the trouble with democracy is that a rich man's vote is worth precisely as much as a poor man's vote. Judy desperately wanted her mother to win the election and yet the people of the Pluckley Green seemed to favour Cuthbert Crookshank.

The only solution was to take matters into her own hands if she was going to get what she wanted.

As the hustings took place, Judy Spiff simply hid in a bush by the open window until she could get a clear shot of Mr Crookshank with her family's pistol, after which, she dropped the gun and returned to waiting outside the village hall.

Judy Spiff is young and her family is well connected. Few people in the village believe that the spoiled girl will see any consequences for her terrible deed.

The eventual winner of the election - to the surprise of many, including the man himself - was August Barey.

If you successfully solved this case of political intrigue, go to entry 81.

38. SIN AND TONIC SOLUTION

When investigating a crime, it is easy to suppose that a perpetrator is a single person - rather than several people involved in a criminal conspiracy. But that is exactly what happened with the attempted poisoning of Lord Pendergast.

Lady Pendergast, Bludger Baxter, Mavis Davis and Reverend Harper - each one full of rage and hatred for Lucien - poisoned a separate ingredient of Lord Pendergast's gin and tonic and then immediately afterwards set about covering up each other's involvement in the crime. This criminal gang hatched their masterplan over drinks at Annie's Tearoom the afternoon before the party. It would have worked, were it not for the fact that the gin and tonic was so overwhelmingly poisonous that Lord Pendergast detected the smell of whipper snake poison immediately.

That evening, Lady Pendergast went home with the reverend to spend a night at the vicarage.

At about 2am, there was a loud knock on the door of Pendergast Manor. Lord Pendergast wearily heaved himself from the bed to see who would have the impertinence to bother him at this late hour.

When he opened the door to his home, he saw a figure, shrouded in a hooded cloak standing before him. Lord Pendergast did not even have time to raise his voice when the figure raised a shotgun to his face - and blasted his head to smithereens.

If you successfully solved this mystery, go to entry 222.

39. A WALK IN THE WESTERN WOODS SOLUTION

As far too many people in Pluckley Green are aware, grief can drive a person mad and force them to commit unspeakable acts.

Perhaps Artemis Baird did not hate Doctor Henery White - but he certainly wanted him dead. When the general practitioner became engaged to his mother - nurse Angela Baird, the undergraduate student was horrified. No man on earth was good enough to replace war hero Bernard Baird - his beloved father.

Artemis' plan was to quickly and cleanly dispatch this usurper to his father's position.

Before the weekly walk in the Western Woods, Artemis purchased a cutthroat razor and took it with him for the stroll - along with a pair of latex gloves to mask his fingerprints.

When he was out of sight of Minerva Arcana (and behind Bathsheba Sharpe), Artemis veered off the path to hide in the undergrowth behind the abandoned cottage.

As expected, Doctor White arrived shortly afterwards and Artemis simply crept up behind him and slashed his throat.

Artemis may have prevented his mother's marriage but it has come at the cost of his freedom and of an innocent man's life.

If you successfully solved this mystery, go to entry 530.

40. THE GHOST IN THE FIRE SOLUTION

There can be no doubt about it. The Ghost has struck again and claimed his or her fourth victim.

Poor Bertrand Mallard was an unassuming and well-liked man who meant no harm to anybody.

And yet, Pluckley Green's most dangerous resident saw fit to burn the man alive. Why?

The Ghost, for whatever reason, must have taken a great deal of time gluing the latches shut on Bertrand's cottage and then padlocking the front door - preventing any possibility of the retired man escaping.

As Bertrand slept downstairs in his armchair by the unlit fireplace, The Ghost climbed the tree and onto the roof. Once there, he dropped a flaming bottle of vodka down the chimney.

The inferno would have spread instantly. We can only hope that Bertrand did not suffer too much before his fiery death.

If you correctly solved this burning mystery, go to entry 146.

41. THE CIRCUS OF BLOOD SOLUTION

When Leonard and Wanda testified that Chip Burlington had no enemies in the world, they were not lying. His murder was committed not as an act of hatred for the strongman but out of jealousy towards Polo the Clown.

A year ago, Bartholomew (real name, Luke) Bostwicke and Dazzle/Wanda Highsmith were in a romantic relationship together; a relationship the acrobat ended so that she could be with Polo/Dominic Tell.

Mr Bostwicke did not recover from this rejection and harboured a resentment towards his newly employed clown (who had taken over from the alcoholic Dropsey/Curran Cornwell).

His plan to permanently end the relationship between Dominic and Wanda was to frame the clown for murder.

Earlier in the afternoon, as the performers rehearsed their routines in the big top, the ringmaster used his spare set of keys to enter the caravans which were home to Dominic and Leonard. From Dominic's caravan, he took some face paints and from Leonard's caravan, he stole a pistol.

When Chip Strongman took to the stage that evening, Mr Bostwicke hurried to his own caravan, applied the clown makeup and, dressed in Polo's spare outfit and took the pistol onto the stage. The ringmaster shot the strongman in full view of hundreds of spectators and then fled the big top.

During the panic and confusion as Leonard wrestled Dominic in his caravan, Mr Bostwicke likely removed his makeup and burned the clown costume in the barrel fire outside the caravans.

Poor Polo the Clown was released shortly after this revelation and Bartholomew Bostwicke was promptly arrested. The future of the circus may be uncertain but there is no doubt that the love shared between Dominic and Wanda is set to last.

If you successfully solved this case, go to entry 360.

42. MURDERING ABOUT ON BOATS SOLUTION

Far too often women are expected to tolerate being jeered at, inappropriately touched and photographed without their consent by lecherous men. They are even supposed to take this unwanted attention with good humour.

But what happens when a woman decides she has had enough? Both Sabrina Danvers and Tess Mudgens had complained to their spouses that Ryan Moon had been objectifying and photographing them but neither husband was willing to do anything about it.

It was Sabrina Danvers who eventually decided on a plan to permanently end Ryan Moon's lecherous ways.

After breakfast that morning, she untwisted a wire coat hanger from her cabin wardrobe and took it with her to the communal bathroom.

Meanwhile, Ryan retired to his cabin, where he was free to watch Sabrina shower by peering through the keyhole in the bathroom door. Sabrina had not just expected this filthy behaviour but had anticipated it. She stabbed the metal wire through the keyhole and into Ryan Moon's eye - and brain.

Sabrina then threw this blood-soaked wire through the window, hoping it would reach the canal. It instead only made it as far as the bow of the boat.

She then joined her friends who were outside Cabin 3 and feigned shock at what she saw there.

However, when the police arrived at the scene, several key pieces of evidence had changed. Tess and Karl now claimed that Sabrina had been with them in the dining room when Ryan screamed and Herb testified that he had seen Ryan with a wire hanger on the unsteady boat - a wire hanger which was now beside his corpse in his cabin.

The case was ruled an accident and all suspects were free to enjoy the rest of their holiday together.

If you managed to solve this eye-watering mystery, go to entry 665.

43. HALLOWEEN: PART ONE SOLUTION

The motive for the murder of Sheila Moribund may have been a surprisingly complex one but at its heart, the reason was plain and simple greed.

The job of undertaker in Pluckley Green is (for obvious reasons) an extremely lucrative one.

Stanhope Jones (who had only recently started working at the funeral home) knew that it would take years, maybe even decades to become the senior assistant to Dorian Moribund but he knew of another means to ensure that he would be in line for the inheritance of his boss' huge wealth and business. If he framed Dorian Moribund for the murder of his wife, the undertaker's business would be passed on to John Jones, his retired business partner and Stanhope's aged and ailing father.

Once nature took its course, Stanhope would be next to inherit a quite staggering fortune.

On the day of the party, Stanhope dressed as the Grim Reaper (the same costume he knew that Dorian would wear) and that evening he had to simply wait for Dorian to leave the house to get alcohol (the wine connoisseur would certainly want to hand-pick the party drinks and he was notorious for always leaving things to the last-minute).

Then it was just a matter of arriving early for the party and suggesting a friendly round of apple bobbing to Sheila.

Once he had drowned Sheila (and was certain that the murder had been spotted through the window - thereby framing Dorian), Stanhope simply had to flee the house via the back door, throw off his black cloak to reveal the werewolf costume underneath and then join the group of guests at the front door.

Stanhope no doubt assumed that Dorian would be hanged for the murder of his wife (and that the funeral business would be handed to his father) but it seems the only person who will swing from the hangman's noose is Stanhope Jones himself.

If you correctly solved this murder, go to entry 261.

44. HALLOWEEN: PART TWO SOLUTION

It would seem that a dog was at the centre of this fiendish murder. Not as the killer, of course, but as the motive.

In January, Helena Turner had attempted to murder Holly Merryfair and rather than face justice, had chosen to flee the village and everyone she knew (including her husband). It was during this period of exile that Bert Turner began divorce proceedings.

Holly may have been forgiving of Helena's murderous ways but Bert could not forgive his wife for abandoning him. Bert's only worry with the divorce is who would gain custody of the couple's beloved dog Crowley. Holly had made no secret that he wished to cast a binding spell upon The Ghost at Samhain and this was inspiration for Bert's murder plan.

In advance of the ceremony, Bert Turner soaked a piece of apple in poison (most likely derived from a whipper snake as the smell of the poison would be indistinguishable from that of the cinnamon the ceremonial apple had been soaked in). He took this piece of poisoned apple with him to the Samhain ceremony in the pocket of his white robe.

When Holly brought the plate of apple pieces to Bert, he ate one slice and while Holly's gaze was directed towards the sky for an incantation, Bert swapped the last remaining apple piece for the poisoned one. The Grand Wizard then took this poisoned slice to Helena - the final member of the Order around the circle.

Bert Turner did not get away with murder but only time will tell if the binding spell will really prevent The Ghost from killing again.

Crowley will live with Gerald Ratchett and his dog Merlin.

If you correctly solved this murder, go to entry 9.

45. THE FALL OF THE HOUSE OF SPARROW SOLUTION

Nobody deserves to be murdered, but some deserve to live less than others.

When Wilma Rogers paid for an announcement in the Pluckley Green Press she thought she was simply informing the village of her sister's engagement. She had no idea that she would inadvertently cause Professor Sole's death.

This is because one person who read the announcement was Mavis Davis - and she knew the name Reginald Sole all too well - as he had been her sister's husband.

Katherine Sole had lived a miserable life with her violent husband and she had once pleaded with Mavis to let her live with her so that she could escape from him. Mavis however, rejected this plea and told Katherine that a divorce would bring shame upon the desperate woman. Katherine was murdered by her husband in the autumn of 1954. Reginald was never brought to justice for the crime. Mavis has lived with the guilt, shame and anger ever since.

On the morning of Reginald's arrival in Pluckley Green, all Mavis Davis had to do to ensure his death was to wait for Mabel Witherspoon to finish baking in the kitchen and to then use her own set of keys to gain entry to the cottage.

Once inside, she simply turned on the gas and let it fill the ancient cottage. When the chain-smoking professor arrived at 4am, his fate was sealed.

Mavis Davis was more than prepared to go to prison for this crime - it would be justice, she believed, for the way she had treated her sister. However, the villagers (upon learning of Mavis' motive and realising that the local gossip most probably saved the life of Daisy Doyle), created multiple alibis for Mavis and the entire investigation simply crumbled away.

If you correctly solved this explosive murder, go to entry 573.

46. A STEP IN THE WRONG DIRECTION SOLUTION

Perhaps the best way to get away with murder is to make it seem as if the death was nothing more than a tragic accident.

That probably would have been the case with Oliver Manville if his murderer - Edgar Minster - had not been sloppy when covering up the evidence of foul play.

Edgar loved Pluckley Green and deeply wanted to stay in the village. Oliver's plans to move the company to London would mean him upending his life to live in the capital - so murdering his boss seemed like the most sensible way to prevent that from happening.

On Monday night, under the guise of "Peter Pepper", Edgar Minster rented a room in the Bloodied Axe Tavern. He even wore spectacles and a fake moustache to avoid being recognised (a disguise he later hid in Michael Doncaster's toolbox - in the hope that if murder was ever suspected, his coworker would be the prime suspect).

Then, early on Tuesday morning, he set up a tripwire on the steps leading to the basement and left the pub before anyone there awoke. He then joined his coworkers outside the door to the tavern at 9am and simply waited for Oliver to enter the basement - and die.

Edgar will most certainly hang for this crime - all because he loved his village too much…

Now with only three men on their workforce, Douglas, Michael and Richmond continued with alterations to the basement for the rest of the week. However, when the men knocked down a section of an 18th century wall, they found behind it the most grisly sight.

A human skeleton had been bricked up behind the wall. Its skull had been partially shattered, as if struck by a vicious blow.

The man must have been murdered centuries ago. But who could have done such a thing?

If you successfully solved this murder, go to entry 311.

47. THE BLOODIED AXE SOLUTION

What was the mysterious treasure which Christopher Aurelius found at Glastonbury Tor? We may never know for sure but whatever it was, it was not the cause of his bloody murder.

Perhaps his death could be seen as some form of celestial justice. The pursuit of untold riches seems grotesque when there are those among us without even shoes for their feet.

When Christopher went to bed that evening at the Feathered Cap, he did not know that the kindly pub landlord's offer to house a freezing beggar would lead to his own demise.

John the Beggar and Peter Slender spent a long night together, getting drunk and exchanging stories in front of the roaring fire - until the pub landlord eventually fell asleep through inebriation.

It was then that John took the axe from the basement and carried it upstairs to the room where Christopher slept. With a single blow, he shattered the man's skull and ended his life.

John the Beggar then dragged the man's corpse to the basement and bricked it up behind one of the half-built walls. The man then cleaned up the mess he had caused (but left the bedroom a bloodied mess) and stole the dead man's leather shoes. He left the pub before Peter even awoke.

A desperate man will be driven to do desperate things. The bloodshed at the Feathered Cap was committed not in the pursuit of untold wealth, but due to the need to survive.

John the Beggar left the village as soon as he was certain that suspicion was falling upon him. Gone to another village, his secret kept forever.

The unsolved murder became a cause of speculation and gossip throughout the village. So much so that it led to the barman renaming the pub in honour of the mystery.

If you successfully solved this murder, go to entry 399.

48. BRIDE AND BOOM SOLUTION

Jealousy has yet again led to bloodshed in the village of Pluckley Green. Phoebe Parks may have acted as if the courtship between her and Winston was nothing more than a distant memory but clearly she was still devastated by their separation all those years ago. She would rather Winston die than be happy with another woman.

Her solution? Explode the newlyweds.

Mabel had earlier left the real wedding cake in the kitchen. During Miss Faversham and Winston's speeches, Phoebe tossed this one into a hedge and replaced it with one she had made herself. Only this wasn't really a cake, it was an explosive device rigged to explode the moment the couple cut into it.

The police arrived later that afternoon to arrest Phoebe Parks. The reception then continued as if nothing had happened.

In the early evening, Miss Faversham requested that her guests convene in the garden - as something splendid was about to occur.

Once the guests were in place, Reverend Amos Harper rode into view upon his horse Nagatha Christie. He hopped from the horse and sank to one knee before his treasured love.

"Mabel Witherspoon, will you marry me?"

"Oh yes!" She wept, "I will!"

If you correctly solved this mystery, go to entry 177.

49. BOXING DAY BLOODSHED SOLUTION

In life, some people turn bitter due to years upon years of disappointments. For others, their bitterness is born from a deep-seated pain. However, some people are just horrible through and through and there is simply no explanation for why.

What kind of petty nastiness would drive one woman to rob another of her beautiful view? Whatever the reason, it was what led to Prudence Roseship's bloody murder.

A few weeks before the 2nd of November (the date upon which she was murdered), Prudence decided that it would be fun to spoil her neighbour's beautiful view of the countryside by planting a fast-growing hedgerow along the edge of her own garden.

The neighbours, Dante and Wendy Finn begged Prudence to reconsider and soon found that they were powerless to stop this vindictiveness. As frustrating as it was for Dante, it was devastating for Wendy - who was a landscape artist of some renown.

Wendy's response was to wait until her husband was away for work and then to steal a shotgun from a neighbour's barn.

At Prudence's house, Wendy simply had to ring the doorbell and as soon as Prudence appeared in the hallway, she fired the shotgun through the letterbox.

Perhaps the courts will be lenient with Wendy. One thing can be certain, nobody will miss or mourn Prudence Roseship and her vindictive ways.

If you correctly solved this murder mystery, go to entry 708.

50. NEW YEAR'S EVIL SOLUTION

Perhaps if Rose Finch - Larry Finch's wife - had been in Pluckley Green, she would have warned her husband to be wary of the note delivered through their door that afternoon.

Larry, however, trusted that the letter writer had good intentions and wanted to hear what information the person had to share. Once he had reached the church graveyard - where he expected to find Perry Gulch - Larry was attacked by The Ghost.

After his throat was slashed, Larry managed to stumble first to the door of his house and then (after realising that he had misplaced his key) to the Bloodied Axe Tavern.

The bloodthirsty mob now descended upon the church - where they were certain The Ghost was hiding.

Larry was rushed to hospital - Perry Gulch rode in the ambulance with him. Despite losing consciousness, he is expected to make a full recovery. Later that evening, Larry woke from a deep sleep and whispered to Perry, who had been patiently waiting by his bedside. "I saw the face of The Ghost! The identity of the killer is-"

If you correctly solved this mystery, go to entry 147.

THE GHOST: THE SOLUTION

WARNING: DO NOT READ UNTIL YOU HAVE COMPLETED ALL OF THE MYSTERIES IN THIS BOOK.

WHO IS THE GHOST?

The motive for why The Ghost is killing the villagers of Pluckley Green has its roots not in 1956, but 1724.

December, 1724 was when Christopher Aurelius brought a treasure with him to the Bloodied Axe (then known as the Feathered Cap). It was a treasure he had unearthed in Glastonbury following an extensive period of research. It was a treasure he believed to be the Holy Grail…

Was the artefact truly the legendary relic? Who can know for sure but Aurelius certainly believed that there was sufficient evidence to trust it was.

Aurelius was murdered that night and his priceless treasure was lost amongst the jumble of the tavern's basement.

That was until sometime in the 1950s, when the new pub landlord, Bobby "Bludger" Baxter found an old, metal chalice in the basement and mounted it atop a piece of wood to make a trophy for the New Year's Eve trivia quiz. Neither he, nor anybody else in the village had any idea just how valuable this trophy was.

By 1956, this trophy had been won five years in a row by the same quiz team - "The Pluckley Bird Brains". Each time, the team's leader was given possession of the trophy for one year. This team leader was postman Larry Finch and his quiz team members were Robin Pascoe, Lucy Sparrow, Penelope Gannet and Bertrand Mallard - The Pluckley Bird brains named themselves owing to a fortuitous fluke wherein each of their names contained a bird.

The true identity (and value) of the trophy remained unknown until one night - New Year's Eve, 1955, when the Tchotchke Triplets spent the night at the pub and saw the chalice.

To their scholarly eyes, the authenticity of the relic was undeniable - and led to Toby Tchotchke murdering both of his brothers so that he alone could possess it. Toby was arrested on New Year's Day, 1956 - before he could get his hands upon the treasure (which was now in the home of Larry Finch).

Over the course of this year, The Ghost has been donning a white costume and killing (or attempting to kill) the members of the Pluckley Bird Brains.

Perhaps the greatest clue to the identity of The Ghost came via a throwaway comment made by Beatrice Beauregard when the historian August Barley went missing. She said that August once lived next door to her - in Crooked Cottage.

When Lucy Sparrow was found murdered, she had marked her calendar "See A about B" - or - "See August about beekeeping" (beekeeping being her newest hobby).

When she visited August that Wednesday, he murdered her before dumping her body down the well on his farm. He then carried this corpse through the tunnels beneath the village and into Crooked Cottage - he knew the passcode to the trapdoor as he had once lived in the cottage himself.

After Toby Tchotchke murdered his brothers, it was August Barley who he was witnessed talking to (about the trophy/Holy Grail) at the edge of the Western

Woods - and it was August who called the police to have the surviving Tchotchke triplet arrested.

August has been spending this year murdering the Bird Brains in hopes that on New Year's Eve, the strongest competition could be eliminated and it could be he who won the pub quiz alone and gained possession of the trophy.

As for the white outfit The Ghost wore (one of the many methods August utilised to suggest that there was a supernatural explanation for The Ghost - including moving the spirit board planchette at the seance so that it spelled "P G".) It was nothing more than the hooded beekeeping suit he wore to tend to his apiary…

If you correctly guessed the identity of The Ghost, congratulations! You are a super sleuth and have successfully won this game!

So what happened next?

The villagers of Pluckley Green had formed a pitchfork wielding mob, a mob which had now surrounded the church from all angles. August Barley had no possible means of escape and desperately climbed the spiral, stone staircase to reach the roof of the church tower.

From atop St Julian on the Edge Church, all August could see was burning torches and angry villagers flooding the streets of Pluckley Green. "KILL THE GHOST! KILL THE GHOST!" they chanted.

"Please!" August begged. "Let me share with you the secret so that you may understand what I did. We could all be wealthy beyond our wildest dreams if you spare me! The quiz trophy is the H-"

But August Barley was silenced by an arrow which was fired from a bow directly into his throat. The crowd cheered and Beatrice Beauregard - bow in hand - curtseyed before them.

August grasped at his blood-soaked neck. He tried to scream some final words but instead stumbled forwards and over the wall atop the church tower. He plummeted to the ground headfirst onto the gravestone of Bertrand Mallard with a sickening crunch.

The Ghost had been defeated and the residents of the village (including Larry Finch - who had made a remarkably speedy recovery) celebrated the arrival of the new year - and the death of August Barley - with the annual pub quiz.

The winners were the Pluckley Green Brights, who will now have ownership of the trophy for one year.

Nobody in all of Pluckley Green has any idea of the story behind the trophy, what it is worth, or why it was worth killing for…

Printed in Great Britain
by Amazon